LOST IN THE MUSIC

Wendy:
I Thank you!

LOST IN THE MUSIC

T. WENDY WILLIAMS

T. Wendy Williams

Gallien G5 Publishing

Contents

For
Joseph, Layla, Miles & Lance
I love you all more than words could ever express

Cover Design: Candice Kilgore
Cover Photo: Gabriela Pereira
Author Photo: Kim Taylor

First Printing, 2021

One

Every June, I fly from Houston to Los Angeles to spend time with my extended family. They always welcome me with open arms. Then, for two weeks, my cousin Cassandra and I along with other sons and daughters of America's Black upper class "rough it" in California's wilderness. This year—1987—is different.

I'm now seventeen and a recent high school graduate. For the first time since my thirteenth birthday, I'm actually getting an opportunity to rest—no camp. As a matter of fact, I'm taking the entire summer off. I owe it to myself. Usually around mid-June, when the first session of camp is over, I return to Houston, and it's back to work. I spend five hours daily studying, playing, and rehearsing on the piano. Since age nine, it's been my constant companion. As a classically trained concert pianist, the piano has taken me to packed concert halls in Houston, Dallas, Cleveland, and Chicago. There have been times when I've had concert engagements and had to fly overnight so I could take final exams for school the following day. Right now, there are no engagements on my schedule, and it surprises me to say that I'm glad.

I can't wait for this plane to land. I look out my window and see it getting closer to the runway. My heart is racing the way it does when I enter the stage before a performance. It's the anticipation, it's that adrenaline rush—something new and exciting is happening and it has me sitting on the edge of my first-class seat.

When I deplane, I spot my sixteen-year-old cousin Cassandra eagerly awaiting me at the top of the Jetway. I just saw her two weeks ago at my graduation, and I swear she's grown a few inches since then. I'm melting from all the love she still gives me. It's refreshing, never stale.

"Maddie, you colored it?" She surveys a strand of my eighteen-inch curly hair in her long fingers. Until a couple of days ago, my hair was dark brown. I wanted a different look, so the hairstylist suggested a lighter shade of brown—chestnut with highlights. She said it complemented my amber-colored eyes.

"You like?" I ask Cassandra.

"I'll have to see it in natural light," she answers.

"I won't care if you don't."

"You know the carpet has to match the drapes."

"I don't understand," I'm really confused by her statement and how it relates to my hair. Cassandra doesn't say a word as we walk a few paces.

"You know?" she continues.

"No, I don't. You've totally lost me," I respond.

"Maddie. You know," she says, her eyes darting from my head to below my waist.

"Ewww," I say when I realize what she's really saying.

"Now, cousin, you have to broaden your horizons—or in this case, brighten your bush."

I just let her talk. There is no way I'm coloring that part of my body. I cringe just thinking about it.

Waiting curbside to help load my luggage into the trunk is Big Cousin Caleb and his best friend, JB.

"Cuzzo."

Caleb lifts me. I'm five-three, and last time I checked, I weighed 155 pounds. To my cousin, who is six-eight and a star athlete at his university, I probably feel more like those heavy medicine balls he tosses during basketball drills. I notice JB standing there with his arms open. I don't want to leave him out. He's the same height as Caleb. He lifts me too. With my nose buried in his neck, I smell a hint of teakwood, a leathery cologne scent, real masculine-like. He puts me down slowly and opens the car door for me to get in the backseat.

Once inside, Caleb hands me a present in a small red box topped with a gold ribbon.

"Hate I missed your graduation."

"It's all good."

I open it, and inside is a sterling silver treble clef pendant complete with a sterling silver chain.

"Cuzzo, this is sweet." I'm touched by his thoughtfulness.

"Allow me," Cassandra says, reaching for the chain. I quickly turn my back to her and grab my hair, holding it in place as she drapes the chain around my neck and fastens it in place. I turn around.

"Thank you." I try to examine it in Caleb's rearview mirror.

"So, you're going to Juilliard," Caleb begins.

"The Juilliard School," I answer.

"Oh, pardon me," he answers.

"I'm only kidding, cuzzo. I remember talking to the school's registrar, and I slipped and said exactly what you said. She corrected me just like that."

"I hope you told her it's not that serious," he says.

"I did not," I respond.

"You really want to know what's serious?" he says. "Winter in New York City. You'll see it's a lot different than winter in Houston."

"I can handle the cold."

"Yeah, you say that now," he responds.

"I'm looking forward to it."

"Don't count on a visit from me if I have to dress in layers," he says.

"The cold won't stop me," Cassandra says. She's a bubbly ray of sunshine in her fluorescent pink and yellow. "Just say the word, and I'm on the first thing smoking."

JB chimes in, "You probably already knew this, but the rats are humongous. You have to compete with them for a good table at a restaurant."

I get a visual.

"And a cab ride," Caleb adds.

"Plus, I hear they make lousy roommates." JB continues, "They eat all your food and skip out on paying the rent."

"Thank you, JB. I'll keep an eye out for the rats."

"New York has a bigger problem than the rats," JB continues.

"What's worse than that?" Cassandra, Caleb, and I ask at once.

"Their basketball team," JB answers.

I hear Caleb chuckling.

"JB, shut up." Cassandra laughs. She reaches over the seat to push him. With his quick reflexes, he dodges her. I hear him laughing.

I find them all quite entertaining.

"The Juilliard School. That's impressive," JB says, glancing over his shoulder at me. "You must be the crème de la crème."

"I'd like to think so," I reply.

"She won't tell you, but not only is she a talented concert pianist, she's also a gifted composer," Caleb says.

JB glances at me. "Wow, fam I had no idea." I notice his eyes light up, and I try not to blush.

We finally pull into the driveway of my extended family's home. It's a grand white structure that sits on a lush green manicured lawn with trimmed hedges, white portico columns, and huge windows. For the next three months, I'll call this place home. Getting out of the car, it has become clear as day why I've always chosen to come here. Los Angeles' weather's second to none, with no humidity unlike Houston. The beaches are less than an hour away, and I have a guest room with a view of the California sunset.

Aunt Teal, who's really Cassandra and Caleb's aunt, is in the kitchen, and whatever she's cooking smells good.

"I'm just in time," I say to her.

"Yes, chère," she greets me with a warm hug.

She opens her pot, and the aroma of onions, peppers, and herbs flood my senses. I nearly cry.

"Go freshen up. I'll have your bowl of jambalaya ready when you return," she says in her Louisiana Creole drawl that never went away.

The room I've been given faces west. When I open the drapes, I look down and see the waves rippling in the pool, and beyond that, breath-taking views of Los Angeles. This is a moment I wish I could hold still and take with me to New York. On cold, dreary days, I want to remember the sun's rays and this L.A. view.

***

I join my cousins, Aunt Teal, and JB for dinner. Aunt Teal sets a bowl of steaming hot jambalaya in front of me and a basket with French bread on the table. She pours fresh-squeezed lemonade for each of us but sets a bottle of Chardonnay on the table for herself. Aunt Teal moved to California in the 1970s to help her younger brother who was an airline pilot and her sister-in-law, a psychiatrist, who happens to be my aunt, raise Caleb and Cassandra. She never left.

"Aunty Teal, we want some Chardonnay," Caleb says.

"Ha. No, no, no, bebby. This is Aunt Teal's. All of it." She sits, pours herself a glass, and holds it up. "When I don't have you, I'm mad. Now that I have you, I'm going to drink the hell of out you." Instead of sipping, she finishes half the glass in one swallow before pouring another.

"Now we really want some," Cassandra says, tapping my leg under the table.

"You children are funny."

Aunt Mary arrives. I hear her raspy nasal tone before I see her.

"Where's my favorite niecy?"

Aunt Mary, my mother's older sister, appears in the dining room, bright eyed, hair styled with bouncy, wispy shoulder-length layers. She kisses me cheek to cheek and stands back to admire me like she didn't just see me two weeks ago at my graduation.

"You colored your hair," she says.

"I did."

"Why? I loved your natural color." The treble clef pendant Caleb gave me catches her eye. "That's nice."

"You have to get used to it being lighter," I say.

"Females are funny," Caleb starts. "JB, imagine if I walked up to you and said, 'Hey, bruh, you did something different with your hair?'"

"You noticed my purple and gold highlights? It's the Lakers special," JB exaggerates, batting his eyelashes and running his hands through his curly hair.

Cassandra winces. "You do that too well."

Everyone, including JB, finds her remark quite amusing.

"Teal, I swear the aroma met me as soon as I got out of the car," Aunt Mary says. She enters the kitchen but returns minutes later with a bowl of jambalaya, and she sits at the opposite end of Aunt Teal.

"Today was a good day," Aunt Mary begins. "A zookeeper stopped by the youth center, and my eaglets got to see an African crowned eagle."

"Wow, Mom. Wish I could've seen it," Caleb says. He seems genuinely disappointed he didn't get the opportunity.

"I took pictures. Remind me to get them developed."

"So, did it spread its wings?" JB asks.

"Of course it did." Aunt Mary smiles. "The zookeeper said the wingspan ranges from five to six feet. Now, it's not as long as the bald eagle, but to see it in person and the looks on those children's faces. They were in awe."

"I'm jealous," Caleb says. "Me and JB played basketball all day."

"I'm jealous too," Aunt Teal adds, pretending to be upset.

I don't know why that's funny, but we all get a laugh out of it.

"How is your father?" Aunt Mary asks me.

"Daddy's good. When we were saying our goodbyes, he was trying hard to fight back a tear," I respond.

"How sweet." Aunt Mary smiles.

"It's different not having anything on the schedule for the summer." I take a spoonful of jambalaya to taste.

"What will you do with all this down time?" Aunt Mary asks.

That's a good question, one I'm not sure I know how to answer.

***

Later that night, after taking a shower, I finally settle into my room. It's only nine o'clock, but my body is still on Houston's time. Cassandra joins me. Her bone-straight hair is done up into a topknot. Her face is free of makeup, her freckles are endearing, her skin, radiant from face cream.

"How's Kyle?" I ask, referring to her boyfriend.

"He's good. We talked just before your flight landed. Of course, it wasn't long. He's volunteering at the youth center."

"Good. Why don't you volunteer with him?"

Cassandra crinkles her nose.

"Why are you giving me that look?" I ask.

"That youth center and those children my mom calls her 'eaglets'."

"What about them?"

"They're interfering with our quality time."

"Just volunteer so you can spend time with him."

She shifts in bed and averts her stare. "No thank you."

"The center is a good place for you and Kyle. It's fulfilling, like music is for me."

"Good for you." Her response is dry.

"You know what else is fulfilling? Writing. Matter of fact, I was about to write in my journal when you walked in."

I hear a long, exasperated sigh from Cassandra.

"What do you like to do?" I ask.

"Shop, party, hang out with the crew."

When she mentions the crew, I'm reminded of our friends from summer camp.

"What do you write about in your journal?" she asks.

"Everything."

"Do you write about Gregory?"

"Gregory." I laugh. "Now he's a character."

"I saw him last week," Cassandra says.

I close my eyes and imagine Gregory Washington III. The last time I saw him, he was a scrawny, horn-rimmed-eyeglass-wearing prankster—a clean, crisp, sharp dresser but full of jokes and mischief.

"Remember in camp when he hid the frog in your bunker?"

"He should've gotten expelled. Had me traumatized."

"Always cracking jokes, both he and Kyle."

"Why aren't you going this year?" I ask.

"Camp's not the same if my crew isn't there."

"You're the only one left. I can see why you don't want to go."

I turn the pages in my journal until I find a group photograph of us at camp. I show it to Cassandra.

"When was this?"

"I think it was two or three years ago."

In the photo, I notice Cassandra and me, shoulder to shoulder. I'm smiling, she's not. Mona and Ursula, the other members of our crew, are standing just to the right of Cassandra. Mona, forever the showboat, is blowing a kiss. Next to her, Ursula's eyes are closed, but her braces are sparkling.

"You look angry," I say to Cassandra.

"I didn't feel like smiling," she says. "Look at Kyle and Gregory, the mischief twins." She points to them standing on the left end of the last row of all boys. We go row by row saying something about each person until Cassandra lets out a tired yawn, and yawns are contagious.

"Good night. See you in the morning." She walks through the bathroom suite we share and into her room, closing the door.

Getting back to my journal, I notice the last entry was two weeks ago, exactly 9:33 the morning after my graduation. I wrote:

May 17, 1987

Wish you were here. I know you would've been proud. You made this moment possible; instilling in me a desire to succeed, teaching me from the time I was three how to read and write. By the time I was eight, we had already traveled to six of the seven continents. I'll forever cherish our elephant rides in Phuket, collecting seashells on the shores of Madagascar, and the smell of the evening rain in Los Cabos. At nine, because of you, I learned to play the piano and master it. Memories of your expressions whenever I played Für Elise and Clair de Lune stay on my mind. Last night, I was a hodgepodge of emotions, each one taking its turn and showing at moments least expected. In the middle of my valedictory address, I remembered your eyes that morning when you collapsed. I paused, thinking what's the use, but I kept hearing your voice mixed with the applause of my classmates urging me to go on. Some days are easier than others, but Daddy and I somehow manage. It's Sunday, and I'm sitting in Daddy's study at the church. They plan to honor me with a congratulatory dinner afterward, but all I want to do is go home and pack. I'm counting down the days.

I write tonight's entry:

June 2, 1987, 9:45 p.m.

I'm here in L.A., and the goal is to rest. For 90 days, I just want to know what it's like to be normal. No concerti and no youth leadership camp. I want to be a normal teenager and experience what teenagers experience: fun, adventures, and new discoveries. I was twelve when my mother died. She was just thirty-five. It was a dreary Sunday morning in November, and she wanted to attend church. At that point, she was wheelchair bound. Ovarian cancer ravaged her body down to a skeleton. Daddy talked a lot about miracles. He said miracles happen if we speak life to them. My mother fought cancer and beat it before. Then it came back. Twice, we were told by doctors to gather the family to say our last goodbyes. After she came home a second time, she had a little more fight than we anticipated. Barely able to speak, she said she wanted to go to church. I remember Gilda, my mother's assistant and best friend, helping me get her dressed. The royal blue jacket and skirt engulfed her weak frame, but she still insisted on wearing it with a string of her mother's pearls.

Daddy spoke, delivering a rousing sermon. My mother, in her frail condition, stood with the aid of her wheelchair. If I wasn't there and someone told me I wouldn't have believed them. She stood and attempted to walk. I remember Daddy so overcome with emotion, he stopped and rushed to her aid. She took one step before stiffening and falling into his arms. Daddy held Mother and gently placed her on the floor where I cradled her in my arms like a baby. Her eyes were wide with wonderment like she saw something no one else was privy to. She uttered a faint cry and stopped breathing, yet her eyes remained open. I refused to move. When the EMT arrived, I remember screaming, "Please don't take her away from me."

That Christmas had to be the worst ever. All the presents in the world couldn't make me happy. Pain came in and made itself at home. The void I felt, I wouldn't wish on my worst enemy. It's an empty, heart-sinking feeling

I get after having seen my mother, alive, in a dream only to wake up and reality sinks in.

I was angry with Daddy for a long time after Mother died. I told him he needed to quit preaching because he wasn't on good terms with God. If he was, Mother would still be alive. He tells me God's ways are not like our ways. I say that's so obvious. All those stories of miracles from the Bible were fairy tales, and if you were gullible enough, you bought into them. Then he says things happen in God's time. I was twelve. Let's just say, God's timing was off.

Daddy employs a staff to help with the household, but no one knows how to handle me. Depression set in, and there were days when I didn't want to get out of bed. In stepped Aunt Mary, mothering from 1,500 miles away. That's when I started rebelieving in miracles. She always knew when to jump on the next available flight—sometimes with Cassandra, sometimes alone. That's when I realized it really was something to God's timing. She was present at quite a few of my piano concerti. For my societal debut, she found a local designer to create a hand-beaded antique lace ball gown for me. Under the ballroom chandeliers, the dress took on a life of its own with an ethereal quality that would have made my mother proud.

Would Mother be proud of me now? I believe she would. Daddy tells me all the time how proud he is of me. Miracles do work; situations change. The world keeps on turning. I'm excited for what's ahead at Juilliard.

After I finish writing in my journal entry, I turn off the lamp and get underneath the covers. I toss and turn before I find a comfortable spot, but I still can't fall asleep. I have songs in my head, and I need to write down the melodies. If I were home and this happened, I'd get out of bed and run downstairs to the piano and let those melodies come to me. I'd play, sometimes for fifteen minutes, sometimes all night. My house in Houston has a rehearsal studio where I can isolate myself and not disturb anyone. That's not the case here. It's frustrating, and I've got to figure out a way to shut my mind off and just relax.

Two

Coming out of my room, I bump into JB in the hallway. He holds up a mixing bowl; a splash of milk from it lands on the floor.

"You're still here?" I ask, following him down the hallway to Caleb's room. At that moment, I regret walking into the room. That locker room sweat odor meets me at the door.

He and Caleb still have on their clothes from yesterday. Sitting in the front of the television, Caleb holds a gaming remote, and JB feeds his face with cereal from the mixing bowl. I step back and hold my breath.

"Cuzzo," Caleb shouts, never taking his eyes off the TV.

He and JB are into the game, their body movements jerking while the colorful visuals from the screen reflect off their faces.

"Pull up a chair," says.

I hesitate but pull up a chair between the two.

"What game is this?" I ask.

"The Legend of Zelda," Caleb answers.

I was never into gaming, but I find it fascinating to watch my twenty-year-old cousin contort, twist, and allow himself to get lost in it.

"Been playing all night?" I ask.

Caleb chuckles. "Don't judge me."

I shift my focus to JB. "What about you?"

"I just woke up like thirty minutes ago," he says. I notice a pillow and a blanket on the floor next to his feet. "Besides, I've mastered the levels."

"Took long enough." Caleb steadies his concentration on the screen.

"It's taking you eight weeks to finish what I did in eight days," JB answers back.

Caleb is unfazed.

"I was hoping we could all go to the beach today." I say.

"We will, after practice," Caleb says.

"When is that?"

"Around seven," JB answers.

"There won't be much daylight left if we go then."

"Evening's the best time. It's not crowded. Hang tight," Caleb says.

"Hang tight. What time does practice start?"

"In a couple of hours," Caleb answers.

"How long does it last?"

"A couple of hours," JB answers.

"Okay. Then what do you do after that?"

"Conditioning and training, and that'll last an hour or two or three," JB adds before drinking the milk from the mixing bowl.

"So, four o'clock you're finished. What do you do from four to seven?"

"Sleep," JB answers.

"Geez, guys. It's my first official day here. I don't want to sit around doing nothing. I want to go to the beach. I want to cruise the strip, go to the mall."

"And you'll have more than enough time to do all that," Caleb says.

I get up and walk toward the door. "You guys could use a shower," I say before walking out of the room.

They both say something that I can't clearly make out. I knock quietly on Cassandra's door and open it slightly to see if she's up. I peek inside. She's sound asleep. Her eyes are hidden under a satin eye mask.

Downstairs at the end of the hallway in the entertainment room sits a black baby grand piano. In the corner is a trumpet encased in thick glass. It sits on a mantel, and the plaque reads, Louis "Satchmo" Armstrong. There's the fleur-de-lis hanging prominently over the fireplace accompanied by photos of the family from their travels around the globe. There's a photo that includes me when I accompanied them to Rio. We were at the base of Cristo Redentor, its outstretched arms guiding us.

In the kitchen, Teal sat.

"Good morning," I greet her with a warm, tight hug.

She has a spread of fresh-cut strawberries, blueberries, strawberry jam, and a plate with bagels meticulously arranged. Teal sips on something that smells of vanilla.

"Did Aunt Mary leave already?"

"Not yet, bebby."

Aunt Mary enters. "Hi, niecy." She kisses my forehead. Studying her, I notice she's wearing lip gloss and eyeshadow. Her lashes are lush and elongated, highlighting her sparkling brown eyes—eyes just like my mother's.

She picks up a bagel, cuts it in half, and slathers a layer of strawberry jam on one of the halves.

"What you're sipping on smells good, Teal."

"It's chicory with vanilla cream."

"I'll stick with coffee." She pours a cup. "Niecy, there's a variety of juices in the fridge. Help yourself. This is your home now."

"Thank you. I will. What time do you have to be at the center?"

"I like to get there around 9:30. The children start pouring in around ten. You should come with me."

"It's 8:35, and I'm not dressed."

"The place is only ten minutes away. You can eat, shower, get dressed, and we'll still make good timing."

I didn't want to refuse.

Forty minutes later, we're in the car driving through the neighborhood where the homes sit high atop the hills, and the street names start with Don. We drive a short distance, and it seems like every Black neighborhood in America has an MLK Boulevard, lined with churches, storefronts, and fast-food restaurants, and someone standing on the corner selling something. Today, there's a man wearing a suit and bowtie, holding a newspaper with the words The Final Call. There's a different scene from the affluent neighborhood we just left and where we are currently. I feel frightened for Aunt Mary, but she's unfazed by it. At one of the intersections, I can't resist the urge to lock my door.

Aunt Mary pulls her Chevy Caprice station wagon into a fenced-in parking lot. On the building is a mural of art depicting children running with their arms spread wide and an eagle soaring above them.

"One of my eaglets did that."

"Talented eaglet you have," I respond, remembering the conversation I had last night with Cassandra. I hardly noticed the door when Aunt Mary opened it. Inside, the air is cool, and when she flicks on the lights, we're standing in a corridor where pictures and accolades cover the walls.

"Is this your first visit?"

"I think I came once when I was ten."

The walls are painted a golden color. The floors are the industrial types you usually see in places like hospitals and schools. The odor, though not overwhelming, smells with hints of lavender.

On the wall leading into her office is another mural, this one of someone near and dear to the both of us. It is my mother, dressed in a white flowing gown. She has a look of pride on her face, and there is a little boy and girl about eight years-old, on each side of her holding her hand with bright smiles.

"It looks just like her," I say.

"Every little detail is captured."

"Same artist?"

"Yes. Isn't she something?"

"She's gifted."

"That's my office. Nothing in there but a desk, bookshelves, paperwork."

I look on the wall and see her qualifications. There's a medical degree in psychiatry from University of Southern California and other certifications. I follow her past more offices and into what is an open room with round tables. There are working stations, a chalkboard, a kitchen, and a dining area. Near the main entrance is the receptionist's desk. There are windows, so the place doesn't feel like a prison. Some sunlight can get in.

"This place gives me meaning. It's flourishing. I just wish your mother was here to see it."

"Me too."

The front door opens, and in walks one of the staff members. Aunt Mary introduces us. She's Leah, the assistant. The door opens again, and in walks more staff members. It's like they carpooled. I'm introduced to the receptionist, the secretary, and the lady in charge of the food.

Around ten, children start pouring in, and what was once quiet becomes rather noisy. Kyle, Cassandra's boyfriend, enters, and behind him more children. He spots me, and we embrace.

"Cassandra told me you were coming, but I wasn't expecting you here, though," he says.

"I heard so much about these eaglets."

As we talk, I notice a couple of the children horseplaying. Kyle spots them too.

"Damon and Blaze," is all he says along with a look. Kyle checks his watch. "What are you doing?"

"I'm not sure," I answer.

"For some reason, both volunteer teachers are running late. I'll need you to take some of the children."

"Sure."

After we divide them up, I have ten children staring at me. They look like nine and ten- year-olds. I haven't a clue as to what to do with them. I glance at Kyle. He has a group of mostly girls and a couple of boys. They look around twelve and thirteen. Some of them even look close to my age. I hear one of the girls and both boys ask Kyle about his shoes.

"Are those the new Air Max's?" one of the boys asks.

"Yeah," Kyle answers.

"As soon as I leave here, I'm going to Fox Hills Mall," he says.

"My brother got a hookup at the Slauson Swap Meet, He can get us both a pair," the other boy says.

"Can he hook me up too?" the girl asks. She looks about seventeen. I notice all of them seem excited about getting new shoes—all except one. Her focus was on something else. Her concentration is deliberate, and the pencil in her hand seems to be dancing. She looks up briefly like she's studying the subject before burying her nose back into her task.

"You new, huh?" a little boy with curly sandy hair and sun-kissed skin asks me.

"So what if I am?" I ask.

"You don't have no activities for us?" a girl about nine with a heart-shaped face and cornrow braids asks.

"I do. As a matter of fact, let's play the Get-to-Know-You-Better-game."

"What kind of game is that?" the little boy asks.

"I never heard of it before," the little girl says.

"Sounds like something she made up," the boy named Blaze responds.

"Can I tell you about myself?" I begin.

"This is going to be boring." Damon rests his face in his hands.

"Let's give it a go here. My name is Madeline. You can call me Maddie."

"I like Maddie," the girl with the heart-shaped face says.

"How old are you, Maddie?" the little boy with the sun-kissed skin asks.

"I'm seventeen," I answer.

"You look like the lady that's painted on Mrs. Mary's wall."

"I do?"

They are talking about the mural of my mother and the children outside of Aunt Mary's office.

"She doesn't look like that. That's not even a real person," Damon says.

"Maddie, you live around here?" Blaze asks.

"No."

"What's your favorite color?" another cherub-faced girl, about nine, with sparkling eyes asks.

"It's a variation of blue."

"I like purple," she says.

"Most girls like purple. I like black and silver like the Raiders," Damon answers.

"Me too," Blaze says.

"I'll give everyone a chance here. Is there anything else you want to know about me?" I ask.

"Are you going to give us something exciting to do?" the boy with the sun-kissed skin asks.

"What do you usually do?" I ask.

"We make projects," he answers.

"I want to paint," the girl with the heart-shaped face says.

"Yesterday we saw an eagle. It was big and scary," a girl, age ten, with long braids announces.

I moved them to the workstations—the girls at one table, boys at another table. There were crayons, markers, and pencils stashed in metal coffee can containers. I found sheets of manila paper and passed them out to each one.

"Draw a picture of the person you want to be when you grow up."

"I want to be pretty just like you when I grow up," one of the girls says as she draws a circle.

"You're too kind. What's your name?"

"Dee," she answers. She's adorable with round, sparkling eyes. Her hair is parted and brushed neatly with two braids. She reminds me of myself at that age.

"Dee. How pretty." I go to each child asking for their name. LaToya is the name of the girl with the heart-shaped face. Jakwon is the name of the boy with the sun-kissed skin. The cherub-faced girl's name is Raquel, and the girl whom I assume is ten, is named Vicky. When I get to Blaze and Damon, Blaze tells me his name is really Marvin, and Damon says his name is really Rodney. They almost have me until they start laughing.

While my group of children draw rather quietly, I hear Kyle's group still chatting. "Raise your hand if you've been in trouble with the law?" Kyle asks.

Both boys raise their hands. One of the girls, dressed in an acid-wash skirt with fluorescent socks raises her hand. Everyone in the group stares at her.

"What did you do?" Kyle asks.

"I went joyriding with this dude."

"How old were you?" Kyle asks.

"Thirteen," she answers.

"How old are you, now?" he asks.

"Fourteen," she responds.

She looks much older. More like seventeen. Eighteen, easily.

Kyle stands before them. "I've never been arrested, but I have been pulled over, like ten times. I have a clean driving record, so they let me go once they check my ID."

"Why do they pull you over?" one of the girls asks.

"They say I fit the description," Kyle answers.

I turn my attention to my group of little artists.

Dee holds up her finished picture. On the page is a round face with curly brown hair, pink lips, and almond-shaped brown eyes. The person she drew is chesty—almost caricature-like with a small waist and round bottom. She drew her very best version of me.

"That's so pretty, Dee."

"Here. You can have it."

"Thank you." I retrieve it, and part of me wants to laugh. The other part is thinking I need to start an exercise regimen.

Blaze draws a picture of what looks like a police officer. Damon draws a man wearing a brown uniform holding what looks like a bird on his arm.

"What's this, Damon?"

"A zookeeper."

The rest of the pictures are of a nurse, a schoolteacher, a fireman, and a truck driver. The receptionist puts a tape inside a boom box, and relaxing sounds of classical music play in the background. I'm wishing for a piano now.

The volunteer teachers arrive, relieving me and Kyle of our teaching duties. My group each gives me a hug, and I feel a celestial energy from each one.

"Are you leaving us for good?" Dee asks.

I take her hands. "No. I'll be here."

With that news, the tense expression in her eyes relaxes.

It seems there's no time for idleness. One minute, I'm hands-on with the children. The next minute, I'm in the kitchen with gloves, helping the food lady prep sandwiches.

When I'm finished, Kyle joins me at a table in an area set aside for dining.

"My intentions were to come here once a week, volunteer an hour or so just so it'll look good on a résumé."

"What changed?" I ask, biting into an apple slice.

"I've become attached to them. I look forward to the time I spend here."

"Some of the kids here seem pretty cool."

"Yeah. What's up with you? Cassandra tells me you're going to Juilliard." He notices my pendant—my graduation gift from Caleb.

"I am. What about you?"

"Fisk. Family tradition."

"Nashville is a long way from Cassandra."

He chuckles. "Isn't her father a pilot? She can use his flight benefits to see me."

"Oh, really?"

"Or she could give me a buddy pass, and I'll fly home. Works for me."

"By now, she's probably wondering where I am."

"You didn't mention you were coming here?"

"She was asleep when we left."

"I'm leaving here in a second. I can take you home if you're ready."

"Just let me say bye to Aunt Mary."

On the way to Aunt Mary's office, I stop to look at the mural of my mother and can't resist the urge to touch it like touching it will magically bring it to life. Aunt Mary walks out of her office. Me being there startles her a bit.

"I'm sorry."

"It's okay." She's staring at me, gauging my emotions. "She's our guardian angel watching over the place," she says, taking my hand. "The artist is here. Would you like to meet her?"

Aunt Mary has a charming way of making it hard for me to say no. When I meet the artist, I am speechless. She's the girl in Kyle's group whose laser focus on her task had me drawn to her.

"I'm Rosie," she says with a firm handshake. Her eyes are bold and bright. Throughout the morning, I kept stealing glances at her.

"May I see?" I ask, referring to her sketches.

She shows me three. One is of Kyle, one is of the other volunteer teacher, and one is me. I take in every detail. Just like Dee's drawing, my long, curly hair is prominent, hanging past my shoulders. She notices everything about her subjects in her sketches—my eyes, they're almond shaped and amber.

"She's masterful, isn't she?" Aunt Mary says. "I love how she captures the emotional nuances of her subjects."

"Captured me to a tee," Kyle says. Got my gap teeth and my sportin' waves." He rubs a hand across his head.

"It was a pleasure to meet you, Rosie. I am such an admirer of your work."

"Thank you. It was nice to meet you too," she says before excusing herself.

I turn to Aunt Mary. "Aunty, Kyle and I are leaving."

"Oh. What do you think about the place? Think you can come in and help out sometime?"

"Sure. I would love to help you out. May I make a suggestion?"

"Of course." Aunt Mary replies.

"You need a piano."

"Okay. I'll work on that."

She instructs all the children in the room to say goodbye to us. They are demonstrative and animated with their shrill voices.

"Make sure you come back." I hear a little voice floating above the others.

"Okay, okay. They heard you," Aunt Mary says as the door closes behind us.

Three

Kyle and I find Cassandra outside lounging by the pool flipping through pages of Seventeen magazine.

"Well." She puts down her magazine. "The eagles have finally landed." She rolls her eyes at us.

Kyle joins her on the chair. He leans in for a kiss. She turns her head. Kyle is visibly flustered.

"What did I do?"

She ignores him and glares at me. "You could've left me a note or something."

"I apologize. I had no idea I was going. I mean your mother asked, and I really didn't want to say no to her."

"Are you going tomorrow?"

"Yes. I actually like the youth center."

She sinks into her lounge chair. "You too?"

"When was the last time you volunteered?" Kyle asks.

Cassandra holds up a finger to silence him and turns her attention to me. "I thought we were hanging out this summer."

"We will," I assure her.

"I'm letting the two of you know right now, I'm not competing with those children. Either you roll with me or roll down this hill."

Kyle and I glance at each other. "I live here now, so I'm not rolling anywhere," I tell her.

"I'm rolling out in five minutes," Kyle begins. "Before I do, let's clear the air."

"I'll call you. We can talk about it then."

"Listen, I'll give you two a moment," I say before I get up and go inside. I need to unpack the rest of my things anyway.

***

Caleb and JB roundup Jake, a teammate with a Jeep Wrangler. I'm in the backseat crammed in the middle between JB and Cassandra. Jake is six-four, Caleb and JB are both six-eight. Of all the vehicles to choose from, this is it, and it has got to be the most uncomfortable. JB has one leg hanging off the side of the jeep—his left knee is almost to his chest. It doesn't help that my thigh is rubbing against his leg, and the sensation gives me butterflies.

A car horn blares. Everyone looks over and notices three girls who look like fashion models, screaming in a convertible riding alongside us.

"Is that the Soul Train dancer we saw at Total Experience last weekend?" Caleb asks JB.

I hear a girl from the car yell, "It's them. Omigod."

JB glances their way and gives a slight nod.

"I lost your number," the girl driving says to him.

"If you want, I can pull over," Jake says to JB.

"No, man. Keep driving. I'm chilling. I'm not trying to entertain her," JB answers.

"Are you sure? They're freaking hot," Jake says, trying to steer and look at them.

"I'm scoping out the one in the backseat," Caleb says.

"Did you score last weekend?" Jake asks, glancing over his shoulder at JB.

"I plead the fifth," JB answers.

"So, you're not gonna give me your number?" the driver asks JB.

"I'll call you," he answers.

"I don't remember giving out my number," she says.

"JB, she's a gnat brain. Please ditch her," Cassandra says.

I stifle a giggle.

JB makes a signal once more that he will call her before Jake speeds through the intersection. The girls make a right turn, driving in another direction.

"The girl in the backseat looks like Vanity from the singing group Vanity 6," Caleb says.

"Where's your girlfriend, Basha?" Cassandra asks JB.

"Basha? Who's that?" He smiles.

"Don't pretend you don't know," Cassandra says.

"He has so many. It's hard to keep track," Caleb says.

A song on the radio catches JB's ear. "Jake, turn that up." He bobs to the rhythm. "Remember that jam?" he asks Caleb.

I see Caleb bobbing along.

"Sophomore year on the yard, when this song came on, all the brothers lined up for the stroll."

"What's the name of the song?" I ask

"'Juice' by the World Class Wreckin' Cru," JB answers.

He and Caleb perform. They are in sync using identical hand gestures. Both are extremely animated.

"I didn't see this much energy in practice," Jake says.

"Coach was on our asses," Caleb says.

"You were a zombie," JB teases him.

"Blame it on Zelda," Caleb replies.

"And you still haven't mastered it," JB fires back.

"I will before the day's over," Caleb assures him.

For the duration of the drive, I listen to conversations ranging from USC basketball with inside jokes and banter about workouts to the Lakers versus the Celtics. I learn JB's and Jake's fathers were once teammates for the Lakers in the late 1960s and 1970s. I heard about JB's father playing professionally, but it was a conversation heard in passing. In my household, we seldom pay attention to sports.

Cruising along Pacific Coast Highway, we pull into a gated community and arrive at a Malibu beachside retreat belonging to Jake's parents. Inside, the back wall of the home is floor-to-ceiling glass with a view of the rolling tide coming onto shore. I'm so captivated by it that I forget about everything else.

"Our own private beach," I scream, opening the door and shedding my top and shorts, exposing my swimsuit underneath. I'm unrestricted, screaming and running to embrace the chilly waves that greet me and sweep me off my feet. Cassandra joins me, and together, we allow the waves to carry us back to shore.

"That was fun." My chest is heaving from all the excitement.

"Let's do that again," Cassandra shrieks.

We rush back bouncing on top of each oncoming wave until we see one large and strong enough to carry us back to shore. This goes on for minutes, and I savor every moment of it. Then I just lie there gazing at the sky with the rich wet sand underneath me and salt sticking to my skin. Cassandra is resting on her elbows with her right leg up and left leg down, appearing as if she's posing for a spread in a magazine.

I glance over my shoulder. The guys are sitting on the deck. I hear laughter and banter floating in the air punctuated with the cries of seagulls and the crash of the waves.

"Did you and Kyle make up?"

She smiles.

"I'll take that as a yes." I close my eyes.

"I don't know why I'm trying so hard. Once he leaves for Nashville, that's the end for us."

"Hello? You have Uncle Frenchy's flight benefits. You can see him every weekend if you'd like."

"Long-distance relationships never last."

I hear footsteps running toward us, and before I get a chance to react, I'm lifted up and tossed over a broad, muscular shoulder. I'm screaming, looking around to grasp my bearings, and whoever's holding me has a firm, tight grip as I feel us moving toward the chilly waters.

"Put me down," I scream.

I see Caleb standing on the deck laughing and pointing. I glance and see Jake with Cassandra tossed over his shoulder. JB pulls me down until we're eye level.

"Why'd you do that?"

He removes a strand of hair away from my eyes. "Just having fun. No harm, no foul."

"Sure," I respond.

Cassandra is sitting on Jake's shoulders coming in our direction.

"Let's see who'll be the last one standing," she screams.

Waves and buoyancy allow me to get on JB's shoulders with ease. At the count of three, we charge after Cassandra and Jake, wrestling at arm's length, testing our battle of wills. Cassandra is taller and maybe more athletically inclined, but I have a steady base on JB, and my arms are sturdier. She and Jake crash into the water with a huge splash. I raise my hands in victory. Jake and Cassandra come up for air.

"Rematch," they scream.

"Didn't get enough the first time?" JB quips.

A huge wave ascends on us, causing everyone to lose their balance. I fall off JB's shoulders, but he never lets go of my hand. We all come up for air and swim to shore. That was an adrenaline rush. Caleb walks up.

"A point for Team JB and Maddie, a point for Mother Nature, and a big round goose egg for Team Jake and Cass," Caleb announces

"We're not done," Jake declares.

"Yes, we are," JB says, speaking for both of us.

"My beach, my rules." Jake kneels so Cassandra can get on his shoulders. "At least even the score."

JB looks at me. "They actually believe we're going to let that happen?" He chuckles. "If you ever dream of kicking my butt, you'd better wake up and apologize."

"Not up for the challenge?" Cassandra taunts.

"Let's get this over with," JB says, effortlessly positioning me atop his shoulders.

I'm impressed because he doesn't wince or buckle underneath my weight. He is steady and calm. As soon as we get in the water and count to three, Cassandra and I tussle. This time, she uses her long arms to her advantage, but I hold firm.

Underneath me, I hear JB shouting, "Get her, Maddie."

"Look." Cassandra points off, but her attempt at distracting me fails.

"No cheating," Caleb referees from the side.

"Finish her, Maddie," I hear JB say.

I find that spot underneath her armpits where she's ticklish and hone in.

"Maddie, stop," she squeals and falls into the water.

"Damn." Jake pulls her up.

"She cheated. You saw it, Caleb."

"Victory for Team JB and Maddie," Caleb declares. "I'm going inside to play Legend of Zelda."

JB and I revel in our small victory. "Let's go for a victory lap and wave to our fans," he says.

Jake and Cassandra wave us off and follow Caleb inside.

JB turns so my chest is pressed against his back, and I hold on to his shoulders, and together, we swim parallel to the shore.

"Listen to the roar of the crowd." He imitates a sports announcer and the crowd's roar.

"I think they like us." I play along with him.

He releases my hold and swims a few strokes ahead of me before turning over. He takes my hands and pulls me closer to him, wrapping my curvy body against his lean, athletic, muscular build. Not a word exchanges between us, but looking into his brown eyes, I notice they travel from my eyes to my full lips to the pendant around my neck and down to my size 40 DDs. My spine quivers as it did in the jeep, and I feel my nipples coming alive through my swimsuit. I never imagined I'd be in this position—not with JB. I think he wants to kiss me.

"Having fun yet?" he asks.

"All depends on what you consider fun."

He takes my hand, and we capture the minutes, jumping over waves, and riding them until the thrill wears off and we end up on the beach, spent, laughing at ourselves. The chill of the evening settles in, but I'm not ready to go inside just yet. JB grabs a blanket and wraps it around me.

"Thank you," I say, eyeing him. This whole exchange and interaction feels odd.

He grabs his own blanket, wraps it around himself, and sits next to me.

"What kind of music are you into?" he asks.

"Classical," I answer.

"I can dig classical."

"Really?" I'm a little skeptical. I bet he doesn't know a composer aside from Beethoven. "Who's your favorite composer?"

"I'm not sure of the composer, but I can play a little of the 'William Tell Overture on piano."

My ears perk up. "That's not an easy one."

"Why not?" he asks.

"It requires a lot of coordination." I reach for his hands; they are large in comparison to mine.

"Your hands can amass the span of the chords. It's easy for you to play."

As I talk, I notice him watching me quietly.

"I'm impressed you actually know its proper name. Most people just call it the Lone Ranger song." I say.

He chuckles, displaying a row of straight white teeth. "My pops watched Lone Ranger reruns. Catchy theme music."

"So how old were you when you started lessons?"

"I taught myself."

"You taught yourself?" I almost leap out of my skin.

"Yeah," he replies like it's no big deal.

"Brilliant. So, you have no formal training?"

"My mom saw my talent and decided to put me in lessons when I was eleven. It didn't last because my dad made me quit to focus on basketball."

"Unbelievable."

We now stare at each other in yet another awkward moment of silence. The summers I spent in the past when JB came around, he was that friend tagging along with Caleb whom I never gave a second look. Not that he wasn't attractive. He was just the boy next door. Now, looking at him, I see symmetrical features, smooth tan skin with firm muscles, and soft brown eyes. Tonight, as we talk and he occasionally looks out into the vast sea, I study his profile. His cheekbones are defined, his nose is narrow and tapering. I notice for a guy, he has long eyelashes, and while we talk, and he's gathering his thoughts, they flit, and I find that oddly enchanting.

"All this time, I had no idea about this side of you," I say, breaking the silence.

"Basketball's just the tip of the iceberg."

"How old are you?" I ask.

"Same age as Caleb—our birthdays are a day apart."

"You just celebrated your twentieth birthday in January—?" I ask.

"The thirteenth," he answers.

"How did you celebrate?"

"Me, Caleb, and our line brothers hung out. Got wasted. We had a game two days later and lost. Everyone blamed me because I was still recovering."

I notice a scar on his upper arm. It looks like a brand you see on cattle.

"That looks painful," I say, pointing.

"I just crossed over. I was so hyped; I don't remember feeling it," he says, looking at the scar.

"Crossed over?" I ask

"It's the process of going from a pledge to a full member of a fraternity."

"Guys are just weird. Why would you do that?" I ask.

"You'll see when you get to Juilliard. You might have an interest in a sorority and go through the process. Only then will you understand."

"I doubt if there's anything like that at Juilliard. I only care about one thing: classical music."

"Hey, you guys," Cassandra shouts from the deck, "let's grab a bite to eat."

With that, JB offers me a hand, and we walk back. As we ascend the stairs to the deck, I look down and see my shirt and shorts are exactly where I left them.

After dinner at a popular Malibu diner on the pier, Jake takes us for a ride down Hollywood Boulevard. We pass Mann's Chinese Theater where even at this late hour, throngs of pedestrians and tourists mill about. Across the street is the Hollywood Pantages Theater where more pedestrians gather and the bright beams from an array of search lights ascend into the night sky. The strip has its share of sights, and being in the Jeep Wrangler with the top removed, we are privy to its sounds. There is the screech of car brakes, loud car horns, rock music blaring from speakers, and women walking the street blowing us kisses while we wait at a traffic light.

"Hey, baby." One blows a huge pink bubble until it pops. "Roses are red, your balls are blue. Twenty dollars to suck; fifty dollars to screw."

JB, Caleb, and Jake are amused. She stands popping her gum and licking her ruby-red lips, anticipating one of them saying something. I'm praying the light changes soon.

Cassandra leans in and whispers, "I feel really bad for her."

Finally, when the light turns green and Jake drives off, she yells, "Lame-ass losers."

"Hey JB, you peeped her spitting bars like a pro?" Caleb asks.

"Definitely missed her calling," he quips.

I listen as Caleb, JB, and Jake banter before I feel myself nodding off.

Four

I glance at the clock on the nightstand, and it's 7:34. I imagine Daddy's fully awake and in his study pouring over scripture. Mornings are his time with God. I force myself to get up and open the drapes so I can feast my eyes on my view. Early mornings in L.A. are usually overcast. Smog is a real thing here. I grab my pen and journal and immediately pour out my thoughts.

A sharp knock on the door interrupts me.

"It's open," I answer before putting a period at the end of my sentence.

Aunt Mary appears wearing bright yellow. The color against her honey-bronze complexion gives her a glow. If she wants me to go with her to the center, I am willing to go and commit a few hours. I really want to see Rosie, the artist. I sense something special about her.

"Good morning, niecy." She sits on the bed. "What time did you guys get in?"

"After midnight."

"I see." She nods. "I realize you're a high school graduate, bright, and intelligent as they come, but you're only seventeen, and in the state of California, that makes you a minor."

I nod, totally not expecting this, but totally getting it.

"I don't have a curfew per se, but I do have respectable hours I feel a young lady should adhere to."

I listen quietly as she proceeds.

"My house rules are simple and straightforward: no drugs, no sex, no strange characters." She stops. "That last rule may be a little hard to follow. I believe 11:30 is a respectable time to be home. I had the same talk with Cassandra. I hope this is the last time we have this discussion. Frenchy and I promised we'd look after you like we would our own."

She runs her hands through my hair. "This color is starting to grow on me."

"See, I knew it would."

"Why did you choose that color?" she asks.

"I dunno. I wanted to do something different."

"I see."

"Quick question," I begin, changing the subject. "Even if we're out with Caleb and JB, we still have to be inside by 11:30?"

"Yes." Aunt Mary's arms are folded, and her expression tells me no further explanation is necessary. "Only legs and liquor stores are open after midnight."

I sometimes forget how she sprinkles droplets of unexpected humor.

"Take the day off. Enjoy the city."

With that, she leaves the room. I wait a beat before I get out of bed to knock on Cassandra's door.

"I'm up." I hear the grogginess in her voice.

I climb in bed and remove the sleep mask from her eyes. She grabs a pillow and plops it over her head.

"I got the curfew lecture."

She removes the pillow. "What did she say?"

I recalled the conversation, and when I'm finished, Cassandra places the pillow back over her head.

"What's the game plan today?" I ask.

"You're not volunteering?"

"Aunt Mary gave me the day off."

"Cool. I talked Kyle into taking the day off too. Let's hook up with Gregory."

I almost forgot about Gregory. He's part of the crew from our camp days. I'm not sure if I want to spend the day with Gregory. He's cool when he's not annoying you with his jokes and pranks. My mind drifts to last night at the diner. When everyone else was busy laughing and feeding their faces, JB and I played footsies. At first, it was an accident —my foot brushed against his long legs while in conversation. Then it happened again. This time, when the owner, who knew Jake, stopped by to chat. JB and I locked eyes, and a look of confusion was displayed in his expression. He didn't know how to read me, didn't know whether my bumping him was a nervous tick or me being flirty. As I sipped lemonade from my straw, I felt the hairs of his legs tickling the smooth-ness of mine. I slipped off a sandal and allowed my foot to travel up his leg in a slow, deliberate fashion. The sensation gives me goosebumps when I think about it.

"Where are we going? What are we going to wear?" I ask.

"I don't know, but I always pack a bikini and an extra change of clothes in case we go to the beach."

"When you saw Gregory last week, how did he look?" I ask.

"You'll see when he comes."

"Is he still skinny?"

"You'll see" is all she says.

Around noon, Gregory and Kyle show up at the house at the same time as Uncle Frenchy. Although I'm happy to see my uncle, I'm distracted at how much Gregory's changed in a year. He's filled out and muscular. His chest is firm and not sunken. He feels different. I'm impressed, but I don't want him to know that.

"Niecy, bebby." Uncle Frenchy and I embrace. He's still in his pilot's uniform. "I found these two wandering in my yard," he says of Kyle and Gregory. "I was coming in here to call the dog catcher."

"Man," Kyle says, "I don't get any love when I come around."

Gregory is preppy, sporty, wearing cargo shorts, a polo shirt, and boat shoes. He greets me with a warm embrace and smells like fresh scented soap, airy and clean.

"Stay put. Don't you go anywhere," Uncle Frenchy says just before leaving the room.

"Frenchy." Cassandra's giving him the evil eye. I've always found it quite amusing that everyone, even his own children, call him Frenchy.

Gregory gives me another hug; this time it lingers. "God, you're beautiful," he whispers in my ear. His voice has gotten deeper since I saw him last. I pull back and offer him a seat.

"How have you've been?" I ask.

"Miserable," he says with a deadpan expression. "I wrote you letters, I sent you flowers, I heard a poindexter escorted you to the ball."

"He was not a poindexter," I protest.

"I didn't get an invitation to your graduation, and you had several concertos I didn't get invites to. What did I ever do to you?"

"You know what you did."

Gregory's eyes grow wide behind his horn-rimmed glasses. "Enlighten me, please." He chuckles.

"Tell him," I summon Cassandra and Kyle.

"Was it the frog in your bunker?" Cassandra asks.

"Among other things," I reply.

"Ahhh, that wasn't me?" He sounds surprised.

"Don't try it," I respond. "I kept feeling something cold and slippery, then I heard a loud croak, and when I pulled back the covers..."

I recoil thinking about that moment. He played countless tricks, but that trick had gone too far. It didn't help that I got teased afterward from anyone who was within earshot of my blood curdling screams.

"Wow" is all he can say. "I am truly sorry."

"I didn't care if I ever saw you again."

"Was it that serious?"

"You traumatized my cousin." Cassandra comes over to give me a hug. "Even Kermit the Frog's a trigger." She holds back a laugh.

I move her away. "Ha. Ha. Ha."

Gregory's looking at me with pitiful puppy dog eyes. I find it quite amusing.

"Other than the frog experience, how have you been?" he asks.

"I'm happy to be here."

"I'm happy you're here too," he says.

Uncle Frenchy enters the room with a camera. "Can I get my lovely daughter and my lovely niece to stand for me, please?"

"Frenchy, we have someplace to go," Cassandra says.

"Just do what I tell you, chère," he says in that Louisiana Creole drawl.

He gathers me and Cassandra together. Neither of us wants to take pictures but manage to give our best poses.

"Gee, Frenchy. What are we, chopped liver?" Kyle asks.

"I don't want to crack my lens. I paid good money for this camera," Uncle Frenchy quips then motions them to join us for a picture anyway.

Gregory stands next to me. I feel his hand on the small of my back. I'm hesitant about my hand placement, so I leave them at my sides.

"Where did you fly in from?" Kyle asks.

"Beijing." Uncle Frenchy reaches into his back pocket and pulls out what looks like tickets. "From one of my passengers."

Cassandra takes them. "Playoff tickets. Thanks, Frenchy."

"You're lucky there's four and I'm jet-lagged. My plans were to take Mary and the girls, but you four make a date of it."

"I don't care what they say about you, you're all right with us," Kyle says.

Kyle and Gregory show their appreciation, slapping hands with Uncle Frenchy.

"I want to talk to my niecy, but you all run along. We'll have plenty of time to talk." Uncle Frenchy walks with us outside.

"That's a fine automobile," Uncle Frenchy says, walking up to admire it. "Is this yours, Gregory?"

"Yes," Gregory says while opening the front door for me to sit inside.

"I know it's a Rolls but what?" Uncle Frenchy asks, eyeing its design.

"Corniche," Gregory answers before closing the door.

"What color is it?"

"It's called magnolia."

"That's nice. I'll need to work on my portfolio. Tell your old man to schedule me into a meeting." He shifts his focus to Kyle and Cassandra sitting in the backseat. "Tell your pops to brush up on that swing. Tee time is eight o'clock."

As Gregory puts the car in reverse, Uncle Frenchy backs away. "I got my eye on both of you." He points to Gregory and Kyle. They chuckle.

"Frenchy's a trip," Cassandra declares. "Gregory, why did you tell Frenchy this is your car, when you know it's your mother's."

"Why would I lie? Besides, I couldn't fit you all into the Testarossa."

"You could have. Cassandra would've made a nice hood ornament," Kyle says. He and Gregory think the comment is funny.

"Keep talking. You might end up being a spare tire," Cassandra says.

"Ohhhhh," we all say. Cassandra always has a quick comeback.

We arrive at Marina del Rey, where a valet attendant greets us, and Gregory casually hands him the keys to the car. We follow Gregory across a boardwalk where rows of boats are docked. As we walk, my eyes meet the stares of others whom I assume are boat enthusiasts. The looks on some faces are pleasant. Some Gregory introduces us to. Others are curious, *wondering*. I know that look all too well. I've dealt with it all my life. It's a look that says you don't belong in their spaces. I grew up in a predominantly white neighborhood, and I attended predominantly white schools. I perform classical music and I see the conductor and other musicians don't look like me. My response: I smile and keep walking. We arrive at a boat I guess is about fifty-feet-long.

"Gregory, this is a nice boat," Cassandra says. We all board it and stand on deck.

"Thank you."

"It smells new," I say.

"Just got it this past April for my eighteenth birthday. I've only been on it twice. Maybe the third time will be a charm."

"Your boat doesn't have a name," Kyle says.

"Yeah, I kept looking on the side of the boat for it," Cassandra says.

"I'm waiting to name it after someone special," he says looking at me. I try not to blush.

"Just name it after your mother," I say.

"She already has a yacht named after her. We keep it in the South of France," he says.

"Let's see how she rolls." Kyle rubs his hands together in anticipation.

Gregory begins a preparation that only a skilled boater goes through. I remember in camp he liked canoeing and rowing. Being on water is his thing.

Cassandra and I each packed totes with an extra change of clothing and toiletries. I was anticipating another day of hanging out at the beach, but Gregory's boat catches us totally by surprise.

"What type of boat is this?" I ask.

"It's a fifty-foot-Beneteau yacht. Perfect size to bareboat."

"Can we look around?" Cassandra asks.

"Sure. Just stow your totes in the berth quarters."

He opens a door, and inside are sleeping quarters, a dining area, a galley, and a tiny restroom he calls a lavatory. I notice when he speaks, he uses a lot of boating terms that go over our heads, but nonetheless, we locate our life vests. He and Kyle leave so Cassandra and I can change.

"He might name his boat after you," Cassandra begins. "How freakin' cool is that?"

"Flattering."

"You don't seem too excited."

"I'm not sure how I feel about him."

"Gregory's a good guy. He comes from a good family. Sure, he can be a pest, but what guy isn't?"

"He's like a fly that buzzes around your ear." I study myself in a mirror. The swimsuit I picked out is a lavender 1950s style that I remember my mother being fond of.

"That's pretty. Like vintage Hollywood glamour."

"It's modest."

"Maybe down there, but up top those girls are saying, 'Yoo-hoo. Look at us. Aren't we a nice perky pair?'"

"I should've packed a cover-up." I'm feeling a bit self-conscious.

"Please. If I had big, round breasts like yours, I'd flaunt them too. That's probably why I don't have them."

Cassandra's swimsuit is neon yellow with pink trim. We couldn't be more different with our styles. She grabs her hair and pulls it into a top knot. I pull mine into a ponytail. We hear the engine of the boat, and I feel us move, slowly.

Gregory and Kyle are on the top deck, and Gregory is at the helm. He pulls the boat away from the docks and controls it down the waterway and out into the open waters.

"Neon. What a sight," I hear Kyle shouting at Cassandra.

"Why are you shouting?" Cassandra says.

"'Cause you can't possibly hear me over that swimsuit."

Cassandra's mouth drops. Gregory and I giggle.

"I like it. That's all that matters," she says.

"God forbid anything happens. We won't have to worry about search and rescue. You wave, they'll spot us."

"I like the colors. It looks really nice against her complexion," I say, coming to her defense because I know she would do the same for me.

"Thank you, Maddie. Kyle, if you want to get in my good graces, I suggest you stop teasing me."

He slips on a pair of sunglasses. "Sure is bright out here."

Cassandra takes off his glasses and runs with them, descending the boat stairs with Kyle close behind, leaving me and Gregory alone.

"Sit." He motions to the chair across from him.

I sit and take in the scenery. Other boats are out. The weather is perfect—not too hot—and the winds are subtle and not too breezy.

"You love to sail," I say.

"Boating is life. The rest is just details."

"I feel that way about performing."

"Are you still performing?"

"I am. Right now, I'm on a break."

"You, too, huh."

"I've been constantly performing for the last five years."

"Would've been nice to see at least one."

"Back to you. So, what are you doing on your break?" I ask.

"After graduation, I'm jumping on a red-eye to London. Once I'm there, I'm meeting with a crew of guys from the yacht club."

"Why?"

"We're summer racing in the English Channel."

"The English Channel? Wow. And what will you do after that?"

"I've got a regatta in Sardinia," he says.

"What's a regatta?" I ask.

"Boat racing," he answers.

"Doesn't sound like you're getting much of a break to me."

"It's just two races. The rest of the summer I'll be in Nice."

"Why don't you sail around the world?"

"That doesn't sound like a bad idea." He steers the boat. "Thank you, Madeline May Richardson. I just might do that."

I don't know what it is about Gregory. In my mind, I still see that scrawny kid with the glasses pulling pranks and running wild through the woods chasing after me screaming, "Me Tarzan, you Jane." We kissed once, if you consider a puckered-up, dry peck on the lips kissing.

"What are your plans for the summer?" he asks.

"Plans. What's that?"

"One who doesn't plan will find trouble right at the door."

"You can say that again. I didn't plan to see you today."

"I'm good trouble, though. Don't you think?"

"There's nothing good about you."

"Madeline May Richardson, you're breaking my heart."

"In camp, you used to pull my braids. One time I was walking back to the cabin, and you jumped out of the bushes. You startled me so I wet myself."

He covers his mouth, stifling a giggle. "I'm sorry."

"You liked tormenting me, didn't you?"

"You were too serious and uptight. You needed to loosen up," he says. "Camp is where you have fun; tell scary stories by the campfire, sneak off and go skinny dipping in the lake."

"You went skinny dipping in the lake?" I ask.

"All the time."

"I was never wild like you."

"Do you have a wild side?" he asks. I feel the boat slowing down. I watch Gregory push buttons, and the boat comes to a stop.

"I don't know," I answer.

He turns off the boat, and the sensation of the waves and currents gives me a queasy feeling.

"I think you do," he answers. I notice his eyes are dreamy and hazy behind his glasses. "You just never had an opportunity to show it."

"I go wild on stage, I guess, when I'm really into the music."

We both hear Cassandra scream. My heart races immediately. There is a confused, alarming look on Gregory's face as he leaps from the top deck to the lower one. I follow close behind descending a ladder, not sure what to expect, but praying everything is okay.

Five

We find Kyle and Cassandra splashing and playing in the ocean.

"We heard you scream. What happened?" I ask.

"This water is freaking cold when you first dive in," she says.

I see Kyle now floating on his back.

"It's nice once you get over the initial shock," he says.

"You're okay, now?" Gregory asks. "That scream had me spooked for a minute."

"Yes, we're good," Cassandra says, lying on her back, splashing her toes.

I stick my toe in to get adjusted to the temperature—testing the waters, if you will.

"Quick joke," Gregory begins.

"Here we go," I say.

"What did the ocean say to the shore?" he asks.

"You got us," Cassandra answers.

"Nothing. It just waved."

He gauges my reaction. I give it a thumbs down. Kyle and Cassandra give fake laughs. I take a plunge into the chilly Pacific, going down about twelve feet before swimming back to the surface. Gregory is now sitting on the edge of the boat with his feet in the water.

"Watch out for that shark," he screams.

"Quit playing." Kyle straightens up.

Gregory is amused. We are far enough out in the waters that I wouldn't rule out the possibility of sharks nearby.

"Move out of the way," I say, slapping his feet. He stands and gives me a hand.

"What's the matter? Don't tell me you're afraid of a little shark."

I felt a lot safer on the boat. Kyle and Cassandra frolic a few minutes more before joining us on the boat.

"Do you have anything to eat?" Cassandra asks.

"Twenty-feet below us, there's rockfish, bass, halibut, and yellowtail."

"I hate you, Gregory. How dare you bring us out here and you don't have anything to eat?"

"Are you hungry?" he asks me.

"I sure am," I say with a quickness.

"Kyle and I can jump in and catch a handful of sardines to tide you over."

"Gregory Washington, if you don't turn this boat around and get us back," Cassandra says.

"All right. All right. Jesus Christ."

Sailing back, Cassandra and I find a spot on the deck to sunbathe. Kyle squeezes between us, and we crack jokes about hearing our stomachs growl over the waves. Suddenly, the urge to jump in for a fresh catch doesn't seem like a bad idea.

"I wish Gregory wasn't going to Europe this summer. I could get used to chilling out here doing nothing," Kyle says.

"Me too," Cassandra responds before she turns to me. "Think you can talk him out of it?"

I glance at Cassandra like she's lost her mind. "No way. He's got the summer all planned out."

I hear Gregory call my name, and I sit up. "I'll be back." I climb the ladder up to the second deck where I find him steering with one hand and talking into a CB with the other.

"I'm ordering pizza. What would you like on yours?" he asks.

"I like Italian sausage with peppers, mushrooms, and anchovies on a thin, crispy crust." He repeats my request into the CB before placing it in its cradle.

"I've ordered pizzas for all of us. I hope you don't die within the next hour waiting on them."

"We'll just dive in the ocean like you said and find something," I joke.

He smiles. "I like your swimsuit. I meant to tell you that earlier."

"Thank you."

The boat we're on gets closer to the marina. Gregory steers it back into the spot where it was docked earlier. He turns to me. "We can go inside, or we can hang out here."

"I like it here," I say watching other boats come and go from the marina.

"Hey." Cassandra and Kyle appear. "What are we waiting on?" she asks.

"Pizza," Gregory answers.

"Cool. You've known us long enough, so you already know how Kyle and I like ours."

They sit across from us. "Can we hang out on your boat while you're in Europe?" Cassandra asks.

"H—Hell no," Gregory answers with a deadpan expression.

"Awww. Come on."

He adamantly shakes his head.

"You'd rather it sit and collect dust?" she asks.

"Absolutely" is Gregory's response.

An hour later, our pizzas arrive, hot and fresh with several eight-ounce bottles of Coke in a bucket of ice. We literally stuff ourselves. I feel drowsy and tired. When we finish eating, Gregory and I lie right there on the deck staring at the clouds. Cassandra and Kyle are inside the cabin.

"I think I'm going to dream about pizza tonight," I say. From my peripheral I see Gregory's head turn, and I feel his eyes on me.

"You don't dream about me?" he asks.

"No."

"Why not?"

"I just don't."

"You keep breaking my heart, Maddie."

"I'm sorry. I do like you as a friend, though."

"That's it? A friend?"

"Yes."

He focuses on the clouds again.

"Are you okay?" I ask.

He looks at me. "What do you think?"

"I say you'll be just fine."

We lie quietly for a moment, staring at the clouds.

"What do you want more than anything?" he asks.

"I want to be the best concert pianist and composer to ever live," I respond.

He sits up, his eyes still focused on the clouds. "You see that cloud? It's giving us the finger."

"No way. Where?" I look, leaning in closer to see what he sees, and at that moment, I feel his lips press against my cheek. His lips are soft and tender. I pull away.

"I should've known. You play too much," I say before I stand.

He chuckles. "I can't help it. Look, it won't happen again."

"I don't believe you."

"We're just friends, okay? Is that okay with you?" he asks with a fake smile and extends his hand for me to give him a lift. Instead, I turn and open the door to the cabin. I can hear him say, "Oh, you're just going to leave me hanging" before the door closes behind me.

Gregory says it's halftime with an attitude. Whatever. That's when we arrive at the Forum and run into Mona and Ursula, more of the crew from camp. Cassandra spots them right away. We greet each other with cheek-to-cheek kisses.

"I see, I see." Mona eyes me and Gregory.

"We're just friends." He says it as if it were a joke.

"Why don't you join us?" Mona asks.

"I hope you have floor seats," Gregory answers.

"What's that? I have a suite, darling." Mona declares with a flip of her hair.

"You ladies take the suite. We'll be courtside," Kyle says.

"Let's meet here in the fourth quarter around the five-minute mark," Cassandra says.

The boisterous noise from spectators and the music grow to a deafening pitch.

"We'll see you then," Gregory shouts over the noise.

Just like that, he and Kyle walk off chatting, meandering through the crowd until they are out of sight.

"We've got some catching up to do." Mona grabs my hand. I remember how animated she was from camp, always rallying us together for some reason or another.

Inside the suite are other guests intermingling and drinking. I walk to the balcony and see the immense crowd, and below us are the players on the court. I'm trying to pinpoint Gregory and Kyle, but I might as well be looking for a needle in a haystack.

"Sparkling water?" A waiter with a tray of flutes garnished with fresh strawberries approaches me and Cassandra.

We each take one and sip. Ursula has a flute in hand, and she offers us a seat. Mona breaks with us to join a group of people. One of the faces I recognize from a popular television show.

"Cassandra tells me you are in L.A. for the summer. How fabulous is that?" When Ursula smiles, I notice how straight and white her teeth are. When we were in camp, she wore braces, and sometimes when she spoke, spittle would seep out.

"It seems different, not performing and not being at camp."

"I entertained the thought of being a camp counselor, but once I found out you guys weren't going, I decided I wasn't either." Ursula says.

Mona joins us on the sofa. She looks mature for her age, and a slight glance at her chest, it appears as though she's been under her father's knife and gotten plastic surgery. I see cleavage popping up from a sequined bustier. She's wearing a white jacket with shoulder pads and white shorts to match. Her lips are blazing with pink gloss, and her eye makeup is popping with jeweled tones.

"I like that top," Cassandra says.

Mona sits erect and pushes up her bustier.

"And I see there's more than just school out for the summer," Cassandra adds.

"Oh, you noticed?"

"Daddy did those?"

"No. Jerry, the other doctor on staff."

Without missing a beat, she lowers her top, exposing round perky breasts. Luckily, our backs are turned to many of the guests in the suite. She carries on like exposing breasts in public is a natural thing. She pulls up her bustier.

"Every girl is not as fortunate as Maddie to have nice, voluptuous, breasts." She winks at me. "So, what's happening with you and Gregory?"

"Nothing," I answer.

"There's something you just don't want to tell us." Ursula sips her sparkling water.

"I'm serious. He's just a friend I hang out with."

"Speaking of hanging out, I was just with your brother and JB. They're a couple of suites down from us, and they were with the girl from that popular tv show."

"Oh yeah, her," Cassandra begins. "She's actually cool."

"You've hung out with her?" Ursula asks.

"Once. JB's mom invited us over for dinner, and she was there with JB."

"Are they dating?" I ask.

"I don't really know the nature of the relationship. Now, I've seen her around town with a gorgeous hunk who has dreadlocks. I think he's a musician or something."

Mona begins, "I saw that movie she was in."

"What did you think?" Cassandra asks.

"You couldn't have paid me all the money in Hollywood to play that role. And that sex scene? It was graphic."

I had no clue who or what they were talking about, but the mentioning of JB's name sent butterflies fluttering.

Mona leaves and returns with the actress girl I recognize from a television show I saw once or twice.

"Ladies, this is, Raven." Mona sits her next to me. "Raven and I met playing tennis."

"Hi, ladies."

She's pretty and petite with a small, svelte frame like a dancer. She has the prettiest cocoa brown skin, and when she smiles, the dimples in her cheeks are pronounced.

"You played an actual match with Mona?" Cassandra asks.

"Of course," she replies.

"I've partnered with her in doubles. She's not that good." Cassandra's way of breaking the ice.

Raven doesn't reply, but her facial expression signals she agrees with Cassandra.

"Don't listen to her," Mona says.

"You could improve a little on your backswing," Raven says, as if the thought was tucked away and she was just waiting for the right moment to address it.

Mona's mouth drops. "Raven, I thought you were my friend."

"I'm sorry." Raven giggles, showing off her deep dimples.

"You need a real partner," Cassandra adds.

"I partner with my sister."

"Sounds like a real player. Look, my brother and I against you and your sister at doubles." Cassandra says.

"I will definitely take you up on the challenge."

Raven and Cassandra shake hands.

"Bring it," Cassandra says.

"Oh, we will," Raven says with confidence.

"I don't believe this. How are you scheduling a tennis date without me?" Mona says.

"No one's leaving you out. As a matter of fact, you keep score," Cassandra says before taking a sip.

Mona narrows her eyes into slits. "I used to like you."

"What? Either you keep score or be the ball girl. Stay off the court."

Mona flips her hair. "You're in my suite, guzzling my Perrier, and talking noise to me?"

Just like that, the energy in the room goes from airy and playful to chilly enough to freeze the Perrier in the glasses.

Cassandra calmly places her flute on a table nearby and wipes her hands. "We were just about to leave anyway."

Ursula holds out her hand. "No one's going anywhere. Look, Mona, she was just joking. Ha, ha. Loosen up."

"Maddie, you stay. Cassandra, bye, bye." Mona dismisses her with a wave of the hand.

"Oh, she's serious," Raven says before she and Cassandra exchange numbers. Mona puts her arm around Raven. "You're my friend, not hers."

Cassandra finds the situation humorous. Raven removes Mona's arm. "Is this how you treat your friends?"

"It's cool." Cassandra smirks. "We fight all the time. Trust me, she'll call me by the end of the week."

"Slim chance," Mona answers.

"Don't kid yourself," Cassandra fires back.

I say my goodbyes to Ursula. She gives me a contact number and an invitation to lunch. Mona approaches. "You don't have to leave."

"Listen, I'll be the ball girl if you keep score," I say.

Mona rolls her eyes. "You've got jokes. Bye."

"Just think about it."

"Bye, Maddie. I don't want to not like you too."

"The feeling is mutual," I say before the door closes in my face. Cassandra and I look at each other and erupt in laughter.

She locks arms with me. "Another adventure awaits."

"What do you have in mind?"

"Let's see if we can buy a drink."

"Oh, Cassandra, I don't know about that."

"What? Follow my lead."

My heart starts beating at a frantic pace, and my palms start sweating.

"How much are you willing to bet I walk up to the bar, order a drink, and won't get asked for my ID?" she asks.

"Let's see."

She walks up to a crowded bar. Several bartenders are busy mixing drinks and taking orders.

"Let's see if they're asking for ID," she whispers. We check out the scene of Laker enthusiasts ordering rounds of spirits, beer, and wine.

A gentleman in a spectacular mood, feeling quite generous shouts, "A round for all of my friends who love purple and gold." Before you know it, Cassandra and I are holding bottles of Budweiser.

"See, I told you. Cheers." We click bottles; she sips. I just hold mine.

"You can have this one, too, when you're finished."

"Take a sip. It won't hurt."

"Since when did you start drinking beer?" I ask.

She's only a year younger than me, but she's always carried herself as the older, carefree, streetwise cousin to my sheltered, regimented existence.

"You really want to know," she says, giggling.

"I asked you, didn't I?"

"Let's find Caleb and JB to see if they can get us more drinks."

"Bad idea."

"You're no fun."

I find the ticket stub that has our seats. "Let's watch the game."

"First, let me finish my beer." Holding a finger, she turns up the bottle.

"And to think you went to charm school," I say, shaking my head.

The energy inside the arena is electrifying. I spot Kyle and Gregory seated courtside, and inches in front of them are the Lakers and the Celtics players handling the ball, and all you can hear are the bottom of their sneakers squeaking against the floor.

"Glad you could join me," Gregory says.

Kyle moves over so Cassandra sits next to me.

I don't follow sports, but the atmosphere is wild with people shouting expletives at the referees whenever a bad call is made. I hear the players spouting expletives too.

"Rowdy bunch." I find myself now having to shout.

"Intense." Gregory is sitting on the edge of his seat. "I wasn't expecting you back so soon."

I didn't want to go into details as to why the whole thing seems trivial. "You're my ride, so I'm hanging out with you."

Gregory nods, and behind those horned-rimmed glasses, I see a guy who really wants to be with me. I see it in his eyes and the quiet way he stares at me.

"What?"

"Nothing." I smile.

***

Riding home that night, everyone is in a celebratory mood. The Lakers beat the Celtics 141 to 121. Aunt Mary's lecture is in the back of my mind. When I glance at my watch, it reads 10:22.

I look in the side-view mirror and see cop lights. Gregory notices them, too, but then the cop's siren blares, signaling for him to pull over.

"What the f—" Gregory reduces his speed.

"Pull over, man." Kyle's tone is serious.

Gregory pulls the car over. He glances at me, and for the first time, I see fear mixed with confusion registering in his eyes.

Moments later, two white cops approach the car. Gregory presses the down button on his window.

"What's the problem, officers?"

"Any drugs or weapons in the car?" one of them asks.

"No," Gregory replies

"License and registration." The officer's tone is dry and routine.

There was one other time I'd been a passenger in a car pulled over by the police. My friend, Lauren, who's white, was pulled over for going ten miles over the speed limit. She even admitted it, and the officer was sympathetic and allowed her to go with a warning. Gregory has one hand on the steering wheel while the other fumbles nervously to open the glove compartment. He retrieves the registration paper and hands it over to the officer who gives it to the other officer who walks back to the squad car.

"Can you tell me why you pulled me over?"

"Vehicle looks suspicious." He shines a bright light on us. "Where you headed?"

"Taking my date home," Gregory answers, shielding his eyes from the blinding light with his hand.

Minutes later, the other officer returns with Gregory's license and registration.

"Checks out. You're a long way from Beverly Hills. What business do you have in this part of town?" he asks.

"Says he's taking his date home," the other officer answers.

"How can you afford a car like this? What do you do for a living?"

The question catches us off guard. I hear Cassandra gasp, and Kyle scoffs from the backseat.

"Am I free to leave?" Gregory has both hands on the wheel.

"You kids stay out of trouble." The officer waves and walks away.

Gregory slowly drives off, checking his rearview mirror, I notice his temple jumping. I take his hand and clasp it.

"I hate these bullshit L.A. cops."

"That was a shitty ass reason to pull you over," Kyle adds.

"Harassment, plain and simple. I got badge numbers. They messed with the wrong one," Gregory says.

My heart is still pounding. "Are you okay?"

"Oh, yeah. It's a rite of passage to get pulled over out here."

"Caleb got pulled over and searched once. What saved him was one of the cops apparently went to USC and recognized him from the basketball games."

"Last week, they pulled me over in my neighborhood on suspicion of driving a stolen vehicle. If my friend, Ruger, hadn't been in the area, they would've taken me into custody." Gregory says.

"They are relentless out here, especially if you're Black," Kyle declares.

"Especially if you're Black." Cassandra backs him.

Gregory starts speaking in French.

"I'm afraid to ask what that means," I say.

"Trust me, you don't want to know."

When we arrive in the driveway, it's 11:24. I lean in and give Gregory a kiss, this time a real one. His lips are soft and his kisses gentle. When we pull away for air, I see a reflection of the moonlight bouncing off his glasses. At that moment, I'm grateful that the traffic stop didn't go south.

"I'm having a graduation celebration this Saturday. I want you to come," he whispers.

"I'll be there."

We kiss once more before Cassandra and I both grab our things and get out of the car. Without missing a beat, she sticks the key in the door and opens. It's 11:30, without a minute to spare.

Six

"Ta-da."

Aunt Mary shows me a shiny, black baby grand piano. It is absolutely gorgeous.

"She's a beauty. Thank you." I walk over and sit down in front of it, pressing middle C, listening for a clear rich sound.

"As soon as you told me you needed it, I made some calls. I found someone willing to donate one, and here she is."

I play scales and arpeggios, listening for buzzing and twanging. The sound is sweet and clear. Then I proceed to play one of my favorite compositions by Chopin, "Prelude in E Minor," such a somber tune.

"I'm going to start crying here in a minute," she says.

I switch up and lighten the mood by playing the intro to Scott Joplin's "The Entertainer."

"Now that's more like it." In a split second, her whole demeanor changes.

"I'm glad you made the suggestion."

"Thank you for jumping on it."

Moments later, when the children see me, they rush me, all ten of them—or so it seems.

"Where were you?" Raquel, the cherub-faced girl asks.

"We thought you'd never come back," Damon says.

"Don't leave us like that again," Jakwon, the boy with the sun-kissed skin tells me.

"I was only gone for one day."

"That's too long," Blaze says.

What's going to happen when it's time for me to leave for Juilliard? "What did you do when I was away?"

Blaze raises his hand. I notice he has a fresh haircut.

"A fireman came and talked to us."

"Good. What did you learn?"

Damon raises a hand. "When there's a fire, you stop, drop, and roll."

"Absolutely."

"I knew someone who caught on fire. They were running down the street, and people were screaming, 'Drop and roll. Drop and roll,'" Damon says.

"My babysitter's house caught on fire. She left a cigarette in an ashtray, and one of her children picked it up and dropped it," Blaze explains.

"Oh dear" is my response.

Dee raises her hand. "I saw a car fire on the expressway," she tells me in a singsong voice.

Everyone wants to share just as Rosie the artist walks up and greets me with a hug. Her hair is combed into two French braids that stop at her shoulders.

"We missed you yesterday," she says, pulling up a chair to sit with the younger group of children.

"We had a dentist come and tell us about cleaning our teeth too," Blaze begins.

"Maddie, I got a cavity." A girl with mouth wide open and drool falling off her lip walks up to show me proof.

"I bet you don't know how to floss your teeth," I hear a little voice say behind her.

"You suppose to floss every night before you go to bed and after every meal," says Raquel, with the pretty, cherub-face.

"If you eat a lot of candy and don't brush your teeth, you'll have a cavity just like Jessica," Damon says.

"Cavities can be very painful if they aren't removed," I say.

"My cavity doesn't hurt," the little girl named Jessica says to me.

I let them talk among themselves for a couple of minutes before I motion them to follow me to the piano where they gather. They can't keep their little fingers to themselves, banging and punching the keys, especially Blaze and Damon.

"No touching the piano until I say it's okay to do so."

Dee raises a hand. "Can you play us a song?" she says in her cute little singsong voice.

Sitting at the piano, I began to play Chopin's "Nocturn in E Flat." As I play, I glance at my little audience.

"Wow. How did you learn to play like that?" Dee asks.

"Years of practice." Their expressions light up.

"I want to learn how to play like that," Dee says.

"Me too." Damon says.

I stop and spin around on my bench. "I'll teach you all the basics. Remember these important keys—E, G, B, D, F. These are the keys of the treble clef. Or you can remember it by saying, 'Every good boy does fine.'" I spend an hour telling them about the components of the piano, and I allow each of them the opportunity to touch the keys and listen to the sounds.

Kyle even drops in for a minute. He gathers the boys and goes outside to play basketball. After the lessons on the piano, I grab a little snack and join Rosie and Dee. Rosie has her sketch pad and tears out a sheet to give to Dee.

"What grade are you going to?" I ask Rosie.

"The ninth grade," she says. She's sketching a picture of an eagle in flight with children riding on its wing.

"How long have you been coming here?" I ask.

"About three years. I like it here. I love Mrs. Mary. She's like my second mom. I always tell her, 'Mrs. Mary, I wish you could adopt me.' She says that always makes her sad when I say that."

She concentrates on her sketch, adding details to it. She stops to admire it—or maybe even scrutinize. In my opinion, it's a genius work of art.

"Does she ever tell you why?" I ask.

"'Cause my real momma is a trip. Mrs. Mary don't want to feel like she's trying to take her place. I tell her all the time, my momma does not care. I'll be one less child she deals with."

I really don't know how to respond to that.

"Look what I did." Dee shows me her picture. She drew stick figures.

"Nice. Tell me about it."

"Well, this is the cop with the gun pointed at my daddy. He said 'freeze, don't move, or I'll blow your ass off.'"

I sit speechless, hearing this coming from her sweet voice. "This is all of us crying." She points to three stick figures with teardrops spewing like water sprinklers from their circle heads.

At that moment, I want to give her a hug. On the drive over, Aunt Mary and I talked about the children. For as many success stories, she's also had her share of disappointments.

"One of my eaglets who I nurtured from the time he was ten was no longer showing up. I found out he's joined a gang."

I listened to her beat herself up for being too busy and not listening and watching for signs. She said she made it her mission to hire more workers so she could spend more time focusing on the needs of the children. She couldn't control what happened to their lives once they left her care, but while they were with her, they were loved, nurtured, listened to, and affirmed.

Rosie held up her picture for me to see. "This is really nice," I respond.

She is such a gifted artist. Her sketches look so lifelike.

"What do you think about my drawing?" Dee asks.

"Your drawing tells an interesting story. When did this happen?"

She shrugs.

"Is your father okay?"

"He's still in jail," she answers. I notice her fidgeting with her knees and rubbing her side.

"How's your mother?"

Again, she shrugs.

"Who drops you off?"

"Sometimes I ride with Miss Vanessa."

"Who's Miss Vanessa?" I ask.

"She's one of the teachers," Rosie answers.

"How do you get here?" I ask Rosie.

"I usually walk or ride the bus."

I want to ask, Aren't you afraid to walk in this neighborhood?

Aunt Mary enters the room, accompanied by a visibly pregnant woman and a trio of dancers.

Aunt Mary claps. "May I have everyone's attention?" The constant talking and movement ceases.

"I want to introduce a very dear friend. We go way back to our days in Houston, Texas. I was her babysitter once, and I have watched her grow and blossom into a force to be reckoned with. She's a dancer, she's an actress, she's a director, a producer, she sings."

"Child, I do it all," she adds.

"I've been trying to get her to stop by for a while, but she's been so busy."

"Yes, I have, honey." She rubs her stomach. They share a girlish inside joke.

"Show of hands, how many of you love to dance?" Aunt Mary asks.

Almost everyone in the room raises their hand. "She's going to show you all some dance moves. Please welcome my friend, Mrs. Nella Harobed."

"Thank you, Mary. As you can clearly see, I'm in no position to perform, but anytime I get an opportunity to share a teaching moment for the babies, I'm all in."

She stands aside as one of the dancers gets into position. I get up and sit before the piano. She had music recorded on a cassette, but during the performance the player chewed it. That's when I began to play. Classical for the ballet performances, and because I saw the Tap Dance Kid on Broadway, I knew the tune by memory to accompany the performers during their tap routine. My timing is impeccable. Someone fishes the cassette out of the player and tries to wound it back and give it to Mrs. Harobed.

"Child, throw that thing away." She waves with a dismissive hand and encourages the children to clap. I watch carefully, following the movement of the dancers as they perform the latest dance moves. They encourage some of the children to join them. The boys come in from outside smelling of sweat, but the dancing continues. The atmosphere is festive. Aunt Mary even joins in, displaying an array of moves I'm much too clueless to name.

After the performance, Aunt Mary introduces me to Mrs. Harobed as the virtuosa then proceeds to tell her of my performances with the Houston and Dallas orchestras and all my accomplishments that probably would have bored anyone else, but Mrs. Harobed seems delighted. She gives me her number and says she will keep in touch, and in her down-home Houston way of flair, she says, "Honey, I know you will do well. We're cut from the same cloth." She winks.

***

Saying goodbye to the children isn't easy. Dee doesn't want to leave, so Miss Vanessa bribes her with a promise of ice cream.

Rosie turns to me. "Are you going to be here Monday?"

"Yes," I answer.

She gives me the sketch of the children riding on the wings of the eagle.

"Thank you." I retrieve it and study every detail.

A smile glosses across her lips. "I'll see you then. I've got a bus to catch."

Aunt Mary enters just as Rosie makes a dash for the door.

"Rosie."

Rosie turns around.

"You're leaving without giving me a hug?"

"I'm sorry, I'm tripping." Rosie sheepishly walks up and gives Aunt Mary a hug, the type with a warmth that's usually shared between a mother and daughter. They are eye level with each other.

"Have a good weekend. You have my number. Call if you need me."

When Aunt Mary says that, instantly, I realize that when her children walk out the door, there may be a possibility she'll never see them again.

Seven

Cassandra and I show up to the Washington family home. When the door opens, we are greeted by the butler. He leads me and Cassandra through a great sprawling area. The furniture is ornate with gilded arms and legs. The marble floors are polished with a gleam so impressive I find myself resisting an urge to kneel and touch them. Most of the guests are assembled outside by the pool. I spot Gregory. He's impeccably dressed and conversing with his guests. We lock eyes, and he immediately excuses himself to walk over and greet me. We hug and kiss. Kissing him is starting to feel right, but why now? He's leaving for Europe in a matter of hours.

"Your fragrance reminds me of rose petals," he whispers.

I look around. It looks like most of his friends from the yacht club are here. Kyle is here along with his parents. Cassandra splits from us to join Kyle. Gregory leads me to his parents who are engaged in lively chatter with another couple. His mother turns, looks at me, and it takes a second until she realizes who I am.

"Madeline, darling," she greets me with a warm hug.

She is casual but still elegant, and in the back of my mind, I can hear the name and see it in lights—Celeste Nobelle, beaute noire of Broadway. She is larger than life on stage, but when we embrace, she is tiny and delicate, and if I squeeze too hard, I'm afraid I may break a bone.

"Mr. Washington."

We embrace. He's Gregory twenty years in the future, with salt-and-pepper hair, mustache, and goatee. He's sporting similar style horn-rimmed glasses, but his dress is casual and quirky—polka-dot lapels and expensive loafers with no socks.

"You're the concert pianist," he says to me.

"Indeed I am."

Then he proceeds to tell the other couple-whom I come to learn are business partners about my playing for various orchestras, and I just know he got all this information from Uncle Frenchy or Aunt Mary. They tell me how much they love L.A. Phil concerts. They mention Andre Watts, a famous Black concert pianist and how his spellbinding performances capture their hearts.

"I never got the chance to see you perform. Maybe you can bless our graduate," Mrs. Washington says.

I glance at Gregory. "Would you like that?" I ask.

Gregory cocks his head slightly to one side, and his expression tells me he wishes he was somewhere else. This send-off graduation party was his parents' idea, and if it were left up to him, right now he'd be on that flight to London.

I meet the rest of his guests and even some of his family from his mother's native country, Haiti. Aunt Fabionne or Tante Fa-bee as Gregory refers to her is his mother's oldest sister and the matriarchal figure of the family. When she looks at me, it's like her eyes see right through to the soul.

"Tante Fa-bee, Je vais l'épouser un jour," Gregory spouts, leaning into his aunt in a conspiratorial fashion.

She nods. "J'approuve."

"I know."

My generic response was used in a way to throw them off course. Have them thinking I knew what they were saying when I actually didn't. You should've seen their faces.

"Vous parlez français?" she asks, somewhat shocked.

I'm no dummy, but I picked up on some of the language, and I respond naturally with, "Oui."

"She's pulling our legs, Tante. Elle ne sait pas parler français. If you know, what did I say?" he asks.

"That I'm really nice and you really like me?"

Gregory takes my hand. "Stop." He chuckles and shakes his head. "I told Tante Fa-bee that I'm going to marry you one day, and she said she approves."

"I'm glad you approve of me," I say to his aunt, "but I cannot marry him."

"Why not?" Gregory asks.

"You've been tormenting me since I've known you. Who wants to be tormented? Not me."

"I wouldn't do that. Though, I might slip a Whoopee cushion on your piano bench right before a performance." He laughs.

I stand there, not finding him funny in the least bit.

We move on to other members of the family. I meet the uncle who's a leading heart surgeon at Cedars-Sinai and the cousin who's an appellate judge. I'm introduced to Ruger, Gregory's friend since elementary and a member of the yacht club. Ruger has piercing gray eyes, chiseled features, and a dimpled chin. He has a bright smile but a laid-back demeanor.

We move on to acting friends of Gregory's mother, gathered, sipping on cocktails, conversing. I notice an actress, legendary in her own right, but now known for her sultry role on a nighttime soap with a stellar ensemble cast. Gregory calls her Aunty Carolyn. She showers him with adoration and affection. Gregory's dark brown skin is the color of roasted chestnuts, and I notice him blushing.

"Seems like yesterday you were running around in diapers." She looks at me. "Yes, I changed them."

I'm smiling, picturing her and Gregory's mother, two legends who you wouldn't imagine being hands-on mothers changing dirty diapers.

"I called him Skippy because he was always skipping and getting into mischief."

"Speaking of getting into things," he mumbles under his breath, winking at me.

We excuse ourselves, and I realize we talked to almost everyone on the terrace and I've worked up an appetite. I eat sparingly, but I can't resist a small cup of corn soup poured over fresh crab, followed up with a small truffle chopped salad, and a slice of lobster pizza.

When the time came, Gregory's mother sat me down before a white Steinway in an entertainment room with clear views of Los Angeles and the Pacific. She gathers all the guests into the room. Gregory stands just off to my right.

"To my dear friend," I begin. "Congratulations on closing one chapter and moving on to the next. My hope is that in this new chapter, you embark on new discoveries that will be revelatory and rewarding."

I searched myself for the appropriate song, then it comes to me in a series of medleys beginning with Elgar's "Pomp and Circumstance March No. 1" in the key of D. I hear a few chuckles in the room. They've heard this at many graduation ceremonies. I try not to go overboard in theatrics, but sometimes I'll come to a section in a piece of music, and I may get a little animated with my fingers, or I may have eye contact with whomever is present and make them feel like they're the only one in the room. I segue to Brahms' "Hungarian Dance No. 5," dazzling them, mesmerizing them while my fingers take on a life of their own and the portals open up and the room is whirling like dervish at a Turkish ceremony. I segue into my last piece that I saw once in the cartoon Tom and Jerry. It is one of my favorite compositions, "Hungarian Rhapsody No. 2" composed by Liszt. I take everyone in the room on a journey with me. When I finish, I stand, take a bow, and receive the applause.

"Merci."

Gregory walks up to me and takes both of my hands. He brings them to his lips and kisses them.

His parents are pleased as is everyone else in the room.

I hear, "Bravo! Encore!"

With applause still ringing in the air, Gregory leads me outside to a quiet, secluded spot and kisses me passionately. My heart and breathing intensify. His breathing is heavy, and his kisses taste like peppermint. We pause for air.

"Leave with me tonight," he whispers against my lips.

"Go with you to Europe?"

"Yes."

"I can't."

"Why not?"

"I can't leave like this."

"I need you with me."

"Gregory, I can't."

An opportunity to travel Europe with Gregory sounds exciting, like a plot straight from a romance novel: Friends set sail on a journey across Europe, fall madly in love on the waters of the French Riviera. I picture it now, us standing behind the helm of a luxury yacht and him guiding my hand while whispering sweet nothings in French in my ear. I just can't. I hear myself repeat it. I just can't. Not now.

"Give me time to think about it. Can you send me a ticket later?"

"Later? When? Tomorrow? A week from now?"

"I don't know." I'm searching for the right words.

"I really like you, Maddie. I know when we were younger, I wasn't always the nicest to you. I'm sorry about all the frogs and all the crazy pranks I used to play. I know it was childish and immature and I was a pest, but out of all the girls in camp, you were the prettiest, and I wanted you to be my girl. I still want you to be my girl."

He looks magical standing in front of me with the sun just going down behind the horizon and the lights from the city twinkling behind him. He takes off his glasses and comes closer for another kiss.

"Promise me you'll be my girl."

I look into his eyes as if I'm seeing him for the first time.

"I promise," I whisper.

We hold each other, and as I look up, I see a shooting star zoom across the L.A. sky. In two hours, he'll board a plane and fly cross country to New York. Five hours after that, he'll land in London. I give him my current address. He says he'll send a postcard or write a letter.

He tells me to keep an eye out for a special telegram. Summer is still two weeks away, but something tells me it's going to be one where the days are long and the nights are even longer.

Eight

"Was wondering when I'd hear from you." My dad's voice is rich and calm. He's been up a couple of hours, had his morning coffee and a hot bath. Church starts in an hour-and-a- half. Right now, he's adding the final touches to his sermon notes. I know the routine.

"Sorry I took so long."

"Everything alright with you?"

I want to tell him how little I slept. How after we left Gregory's place, the minute Cassandra and I got in the car, I became a complete mess. From nowhere, emotions erupted, and I cried the entire ride back. Cassandra held my hand. She cried too.

"I'm good."

"Sounds like you just woke up. What time is it out there?" Then he answers his own question. "It's about 6:47. Shouldn't you be getting your beauty rest?"

"I'm rested. Just wanted to hear your voice."

"L.A. Phil reached out to Gilda. Someone saw your solo with the Houston Symphony Orchestra and wants you to do a guest performance." With this information, I sit up at attention like a soldier.

"What did she tell them?"

"She'll give you the details."

I sigh, sinking back into my pillow. I'm supposed to be using this time to rest—God knows I need it—but this is the Los Angeles Philharmonic. They could've asked a number of pianists—there are literally hundreds of them—but they want me.

"When's the date?" I ask.

"August."

"I'll do it," I answer, then I realize I leave for Juilliard around that time.

"Are you sure?"

"I am."

The life of a concert pianist: You tell yourself to rest, but too much rest gets you off track. What was I thinking? Coming to California to rest.

"Daddy, what's the piece?" I ask.

"Gilda has the details."

I think of Gilda. She was my Mother's assistant, and when my Mother died, Daddy hired her.

"When should I expect her to call?"

"Today, after services. Speaking of which, are you going to worship today?"

I haven't given it much thought. "Of course I am," I say in a tone that sounds convincing.

"I love you, Maddie."

"I love you too. Are you dating anyone?"

I hear a sarcastic laugh. "Only the ministry."

"Besides that?"

"No, baby, and when the opportunity arises, I wouldn't proceed without your blessing."

"Thank you. That's very thoughtful of you, Daddy."

"Call me anytime. I'm never too busy to hear your sweet voice. Tell everyone I said hello."

I hang up with L.A. Phil on my mind. God knows I love classical music—the complexities of the compositions, the blended notes arranged in ways to produce feelings ranging from melancholy to extreme euphoria. Each time I hear "Clair de Lune" by Claude Debussy, I long to rest my head in my mother's lap as I did as a child and feel her fingers massaging my crown until my eyelids are heavy and I fall into a peaceful sleep. Last night when I left Gregory's, all I could hear was

Chopin's "Nocturne No. 20 In C Sharp Minor," especially the first two measures. Hearing them play over and over in my head gave me chills. I held it together for a moment, but the dam burst, and the overflow of emotions came. I can't go to Europe, as much as I think I want to. I imagine a conversation with my dad will sound a little like this:

Me: May I go to Europe?

Dad: What's in Europe?

Me: I'm going sailing with a friend.

Dad: Sailing? Who is this friend? Do I know this person?

Me: No.

Dad: I need to know who this friend is.

Me: His name is Gregory.

Dad: I don't recall meeting Gregory, and furthermore the answer is no.

The same dialogue would play out with Aunt Mary and Uncle Frenchy, and they knew Gregory.

Downstairs, the vanilla smell in Aunt Teal's chicory permeates the air along with the aroma of cinnamon and fresh-baked bread. Uncle Frenchy's distinct laughter, Aunt Mary's raspy voice, Caleb's baritone, and Cassandra's nonchalant shrill are doing a dance to see who is the loudest.

"You're just in time, niecy." Uncle Frenchy extends a hand to the empty seat at the table.

"Good morning." I sit next to Caleb.

Aunt Mary gives me a basket with golden brown, flaky croissants inside. Aunt Teal's over my shoulder.

"Good morning, chère."

"Good morning."

"I'm making omelets. What do you want in yours?" she asks.

"I want it fully loaded," I say.

"Okay." Her tone is like be careful what you ask for.

"On second thought, just fill it with vegetables. I don't care—mushrooms, onions, green peppers."

I glance at the omelet on Uncle Frenchy's plate. "What's in yours?"

"Everything but the kitchen sink," he answers.

"I like mine plain," Cassandra says.

"Make mine like Frenchy's. You can even add the sink." Caleb tosses a strawberry in his mouth.

"Daddy says hello." I tear a piece of croissant and savor the rich buttery flavor.

Aunt Mary sips orange juice from a champagne flute. "How's my brother-in-law?"

"He's good. I asked if he was dating. I got the usual reply."

Aunt Mary chuckles. "My parents—God rest their souls—they thought the world of your father. Said he was the perfect man for my sister."

"Remember what they said about me?" Uncle Frenchy adds.

"You were too common." She giggles at the memory.

"How many common negroes do you know flying 747s?"

"You proved your worth."

Cassandra sticks her finger in her mouth, pretending to gag.

"What was your father's reply?" Aunt Mary asks me.

"He's all about the ministry."

Aunt Teal sets plates before me and Cassandra. "I can only imagine the women at his church."

"He has his pick," Uncle Frenchy adds.

"On another note," I change the subject, "there may be a performance with L.A. Phil in the works."

I notice everyone perks up. "That's wonderful news, Maddie. When?" Aunt Mary asks.

"August. I'm waiting on a call from Gilda with more details."

"L.A. Phil always gives good performances," Aunt Mary says.

"I'm excited."

"The life of a concert pianist is a many-splendored thing," Uncle Frenchy says. "You don't see too many of us in that field."

"I can say the same for you, too, Uncle Frenchy."

"You know in our positions we have to stay on our A game at all times. Eyes are watching us, waiting for us to slip because you know in the back of their minds, we had no business being where we are in the first place."

"Are you referring to you and Maddie being the only people of color?" Cassandra asks.

"Yes, chère."

"Which is unfortunate because no other race carries that burden," Caleb adds. "If one white person makes a mistake, the next white person comes along, and all is forgiven. God forbid, you make a mistake, the whole race suffers."

We all quietly agree. Caleb gave us something to ponder.

* * *

Lounging by the pool, Cassandra and I look through a stack of her Seventeen and Mademoiselle magazines. I find the articles mindless and the fashions not something you'd find on the everyday person.

"Check this out." Cassandra shows me an editorial spread, and the model looks like our friend, Mona. "With her fake boobies."

"That's her," I say upon closer examination. Mona had that racially ambiguous look—

not quite Italian, not quite Black but something not easily checked off in a box. I give the magazine back to Cassandra who studies the page.

"What's up with Raven and the tennis match?" I ask.

"Please. Typical Hollywood-speak. I don't expect to hear from her, and I'd be surprised if she and Mona are still friends."

"Ursula gave me her number. She wants to have lunch."

"Ursula's cool. I'd have lunch with her."

My thoughts drift to Gregory. By now, he's in Europe. A week ago, he was the furthest thing from my mind, but now he's all I think about. I feel myself getting misty-eyed. Maybe I should have left with him.

"You okay?" Cassandra asks.

"Yes," I lie.

"Let's go for a walk."

I need a distraction. The neighborhood itself is quiet with the exception of the constant buzzing of helicopters overhead. Cassandra stops to chat with neighbors who happened to be outside. She definitely doesn't meet strangers. Some of the homes are modest in design with flat roofs and split levels; others are expansive with stately facades and large manicured yards. She points out which house a celebrity lives in.

We walk by a house, and I comment on the car in the driveway or an occasional baby grand sitting behind a bay window and she says, "Oh yeah, so-and-so lives there."

In the distance, I notice a tall, shirtless gentleman walking a dog. His gait signals a quiet confidence, and his athletic build is one of a highly skilled basketball player.

"That's JB. I know that walk," Cassandra says.

We get nearer, and his features are more pronounced. He recognizes us and crosses the street with the dog leading the way. The dog—my guess is a hound of sorts—happily wags its tail and rushes Cassandra, licking her face. The dog's lean and agile with a smooth golden coat. It sniffs me, and I kneel to pet it.

"Smitty's starting to look like you, JB," Cassandra says.

"Of course he's good looking," he quips, and our eyes meet.

"What breed is he?" I ask.

"Ibizan Hound."

"Where did you and Smitty go walking?" Cassandra asks.

"Just around the neighborhood, and I've worked up an appetite. Speaking of which, Mom's in a cooking fit right now. She's preparing pancit, chicken adobo, kare-kare, cassava cake."

"What's the occasion?" I ask.

"Don't need a reason. That's just what she does."

"Say lumpia, and I'll race you home," Cassandra says, still petting a panting Smitty.

JB chuckles, shaking his head. "Let your folks know she'll have everything ready by six."

"We'll be there at 5:59," Cassandra says.

I'm trying not to stare too hard at JB, but the sweat glistening over his muscles is stirring unwarranted thoughts in me. It doesn't help that when we lock eyes, I get butterflies. This was never the case—until last week in Malibu. When he walks away with Smitty, I smell a hint of teakwood mixed with sweat. I'm all confused now.

***

When I return, there's a note waiting for me by the telephone. I call collect, and Gilda's voice answers by the third ring.

"I know you said you wanted a break this summer, but it's L.A. Phil, and let's just say it was really hard to tell them no."

"It's okay. I should be well rested by then."

"Performance is for one show on August 18. It's Schumann's 'Op. 7, Toccata in C major.' I'll send you the contract as well as the sheet music certified mail."

"Great. 'Op. 7 Toccata in C major.' That's awesome."

"How are you, Maddie?" she asks, and coming from Gilda, that's a genuine question, not just small talk.

"I'm wonderful, but what's really funny: All I've been doing is eating."

I hear a light-hearted chuckle on her end.

"I may need to buy a couple of Jane Fonda tapes and start a regimen before August."

"You're in the perfect place to make it happen."

"I'm so fortunate."

"Indeed, you are."

"Thank you, Gilda."

"My pleasure, Maddie."

I hang up feeling grateful for Gilda's assistance. She's been a major part of my life since I was nine years old. I sometimes overlook the fact that when Mom died, Gilda stepped in during times when Aunt Mary wasn't there. She was a quiet presence, always willing to help.

I open the closet to search for something cute to wear to JB's house. I'm seeing a lot of girls here in California wearing acid wash mini-skirts, jeans, and neon midriff tops. They love fringes on their jackets and on their boots. I reach in and find a pair of Calvin Klein jeans and a Coca-Cola shirt that hangs off one shoulder. When I put on the jeans, I must lie down on the bed to zip them. When I look at myself in the mirror. The jeans are so tight, I can barely walk. I lie down to take them off, but it's a struggle.

"Cassandra," I yell for help.

"What?" she yells from her room.

"Come here, please." I'm lying on the bed when she stands in my doorway.

"Omigod," she says, laughing.

"Get me out of these," I say.

She grabs one pant leg and wiggles it off, laughing the whole time.

"What were you thinking?" she asks.

"I thought they were really cute, but they're too tight."

She grabs the other pant leg and wiggles it off. "There," she says. I notice she's wearing acid wash shorts and a Coca-Cola shirt.

"Thank you." I look at her shirt. "We're twins."

"I know you have a cute pair of shorts you can wear," she says.

"My thighs are too big, and the shorts will crawl. All night I'll be pulling them down, and that won't be good."

She searches through my closet. "If I were you, I'd wear something loose, because when you eat JB's mom's cooking, you won't stop until you're about to burst."

She pulls out a pair of Gitano jeans. "These are cute."

I grab them and put them on with no problem, checking out myself in the mirror.

"Do these make my butt look big?" I ask.

"They make your butt look cute," she responds. "Let's go. There's a plate of lumpia with our names written all over it."

Me, Cassandra, Caleb, Aunt Mary, and Uncle Frenchy get there around 6:30. Of all the summers I've spent coming to L.A., this will be my first time in JB's family's home. They live a couple of streets over in one of the highest points of the neighborhood. I notice other guests already gathered in the spacious living room with the sky lighting. Uncle Frenchy comes with a couple bottles of his best brandy in hand. Aunt Mary brings two bottles of wine—one white, one red.

JB's mother, Judy, is not what I expected. I was anticipating a modest dressed—sort of how Aunt Mary carries herself—type of woman. Instead, she is high-spirited, vibrant, and dressed in a short black halter dress that clings like a glove. In my opinion, she looks like a twenty-something, not a mother with a son in college. His father, James, is tall, broad shouldered, still with an athletic build but long retired from playing basketball professionally. The way his large hands hold on to the small of her waist seem protective. I also notice a look of pride in his eyes whenever she walks away from him.

"Ain't no woman like the one I got," he says, biting his bottom lip.

Cassandra does the finger with the fake gag, and I simply giggle, finding it all too funny. The other people in the room I find out are neighbors who have known the family for years. There's jazz music playing—brass instruments with a feel of being on the streets of New Orleans. I look around the room and see black-and-white photos and abstract paintings. The house is decorated with an eclectic mix of modern and contemporary pieces, and the feel of the place is earthy and calm. Smitty's standing outside the glass wall leading to the pool with tail wagging and mouth panting, waiting for an opportunity to be let inside. Meanwhile at the bar, Uncle Frenchy and James and a couple of male neighbors have gathered to talk about the Lakers losing to the Celtics. I follow Cassandra into the kitchen where JB sits feeding his face. Caleb has a plate and is pulled up at the table about to feed his face.

I wash my hands and grab plates for Cassandra and myself. JB's mother enters the kitchen.

"Ma'am, I'm going to need your help," I say as calmly as I can to her.

"Please, call me Judy, she says. "You had Filipino food before?" she asks.

"No, I haven't."

She proceeds to patiently show me every single dish she prepared as well as the story and meaning behind each one. I have a plate and a history lesson.

"Try this," she says, and I try it.

"You like food, I can tell," she says, and I'm sure she means no harm by that statement.

"The lumpia is everything," Cassandra says.

"What are you talking about? Everything is everything," Caleb says.

I bite into what looks like a skinny egg roll, and the taste is a blend of carrots, ground pork, onions, and whatever else she added to give it flavor. I close my eyes and savor every moment of it.

"Delicious, right?" Cassandra bites into her own.

I give it a thumbs up. JB offers me his seat so I can sit and enjoy every bite, which I do while being thoroughly entertained by Uncle Frenchy and James. Aunt Mary just shakes her head and sips on a glass of wine while talking with a couple of ladies she knows from the neighborhood.

Judy sits next to me with a glass of wine in hand.

"Everything is so delicious," I tell her, and it really is.

"I cook when I get homesick," she says before taking a sip. "I miss my nanay's cooking back home in Manila."

"Is that your mother?" I answer.

"Yes," she responds. "I watched her cook, and she let me help."

I nod, as I think about my own mother.

"You cook?" Judy asks.

"No," I respond.

"How old are you?"

"Seventeen."

"It's never too late. I was cooking at ten. My nanay worked all day in a candle factory, so I cooked for my brothers and sisters."

"You were just ten?" I respond.

She sips. "Yes. I came to America when I was twenty. I met James when his basketball team ate at the place where I worked. I fried fish, he said I put something in the fish because after one bite he was ready to marry me." She laughs. "JB cooks too. I taught him well."

"Maybe I should come over for cooking lessons," I suggest.

"Yes. I'll teach you, and when I'm finished, you'll cook anything," she declares.

A song comes on, and some of the guests start to dance. I see Uncle Frenchy and Aunt Mary dancing as well. JB's father, James walks over to the table where Judy and I are sitting.

"May I have this dance?" he asks Judy.

"I think I've talked your head off enough," she says to me before standing up to take James' hand. I watch him lead her to an area in the living room where the rest of the guests are dancing. I take one last bite of lumpia before I push my plate aside.

Outside by the pool, Smitty rushes me. I kneel to pet and rub his coat and watch the sun disappear behind the horizon. Remembering when I took in a similar view across town less than twenty-four hours ago. The lights in the pool are a pristine blue, highlighting a mosaic design.

"Maddie, I want to show you something." JB walks past me. Smitty and I follow him across the other side of the pool to a guest house. He flips on the lights, and I immediately hone in on a Yamaha keyboard. There's a massive stereo system with reels and gigantic speakers, a pool table, wall-to-ceiling mirrors, a living area with a kitchen, and a wet bar.

He sits in front of the keyboard, which has various instrumentations to choose from. He powers it on, hits the piano selection, and proceeds to play his interpretation of the "William Tell Overture." His right hand moves on the edge of the keys while the left hand dances between the high and low notes giving the tempo its galloping effect. Not bad for someone who plays by ear. Cassandra and Caleb enter. Caleb leans over and taps a random key. JB waves him off like an annoying fly.

"I didn't know you play," Caleb says.

"Is that the Lone Ranger song?" Cassandra asks.

JB stops mid-play and presses a few buttons, and his fingers search the keys for notes until he finds the chords. He also does this thing where he leans into the keyboard, listening, and with his eyes, he searches, then he proceeds to play a melody. He looks at me.

"Sound familiar?" he asks.

I listen, and I'll admit, it doesn't. If it isn't Chopin, Liszt, Schumann,

Rachmaninoff, Mozart, or Beethoven you've lost me. People look strangely at me when I tell them I don't know any Michael Jackson songs besides "Beat It," "Thriller," and "Billie Jean." My ears are attuned to complex arrangements backed by an orchestra. Ask me about soul music, and I'm clueless. I know a couple of Stevie Wonder tunes. There's a couple of songs I like by Prince. If you really want to know the truth, listening to popular music just isn't my thing.

"Maddie, you haven't heard 'Hello' by Lionel Richie?" Cassandra asks, almost dumbfounded.

I shrug. JB continues to play his interpretation, and before long, he starts to sing. He has a rich tenor tone.

"You sing too?" Caleb is shocked.

"If basketball doesn't work out, there's always Star Search." Cassandra grabs a pool stick and cue chalker. JB continues to sing, and I am hypnotized by the sound of his voice. I nearly melt right there. Caleb, in all his silliness, pretends he's a screaming fan, fawning and rolling on the floor.

"Take me, JB. Take me right now," he screams.

Even JB stops to laugh at the foolishness.

I'm impressed.

"Maddie, are you blushing?" Cassandra asks before she hits a ball into a corner pocket.

"It's a little warm in here," I admit.

I glance at a massive record collection and reel containers. "This belongs to you?" I ask.

"Some of it. Most are Mom's and Pop's."

I randomly select an album, and I see Genesis Live: Seconds Out. I randomly select another album and read Queen, A Night at the Opera.

"Cuzzo, I can't believe you haven't heard 'Hello'." Caleb says.

"What can I say? I've been living under a rock."

"Play something for me," JB says, moving over to join Smitty on the floor.

I sit and study the keyboard a bit, locating all the buttons I need to push. There is a button with a grand piano effect. When I play, I still want to hear the organic richness you get from playing an actual piano. There's a sustain pedal. Cool. I close my eyes and play the first movement of Beethoven's "Moonlight Sonata."

"I've heard that song before," Caleb says, cueing up to shoot a ball in one of the pockets.

"Why does that one part remind me of Halloween? Eerie," Cassandra says.

"The movie?"

"Doesn't it sound like that creepy theme music?"

I open my eyes and see JB standing by studying the chords. "Who wrote that piece?" he asks.

"Beethoven."

"That's dope. Sounds like he was on the verge of insanity."

"Interesting you say that because he eventually went deaf and experienced a great deal of internal turmoil from that."

"I can't imagine not being able to hear music," he says.

"Neither can I," I respond.

Caleb goes to the stereo system and presses the power button. There is a song playing on the radio that causes him to bob along.

"Hey, Wolf," he shouts to JB.

"What, Floyd?" JB answers.

"What's it called when you're busting loose?" Caleb asks.

"Juicy. Juicy," JB moans.

They launch into a dance routine with a lot of jumps and kicks. JB grabs a walking cane and twirls it effortlessly—tossing it to Caleb who twirls it and flips it over his shoulder before tossing it back to JB. When they're finished, they slap high fives, like a secret handshake. Cassandra continues to play pool, unfazed by it all. Me, on the other hand, I find it entertaining.

A new song comes on the radio. This one has a slower tempo but Caleb and JB find the rhythm and start dancing along with it. I'm checking out JB's moves and the confident expression on his face. He notices me watching, and in a very sensual way bites his bottom lip and winks at me. I shift in my seat, feeling my heart race, hoping it doesn't seem too obvious that I'm really enjoying what I'm seeing.

They finish dancing, and Caleb goes to the pool table to play with Cassandra, and JB joins me at the keyboard.

"You're so talented," I say. "You sing, you dance, you play by ear. I hear you're a really good basketball player."

"What else have you heard?" he asks.

"All good things so far."

"I still can't believe you haven't heard 'Hello' by Lionel Richie," he says. "All you listen to is classical music?"

"That's all, and the gospel hymnals that I play at my father's church."

"I see. That explains everything. Your father's a minister and you grew up in a strict household. If it isn't gospel or classical, it's considered 'devil's music,'" he says with air quotes.

"That's not it. Growing up, my mom always had classical music playing. It's what I love."

"I have some music I think you will like." He walks to a shelf of records and notices the two that I randomly selected. He picks up one of them, takes the record out of the sleeve, and places it on the turntable. He moves the arm to the spot where he wants to play. Over the speakers, I hear a crowd cheering and an announcer's voice speaking in a foreign language and then I hear a series of rapid arpeggios played with a moderately fast tempo on a synthesizer. The synthesizer produces a trill effect that slows for a beat then escalates. The crowd cheers when the guitar roars, the drummer kicks, and the singers start with the first verse. The song is a rock song and I admit, I like it.

"Are you guys having a concert?" Cassandra asks. I notice she places the cue stick back in its holder.

I look at JB. "Are we?" I ask.

He's nodding and singing the song. I turn to Cassandra. "I guess we are, then."

"I'm going inside, I haven't had dessert, yet," she says, leaving Caleb at the pool table with a stick aiming at one of the balls. I hear him say, "Center pocket" before he strikes the ball.

"What's the name of the song?" I ask.

JB picks up the album and reads the song title. "'The Lamb Lies Down on Broadway' I prefer this live version of it."

"It's nice. I like the dynamics of the synthesizer."

"Me too," he says. "I like how the notes are fast and they blend together."

"What else you got there?" I ask, wanting to hear more.

He lets the song play to the end before he picks up the other album I chose at random from the shelf.

"It's crazy, out of all the albums here, you pick two that I actually considered to use as examples. I like progressive rock. It has a blend of the classical music that you like, mixed in with guitars and synths-and drums—instruments you hear in a typical rock song."

"Oh shit," Caleb says. "I've got a phone call to make. Can I use the phone in your bedroom?" he asks JB.

"Fa sho." JB places the next record on the turntable. Caleb hurries out of the pool house, closing the door behind him.

"Is everything okay?" I ask.

"Your cousin met a girl," JB says.

"I see."

I find a spot on the floor next to Smitty to relax and listen to the music. I hear voices singing a capella, then the song drifts into a piano-driven ballad. The piece is somber, and it tells the story of a guy who murdered someone, and he wishes he were never born, and nothing really matters to him anymore. Then the song segues into an operatic passage, with the subject of the song agonizing over his fate. The operatic part is followed up with a hard rock part before it ends with a reflective coda. The singer echoes how the subject feels, that nothing really matters. At the end of the song, his voice mellows out, then he sings, "Any way the wind blows," and I hear the light sound of a tam-tam. I am mesmerized. I've been taken on a whirlwind of a journey but somehow managed to be dropped off in one piece. I have JB replay it again.

"You like that?" he asks.

"Yes."

"I knew you would," he says.

While rubbing Smitty's coat, I close my eyes and listen. JB doesn't say a word, but he sits there quietly nodding. There are moments he'll ask me about a particular way a song is structured or what key the song is being played in, but for the most part, he's quiet. I think I've found someone who loves the sound of music as much as I do.

Nine

June 7, 1987 11:52 p.m.

I can't sleep. My mind does this when the creative portals are opened. I'm inundated with words and melodies, and I have to jot them down. I write a piece entitled, "Dawn Is Here." The words come to me like this:

Dawn at last

No more darkness prevails

Light is all around me

Free from this living hell

I open the drawer to the nightstand where I keep sheets of staff paper for moments like these. I fill up a sheet with notes for the piano. I hear violins and cellos, so I fill in the notes for them too. This piece reaches from the depths of my being, pulling from within feelings of accomplishment. I hear victorious woodwinds like flutes, clarinets, and oboes. A line of timpani drums brewing to a dramatic climax with cymbals clashing. When I'm finished, I fall into the pillows, close my eyes, and see Gregory. I imagine what he's doing and if he's thinking about me the way I am about him. Then my mind drifts to JB. I never knew he liked such an eclectic mix of music. When we leave around eleven, I have three albums for my listening enjoyment. His father, joking of course, mentions he's going to charge me a rental fee. I show him the albums—Genesis, Pink Floyd, and Queen. He frowns.

"These must be Judy's." Handing them back to me he says, "She won't miss them."

Whenever I get an opportunity to hear them, I'm reminded of sitting on the floor with Smitty and allowing the music to penetrate the essence of my soul. I toss and turn until I find a comfortable spot before I drift off.

The following morning, Aunt Mary and I arrive at the center. Sitting behind the wheel, I notice even with makeup, she still looks exhausted. Bags are difficult to hide.

"Morning came too quickly," she says. "I could use two more hours of sleep."

A hard knock on her window startles us both. I look and notice a woman, disheveled in appearance, dancing and motioning for Aunt Mary to roll down her window.

"No, darling." Aunt Mary speaks loud enough for her to hear.

"But lady, listen," she shouts.

Her dancing and pacing give me cause for alarm.

"Lady, listen. I got four children. I need twenty dollars to buy them something to eat."

I open my pocketbook, and before I grab a twenty, Aunt Mary slaps my hand.

"Lady! I swear to God. My children at home starving."

She walks in front of the car and makes her way to my side where I get a good look at her. She leans forward, and the look in her eyes is hollow and cold, and there's white froth on one corner of her mouth. With a faint smile, she tries to garner sympathy from me.

"You got twenty dollars?" she asks.

I glance at Aunt Mary. "Don't do it" is all she says.

"I'm sorry. I can't help you," I say to the woman.

The resigned expression on her face is crushing. She hurries off with great speed, dashing out of view.

Aunt Mary sighs. "You'll be seeing a lot of that around here."

"What if everything she said was true?"

"Maddie, Maddie, Maddie. You've never been exposed to the harsh realities of the ghetto. Your twenty would've done more harm than good."

I never looked at it that way.

Hours later, when the children arrive, I give them a brief lesson on Black composers. I tell them about Scott Joplin and play "The Entertainer" for them. Some are attentive, then there are others like Damon and Blaze who want to arm wrestle instead.

"This is boring, Maddie," Jessica, the girl with the cavity says.

"Can we talk about something else?" Raquel, the girl with the cherub face suggests.

"Why do you find this boring?" I ask.

"Nobody cares about that kind of music. I like Michael Jackson. Beat it. Beat it." Blaze stands and proceeds to kick and spin.

"That's not how he does it." Damon moves him aside and does his kick and spin.

"Damon and Blaze, sit." I say. They don't listen.

Dee is drawing. I guess my talk on Scott Joplin is boring her too. I gather my group of ten around the piano and show them the basics again until they start to get restless. Next thing you know, a couple of my girls are shoving each other. Damon and Blaze are now on the floor having a full-on wrestling match.

I separate the girls. Vanessa, one of the other teachers, separates Blaze and Damon.

"He started it," Blaze says.

"It doesn't matter. If we have to tell you one more time, your behinds are going home. Is that understood?" Vanessa gives them a look like *I dare you. Act up again.*

"Yes," they mumble.

She walks up to me. "These children will try you if you allow them."

"Thanks," I say.

"Don't be afraid to put your foot down."

"Miss Vanessa, why are you so mean?" I wasn't sure if the voice was one of the girls or boys.

She stops. "Who's asking?"

No one wants to confess.

"Don't worry. I'll find out," she says.

She leaves, leaving me scrambling for an idea for the children.

"Can we go outside and play?" Dee asks.

With that, I gather my precious ten and open the door for them to play. They seem restless and agitated, and a breath of fresh air usually does the body good. Just beyond the chain-linked fence, cars speed by blaring music while helicopters buzz overhead like flies. Rosie joins me with her sketch pad.

"Why aren't you with your group?" I ask.

"They annoy me."

"So, you just leave them?"

"I do it all the time. If I don't want to be inside, I come here and sketch." She opens her pad.

"What are you about to draw?" I ask.

"The kids playing."

"You can draw that fast?"

"Yes. Once I get the image down, I just go from there."

I notice her studying the children before she begins the sketch.

"What did you do this weekend?" I ask.

"I hung out at the mall with some girls from my hood."

"Do you hang out with the girls from the center?"

"No" is her reply. She continues her sketch. "Can I tell you something, and please don't say anything."

"Yes. Sure."

"One of the girls, she always flirts with Kyle."

I'm alarmed by this bit of information.

"How does she flirt?"

"She'll say something like 'Kyle, you smell good enough to eat' or 'Kyle, you're so fine you gon' mess around and make me give you some.'"

My eyes widen. "Some?"

"I know you know what I'm talking about."

"And what does he do?"

"He doesn't say anything, but you can tell he's uncomfortable."

I know Aunt Mary thinks the world of her eaglets, but she may need to be aware of this. My next thought is having a conversation with Kyle.

"I don't know about this, Rosie. I think we should tell Mrs. Mary."

"If we tell and she gets kicked out, I don't want to be responsible for that."

"She won't get kicked out. Maybe more like reprimanded."

"I dunno."

"Let's see if Kyle and I can switch groups instead," I suggest.

Rosie's eyes light up. "I like that idea."

"What do you guys do in your group?" I ask.

"There was a lady who came in and taught us etiquette rules. I know the difference between a dinner fork and a salad fork, and I know how to butter my bread, one piece at a time."

I nod and listen as she continues. "Another person came in to teach us typing skills with typewriters and computers. I swear, if it wasn't for this place, I'd be getting into all sorts of trouble."

"Trouble? Like what?"

"Where I'm from, you're either gang banging, selling dope, selling your body, or working for minimum wages."

"I see."

"Every day is hard just to walk down the street. I don't know if I'm gon' get jumped, shot at, or raped."

I feel my heart racing as she tells me this.

"You know what gets me excited?" she asks.

"What?"

"Coming here. Mrs. Mary makes me feel like I matter." I notice her eyes getting moist with tears.

"Is it okay if I give you a hug?" I ask. I feel my eyes misting.

She laughs as a teardrop rolls down her cheek and reaches out to give me a hug. We are both wiping our eyes and fanning our faces.

"I was so happy when she let me do that mural on the wall outside and the one inside."

"How long did it take?"

"About a month, and I did it all by myself."

"You did a wonderful job."

"Thank you." She smiles.

"The mural you did in the hallway is very special. That was my mother."

"She was pretty."

I smile. In addition to all the other super kind adjectives ever used to describe her, pretty often slides its way in. I look up and see Dee and the others approaching me, sweating, trying to catch their breath. Dee's holding her side. That's my cue they've had enough playtime.

I admit, I'm exhausted when the last child leaves. Waiting on Aunt Mary to finish in her office, I sit at the piano. Closing my eyes, I hear a melody in the form of a feather that lifts off the back of an eagle floating aimlessly in the air. The thing about a feather is it doesn't stay in one spot; it's constantly moving. Where do feathers go? Where do they ultimately land? Is it crazy to envy a feather? After all, they have the kind of access one can only imagine in a dream. I don't believe in reincarnation; I'm the daughter of a Methodist minister who preaches the Gospel. However, if at all possible and in some crazy way, I emerge in a new life as an eagle's feather, I would be as grand as ever. I grab a staff sheet and a pencil and draw a treble clef, bass clef, whole notes, and half notes. I hear violins producing a stylish trill, and I write a signature for them. I hear a flute fluttering in the wind, and I write a signature for it. The lyrics I hear go something like this:

Winds carry me off to places I long to go

Across skies so vast and worlds unknown

Where every good feeling is built to last

In nests on mountains and streams a-flow...

I continue to play, stopping to write a measure here and there. The room where I sit is transformed into a tropical rainforest with macaws and crimson topaz. Everything is fluorescent green and lush, vibrant and succulent. Nothing could go wrong in a situation like this. I thrive in it. It gives me life. Falling from a nest, high above the forest floor is a red feather, and it lands in the palm of my hand—a blow from my lips, and it's off to who knows where.

"Niecy, honey." I hear Aunt Mary's soothing voice over my shoulder.

I write the last of the notes I hear on the staff sheet before they vanish and I won't hear them quite the same again.

"Yes," I answer.

"What's the name of the melody you were playing?"

"I don't have a name for it yet."

Her brown eyes widened. "You wrote this?" She glances over my notes.

"I did."

"You are something else." Her eyes are brimming with tears. "My baby sister would be so proud." A tear flows down her cheek. "This is truly a gift from God, Maddie." She holds the paper in her hands. Wiping away tears, she chuckles, realizing she's gotten a teardrop on my composition.

"I'm sorry." She gives it back. "I didn't mean t—"

"It's okay. There's more inside."

"You children never cease to amaze me. When it comes to talent, you and Rosie are in a league of your own."

Her esteem for me means the world right now. Even as I walk outside the door and get in the car, I have this feeling there's nothing I can't do.

Unlike the lush, green forestry I visualize in my music, riding in the car, I see the reality of the neighborhood that surrounds the youth center. There is tarp of palm, banana trees, and begonias and wall-to-wall 1950s-era courtyard apartment buildings. I imagine Rosie and the other children from the center walking these streets and encountering people like the girl Aunt Mary and I saw this morning. In this environment, with all the liquor stores, pawn shops, and fried food places, how does one find beauty and capture it the way Rosie does?

"Aunt Mary, aren't you afraid of this neighborhood?"

"You sound like my highfalutin' friends," she responds. "'Mary, why don't you leave and let someone else deal with those children?'" She imitates their voices. "'Just because your name is Mary doesn't mean you have to go around behaving like a saint.'"

"Well?"

"I love what I do. I just happen to be in the ghetto doing it."

At the traffic light, I look out and see an elderly man holding a cup. A group of boys, one carrying a loud boom box, walks past and brushes him aside. He loses his balance and falls back on the sidewalk. Even with the windows rolled up, I can still hear their roaring, sinister laughter.

"If you can make a child feel they can conquer the world, they will. That's what I do at the center. I give them a place where they can look beyond what they see around here." She pauses. "That's why I call them my eaglets. Eagles are taught to fly at an early age. Once in flight, they soar above anything like poverty and low self-esteem."

"I don't want to sound highfalutin,' but in the back of your mind, aren't you just a little afraid?"

"Niecy, I pray for God's protection, and after ten years, He's never let me down."

As we drive away, I notice the man now sitting up on the sidewalk with a defeated look. His cup has spilled, and the few coins he had are scattered on the sidewalk. All the while, people are walking, stepping over him, ignoring him.

When Aunt Mary pulls into the driveway of her home, we both notice Kyle's car parked at the curb in front of the house.

Once inside, the television in the den is on but Uncle Frenchy and Aunt Teal are on the opposite ends of the sectional asleep, both snoring loudly.

"I have to get the camera," Aunt Mary whispers.

I stifle a giggle, covering my mouth at the sight. Aunt Mary leaves and returns with her camera, snapping shots from many angles. She gives the camera to me with instructions to press the flash button once I get a good shot. I look in the view and see Aunt Mary plant rabbit ears with her fingers above Uncle Frenchy's head. I snap two shots.

Uncle Frenchy's snore hits a high pitch, and he mumbles something in gibberish.

Aunt Mary and I are trying not to laugh out loud, and we both leave the room.

"My God, they must've eaten themselves into a stupor." She walks into the kitchen to wash her hands before lifting the pots to see what goods Aunt Teal has in store.

"Red beans and rice with andouille." She sniffs the aroma. "Thank God for Teal."

I excuse myself and go upstairs to my room to unwind. I look out the window. It's sundown, and lights are sparkling in the distance. I look down and spot Cassandra and Kyle swimming in the lighted pool. I find a swimsuit to change into and join them.

"Hellooooooo," I shout.

They scramble to get themselves together. I think I interrupted something.

"Wow. If it isn't Maddie the eagle princess," Cassandra says.

I find a spot on the edge of the pool to sit. "Where were you today, Kyle?"

"Who are we, FBI?" he answers.

"Just asking," I reply, sensing a bit of agitation in his tone.

"I've been right here," he says.

"Kyle has a life outside of volunteering, Maddie," Cassandra adds.

"I'm just asking a simple question."

"I've been here, relaxing with my girl."

"I totally understand," I answer.

"Did Mom say something about Kyle?" Cassandra asks.

"No." I splash some water with my toes. The conversation I had with Rosie is still in the back of my mind. "The boys missed you. They were restless today."

"Take them outside, let them run. That always works."

"Believe me, I did."

"I tried to give those children a chance," Cassandra begins. "I got into an argument with a girl. She said I talk white." Cassandra frowns. "What? Just because I don't use slang, I talk white?"

Kyle and I listen.

"It was like they resented me. I couldn't connect with them, and as time went on, I didn't want to."

"So far, I don't have that problem," I say.

"I'll take the younger group any day," Kyle begins.

"I'll be happy to switch with you." I say.

"Yes. Thanks, Maddie. There's a couple of the girls."

"What about them, Kyle?" Cassandra is curious.

"They're relentless. The final straw for me was when one of them wore a skirt with no underwear."

Cassandra and I both gasp.

"Did you tell Mom?"

Kyle looks uncomfortable, searching for the right words.

"The easiest thing for me is to switch to the younger group or not show up."

Cassandra's café au lait complexion turns beet red, and she's glaring at him.

"What?" Kyle is visibly flustered.

"Either you tell Mom, or I will."

"I'll tell her."

"When?"

"I'll tell her."

Cassandra studies him for a beat, carefully analyzing his expression.

"Stop looking at me like that."

The mood in the air is heavy and in dire need of a shift. "Cassandra, Kyle does an amazing job with the children, especially the boys."

"Thank you, Maddie." Kyle nods. "Have you heard from Gregory yet?"

My heart flutters at the mention of Gregory's name. It's Monday night. Shouldn't I have gotten a phone call by now? I think constantly of how I arrived at this point, feeling this way, falling for Gregory. What if I had said yes when he asked me to go with him to Europe.

"No, I haven't," I reply.

"He'll call." Kyle's tone gives me assurance.

"He asked me to go with him." As I speak, I feel a lump in my throat.

"Really? That's a big deal. When it comes to sailing with his yacht buddies, even I don't get an invite." Kyle says.

"Right now, while he's out sailing, I'd be in a suite ordering room service or shopping at Harrod's."

"Now that you've had a little time to think about it, would you go if he sent you a ticket?" Cassandra asks.

"Without question."

"If your dad objected, would you still go?" Cassandra asks.

"As difficult as it sounds, I'd still go."

"Just the other week, he was annoying. Now, you're willing to follow him halfway around the world. What changed?" Cassandra asks.

"Not having him around makes me want him even more."

Cassandra and Kyle's blank expressions are clear indicators they don't understand the level of longing and frustration I'm feeling.

Aunt Mary walks outside. "Hi, Kyle. I missed you today," she says.

Kyle has a sheepish grin. "I was running errands and lost track of time," he answers.

"Really." Aunt Mary gives him a side glance.

For the strangest reason, I feel nervous and anxious for Kyle. I'm wondering if he's going to tell her what he told us. Or will Cassandra tell?

Ten

My sheet music and contract arrive by courier just as I walk out the door with Aunt Mary. I'm too excited to go to the center with her, and she understands. I immediately get on the phone with Gilda, Daddy's assistant, who's well versed in reading contracts. I trust her just as my mother did and Daddy would to handle all my professional affairs.

"I wouldn't have bothered if I didn't believe it was a good move," she says.

"Thank you. I needed this."

"It's Schumann. I know you relish the challenge."

I glance over the sheet music to see the chords are bold. It's cast in a sonata-allegro form. Mastering this piece requires exceptional digital abilities.

"I'm starting asap," I say, studying the chords.

"If you have any more questions, call me," she says.

"Don't be surprised if I call you at three in the morning."

"Don't be surprised if I don't answer." Gilda's response and light-hearted chuckle makes me laugh.

"I know Daddy's out golfing, but tell him he can call me sometimes."

"I will," she says.

With that, I hang up and stare at the piece before me, studying it as I make my way into the entertainment area to the baby grand. I find a spot on the piano bench and place the sheet music on deck. Like a surgeon, I sit and analyze and interpret each note. I look at my fingers, God bless them. After playing this piece, they will require much therapy.

As I do before every practice, I play the scales, listening to the quality and tone of the piano. I bring out my metronome, which helps me keep rhythm, and do finger exercises. I know this piano doesn't get much use until I touch it, but I'd like to hear what I'm working with. I close my eyes and play. And play. And play. I imagine what Schumann was feeling when he wrote this piece. He seemed angry at the world and frantic with every changing episode of thought. He was suffering from a debilitating hand injury, and after looking at this toccata and studying similar toccatas of his, I see why. When I open my eyes, I notice JB, Caleb, and Cassandra. I wish I had a camera to capture the looks on their faces.

"We're here to do a wellness check," Cassandra begins.

"Why? I'm fine," I say.

"But the piano, though," Caleb adds.

I chuckle. I imagine it must have sounded like I was battering the keys.

"Your hands were moving faster than the crackheads I saw on Crenshaw the other night." JB sits beside me and glances at the sheet music.

"I hope it wasn't too loud."

JB holds the sheet. I notice him scanning over the notes. "Dude, what the hell—"

"I know."

"Was he going deaf, too?"

"No. He was suffering from a hand injury and bipolar disorder."

"What is it with these composers? They don't know how to create with a clear head. There's always a handicap or a burden or some kind of conflict." JB says.

"All that fuels the genius inside of them," Caleb adds.

"And as the saying goes, there's a fine line between genius and madness," I say.

With his large hands fumbling over the keys, JB attempts to play.

"Sounds close enough?" he jokes, glancing at me. "What do you think?"

"Hope springs eternal," I answer.

He pretends he's upset with my answer. "Hey, I'm always up for a lesson."

"We'll see."

"Let's go." Caleb rattles a set of keys.

"I'm serious." JB taps my thigh before all six-eight of him rises up from the bench and walks calmly out of the room. Cassandra sits next to me on the bench. I notice she's wearing a casual white linen top with denim jeans and strappy sandals. Her hair is done in a top knot, and pink lip gloss glistens on her round lips.

"Sorry to disturb you." She says.

"It's okay. I could use a break. You okay?"

"Just thinking about our talk. You remember the one about finding something fulfilling?" Cassandra asks.

"So?" I answer.

"I'm still searching," she says. "It's really messed up when you don't have a clue."

"You're only sixteen. Still trying to figure things out." I say.

"You are focused and driven, and doors are opening for you, and your future is certain."

"I don't know if I want to spend the next twenty years playing two-hundred-year-old songs by crazy, dead White men."

I manage to get a giggle out of Cassandra. It's refreshing.

"I thought you and I were actually hanging out this summer. Another reason why I didn't go to camp." Cassandra says.

Now I'm starting to feel a sliver of guilt for taking on this assignment. I'm asking myself what really matters. Is it spending quality time with family, getting the rest I so badly need, or accepting the invitation to play with one of the most prestigious orchestras in the country? It's a delicate balancing act.

"It's okay, though. I'll get through the summer. I may even tag along with Frenchy."

"That might not be a bad idea. Where's he flying these days?"

She shrugs. Cassandra is one who uses words. These gestures are worrisome.

"Talk to me. Everything okay with you and Kyle? Has he talked to Aunt Mary?"

"We had a fight."

"What?"

She lays her head on the piano. "Big girls don't cry, big girls don't cry," she repeats like an affirmation.

"Is it because of what happened at the center?"

"He says he didn't do anything, and I have to trust him, right?"

"Of course. Kyle's not stupid. He's professional. I've seen him."

"Why hasn't he said anything to Mom?"

"Maybe he's trying to figure out a way to approach her. Telling her that one of her beloved eaglets is enticing him isn't an easy conversation. Just look at it from his perspective."

"The writing's on the wall, Maddie."

"What? Not because of that."

"It's a combination of things. I don't want to get into it. I don't think we're going to make it through the summer."

"You think so?"

"Yes, I do."

"I'm sorry."

She takes a deep breath. "I'll be okay."

"Where are you going?" I ask, changing the subject, admiring her crisp white linen top.

"I didn't tell you? Mona called as I expected she would. She invited us to go shopping with her."

"Wow." I find this information amusing. After the spat Cassandra and Mona had at the Lakers game, I really didn't expect Mona to be reaching out so soon.

"She's on her way over. I don't want to seem as if I'm dragging you away from your assignment, but you're welcome to come along, seeing as she extended an invitation to you as well."

"Maybe next time," I say, glancing at the sheet music.

With that, I hear the doorbell ring.

"This should be interesting," I say, getting up to follow Cassandra.

Aunt Teal opens the door, and Mona appears, dressed in an oversized crisp white shirt with a designer belt hugging her slender waist. She greets Aunt Teal with a hug.

"Where's the rest of your outfit?" Aunt Teal lifts up the back to get a peek.

"You are hilarious," Mona says and does an air cheek kiss with Cassandra and me.

"You eighties girls are bold with your style."

"It's chic and provocative, like yours truly."

"Good thing you have long, pretty legs to pull that off. That would be hard for the average girl."

Mona soaks up the praise like a sponge. In all the time of knowing her, there's nothing she likes more than to be showered with compliments.

"I'm curious," Cassandra says. "What are you wearing underneath?"

If showing her breasts in public isn't a problem, lifting her shirt to show us what she has underneath won't be either.

"Pom-pom shorts." She turns and shows us from all angles.

"Cute." Cassandra looks at herself in the mirror. "Compared to you, I feel overdressed."

"Nonsense. I like your top. Who is that?"

"I don't know."

Mona looks at me from head to toe. "Where's your white?"

"Maybe next time. I have some business I need to attend to."

"Okay." Mona gives me another air-cheek kiss before she and Cassandra grab their designer pochettes. "Must be really important business."

Cassandra opens the door, and while Mona's back is turned, she sticks her finger in her mouth pretending to gag. I'll never understand their friendship.

***

It's six o'clock when I finish with Schumann. The house is still and quiet. I look outside by the pool. Aunt Teal sits at one of the round tables sipping on a glass of wine and writing on a yellow legal notepad. I join her. I gauge her mood.

"Tell me the truth, Aunt Teal. Did my playing run you away?"

"No, bebby. Aunty needed some fresh air. I had to turn off the television. I was tired of seeing that Iran-Contra mess. It's on all the channels. I haven't been able to watch my stories."

"What are you doing?"

"Looking over my catering notes and making sure we have everything on the menu in time for next Saturday."

"What's happening then?"

"That's Juneteenth."

"What's on the menu?"

"Frenchy introduces a lot of the foods from back home. I have andouille, boudain, and stuffed mirlitons on order."

"Sounds delightful." But none of it is food I recognized.

"Catered barbecue for the less adventurous eaters."

"I see. So where's this taking place?"

"At the center."

"Growing up, my family didn't celebrate Juneteenth." Admitting this makes me ashamed. I grew up in Texas, and you would think the family would have at least taken me to a parade. It wasn't until I came to California in June to camp that we celebrated Juneteenth. Even then, we had only a minute set aside to sing a Negro spiritual.

"Your family is an exception to the norm," Aunt Teal says in a tone to suggest that she knew the family dynamic all too well.

"What's in store at the center?"

"Mary and Frenchy put together a program with local singers, dancers, poets, and actors. She may have some of the children from the center put on a little skit or have a historian talk for five minutes. All that takes place inside. Outside, there's vendors from the neighborhood selling merchandise. It has a carnival-like atmosphere to it."

"Wow. She never mentioned anything to me about it."

"Bebby, Mary's got a ton of things going on right now."

"I'm always willing to help."

"Thank you, chère. That's what I love about you."

**

Sitting on my bed, I read over the contract for the upcoming shows. With L.A. Philharmonic, I will earn more in one night than I did with a week's worth of performances with other orchestras. Not that they weren't stellar companies, but they don't carry the weight and prestige as L.A. Phil. I visualize myself walking out on stage and hearing the applause of the audience. I'm dressed in a simple but elegant black floor-length performance dress with black ballet flats. My hair is brushed into a curly chignon, and on my ears are my mother's diamond studs. I sit at the piano and begin to play.

A knock on the door interrupts my thoughts. Cassandra enters with a shopping bag.

"I saw this and immediately thought of you," she says, plopping on the edge of the bed.

"You shouldn't have." I look inside, and underneath the intricate wrapping paper, I see a cotton candy pink cashmere sweater. The material is delicate to the touch. I hold it next to my skin.

"It's gorgeous against your complexion," she says.

I get up to look at the sweater in the mirror, eyeing it from different angles.

"I like it. Thank you."

"*Whenever* we get a chance to go out, that would look really cute paired with a skirt or a pair of jeans."

"Don't say *whenever* like that," I say, imitating her voice.

"It's true."

"Listen, here's the deal: I volunteer two days at the center, I rehearse three days, and weekends will be our time together. Sounds good?"

She contemplates. "Noon on Fridays is when the weekend officially kicks off."

"Okay. That's fine. There's one problem."

"What?"

"Aunt Mary's curfew."

"We can work around that."

"I gave her my word I wouldn't violate it."

"And we won't."

"So, say we're out partying and having a good time and forget?"

"Let me handle that, Miss Goody Two-shoes." Cassandra winks and trots through the bathroom that separates our bedroom suites. I follow and enter her room where I see more shopping bags sprawled on the floor.

"Oh my."

She reaches inside one of the bags and pulls out a pair of shoes. "Aren't these hot?"

"Nice," I reply. "I see you're spending your trust fund wisely."

"Gotta spruce up my summer wardrobe." She opens another bag to reveal a mustard-colored halter dress.

"You and Mona, one day you're speaking, the next you're not. Then suddenly, she shows up, and you go shopping. Explain."

"Do you know the moment when you fall asleep?"

"No."

"Neither do I. Why is it your feet smell and your nose runs?"

I shrug. She's waiting for me to answer.

"Some things you can't explain."

"You better hope Aunt Mary doesn't see all these shopping bags. How will you explain that?"

"Touché, cousin." She gathers all the shopping bags to hide in her closet and tries to close the door but can't.

"I'll hide some in my closet," I say, taking a few bags.

"Please remind me about these. I don't want to find you wearing my jeans."

"I can't wear them anyway," I say before I turn and walk back to my room.

Later that evening, Cassandra and I come downstairs to grab a snack and find Uncle Frenchy, Aunt Mary, and Caleb sitting at the bar.

"How did the Lakers do?" Cassandra asks, hugging her mother and father. I do the same.

"They won," Uncle Frenchy announces.

"Barely," Caleb adds.

"Magic came through with a baby sky hook with two seconds left in the game," Uncle Frenchy says.

I notice a small stack of photographs sitting in front of Aunt Mary. Her hair is pulled into a bun, and glasses are perched on the tip of her button nose. Cassandra picks up a photograph. I glance over her shoulder and see a picture of a man holding a bird whose wings are spread out and the awestruck reaction on the children's faces. I notice Dee's sparkling eyes and recognize some of the others.

"Mary and I are getting a Juneteenth festival in order." Uncle Frenchy looks at the three of us.

"I'm in, coach. What's the game plan?" Caleb leans in.

"See if you can gather some of your teammates to make an appearance."

"That's it?" Caleb looks shocked.

"Yeah. Don't want you jumping around getting hurt. Not when the NBA's knocking on the door."

Caleb does a half swivel on the barstool. "How does the team tie in with Juneteenth?"

"The children get a chance to interact with you. It's a big deal to them."

Aunt Mary picks up a photo and examines it over top of her glasses. "Cassandra, I'm going to need you to introduce our keynote speaker."

"Who is it?" she asks.

Aunt Mary gives her a folder, which she opens. "Oh, nice." She slides it over to me. I look at the name and a photo attached to it, and it looks like someone famous. It's assumed I should know who this person is, but I haven't a clue.

"Niecy, if you're feeling up to it, dazzle us with the piano." Uncle Frenchy says.

"Of course," I reply.

"Great." He glances at Aunt Mary. "I feel good about this."

Aunt Mary winks at him. "Frenchy honey, I declare when this event

is over, you will be the crown cultural ambassador of Black excellence."
She high-fives Uncle Frenchy.

"That's why I love you, Mary May Honoré." Uncle Frenchy leans over
to give her a peck on the lips.

I watch Cassandra and Caleb's reactions. Cassandra pretends she's
about to throw up. Caleb only shakes his head.

I love my family with all their quirks and personalities. Some of the
best times of my life have been spent in this house. Before Mother died,
it was rare outside of church for my parents and I to get together. We
had our trips we took, but if I had to recall a moment where I joined
my parents at the table and I remembered the conversations, I can't.

"Did Kyle tell you he was looking for a job?" Cassandra asks her
mother.

"Yes. He mentioned it."

"Did he tell you why?"

"He doesn't owe me an explanation." Aunt Mary continues to flip
through the photos.

"He was too afraid to tell you that one of your girls came to the
center wearing a skirt and purposely forgot her undies."

Aunt Mary stops flipping, and I notice her stare shift to Cassandra.
She doesn't bat a lash. Uncle Frenchy and Caleb study Aunt Mary for
a beat, gauging her reaction.

"Go on."

"That's all I have." Cassandra shifts her weight to one side.

"Mom, some of your girls are rough," Caleb adds.

"Is that why you and JB stopped volunteering?" Aunt Mary asks.

"Yes."

"Describe rough."

"I was teaching a basketball drill once. When no one was looking,
one of the girls copped a feel."

Aunt Mary and Cassandra gasp.

"And Mom, if you ask them, I'm sure they will deny it." Cassandra's
face appears flushed.

"Why didn't you come to me when this was happening?" She looks at Caleb for an answer.

"What would you have done?" he asks.

"Gave her a gut-wrenching lesson on what it means to respect boundaries."

"I wonder who she is," Cassandra says.

"Maddie, did you know about this?" Aunt Mary asks.

"Rosie mentioned it to me, she didn't want to say anything because she didn't want to get anyone in trouble."

"Did she tell you which girl?" Aunt Mary asks.

"No. She didn't," I answer

Caleb and Cassandra shake their heads. Aunt Mary looks to Uncle Frenchy who's been quiet, taking in all the information. He swivels slightly on his stool. "You've got to do some investigating," he says.

"I'll get to the bottom of this." She raises up from the bar and walks out of the room without telling any of us goodnight.

Eleven

Aunt Mary is quiet this morning on the drive to the center. When we arrive, I notice Kyle's car. We pull in the parking spot next to it, and I see him sitting in the front seat. He gets out immediately and hurries to the driver's side to open the door for Aunt Mary then walks back around to open the door for me. I really wish Cassandra gave him a chance.

"How long have you been waiting?" Aunt Mary asks.

"Just a minute or two before you pulled up." He seems anxious.

Once she opens the door and turns on all the lights, she tells Kyle to have a seat in her office, then she tells me to check all the rooms, a ritual I notice she does when she opens and closes the place.

"The staff will start coming within the next ten minutes or so. If anyone asks, I'm in a meeting."

She hurries down the corridor to her office and closes the door. I have the urge to run down and prop my ear against the door, but that mural of my mother is there, and the expression on her face says, Maddie, I taught you better.

Once the doors open and the children pour in, I notice Aunt Mary summoning each girl one by one to her office. I'm surprised she summons Rosie, but when Rosie returns, she shares with me why.

"She wanted to talk to everyone and see what we knew."

"You tell her what you told me?"

"I did."

"Was Kyle there?"

"No."

I'm thinking he must've made his exit out the back door. I'm curious as to how the meeting went with him. My hunch is there's nothing Aunt Mary can say to convince him to stay on and volunteer. I guess he really is looking for a job, otherwise he'd still be here.

"She thanked me for speaking up."

"I'm glad you did too," I say.

Our conversation is interrupted with loud yelling. Every person in the room, including the children, stop.

"I don't need this," I hear.

One of the teens appears. I recognize her as the girl who said she was arrested for joyriding. She's the fourteen-year-old who can easily pass for my age or older.

"Everybody in here can kiss my ass," she yells.

Aunt Mary; her assistant, Leah; and the secretary herd her toward the front of the entrance, all the while the girl spouts out more obscenities. Leah opens the door, and Aunt Mary stands there, and the way her shoulders are hunched, I can tell she's hurt. Even as the door shuts, I can still hear the girl cursing. Everyone is staring at Aunt Mary like *What now?* The room is dead silent.

"I hope I never have to put anyone else out." She scans the room before calmly walking down the corridor to her office with Leah and the secretary following.

"Was that her?" I whisper to Rosie.

"Yes," she whispers back.

The other teens resume talking in hushed tones amongst themselves. Rosie and Dee and some of the other younger children join me at the piano. I play what little I have memorized from the Schumann piece before I play a little of Mozart's "Rondo Alla Turca."

"Where were you yesterday?" Dee asks, I notice her rubbing her knees and her side.

"I was home." Then the thought occurs: *tell them what's happening in your life.* "Do you all know what a concert pianist is?" I ask the younger children.

"Duh. Someone who plays piano at a concert." Rosie gives me a sideways glance.

"I wanted to give the younger ones a chance to answer," I tell her. "Anyway, there's more to it than that. I am a classically trained concert pianist, and I play with large orchestras and sometimes chamber orchestras. I spend a lot of time practicing—sometimes two hours, sometimes all day. Like I literally wake up, eat breakfast, practice, eat lunch, practice, eat dinner, practice, and go to bed."

"Wow." Dee's eyes grow wide. "How do you do it?"

"Funny, I ask myself the same thing," I say.

Suddenly, she grabs her side and leans over the piano. "Ouch," she cries.

I look at her to see if she's playing or joking. Her eyes are wide, and there's fear in them.

"Dee, are you okay?" I ask low and softly.

While still holding her side, she stares at me and Rosie. "Yes," she replies.

I glance at Rosie, and she looks at me like, *what just happened?*

"Are you hurting really bad?" I ask again in my low, quiet voice.

She looks down as if she's too embarrassed to admit it. This crushes me inside.

"What hurts?" I ask.

"My side."

"How long has it been hurting?"

"I don't know."

"Did you fall?"

"No."

"Has someone hurt you?"

"No."

"Are you telling the truth?"

"Yes."

She seemed fine when she walked in this morning. She received a lot of compliments on her matching bright yellow short set.

"Let's go talk to Mrs. Mary." When I stand, I notice she doesn't move.

"If we talk to Mrs. Mary, maybe she can get us a scoop of ice cream."

That isn't enough to convince her. I turn to Rosie.

"See if you can find Miss Vanessa, please." I say.

Rosie swivels around, leaving her drawing pad and pencil in the chair.

I sit back down, trying to gather my thoughts but unable to. Miss Vanessa arrives with a concerned look.

"What's wrong, Dee?" she asks and immediately kneels to Dee's level.

She's still holding her side.

"What happened?"

"My side hurts," she answers. The singsong quality in her voice is now flat and weak.

"Let's go check you out."

She doesn't move.

Miss Vanessa looks at me. I explain to her and even demonstrate with Rosie what happened.

By now Damon and Blaze stumble over with curious gazes.

"Dee, you okay?" Damon asks.

She bursts into tears, sobbing.

I run quickly to Aunt Mary's office, interrupting her meeting with Leah and the secretary.

"Aunt Mary, hurry. Dee needs you."

We rush back to find Vanessa is doing her best to calm Dee. Some-one must've dialed 9-1-1 because twenty minutes later, the paramedics arrive. They examine her for bruises, and there are none, but when they touch the area, she screams. Aunt Mary, calm as a summer sea, holds on to her hand as the paramedics put her little body onto a gurney. The sight of it and the hospital smell on the clothes of the paramedics stirs emotions. Miss Vanessa and Leah grab their purses.

"Wait. I'm coming with you," I say to them. I don't have to grab a purse because I always keep my backpack with my sheet music and wallet on me. I follow them down the corridor past Aunt Mary's office. I look behind me and see Rosie.

"You're not leaving without me," she says.

The four of us get into Leah's car.

Miss Vanessa turns to Leah. "Before we go to the hospital, we need to stop by her mother's."

"Where is that?" Leah asks.

"She's off Santo Tomas" is Miss Vanessa's answer.

"That's the Jungle." Leah replies.

"Yeah, I know," Miss Vanessa says.

Leah hesitates and takes a deep breath before she turns the ignition.

"How about you get out and drive over there?" Leah suggests to Miss Vanessa.

"But she has younger children, and she needs me to babysit so she can ride with you."

Leah sucks in her breath and drives. She's silent the entire drive over. When she pulls up to the apartment complex, Miss Vanessa runs up to the door and knocks. As she waits for it to open, there are a couple of guys standing at the adjacent apartment. When it finally opens, I see who I assume is Dee's mother with a baby on her hip. I watch Miss Vanessa engage her in conversation, and the expression on her face shows horror. She looks over Miss Vanessa's shoulder at us waiting in the car. Miss Vanessa goes inside, closing the door behind her.

"Hurry." Leah nervously drums her fingers on the steering wheel. In the rearview mirror, her eyes are anxious and alert.

When Dee's mother emerges, she runs to the car, opens the door, and sits inside. "Thank you, Leah."

Leah hits the accelerator so hard I see smoke trailing her car.

"I pray my child is okay. I took her to two different doctors, and they couldn't find nothing wrong."

"She kept holding her side, so the paramedics checked for bruising," Leah explains

"God knows I wouldn't hurt my child."

"I know," Leah says.

"I want the best for Dee. She's my little superstar," her mother says.

I reach over and touch her shoulder. "Hi. I'm Maddie."

"You're Maddie?" Her eyes light up.

"I am."

"It's nice to finally meet you. I'm Felicia. Dee talks about you every day."

"She's my sweetheart. We were talking and joking about the piano, and the next minute she started complaining about her side."

"Was she in a lot of pain?"

"Yes, she was."

Felicia turns to face forward. "I hope they find out what's wrong with my baby."

"I do, too," Leah says, sounding as soothing and calm as Aunt Mary.

"Her daddy's in the county. They got his bail set so high, I can't afford to get him out."

I remember the picture she drew of her family. I see the place where she calls home.

"People assume the worst about you when you live in the projects," Felicia begins.

I hear Rosie agreeing. "Hi, Felicia. I'm Rosie. I'm in the Coco Capri Apartments."

"Girl, what? Somebody got smoked there last night," Felicia says.

"I heard the shots." She looks at me, noticing the horror flashing across my face. "No. For real. I heard shots."

I can't imagine living like that.

Once at the hospital, we go to a waiting area where we see Aunt Mary. She and Felicia embrace and hold each other. Aunt Mary rubs her back and allows her to sob. Felicia's cries sound like they've been locked behind those steel burglar bars used to protect her, and now they finally have a chance to roam.

Aunt Mary holds Felicia's face in her hands and wipes her tears. "She's going to need you to be strong."

"How is she? What did the doctor say?"

"A nurse is checking her vitals."

Felicia takes a deep breath. "I hope somebody can finally tell me something."

"How was she this morning before she left?" Aunt Mary asks.

"She was fine, but I noticed she kept rubbing her knees and side."

"You've had her examined before?" Aunt Mary asks.

"Yes."

"What did the doctor say?"

"They couldn't find anything, but they're still looking at me like I'm Penny's abusive momma from Good Times."

We all find a set of chairs where the four of us sit in a crowded waiting area. The place is busy with nurses and patients alike drifting like logs down a river. I don't like the smell, the look, and the feel of these places. I get my notebook of staff sheets, and Rosie opens her sketchpad, and without saying much, we each do our thing. I notice Rosie tracing what looks like a girl holding a tennis racket. It's amazing how much life a sharpened number two pencil adds to a blank sheet of paper.

"Who is that?" I ask.

"A little girl I saw on the tennis court in Compton."

She looks at my staff sheet at the notes and melodies I have written out. I titled this piece, "Catastrophe in G."

"What does 'Catastrophe in G' mean?" she asks.

"It's the sound I hear when the song is played."

"How do you know what sound you want?"

"I don't."

She nods. "It just comes to you?"

"You understand."

"Yeah, I totally get it."

A nurse asks for the mother of Delight Morris. Felicia stands. "I'm her." Aunt Mary and her assistant, Leah, stand alongside her. The nurse explains that an X-ray is needed.

"Can I see her?"

"You will after an X-ray is taken and the doctor has had a chance to analyze it."

Felicia cups her hands together like she's praying. "How is she right now?"

"Compared to earlier, she's in good spirits."

Felicia's shoulders seem to loosen with that bit of information. When the nurse leaves, she turns to Aunt Mary and Leah.

"If it weren't for you all," she says, her bottom lip is trembling, but she has her emotions under control.

Aunt Mary is calm and gentle as she holds Felicia's hand.

"She looked so adorable in her yellow outfit today," Aunt Mary says, making Felicia smile. "I just want to tell you how I appreciate you allowing us to work with her. She is a joy to have around."

"Every day, she sits by the door waiting on Miss Vanessa to pick her up, and don't let her be late."

Aunt Mary, still holding on to her hand, smiles. "Miss Vanessa told me she can be a little firecracker."

"When she comes home, I can't get her to stop talking about you all, especially you, Maddie."

Felicia reaches for my hand. "She says to me, 'Mama, I want to play the piano like Maddie.'"

"I was her age when I started."

"She sits at the table pretending it's a piano, and her little fingers are just going and going."

Aunt Mary and I make eye contact for a brief second. We don't say a word; we listen, and we take it all in.

"She helps me out a lot with her brother and sister, especially now with her daddy locked up."

"Why is he locked up?" Aunt Mary asks.

Felicia blinks back tears.

Aunt Mary stands quietly, waiting for her to answer.

"We have to eat. Rent's gotta be paid. Dee gotta keep looking her best every day."

Aunt Mary doesn't say anything. My guess is that she may already know the answer. When it comes to dealing with the children at the center and their families, she's seen and heard it all.

The nurse appears. "Miss Morris, you can see your daughter now," she says.

Felicia grabs Aunt Mary's hand. "Can she come too?"

The nurse doesn't object.

"I'll be right with you, Felicia. Just let me talk to Leah for a minute."

Aunt Mary turns to Leah. "Take the rest of the afternoon off. You and the girls have a nice early dinner. I'll call you in a couple of hours."

Aunt Mary opens her arms to embrace me and Rosie. "My girls."

"We were hoping we could see Delight," I say, thinking how much I like that name.

"Maybe in a couple of hours." Aunt Mary seems hopeful. Her calmness seems to ease my anxiety.

Once outside in the car, Leah turns to Rosie. "My goal is to have you home before dark. In case you haven't already figured it out, I'm not a fan of the Jungle."

"Okay, Leah, I get it," Rosie says, rolling her eyes when Leah isn't looking.

"What do you guys want to eat?" she asks, starting up the car.

"Take us to Fatburger," Rosie responds.

Leah glances at me. "What about you?"

"Fatburger it is," I answer.

"I want a king chili cheeseburger," Rosie says to Leah.

"I've never had one so I'm looking forward to it," I say.

"Ever had it with an egg on top?" Leah asks Rosie.

"Yes" is Rosie's response.

"That doesn't sound good." I'm already holding my stomach.

"You have to try it," Leah says.

We arrive at a burger stand, and it's crowded with people, yelling out orders, with most of them wanting the king chili cheeseburger. Minutes later, when I finally bite into my first Fatburger, I see what they all mean. The three of us sit in the car across the street from the burger stand with the radio on, feeding our faces and not saying much.

"What do you think?" Leah asks me.

"It's actually good," I respond.

"What I like about them, there could be hundreds of people yelling out orders, and guess what? They always get your order right," Leah says.

"How do they do it?" Rosie asks.

"They have a mind for it. Pretty much like me with Mrs. Mary's business. I can precisely remember something she told me two weeks ago even when she can't." Leah starts up the car.

"I'm having so much fun. I'm not ready to go home," Rosie says. "Leah, can I stay with you?"

"No." Leah is adamant.

Rosie sighs and sinks back into her seat while quietly staring out the window. I didn't know Leah could be so blunt. Instead of dropping Rosie off at her front door, Leah stops at the corner, adjacent to the apartment building where Rosie lives. Rosie opens the door, and I get out of the car with her.

"Call me, okay?" I say to her.

"Our phone just got turned off," she says.

"Wow, I'm sorry" is all I say before giving her a hug. I sit in the passenger's seat, close the door, and watch her walk across the street, and as Leah drives off, my eyes are still on Rosie until I can no longer see her.

"May I say something?" I turn to Leah.

"Yes, sure," she says.

"If someone is saying to you that they don't want to go home and they're asking to stay with you, shouldn't you be concerned?"

"You know, there are protocols I have to adhere to, and one of them is unless I have proof there is an imminent threat to a child, only then can I intervene, and even then, I have to notify the state. I just can't take in someone's child. As innocent as it was for her to be in my vehicle, if the state finds out she was riding with me without her mother's consent, I get in trouble. Your aunt could get in trouble. There's a lot of moving parts when it comes to dealing with these children."

She turns into the neighborhood. "And as far as the Jungle, I've read too many news stories of innocent bystanders caught up in gang crossfire. I don't want to be another statistic."

"I understand" is all I say, and I see her pull into the driveway of Aunt Mary's and Uncle Frenchy's home.

"Thanks, Leah," I say, getting out of the car.

I have a sick feeling in the pit of my stomach. I don't know if it has anything to do with Rosie's situation, Dee's situation, or that king chili cheeseburger with egg I just ate. At any rate, I feel miserable, and I don't like this feeling at all.

Twelve

I wish I didn't know this. It's something that once you're told, you don't stop thinking about it. You question why and how. When Aunt Mary tells me the news, I sit in the nearest seat I find. Her words to me are: Dee has osteosarcoma—that's bone cancer. This, the same little girl I met just over a week ago, with the sparkling eyes, has bone cancer.

"A diagnosis is not a death sentence," Aunt Mary assures me.

"She needs another opinion."

"The X-rays showed lesions on her bones." Aunt Mary sits at the bar and holds her head in her hand. The air in the room is crisp and smells of lavender. The distraction is brief, welcoming, and pleasant. Then my thoughts drift to my mother's first chemo treatment. She combed her hair in a stylish updo with curly tendrils cascading from the nape. After the third round of chemo, her eighteen-inch hair and perfectly arched eyebrows were gone. She looked alien and cold. Her skin was so thin and pale I could see the coloring in her veins. I shudder when I think of Dee's coarse braids falling on the floor. It hasn't happened, but my prayer is that it doesn't. I remember brushing my mother's hair and seeing clumps of it still on the brush. Images like that stay with you.

I lay in bed, tossing and turning, grappling with the feeling I had when my mother went through her ordeal. There were days when the pain was unbearable. I'd hold her hand, and with every strength she could muster, she'd squeeze it. I turn on the lamp light, open my nightstand, grab a sheet of paper to write the following:

Pain is uncontrollable.

Pain sets the tone for the day.

Pain fights and wrestles with you.

Pain ultimately weakens your will and breaks your spirit.

Notes and melodies pour into me, and I'm writing them down. Sometimes they come so fast I can't keep up with them. I'm erasing, and they don't stop to wait for me, so I run to catch up with them. We're sprinting neck to neck. Daddy quotes a scripture from the Bible that states, "The race is not given to the swift nor the strong but to the one who endures to the end." I write:

Life is a race

stay in your lane

keep the pace.

I write until dawn breaks outside my window. Sheets are scattered on my bed. I'm too tired to gather them.

***

Cassandra finds me and the sheets of music sprawled across the bed. I'm still wearing the clothes I had on yesterday. Clearing away paper, she sits on the edge of the bed, stunned at what she sees.

"Mom told me," she says.

I manage to sit up and gather my papers. All the lyrics and notes are still running through my head. "Do you know her?" I ask.

"No."

"She's nine years old."

"It's unfortunate."

"She's such a beautiful little girl."

"I hear."

"She says, 'Maddie, I want to play the piano like you.'"

"And she will. One day."

"I hardly know her. This really hurts."

"This may sound weird and off the subject, but have you ever swam naked in the ocean?"

I frown. "No."

"Ever flown upside down in a World War II twin engine plane?"

I don't answer.

"Ever been choked out during sex?"

"Ewww, Cassandra. Stop."

My head begins to spin, too busy trying to figure out where she's going with this conversation.

"Frenchy says, 'Life is short. You better get to living because you won't get out alive.'"

We sit there in silence for a moment. My mind is racing with a million thoughts.

"This is going even more off topic, but have you had sex?" I ask.

She stares at me for what seems like an eternity before answering. "Of course I have."

I don't know what to say. I sit there quietly still holding on to all my papers. "What was it like?"

She chuckles. "You really want to talk about this?"

"I thought you'd wait until you got married."

"Who does that?"

"I am."

"My God, Maddie. Let's be real: Do you think our mothers were virgins when they married?"

"I'd like to hope so."

"Nobody waits anymore, unless you're stuck in the dark ages, or like you, living under a rock playing a Steinway."

The jab stings a little, but it's the story of my life: hours a day at the piano, concerts, church, private Christian schools. I don't have very many friends, I don't watch much television, I don't listen to much music outside of classical, and my image is carefully choreographed. I don't drink, I've never smoked, I've never had sex. Cassandra said I was a Miss Goody Two-shoes once. I can't help it. I saw it exemplified in my mother.

She said, "Maddie, you may not always remember what I say, but you will always remember what I do."

I remember how compassionate she was for the less fortunate—that was her full-time ministry in the church. I remember how she never left home without a trace of makeup. I remember how stylish she was—even at the beach she wore a silk cover-up and accessorized it with a layered necklace. For the most part, her hair was always brushed in an updo, but there were occasions where she wore it down, and the waves hung past her shoulders. Her conversation was even-toned and pleasant. She rarely raised her voice. I didn't really hear my parents argue. I watched her cross her right leg over her left leg when she sat down. I saw her give you her full attention when you spoke. Tiffany pearls adorned her neck. She was a throwback to timeless black elegance during the 1970s and early eighties when everyone else was loose and carefree. My mother didn't live long. She was just thirty-five.

"You talked to Kyle?" I ask.

"I have."

"What did he say?"

"He's not coming back. He's working at his dad's firm."

My mind drifts to her having had sex. I assume it was with Kyle, but after her mentioning being choked out, I can't imagine Kyle doing anything like that. I could be wrong.

"Where do you keep your hairbrush?" she asks.

"Look in the bathroom in the middle drawer."

When she returns with the brush, she sits in the bed behind me and takes down my hair, letting it dangle past my shoulders, and begins to brush through it. One hand holds the strands in place while she brushes with the other. I'm still holding on to my music, like I used to hold on to my mother.

"Was it with Kyle?" I ask.

"Yes. It happened this year, right after my party."

"How?"

"I asked Mom if I could spend the night at Mona's. Her parents weren't there, so she slept with Ruger while Kyle and I slept in the guest house."

"Mona slept with Ruger?"

"I know, right?" We shared a laugh with that.

"Back to you and Kyle— Did you enjoy it?"

"I did."

"How did you feel afterward?"

"I didn't feel different. That's not to say it wasn't good. It happened, I enjoyed it, and it kept happening."

I closed my eyes and let that bit of information sink in. I felt Cassandra's fingers gathering the strands of my hair together and brushing it.

"You've never seen a guy naked?" she asks me.

"No."

"Have you at least gotten a peek at his penis?"

"No."

"Not even the tip of it?"

"No."

She sighs in a way to indicate my life is dull.

"Get yourself together. We're going out," she says.

With that announcement, I contemplate whether I want to go. My idea of fun is hanging out on the beach, going shopping, and relaxing by the pool. With Cassandra, there's no telling what's in store.

***

Sunsets just do something to me. It's like the Earth holds the sun in the palm of its hand to admire before it slips through its fingers, and like that, all the natural light gives way to the artificial ones. My hair is blown out straight to a look unlike anything I've ever worn before. I let Cassandra apply my makeup to a point where I don't recognize myself. On my round, full lips is cherry-red lipstick. My eyes are slanted and outlined in black. Shades of orange are layered with gold highlights on my eyelids. My lashes are separated and elongated with the help of a lash curler, my cheeks are so red that when I see my reflection, I don't know if it's the makeup or my nerves that cause my cheeks to flush.

Who is this girl sitting in a stretch limo, wearing a soft pink lightweight off-the-shoulder cashmere sweater? Why isn't she wearing a bra?

Cassandra, Mona, and Ursula are laughing and singing along with the radio.

"I know you know this song," Cassandra says to me as if I should.

I listen to the melody. I don't say anything and just move along with the rhythm like I observe them doing. I look out my window and see traffic at a stop-and-go pace, too much for a Saturday evening. My thoughts drift to the Schumann piece I haven't played since Wednesday. I can't seem to get Dee off my mind. I'm wondering how she's feeling. Right now, I want to be by her side, holding her hand.

"Maddie, I spoke to Gregory's mother today." Mona's voice snaps me out of my momentary drift. I notice her complexion glittering against the limo's lighting. Her eyeliner, with the aid of Cassandra, is done up like mine with the cat-eye effect. To anyone who sees us, the aim is to appear fascinating, maybe alluring.

"Nice," I respond. "Were you visiting? Out shopping?"

"Mom and I were having lunch." She flips her hair off her shoulders, showcasing an off-white silk blouse with a low V-neck in front. "I'll give her props. When Madame Celeste enters a room, she owns it."

Although it wasn't planned, all of us are wearing skirts—theirs are a few inches shorter than mine.

"She says Gregory's in Europe," Mona says.

"She's correct," I answer.

"She said he left last weekend," Mona continues.

"Sure did."

My terse responses seem to quiet her for the moment.

"You miss him?" Ursula chimes in. Her hair is straightened as well, and it cascades past her shoulders.

"I do."

"When is he coming back?" Mona asks.

"I don't know."

"Are you going to see him?" Mona continues asking.

"If he sends a first-class ticket."

They all get a laugh out of that.

"Why settle for a seat? Tell him to send you a plane," Mona says.

"That would be nice too."

I remember the conversation with Cassandra about Mona and Ruger having slept together. If I bring up his name, I wonder how she'll react.

"Did Ruger go to Europe?" Cassandra asks. She must have been reading my mind.

"He did."

"What about you?" Cassandra asks. She discreetly taps my leg. She does that from time to time when she's prodding into someone's business and she wants me to come along for the ride.

"Mum's the word on that," is Mona's response.

Cassandra opens her compact to check her makeup. "Why's it a big secret?" she asks.

"No secret." Mona opens her own compact to inspect her makeup.

Where do four underage girls in a chauffeured stretch limo go on a Saturday evening in L.A.? The chauffeur opens the door, and the four of us step out. The pink pumps I'm wearing have me three inches taller and feeling confident as I stroll into the side entrance of the restaurant. I see Mona slip the maître d' a folded bill. She struts, shoulders back, hair flowing and bouncing. The ambience in the room gives a flair of understated elegance. If you're inside, you're definitely somebody.

"Best table in the house, Miss Palermo." He sits the four of us in a booth with white linen tablecloths.

"The salmon and caviar pizza are the best here," Ursula says after he walks off.

"I wasn't going to eat," Cassandra says, turning to me, "but that sounds scrumptious."

"Why don't we all share one? I'm only eating half a slice anyway." When Mona flips her hair, part of her nipple is exposed. She doesn't seem to mind. Ursula reaches over to cover it. "Can't take you anywhere."

"It's an advertisement for the practice," Mona says.

"You get another procedure?" Cassandra asks.

"You noticed?" She points to her forehead. "Lunchtime procedure, less than thirty minutes, loses wrinkles over time."

"What wrinkles? You're only eighteen," Cassandra says.

"I still have forehead wrinkles."

"That's just your imagination," I respond.

"Ursula, do you see wrinkles?" Mona asks.

"No. Just because you have access to it doesn't mean you need it."

"Listen to her, Mona." Cassandra says.

"Maddie, what do you think?" Mona casts a smoldering temptress pose.

"I agree with Ursula. You don't need enhancements."

"A guy told me my breasts looked like mosquito bites."

"Was it Ruger?" Cassandra asks.

"I'm not saying, but can you imagine how I felt?"

"Is that why you—"

"Yes," she replies before I finish the question.

Our drinks arrive, and at some point during the evening, our salads and pizza arrive. Mona takes two bites, and she's done. I didn't want to seem ravenous, so I only eat a slice. It's the Hollywood thing to do. Just like it's the Hollywood thing to slip into the limo and with no plans just see where the evening takes us.

"Maddie's still a virgin," Cassandra blurts.

I can't believe she is saying this with a clear head. What we discussed was between us. She seems to regret it the moment she sees my reaction.

"Ooops."

"Maddie, awww, that's sweet," Ursula adds.

"You and Gregory never?" Mona asks, shocked.

"Thanks for telling the world, Cassandra, but no."

"She's saving it for marriage."

"What?" Mona and Ursula laugh.

I'm done talking.

"That's so sweet," Mona gushes.

I'm livid.

"Relax, friend. I think it's a beautiful thing to have your cherry intact," Mona says.

"Is that what they're calling it in L.A.?" I ask.

"Maddie, I'm sorry." The puppy dog expression on Cassandra's face doesn't change the way I feel.

"I can totally see you and Gregory getting married. You're the only person I know who can truly wear white on their wedding day." Mona says.

"My issue with waiting until marriage is this: What if he doesn't satisfy you?" Ursula asks.

"That will be a problem for me," Cassandra says.

"A definite deal breaker," Ursula says.

"Grounds for divorce," Mona adds.

I remain quiet, listening to them go on and on.

"Ruger makes really ugly faces." Mona demonstrates, contorting and grimacing. I have to admit, it's hard trying not to laugh. "When I kiss down there, lights out, baby."

"Oh, nooooo." Ursula covers her face.

"Maddie, I need you to pay attention."

Mona grabs one of the Perrier bottles, unscrews it, and sticks the neck of it into her mouth. She moves her mouth up and down the neck of it in a slow, deliberate suggestive fashion. Holding it with both hands, she increases the speed in which she takes it inside her mouth. Her eyes are closed, and the expression on her face is intense. I notice foam bubbling to the surface of the bottle. I cover my face. Cassandra and Ursula's laughter has my ears ringing. Cassandra laughs so hard, she's coughing. Ursula taps my shoulder.

"Lighten up, Maddie," Ursula says.

"You girls are clearly out of my league," I say.

"We're just having fun," Mona says.

"You're a mess, Mona," Cassandra says, wiping away tears from having laughed so hard.

"Funny. That's what Ruger says."

"Look at us, all beautiful and fabulous," Cassandra says.

"Let's go to the Comedy Club. I can get us in. One of my friends is a regular there." Ursula opens up a compact to inspect herself. Soon, we all get out our compacts to inspect. I apply a fresh coat of cherry red to my lips. Once at the Comedy Club entrance, I notice the line snaking around the building. A burly gentleman I'm guessing is about seven feet tall with folded arms is there with no expression.

When Ursula walks up, I notice a hint of a smile across his lips. He opens the velvet rope and allows us to walk inside. The place is crowded yet dark and smoky and smells of cigarettes. We find a spot near the edge of the stage. A waitress comes over to take our drink orders.

Ursula, Mona, and I order Perrier with cranberry.

"Vodka and 7," Cassandra says without flinching. The waitress doesn't ask for her ID.

A comic is introduced. A scrawny black guy walking hurriedly, slue-foot and slouching approaches the mic to applause and cheers. He's sporting a Jheri curl box top cut, and his teeth are big, and his eyes are round and busy.

"Whazzup, L.A.?" he says in a loud, roaring shrill voice. The audience responds. "Would have gotten here quicker if it wasn't for my car. I try starting it up." He imitates the sound of a struggling car engine. "After a while, it just says, nigga, please."

The laughter seems genuine, and the looks on people's faces in the audience anticipate more.

"Got my ass on the bus. I'm from Brooklyn, so I know. I find out real fast in Hollywood you can't mack the babes if all you got is a bus pass. I don't see what the problem is. At least we ain't walking, shit. Wheels better than heels. When I say wheels, I mean Hot Wheels, big wheels, a Good Humor bike."

I chuckle and glance at my crew, my trio dazzling under the haze of smoke and soft lights. The laughter that punctuates the air makes me forget about the things happening outside and be in the moment. During the course of his bit, somewhere in the audience, a voice goes on a drunken rant, slurring words and spitting obscenities. The comedian holds steady on the mic. "I'm sorry. I don't speak alcoholic," he says.

"You don't speak English either. Haven't understood a word you said."

The comedian chuckles. "Hey buddy, ma-me-se, ma-ma-sa, ma-ma-coo-sa. Understand? That's Michael Jackson. Now beat it."

The audience erupts. Drowning out any retort the guy in the audience thought he could muster. I laugh until I can no longer feel my face. Another comedian follows. This one is a lot easier on the eyes. He's tall with a full mustache. The angle of the stage lighting showcases an outline of taut muscles underneath his shirt.

"That's my friend," Ursula says before taking a sip of her drink.

"He'd better be funny." By this time, Cassandra is on her second glass of vodka and 7.

"Show of hands, anyone here got that one aunt, you know the one that gets drunk and spills all the family secrets?"

The room is stirring with conversations and scattered laughter. "Aunt Gladys will walk up to you..." He stumbles in his spot like he's intoxicated, and he says in a woman's voice, "All your brothers and sisters have a gap like Willy B. Where's yours?" He takes a beat to hear the audience's laughter. "Because Willy B is their daddy, not yours, that's why." His facial expressions are just as comical.

"You better hide when Aunt Gladys comes around. She's not satisfied until she's worked the room. What's supposed to be a happy, civilized occasion turns into Thrilla in Manila."

Ursula's smile is glowing. She glances at me and Cassandra who holds up her glass signaling her approval.

"Days later, when you tell her what she did, she acts like your president. You know your president with the C.R.S. disease—can't remember shit." He imitates President Ronald Reagan's voice and mannerisms. "I don't recall. I can't remember."

"I like him," I say to Ursula. She touches her tongue with her thumb and points up making a sizzling sound.

It must be two o'clock in the morning when the four of us crawl into the backseat. I'm trying my best to stay awake. Cassandra had four drinks and is feeling the effects. She turns to me.

"I'm sorry, cousin." She starts sobbing.

I take her face into my hands. "Shhhh. I know. I know. I'm not mad anymore, okay?"

"You promise." Her aqua-colored eyes are pleading with me. I roll my eyes and simply nod, wishing I had tissue.

"Whatever you do, don't throw up in here." Mona opens the sunroof.

Ursula is standing outside the door making out with her friend, the comedian. The door opens, Ursula gets inside, and presses the button to let down her window.

"Wow," he says, looking at the four of us inside. "The night can't end. Where's the party?"

"Malibu," Ursula says. "If you can keep up, you just might get in."

"Give me the address, and I'll beat you there."

"Get in," Mona says to him. Ursula opens the door. He gets in and sits between the two of them. He has an expression like he's the only person at a huge buffet and he doesn't know where to start. We ride off, and he's smiling at Ursula like he's ready to eat her alive. All I hear from Cassandra now are snorting noises. Mona leans forward to check on her.

"You've had enough? You want four more glasses?" she asks.

Cassandra moans.

The comedian leans in. "Hey. I found a message in a bottle. It said you drank too much." He tries humoring, tilting his head sideways to glance at Cassandra whose head is now in my lap.

"You just better not throw up in here. Your ass is getting dropped off on the expressway before that happens." She and Ursula giggle like wicked witches.

A minute more into the drive, Cassandra is snoring. I myself am going in and out of consciousness. I rest my head on Cassandra's back and close my eyes.

Moments later, I'm awakened by loud kissing and low, soft purring. The lights are now dimmed, but I look and notice Ursula, the comedian, and Mona kissing and touching each other. I close my eyes. But that still doesn't prevent me from hearing all the kissing and low moaning. At this point, Cassandra has stopped snoring, but I wish she hadn't. I tell myself, when she awakes and sobers up, don't ever tag along with her on these wild escapades. My life with my Steinway is just fine.

Thirteen

It takes a minute for me to gather my bearings, and then I realize I'm at Mona's family's beach house in Malibu. I look beside me, and Cassandra is sound asleep. She looks as soft and delicate as a baby doll with freckles and long lashes. Her cheeks are rosy and round. The room is bright, and there are no blackout curtains to shield the outside light. This view of Malibu is spectacular because it is right on the beach. I see the morning haze is still in the air, but the Pacific is flourishing, blending in with the gray of the haze. The waves shimmer like tiny footprints. I want to think Cassandra told Aunt Mary our whereabouts. She doesn't seem to think it's a problem when we hang out with Mona and Ursula. God, if she only knew.

My pretty pink cashmere top smells like I've been chain smoking. I explore my settings, getting a feel for what's what. There are no family photos. The walls are ivory with black-and-white photos of nondescript settings. The bathroom suite is grand with a garden tub in the center. I open the linen closet and see terry-cloth robes and bath sheets. I close the door behind me and lock it and start rummaging through the drawers for soap and shampoo. I find something to wash off the makeup.

After I wash my face, I am pleased. I see someone I recognize—amber-colored eyes with no eye shadow, full, pouty lips with no red lipstick. My mother would have been livid had she seen me last night. Aunt Mary, too, for that matter.

After showering, I put on a robe and allow my hair to air dry. I open the door, and Cassandra is sitting up in bed with a dazed look.

"You, okay?" I ask.

"What happened?"

"Too many vodkas and 7."

She gets up and immediately runs to the toilet, hurling and gurgling, hugging it like a long-lost friend. I grab and twist her hair so she doesn't vomit all over it.

"As God as my witness, I promise I won't take another drink." She hurls once more before she rests her head on the toilet seat.

"Where are we?"

"Mona's family's beach house."

"Where are Mona and Ursula?"

I remember what I saw last night in the limo with the comedian. "Occupied," I answer.

"Huh?"

"Never mind. Let's get you back in bed."

"No, no, no. I want to stay here."

I find a spot next to her on the floor and rub her back. "You remember the limo ride?"

"No."

"Good." I wish I didn't.

"Why'd you say that?"

"I'll tell you about it later. Can I get you something?"

"Tomato juice or Bloody Mary mix."

"Or I can get you more vodka and 7."

She waves me off.

Mona's family's beach house is white and sterile, and once I find my way downstairs, the aroma of bacon and the sounds of music beckon me into the kitchen where I find Mona, Ursula, and the comedian dancing like they are at a club.

"Hi, Maddie." Mona is extremely happy as she grabs my hand.

"Hi." Her breath smells fruity, and I notice a magnum of champagne and a glass of OJ sitting nearby. Everyone has on their robes and is in a particularly jolly mood.

"You were always so quiet in camp, all prissy and proper." She places my hands around her waist and circles her hips, pressing against me like we are a couple in a slow, intimate dance.

"You've had way too much," I say.

She grinds slowly and deliberately against me. A sly, cunning smile flashes across her lips.

"You like that?"

"Mona, stop."

She realizes I'm serious and backs away. "Harry made breakfast."

I check out the spread—bacon, toast, eggs, fruit. "I'm good," I say, remembering my original reason for coming down. "You have tomato juice, Bloody Mary mix?"

"Harry, check in the fridge."

"I'm the fucking help now?" he asks, his robe is open around the chest area, and I can clearly see he has nice brown firm pecs. He really isn't a bad-looking guy. I sense he's a little outside Ursula's age dating range. When he opens the fridge and bends over, Ursula flaps the robe over his butt, revealing a brown hairy bottom. I look away, just out of habit.

"Negative on the juices," he says. "You might want to tell your staff to stock up for the guests."

"We rarely use this house," Mona says, picking up a strawberry.

"It's nice," I say, admiring its openness and the view of the Pacific. It isn't as spacious as Caleb and JB's friend, Jake's family's house, but that doesn't matter. It was prime real estate, and soon the wheels in my brain begin to turn.

"You could use a house sitter," I say.

"I'll talk to my people."

"How do you all know each other?" the comedian asks.

Mona sips from her flute. Her hair is pulled into a ponytail. "Ursula, Cassandra, and I grew up like sisters. Our moms are in the same clubs and volunteer with the same charities. Maddie grew up in Texas, but she has ties to our circles."

"Our circle is teeny, tiny. You could call it a bubble of sorts," Ursula adds.

"How's Cassandra?" Mona asks.

"Not well. She sent me down to get tomato juice."

"If it's for a hangover, she'll need an aspirin and a ginger ale." She glances at the comedian and smiles. "Can you look in the fridge and see if there's one?"

He scowls at her in a good-humored way. "I don't live here," he says but looks for the ginger ale anyway. This time his hand is in place to catch Ursula in case she tries to flip his robe up again. He has a can of ginger ale in his hand and sets it on the island bar.

"Anything else?" He's looking like, I dare you to say something.

Mona takes the can. "Thank you." She saunters up a spiral staircase leading to the second level, all the while smiling, winking, and blowing kisses at us.

The comedian walks up behind Ursula and kisses her ear. This time she's coy, waving him off, slightly embarrassed he's being this affectionate in front of company. He grabs a bottle of honey nearby.

"What are you doing with that?" she asks.

Without saying a word, he grabs her foot and squirts honey on top of it then licks it. She squirms in her seat and holds firmly to the island bar.

"I'll leave you two." I get up.

"No, stay. I like company," he says.

"I'm good." I hurry up the staircase to the bedroom where I left Cassandra. I didn't want to see anything I couldn't unsee. God knows I've seen enough already. Mona is sitting on the floor next to Cassandra who's working on the can of ginger ale.

"Feeling a little better?" I ask.

"Did you know the Lakers are playing at the Forum today?" she asks.

"You're here looking like death warmed over, and all you can think about is the Lakers?" Mona asks.

"I'll need something to wear."

"It's an early game," Mona says.

"Do you have anything I can wear?"

"What size?" Mona asks.

"Four."

"I have a pair of Versace hot pants you can wear."

"What time is it?" Cassandra asks.

"Why? You have someplace to be? You might want to hang out with me until you sober up. Besides, don't want your mom thinking I'm a bad influence."

"You are."

"Damn. I know, but still."

"Ursula's asleep?" Cassandra asks.

"She's occupied," I answer.

"I was shocked to see her walking this morning," Mona says

"Why?" I ask.

"Her friend Harry. You've gotta see the length and girth of that unit he's packing."

"Is it lethal?" Cassandra asks.

"When I saw it, I said, 'No way. Goodnight.' I left and went to bed."

"Wait a minute. You saw it?" Cassandra asks.

"Yeah. We were all having a little fun."

"But size matters to most girls."

"No. In this case, you run for the hills. It was three inches from the floor."

Cassandra laughs until she starts coughing.

"Ask Ursula."

"She was getting honey poured on top of her foot," I say.

"What? Mona asks.

"This is wild," I say.

Cassandra stands. "If you guys don't mind, I need to shower and gather my thoughts." She waves us off, shoving us out of the bathroom and closing the door.

"Well," Mona says, "this is a first."

I go to the window to check out the view. "I'm envious," I say to her.

"At sunset, the water's like liquid gold."

"I love sunsets."

"Ruger and I come here sometimes."

"I can see that."

"It's open to you as well, anytime you want. We can watch it together."

I glance at Mona. "I'd rather watch it alone."

"What? Maddie, I'm crushed." She chuckles.

"I don't know what you had in that drink."

She laughs. "I'm just teasing."

Ten minutes later, the door to the bathroom opens, and Cassandra emerges refreshed in a robe, drying the ends of her hair with a towel.

"Mona, I'm calling Leah. She can find us clothes."

"I have my own assistant, thank you." Mona rolls her eyes. "She knows what boutiques I like. She knows I'm a size three, you're a size three, Ursula's a size three. Maddie, I'm sorry, what size are you?"

"Eleven," I say. I notice how silent the other two are.

"You wear it with confidence, cousin," Cassandra says, trying to make me feel better.

"Designers rarely go larger than seven," Mona says.

"It doesn't have to be a designer," I say.

Mona and Cassandra's silence makes me self-conscious. "Stop looking at me like that."

"I'm brainstorming boutiques in Beverly Hills for your size, and I can't think of one," Cassandra says.

"Listen, just find a blouse to go with my skirt."

"Relax. It's handled," Mona says. "Got a phone call to make."

***

Hours later, we're in Mona's bedroom suite trying on clothing that her assistant dropped off. Shopping bags and clothing are scattered everywhere. Cassandra finds an ivory ruffled blouse to pair with an acid wash skirt. The size eleven jeans I attempted to try on don't make it over my thighs. I find an extra-large black top, but the fabric is sheer, and because I'm not wearing a bra, my breasts are on full display. Ursula picks up a red camisole.

"Try this under your top," she says to me. She's walking around totally nude.

"Taking a break from Harry?" Mona asks.

"He left—had to get ready for tonight," she says.

"I'm sure you gave him lots of material," Cassandra says.

"He gave her lots of material," Mona adds.

Ursula fans herself.

"How did you handle all that?" Mona asks.

"With care." She winks.

Once we find outfits and do our hair and makeup, it's time to leave. When the limo arrives in Inglewood, the traffic is bumper-to-bumper. Fans are in a frenzy, standing on top of cars, yelling, honking horns. People are running between cars, getting on the hoods yelling, "We're the champions, baby."

"Lakers won," I hear Cassandra yell. She opens the limo roof and stands up. Mona joins her. The limo slowly makes its way through the crowd of revelers who are in no rush to disperse.

Hours later, Cassandra and I arrive home to a dark and quiet house. Cassandra turns on the light and sees a letter written in Aunt Mary's handwriting. Cassandra reads it aloud: "Teal, Frenchy, and I are at James and Judy's house watching the game and playing spades. Hopefully you make it home before we do. Love, Mom a.k.a. Aunt Mary." Cassandra leaves on the lamp light downstairs before we run upstairs to our rooms. For some reason, I didn't want to talk about this past weekend with Aunt Mary or Uncle Frenchy. Not that I was going to mention it, but I want to forget what I saw and heard in the limo with Ursula, Mona, and the comedian.

Monday, the big win is all over the news. As much as I'm happy for L.A., I want to be equally happy for Dee. Aunt Mary recommended she be moved to UCLA to get the best care and treatment. I want to see her, but Aunt Mary has already left for the center. Caleb is in his room hungover from celebrating. Uncle Frenchy is gone. Aunt Teal is gone. For whatever reason, Cassandra isn't leaving her room. It just so happens that when I open the door to walk outside to get fresh air, JB is standing there with his finger in place to ring the doorbell.

"Hey," he says.

"Hi."

"My boy home?"

"He is." I open the door. JB stares at me with those electrifying eyes before he enters.

"Gotta check on him. Last night," he says, rubbing the back of his ear, "your cousin got buck wild."

"Pretty intense, huh?"

"To say the least." As he walks out of the room, butterflies slowly creep in. Why now? Why this summer? All the previous summers I haven't given JB any thought. Before I'd see him, and nothing happened—no butterflies, no lingering stares, no spine-tingling sensations. What's happening now? Is it the way he lifted me off my feet and tossed me over his shoulder like a feather? Is it the way our eyes connect, like we see straight to each other's souls? He reappears chuckling to himself.

"JB, can I get you to do me a huge favor?" I ask.

"Anything, as long it doesn't involve murder, kidnapping, robbing, or carjacking."

"I guess the search continues for a partner in crime," I play along.

"What would you like me to do?" He leans in.

"Take me to UCLA hospital. There's someone there I'd like to see."

"UCLA? You understand that's enemy territory for me, right?"

"Why?" I ask.

"They're our biggest rivals in basketball."

"I see."

"For you, I'll make an exception."

"I feel very honored."

"Cross your fingers, and hope we get out alive."

He sees the look of horror on my face. "Just kidding, just kidding."

I grab my backpack with my sheets of music and wallet and follow him to his car, where he opens the door for me. I get inside and watch him calmly walk to the driver's side and get in.

"Sorry I don't have classical music for you to listen to," he says, starting up the engine and inserting a tape in the player. Through the crisp, clear surround sound system, I hear a groovy bass line followed by women screaming and a guy with a hip voice sounding like he's ready to get a party started. JB opens the sunroof. "It's about to get funkier than a Trojan b-ball locker room in here." He turns up the volume and starts nodding with the rhythm. A thumping bass line with electric piano carries the groove. I'm speechless as well as entertained.

"What's the name of the artist?" I ask.

"George Duke," he answers.

"What's the name of the song?"

"'Reach for It.'"

"Okay." I say. Interesting title for a song.

"When you hear it, I want you to say 'dance,'" he says. "When my part comes, I'll say 'hey.'"

Listening to the music while riding down the street, checking out the scenery, I hear the part in the song where the female chorus calls out, "Dance" followed by a chorus of men shouting, "Hey."

The feel of the song is infectious, and soon, I'm nodding along with it, singing, "Dance."

JB responds with "Hey." He's shifting gears and grooving at the same time. "Mozart and Beethoven couldn't get this funky if they went the rest of their lives without a bath."

"Dance," I shout.

"Hey." He does this thing where he bites his bottom lip. His eyes are on the road, and his mood is super cool. He breaks out into a rhyme of sorts. It takes a second, and I realize he's singing along with the lyrics to the song. He glances at me and continues with the rhyme.

"Catchy," I say.

"Got to expand your listening ears and hear more than one musical language."

I don't know why, but at that moment, I think of Gregory—his whole French speaking vibe. I want to speak a different language. I think it's fascinating, but of course, that's not what JB's talking about.

"I'm open," I say, "but classical music will always be my first love."

"That first love is everything, I know."

We sit quietly until the next song comes on. It's a ballad with color-ful vocal harmonies. The singer's voice is a soft falsetto, very mellow, relaxing, haunting. JB shifts gears and merges on the expressway with the traffic. He turns up the volume.

"Listen to those keys. Man, I wish I could play like that."

I listen, and I'm drawn to the musician's digital abilities and the blend of the notes, a constant legato like blood flowing through the body.

"You hear that?" he asks.

"I do."

He smiles and nods. "I want to produce a song like that."

"What do you know about musical production?" I ask.

"I can't read music and I can't write it. All I know is when I hear the melody, it's like baking a good cake."

I turn my attention to the cars zooming by us. "But I thought you liked basketball."

"Remember me saying basketball was the tip of the iceberg?"

"Sort of."

"Well, it's like this: Basketball is my wife; music is my mistress."

"Interesting."

"I'm obligated to one, but for both to be beneficial to me, I must find a happy medium."

"If basketball and music were dangling off a cliff, and both were reaching out for you to save them, which one would you choose?"

We come to a slow crawl in traffic, and he shifts the car back to first gear. "As much as I love my wife, that mistress moves me in ways I can't explain."

He pushes a button, and the tape ejects, he finds another tape to insert into the player.

"I think you like music as much as I do," I say.

"I like all music, you only like classical."

"I'm willing to expand my musical ears."

"Are you really?" He glances at me with those dreamy looking eyes.

"Yes. I really like the Queen album you let me borrow, especially the

'Bohemian Rhapsody' song. In the classical world we call a song like that a suite."

"Sweet like sugar?" he asks.

"No, suite, as in a hotel suite."

He nods, shifting gears and focusing on the stop-and-go traffic on the 405.

"In a suite format, the song is broken into sections, but each section shares a common theme. In 'Bohemian Rhapsody,' it's about nihilism. That constant echo that nothing really matters."

"You're using some big words on me. What's that?"

"Nihilism?"

"Yeah."

"It's when you have no morals, and life has no value, and everything is meaningless—even God has no meaning to you."

"I'm going to listen to that song in a whole different way now," he says.

"I had nihilistic thoughts after my mother died," I say.

"I'm sorry about your mother," he says.

"I was only twelve. I was hurt. I was angry. I was mad at God. I was mad at my daddy. I was mad at the world. How do you go on with your life when the person responsible for giving you life dies?"

"I can't say I know how you feel because I haven't dealt with a loss like that," he says, while at the same time, maneuvering through the traffic.

"Some days I wished I were dead. I didn't kill myself because I didn't want to hurt my daddy and Aunt Mary, Uncle Frenchy, Cassandra, and Caleb. Their love gave me a reason to live."

"That's heavy, Maddie."

"I'm sorry. I don't want to depress you with my stories."

"You're not depressing me. Your cousins, they really love you, and they speak highly of you. When Caleb told me you were valedictorian of your class and going to Juilliard, I said this girl is really special."

I feel myself blushing. I look out my window at the scenery in the hopes that he doesn't notice.

Once at the hospital, we stop by the gift shop to pick up a stuffed animal and a coloring book with crayons. Walking down the corridor with JB, I notice people do a double take. With his height and build, they know he's a basketball player, but which one? We get on an elevator and someone says to him, "Better luck next season."

JB simply nods and waits for the person to exit their floor. After the door closes and it's just the two of us, he merely scoffs and shakes his head.

The door opens, and I search for Dee's room with JB strolling behind. I notice on her door is a picture of a unicorn. I knock and enter with JB behind me. When she sees me, she reaches out, forgetting the IV attached to her hand. Her face lights up, and her eyes are sparkling. "Maddie!"

"Dee." I sit gently on the edge of the bed and give her a hug, careful not to squeeze her. She notices JB. "Who's he?"

JB and I glance at each other. "A really good friend," I respond. "JB, this is my friend, Dee."

"Hi, Dee." He waves. I give her the stuffed animal. She takes it, holding it firmly. "Thank you. I like it." I see other stuffed animals lying in bed with her.

"Starting a collection, I see," JB says. "What are their names?"

"They don't have names yet."

'No? May I ask why?" he asks.

"I'm waiting until I get home," she says.

I show her the coloring book, and she reaches for it. "I like the Smurfs. Want to color with me?" she asks.

"I'd love to." I open the first page; she takes the book and flips through it until she sees a page she's satisfied with. She colors the page; I color the adjacent page. She glances at JB. "You want to color?"

"Sure. Why not?" He pulls up a chair and angles it so his long legs won't bump the bed. He reaches into the box and pulls out a color, and we share a page. As Dee shades in her lines lightly with the blue crayon, she steals glances at me and JB's collaborative efforts. I color my Smurf blue. I notice JB colors his Smurf red.

"Smurfs are supposed to be blue," she says to him.

"This one is in college," JB explains. "He goes to 'SC. If I color him blue, that'll B'ruin him."

"You mean ruin." I say.

"I meant B'ruin. UCLA's colors are blue like the Smurfs, and their mascot is a Bruin. Get it?" he asks.

I smile, and we find ourselves smirking at each other. "It took me a minute, but yes. I get it."

"Here, take this. Color him blue." She gives the crayon to JB.

"Awww, c'mon. You're really making me do this?"

Dee finds it amusing.

JB colors over the red. "Dee, we just met, and already we're starting off on the wrong foot." He winks.

"And stay in the lines," I tease.

He gives me a look that says, *don't try it.*

"Dee, how's your mom?"

"Fine."

"Have you seen Aunt Mary lately?"

She nods. "She was here yesterday."

"We love you," I say, feeling my heart about to explode.

"I miss my momma and my little brother and sister."

I nod. Only imagining being nine years-old and away from home, lying in a strange bed. A nurse enters. We exchange pleasantries. She places a thermometer in Dee's mouth.

JB and I stop coloring and sit quietly awaiting the results. The nurse removes the thermometer. "It's 100.1," she says. "You have a mild fever, Delight."

"What does it all mean?" I ask.

Before the nurse explains, she pauses. "Any relation to the patient?"

"I'm her sister." I hear myself tell a bold-face lie.

"I'm her brother," JB adds.

"She may have a reaction to the pain medication."

"I wasn't around initially to get information, but can you tell me what's going on?"

"The doctor has to give you that information. I'm sorry."

She looks at Dee. "Delight, I'll be back with new medication for you." We exchange more pleasantries before she leaves the room.

"Dee, JB and I are leaving but I'll be back to see you soon." I take her hand and hold it.

"I want to go home," she says in her sweet little voice.

I look away at JB.

"We're coming back. Want us to bring you something special?" JB asks. He says *us* and *we're*.

"I dunno," she says.

"Something tells me you like surprises," JB says, lightening the mood.

She nods. I move closer to embrace her delicately and kiss her forehead. JB holds out his large hand. "I think I just made a new friend. What do you think?" he asks her.

She slaps his palm. A bright smile emerges from her lips.

"I'll take that as a yes," he says.

We leave and stand on the elevator, watching the floors light up, not saying a word. Once inside the car, we sit in silence. He turns over the ignition, and there's no music playing, just silence. He puts the car in first gear, and it takes off into the congested medical center traffic. We're cruising down the street, and he shifts to second gear. The car picks up more speed, and he shifts into third. Still silent.

"I'm hungry. You hungry?" he asks.

"I am," I respond.

"What's up with Dee?" he asks.

"Bone cancer."

"Damn."

"I know. It's weird how it all happened."

"Explain."

"Sometimes I volunteer at the center for Aunt Mary. I was sitting at the piano about to teach Dee a song. I remember I was asking a question about a concert pianist, then suddenly she writhes in pain."

I feel JB staring at me as I face forward, revisiting the image of Dee holding her side and the fear, anguish, and pain in her round eyes.

"There's no telling how long she's been in pain. Her mother says she takes her to doctors, and they basically dismiss her. It's criminal."

"She lives near the center?"

"Yes. In the Jungle."

"You don't get the best of anything when you live in the J's."

"I met another girl at the center who also lives in the Jungle, and the three of us have become close in such a short time. I wish I could adopt them and show them a different side of life."

"What's your definition of different?" he asks.

"Access to a quality of life that sets you miles apart from the typical."

"Like yours and mine?"

I ponder it before I answer. "Yes."

We pull up to a popular diner with no wait, and we are seated immediately in a booth. JB's a regular, so already he knows what to order and drink.

"I'm keeping it simple: just a house salad with vinaigrette and fresh-squeezed lemonade," I tell the waitress before handing her the menu. After she leaves, JB and I sit staring at each other. There's definitely chemistry—or I could be reading too much into it. I get butterflies, remembering the last time I sat across from JB at a booth.

"All this time, I never noticed your eyes. What color are they?" he asks.

"Amber."

"Extremely rare."

"So I've been told."

"You like basketball?"

"No," I respond. "I'm sorry."

"I know you're a square."

"Tell me what JB stands for."

"Jelly Bean, Jingle Bell, Jock Boy. Depends on who you ask, Juicy Black."

"You are full of it," I say.

"Truthfully, they're just initials. Ask my dad, he'll say JB means James' boy. Ask my mom, she'll tell you it means Judy's baby."

"Ask what JB means to me."

He chuckles and leans in. "I can't wait to hear this."

"Just bad," I answer.

He laughs. "Not the first time I've heard that."

"Good. I'm not alone."

He doesn't respond. Instead, he sits back and allows his eyes to do the smiling.

"What?"

"Just beginning," he says.

Hearing that flow from his lips set my mind adrift in many directions. I'm too afraid to ask him to elaborate for reasons I'm not sure myself. The tone is light and pleasant like a Mozart Opus, and I want to keep it that way. If I did something spontaneous like take off my sandal and slide my foot up his leg as I did in Malibu, this time, there's no telling how the evening might end.

"Have you had a chance to check out the clubs?" he asks, once our meals arrive.

"No. I'm not a club person."

"You're not?"

"No. I went to a comedy club over the weekend for the first time. I left there smelling like cigarette smoke."

"You go to the one on Sunset?" he asks.

"I don't know. I don't even remember the name." I fork my salad.

"You don't go to clubs, and you only listen to classical music."

"I know, I'm dull."

He smiles. "You said it, not me."

"Cassandra teases me all the time. My friends tease me. I have no life outside of music."

As we talk, I notice a couple of girls sitting at a table not far from us glancing in our direction.

"Don't look now, but we're being watched," I say.

JB waves it off.

"You get that a lot?" I ask.

"People staring at me?"

"Yes."

"Of course. They do that here in L.A. They stare because they think you're somebody famous."

"Are you?" I ask.

"You're probably more famous than me; you're the concert pianist."

"They don't look like fans of classical music."

JB looks over his shoulder until he spots the girls. "How do you know? Didn't your minister father teach you not to judge a book by its cover?" he asks.

I laugh. "They look like sports fans."

"And how does a sports fan look?" he asks.

"Very casual, sporty, and relaxed."

"And the people who enjoy your concerts, they're not casual, sporty, relaxed?"

"At my next performance, remind me to give you a front row seat so you can see the type of people who attend."

"Let me guess: rich white people with snooty attitudes."

"Look who's judging now."

We laugh before we find ourselves staring into each other's eyes again in one of those awkward moments of silence. Only when the waitress brings the ticket do we snap out of our gazes. I reach for the ticket, but his hands are quicker and bigger.

"I got this." The way he says it, resonates. "As long as you're with me, always know I got you." That part resonates all-over-my-body.

Fourteen

JB turns on the light to the pool house. Smitty follows us inside, panting, his paws making a tapping sound on the tiled floor.

"Here's a song I've been working on."

We sit at his keyboard. I see he's scribbled notes on a sheet of diagram paper used to write basketball plays.

"Excuse the presentation. When the music comes, I find the nearest thing to write on."

I read what he's written. I also notice a well-used composition notebook. The cover has a diagonal crease fold across it.

"Play for me what you hear," I say to him.

"Here's the intro." His large hands tickle the keys, starting with a high note then following up with the same note in a lower register until he reaches the same key in the lowest register. As he's playing, I notice his eyes searching the room for that note, and when he finds it, he glances at the keys. The tempo is upbeat at parts and soft at other parts. He stops.

"That's all I remember for now."

I read the words, "Eyes on the Ball." I point to them. "Is this the title of the piece?"

"Yeah. I want to show you something." He gets up and walks to a collection of VHS tapes, pulls one out, and turns on the television and VCR. He inserts a VHS tape, and on the screen, I see a group of basketball players in a huddle. They scream, "Trojans," and JB enters the court. The image shows him walking in slow motion, and the stare in his eyes indicates he's ready to do battle. The next shot shows him effortlessly dribbling with the ball between his legs against a defender and him taking a shot and nailing the basket with the defender in his face. Another shot shows Caleb dribbling at full speed down the court with a defender on his heels as he passes the ball to JB who takes it and slams it into the goal. Teammates are jumping from the bench, and the crowd in the arena is on its feet. A slow-motion shot shows him diving after the ball into the crowd of spectators. The next shot shows him spinning two basketballs—one on each finger—and that smile of his. The final shot is a slow-motion tilt up of him walking toward the camera with the ball resting inside his forearm looking fierce and confident before it fades to black.

"You're writing a piece to go with that video?" I ask.

"Yeah."

"I got it." I start playing off the top of my head, with an intro similar to the way he wrote it but putting my own interpretation on it. When I'm done, I glance at him. "Is that what you were looking for?" I ask.

He stands, mouth open. His expression is a combination of euphoria mixed with jubilant relief.

"Eureka," he screams. "Black gold. Texas tea." He covers his mouth.

"I got a lot more where that came from."

"Oh, man. You don't know how long I've been working on this piece."

He joins me at the keyboard. I play it again. He stands, over-joyed, walking around the room. Smitty is nearby sitting, panting, and following his every move.

"You say I'm bad. You're bad." He points to me. "Bad, in a good way."

I take out my sheets and write down the notes I hear. I look at what he's written on the diagram paper. "Are these lyrics?"

"Yep."

"You're the singer," I say. "Let me hear what you have."

Got the ball

My mind is on a win

Watch my shot

Sinking through the rim

You can't defend me

You're moving too slow

Alley-oop I got us two more.

We spend the better part of the hour hammering the piece out on his keyboard.

"What time is it?" I ask.

"It's 11:05."

"I need to get home."

"O-kay. So, what do you think about our song?" he asks.

"Our song. I appreciate you giving me co-producer credit."

"It isn't classical, but—"

"Doesn't have to be. A good piece can transcend many genres."

Another awkward moment of silence occurs between us. "Guess I'd better get you home," he says.

"This was fun," I say.

We sit in the car in his driveway. We have fifteen minutes to spare, which is good because his house is about four minutes away from Aunt Mary's and Uncle Frenchy's house.

"Thank you. Now I have an original song to go with my highlight footage."

"You know someone with a recording studio?" I ask.

"I know several people," he says with a smile.

"Do you know a good sound engineer?"

He looks at me. "That's one of the things I like about you. You have no idea how big I am in this town. To you, I'm just JB. I love that."

"You're saying whatever you want, no matter how difficult it is, you can get it."

"That goes for studio time, quality engineers, top-tier musicians, a composer to help me with this music." He winks at me when he says that last part.

"I know a composer—one of the best to ever compose a song. She lives, breathes, sleeps, and dreams compositions. She has an engagement with one of the biggest philharmonic orchestras in the country, which means her time these days is limited because she's practicing and interpreting."

"Would she be willing to help out a friend?" he asks before starting up the car.

"She has a manager too," I answer.

He chuckles. "I see she's all business. I like that."

He drops me off in front of the house. I check my watch. I manage to get in without a minute to spare.

***

The crowd assembled at the center is dense. The parking lot is transformed into a marketplace with colorful vendor tents. One vendor has a display of African-themed books for sale. Another vendor sells African garments and handmade jewelry. There are healthcare workers with information on HIV/AIDS. Parents with younger children stand patiently waiting in line for two artists to apply face paint to the cheeks of young attendees. Another vendor sells original art depicting the Black American experience. There is an oil painting of four little black ballerina girls, all in pirouette. Another oil painting shows enslaved men on an auction block in chains. Music is in the air, and there are dancers. Cassandra and I watch.

"What dance is that?" I ask her.

"They're popping and locking." She dances along with them and beckons me to join. I stand in one spot and imitate their hand movements. I have no rhythm. I notice a couple of children from the center dancing. I stop and watch them until the song is over. Cassandra and I walk inside the center where there are more people, and there is a speaker with immense oratory skills behind a lectern. With so many inside, it's difficult to identify just any one person. I follow Cassandra outside to the enclosed playground area and basketball court where there are more attendees. I spot JB, Caleb, and their friend, Jake. There's also a guy with a handheld camera just off to the side capturing JB spinning the ball on his finger and walking into the crowd. JB sees Damon and tries to give him the spinning ball. I hear Uncle Frenchy's laughter over the music, and I turn to see him engaging in a lively conversation with an attendee. This celebration isn't just limited to Black people. I see quite a few white, Asian, and Hispanic attendees as well.

Aunt Mary and Leah emerge from the crowd. Aunt Mary's hair is brushed into a simple ponytail that bounces when she walks.

"Our keynote speaker is running a little behind. You may need to improvise until he shows up," she says to Cassandra.

"Improvise how? Tell Juneteenth jokes?" Cassandra responds.

Aunt Mary does a double take. "Are you out of your mind?"

"I wasn't sure."

"I know you have something informing and entertaining cooking in that brilliant mind of yours." Aunt Mary gives her a quick peck on the cheek and moves on to the next order of business. Cassandra looks at me and just shakes her head. We go back inside where there's a poet at the lectern reciting what sounds like an original poem.

"I am my ancestors' dream," he repeats in a rich tenor voice. The message reverberates and touches a handful of attendees in the audience. Their shouts and praises are electrifying. A small choir follows. They are accompanied by their own musician on piano. Cassandra and I find seats in the audience and listen while they sing first in a cappella before they launch into the song, "Steal Away (Steal Away to Jesus)."

Their beautiful harmonies blend like fabrics woven into a loom. The musician plays softly, directing their voices from the piano. People moved by the performance stand as the energy of the atmosphere elevates to a spiritual level.

Cassandra looks at an itinerary with the scheduled events listed. She's up next after the choir to introduce the speaker. She flips back her hair and walks to the front of the room. She places her notes on the lectern then grabs a handheld microphone and moves closer to the crowd. Gorgeous, tall, and slender, she glances at all the faces in the room before she proceeds.

"I'm really loving the energy in this place. How about you?" She gives the people a moment to respond.

"Before I introduce this next speaker, I want to introduce myself.

I'm Cassandra Honoré. I'm Frances Honoré's daughter. You may know him affectionately as Frenchy. Frenchy, are you in the room?"

I hear him respond followed by laughter from the people around him.

"I have the microphone, Frenchy," she says and allows the laughter in the room to calm. "I'm also the daughter of Dr. Mary May Honoré. If you see her around, please let her know she's doing a wonderful job." The room applauds. "She and my father put their minds together. This is what you have when those minds meet, a celebration to remember the day the message finally arrived to the remaining enslaved that they were finally free." She pauses. "Can you imagine that feeling?" She scans the room in the same fashion Aunt Mary does when she's speaking. "There's a saying we came to the Americas on different ships, but we're here in the same boat. You see me, a product of English, Venezuelan, French, Trinidadian, and Martinican and you ask what does she know about Juneteenth? Thanks to Frenchy and Mary Honoré, a lot more than you think. My mother's mother—my grandmother—her father was English, and her mother was Trinidadian and Venezuelan. They eventually settled in what is now New York City. My grandfather's family has its roots in Pennsylvania, where the family thrived in the textile and insurance business. My father's family was from Martinique and settled in New Orleans. They were all successful, yet, in spite of and at every turn, they were still reminded-they were Black." She pauses to let the words sink in. "Just because the law said you were free didn't mean it was so. So, we're here in the same boat, celebrating, singing, talking, remembering."

I sit, impressed with my cousin. She's only sixteen but has an old soul. We both remember our maternal grandmother, Magdalene May, sharing this bit of history with us. She was proud of her ancestral heritage, showed us pictures of them living stylish and grand. I also remember her saying, "As much as I'm free, I do get a reminder that I'm Black, which subjects me to the same treatment as those whose ancestors were enslaved." She would say it and clutch her pearls at the same time. "America is a motherfucker."

The keynote speaker finally arrives; Cassandra introduces him. He gives a story of why he was late, but with his rich baritone voice reso-nating in the room, he keeps us on the edge of our seats. At one point, he breaks into song, and naturally, I go to the piano, watching him and following along playing softly. His message is We've Come So Far.

"My grandparents were sharecroppers," he begins. "They were two generations removed from slavery. They instilled core values in their children. They told them they were worthy. They esteemed them and encouraged them to reach beyond their circumstances. They often quoted Romans chapter 8 verse 31, 'If God is for us, who can be against us?' They carried that Word with them wherever they went." The crowd in the center shouts praises.

"They passed those values on to me and my siblings. I carried the Word in my heart, handed down to me from sharecroppers." He stands before the crowd.

"I wish they could see me now. I remember as a kid leaving town and going deep into the country to work the fields. The white owner said to me, 'Boy, you's a hard worker. When you get back to town, you make sure you go work for some good white people.'" He laughs. "We've come a long way because right now in 1987, I have some good white people working for me." The crowd applauds, and I notice a couple of people get emotional. The atmosphere is electrifying.

The celebration doesn't end at the center. A more intimate crowd arrives at the house with Aunt Teal pulling out all the exotic foods from Louisiana. Frenchy invites a couple of his pilot coworkers and their wives. The keynote speaker shows up with his wife. JB's parents arrive. JB, Jake, and their friend from school show up with his camera. I'm sitting at the piano playing Gershwin's "Rhapsody in Blue." The friend with the camera, whose name is Paul, is over my shoulder.

I continue playing, absorbing the melodies. "Wow," he says and puts his camera aside and just watches me play.

"Don't stop. Keep it going," he says. "You know 'Flashlight' by Parliament?"

At that moment JB, Caleb, and Jake enter. JB sits next to me. "Listen, whatever he's telling you, don't believe it."

"O-kay." I sit, taking it all in.

"Hollywood, I see you with that camera, checking out my cousin," Caleb says to Paul.

Compared to the other three, Paul just doesn't seem to fit. They're tall, athletically built, and could easily get jobs modeling if they didn't play basketball. Paul, on the other hand, is a foot shorter. His dimpled chin is his only redeeming quality. Aside from that, he looks like a weasel.

"Your cousin is good," he says to Caleb.

"Remember the highlight footage you shot of me?" JB asks him.

"Yeah," Paul answers.

"She and I collaborated and produced a song to go with it."

"Get outta here—" is his response.

JB puts his arm around my shoulder. "You're looking at the eighties version of Ashford and Simpson—solid as a rock."

They got a big laugh out of that.

"Wait until you hear it," JB says.

"When did this occur?" Caleb's tone sounds like an interrogator.

JB and I look at each other and shrug. "Earlier this week."

Caleb has a suspicious look, almost like JB and I are doing more than a music collaboration.

"Let me say this: We are not playing games here. JB is serious about his music," I say.

"Define serious?" Caleb's arms are folded.

"Like I have a million songs in my head, and I need Maddie to help make it all make sense," JB says.

Caleb is still standing with his arms folded—my protector. He doesn't say another word.

Jake chimes in pointing to himself. "In case you need a cool, savvy Jew to manage things."

This breaks the tension in the room. Paul, chuckling, picks up his camera. "I'm out." He holds up two fingers. Jake follows him, leaving me, Caleb, and JB in the room.

"Are we cool?" JB holds up a fist.

Caleb takes a moment before he bumps it.

"Always," he says. He glances at me before walking out of the room.

JB exhales. "Your cousin is tripping," he says.

"Just being Caleb."

"Let me know next time you go see Dee."

"I was thinking about tomorrow."

"Tomorrow's cool," he says.

"Your friend—Paul wanted me to play a song about a flashlight?"

He chuckles.

"What's funny?"

"You."

"Why?"

"I never met anyone like you," he says.

"I know I'm different," I say. "I embrace that."

"I like different," he says.

Fifteen

Remembering Dee's mother telling me about Dee pretending to play the piano on the table really set the wheels in motion for me. When JB picks me up, I know exactly where I want to go.

"Take me to the music store," I say.

"What are you looking for?"

"A portable keyboard player for Dee."

We stop at a shop en route to UCLA medical center to check out their selection. I want a keyboard player small enough to carry around —one she can plug in or use batteries. JB and I search until I find a cute portable Casio.

"This is it," I say.

"For sure?"

"Without a doubt, I want this one."

I make the purchase and they wrap it for me at the music store. When we finally arrive at her room, I see her mother is there holding her hand.

"Maddie." Dee sits straight up in her bed.

"Hi, Maddie." Felicia stands to greet me with a hug. JB is the one holding the gift, a collage of colors with a giant red bow to accent.

"Hi," Dee says to him.

"You remember me?" JB asks.

She nods playfully, and my heart melts as she smiles, even with tubes connected to her body.

"What's that?" She points.

"I don't know. What is it, Maddie?" JB winks at me.

I retrieve the gift from him and set it on the bed in front of her.

"Wow. Can I open it?" she asks her mother.

Felicia nods. She seems just as excited about it as Dee who opens it and sees the keyboard player in the box. Her mouth forms the cutest little O, and her round eyes are wide.

"Say something." JB mimics her expression.

She looks at her mother.

"What do you say, Dee?" she says.

"Thank you, Maddie."

"May I help you open it?" I ask.

"Yes."

Together, we open it, and she searches for the power button. Once she finds it, she bangs a cacophony of notes.

"Thank you, Maddie," Felicia says, giving me a hug and pulling me aside.

"I'm sure by now you heard the news," she whispers.

I did, but I wanted to hear it directly from her. She never gives me the chance to respond before she jumps right in.

"The last time I saw you, Dee had gotten X-rays, and when they returned, the radiologist saw lesions on her side and around her knee. Thank God, your aunt Mary knew somebody here at UCLA, and we rushed her over here to get a second opinion. That's when they did a biopsy and told us she has bone cancer."

"I'm so sorry" is all I can say.

"She begins chemotherapy this week." Felicia's eyes brim with tears.

Fighting back tears, I glance and see JB sitting next to the bed showing Dee what keys to press on the keyboard player.

"I'll check on her and keep her in good spirits," I say.

"I appreciate that."

I grab a handful of tissues to give to her. She dabs her eyes. "I don't want her to see me like this." She straightens her face and joins JB and Dee at the bed.

"I recognize you," she says to JB. "You play for USC?" she asks.

JB takes a moment before he answers. "We look a lot alike," he jokes.

"Maddie, can you play me a song?" Dee asks.

I play "Fur Elise" for her. It's one of my mother's favorite compositions from Beethoven. Given the keyboard player's portable size, it serves its purpose. When I finish, I survey her reaction.

"I like it," she says. "I'm going to play like that someday," she says to her mother.

Felicia blinks back tears. "Yes, you will," she says.

***

Our spirits need uplifting. We agree music is the cure for all the blues. JB pulls up to what looks like a nightclub. Patrons gather when we walk up to the entrance. I hear someone yell JB's name over my shoulder. JB and I walk inside with an attitude like we own the place and dare someone asks us for ID. He takes my hand and leads me through the crowded room to an elevated spot near a stage. Sitting alone in a booth, wearing a top hat and round sunglasses with long curly locks is the actress I recognize from a popular TV show. The sunglasses are pulled just below her eyes. She peers at us over the lenses.

"Brother JB." She stands, and they embrace.

"Hey, sis. This is Maddie," he says once they pull apart.

She puts her hands together like a prayer and bow, then she places a hand over heart and holds it there. I've never had anyone greet me like that before.

"I'm Lilly. Delighted," she says with a smile emanating from naturally pink pillowy lips. JB and I sit together in the booth. She sits across from us.

"He's on in five minutes," she says to JB.

JB taps his hands rhythmically on the table, bites his bottom lip, and nods to an imaginary beat. He looks at me checking him out. He winks, something I notice he does often, which sometimes leaves me feeling like I just ate a plate of butterflies.

"Maddie, I love your pendant." Lilly zeroes in on the treble clef.

"Thank you."

"She's masterful with a piano," JB says. Hearing him say that about me makes me blush. I'm hoping they don't notice in the dim lighting.

"That is so awesome," she says in a sweet, mellow voice. She holds up a tambourine and shakes the zills. "It's no piano, but it's guaranteed to get a crowd moving and grooving."

The lights in the room fade to black as the crowd cheers. Lilly is on her feet, shaking her tambourine. JB puts his fingers to his mouth, letting out a loud whistle. On the stage is a silhouette of a drummer, a keyboard player, and two guitarists. A spotlight shines on the musician standing center stage. His guitar lets out a riff that moves the crowd. He walks to the mic and belts out a tune, mesmerizing the room. His voice is a combination of rocker with a soulful edge. He sings of having found a soulmate—the girl he's always wanted—and how they sing, laugh and dance naked in the rain. Lilly is really into the music, hugging herself and swaying. If I didn't know any better, I believe the song is about her. He caresses the mic like he's holding her face, then steps back and sends a roaring riff from his guitar. His eyes are closed as in the way most musicians do when they allow the music to take over. I knew that feeling all too well. JB's eyes are closed as his head is bobbing. He must feel me staring at him. When he opens them, he looks at me. He traces my jawline with the tip of his finger and stops at my lips. I close my eyes and kiss the tip of his finger. My heart pounds in sync with the drummer's rhythm. I open them to feel JB's gaze, his eyes are dreamy like he's reading my thoughts. I hold back, and with a slight nod, he turns his attention to the band.

"Who's he?" I ask JB.

"Benny Manheim, and that's his band, the Tornadoes."

Lilly beats her tambourine in tandem, forgetting about us and enjoying the pleasure of the experience. After their set, Benny, the lead singer, joins us at the booth. Lilly greets him with a big hug and a shower of kisses. When they finish, he and JB slap palms and lean in to greet each other.

"Always a pleasure, brother."

He notices me. JB introduces us. I see an earring piercing on his nose and a piercing on the corner of his right eyebrow. The four of us sit in the booth.

"What do you think?" he asks Lilly.

"I dig it, baby. Of course you could stand up there and sing about a pet rock, and I'll still dig it."

He touches his forehead with the tip of his finger. "You just gave me a brilliant idea."

"What time is your next set?" she asks.

"Finito," he says to her. "I'm all yours."

We sit engaging in conversation when the stage lights come on, and a guy wearing a white trench coat sings into the microphone, sending the crowd into a frenzy. A band of musicians join him on stage.

"Wow. Look who just popped in," Benny shouts.

"Are you ready to jam?" he asks.

The crowd's response is deafening.

JB looks at me. "Unbelievable."

"I say L.A., are you ready to jam?" He leans with an ear toward the crowd. "One. Two. A-one. Two. Three. Four."

The band starts playing, and the crowd is on its feet. Lilly shakes her tambourine. The noise in the place is so loud, my ears are ringing.

JB is up dancing. Benny's head is bobbing. I notice other people in the room losing control in the excitement of the moment. This guy in the white trench coat on stage knows how to move an audience, not to say that Benny didn't. Benny and the Tornadoes are good. This guy here is stratospheric. The energy in the room is brimming with intense excitement. I don't usually dance, however; I get up and join JB, dancing and following his lead.

"You want some more, L.A.?"

He's met with a deafening response.

"I can't hear you? You want some more, L.A.?"

I can't hear myself think. JB twirls me before he dips me—

maintaining full control, and brings me back up. He turns me around and holds me close to him—our fingers are intertwined—then I turn to face him, gazing into his eyes. I feel his fingers running through my hair. The guy in the white trench coat set the place on fire. When his set is over, we're all exhausted.

Afterward, the four of us stop at a diner and order like we haven't eaten in days.

"The energy you get from a crowd is intoxicating," Benny explains.

"I get it," I respond.

"It's the ultimate high, knowing your music and the time you put in elevates and moves the mind," JB adds.

"You get people together and everybody's vibin' on an equal plane. It's beautiful." Lilly smiles.

"Good music is nurturing for the soul," Benny continues. "I grew up listening to Miles, Led Zeppelin, Prince. They all had an influence from the way I play to the way I express myself."

"Who would you consider your greatest inspiration?" JB asks.

Benny, drumming his fingers on the table, tilts his head sideways to think. "That's a loaded one, man. There's so many: I remember as a kid, going to a Jackson 5 concert. It blew me away."

JB sings a Jackson 5 song. I forgot how nice his voice is.

"Yeah." Benny nods and smiles. "Tito on guitar, Jermaine on bass. Both self-taught, I believe."

"After my dad retired from the NBA, we moved to Alabama, where he's from originally, and he got a job coaching basketball at his alma mater," JB began. "My grandma made me go to church, and that's where I heard real good music. Her church had a pianist, a drummer, and a guitarist, and all were self-taught."

"The hand of God," Benny adds.

"The choir wasn't big, but the voices blended in harmony with the music."

Lilly holds up her hand. "I'm seeing a church hidden in the woods." That mellow attitude of hers is calming and soothing.

"It was. Picture a wooden church on cinder blocks, and hear the sound of feet patting to a rhythm."

"Sounds like a Baptist church," Benny says.

"You know it. After the preacher finishes his sermon, he'd follow up with a song, and before you know, the energy elevates to a spiritual level, man, and you feel that holy spirit and start dancing. It tripped me out the first time I saw it."

"Good music gets all in your bones, makes your spine tingle." Benny glances at Lilly.

"Like your music does for me," she says. I find the two of them fascinating.

We leave the diner, and JB and I follow Lilly and Benny to another nightclub. A performer, wearing dark sunglasses plays a grand piano. Next to him sits a small table with an ashtray, a lit cigarette, and a glass with brown liquid in it. He sings about a married woman who walks into a bar and meets a guy. Meanwhile her husband shows up at the same bar and confronts her. The performer sings as if he's the husband, asking his wife, why is she leaving. The audience must have heard this song before because on cue they all scream, "You bitch. You slut. You whore."

It was jarring and totally unexpected. JB laughs at my reaction. The place is animated with happy, loud, drunk people. The performer is humorous and animated with his facial expressions as he tells stories. Benny and Lilly are enjoying it. Lilly has her tambourine tapping along. When he comes to the end of his performance, he takes a puff from his cigarette and listens as the crowd cheers.

He plays another song that gets the crowd on its feet and everyone singing and swaying along. I'm having so much fun that I look at my watch and notice it's ten-thirty.

"JB, we have to go," I whisper to him.

He looks at his watch. "Oh, shit."

We say our goodbyes to Lilly and Benny. Lilly gives me a hug. "Peace and love, my sister," she says.

"Peace and love to you too," I respond before I turn to hug Benny.

"Good-night, sister," he says to me before he and JB slap palms and lean in for a hug.

"We'll link up again," I hear JB tell him.

JB gives Lilly a hug and a kiss on the forehead. Now the challenge lies in getting home before eleven-thirty.

***

When JB pulls up to the driveway, I notice it's close to midnight. "I tried to get you home sooner. Aunt Mary won't be too happy."

"I hope she's asleep."

JB is silent for a beat. "Let's hang out tomorrow. Bring your swimsuit and your sheet music and a change of clothes in case we go dancing. We might hook up with Benny and Lilly again. Who knows?"

"I had fun with Benny and Lilly. They're cool people."

"They are."

I remember the conversation at the Lakers game between Mona and Cassandra about JB and the girl from the show. It was Lilly they were talking about, and the gorgeous hunk with the dreadlocks was Benny.

"So, were you and Lilly more than friends at one time?"

"Why?" he asks.

"I just picked up on a vibe."

"We made out a few times."

I didn't expect to hear that. "She seems so nice. Why didn't it work?"

"I didn't want to be in a high-profile relationship."

I take in all the information I've gathered. "I'll see you tomorrow."

"Good night, Maddie," he says.

"Good night."

I open the car door and close it before getting my key to open the front door. I hear him drive off just as it opens. The house is dark and silent. I have a musical piece on my mind about this past weekend, and I sit at my desk, turn on the lamp, and start writing the notes I hear. Violins for the drama because, let's face it, violins are dramatic. Aside from the violins, the piece I hear is the piano, the dominant instrument. I hear it swelling with the violin in ocean waves and crashing against the rocks. Two hours later, I name it, "What Lies Ahead." I set it inside a notebook binder with the rest of my compositions and prepare for bed, forcing my mind to go to sleep.

***

I show up around two in the afternoon, ringing the doorbell. I notice there are no vehicles in the driveway, so just as I turn to walk back home, I see him and Smitty. JB is shirtless, wearing only basketball shorts and high-top sneakers. The walk has his muscles glistening; sweat drips down his body.

"Was hoping you'd get here earlier so you could join me."

"I was practicing on this piece." I kneel to rub and pet Smitty.

"Original piece, or dead, crazy white man piece?"

"The latter."

Inside, the chillness of the air is welcomed. He notices my duffel. "You moving? Aunt Mary kicked you out?"

"You are too funny."

He opens the sliding door to let Smitty roam. Smitty immediately goes to the water bowl. I hear him lapping.

"Where can I change?" I ask.

I follow him to the pool house. He opens the door to a bathroom suite.

"Thank you," I say, closing the door with him standing there. I lock it. I stare at my reflection in the mirror and take a deep breath. Slowly, I undress and change into a two-piece bikini. I gather my hair back into a ponytail and search my duffel for a cover-up. I hear music playing in the room and recognize it as the artist we saw last night at the impromptu concert. I apply lip gloss and glance sideways at myself in the mirror. Opening the door and entering the main room of the pool house, I see JB sitting at the keyboard.

"What are you working on?" I ask.

He uses a remote control to turn down the volume on the stereo system. "This came to me last night after I dropped you off."

He plays the melody. I listen, and I notice his pattern. He likes to play a lot of his songs in the key of-G. G major scales are brighter and lighter in sound.

"Can you play it in C?" I say, pointing to the key.

He tries to play but fumbles.

"I'm sorry."

"I like my version. Can we stick with it?"

"Keep it—your song. What's the name of it?"

"'How She Moves Me,'" he answers.

"Interesting," I say, listening to him hammer it out.

It's in her walk

Her walk says everything

Her style, her flow

The confidence she brings.

He writes in his worn-out composition book. I join Smitty on the floor and rub his coat. I gather my notebook to look at my own compositions. This captures JB's attention.

"How many songs you got there?"

"Close to two hundred."

"How long have you been writing?"

"Since I was twelve. It's my therapy—keeps me sane."

"I've always had a passion for music, but Pops was on my ass with basketball. He said I had too much height to be sitting at a piano. Then I saw you play."

I continue to rub Smitty's coat. It's just as relaxing and therapeutic for him as it is for me.

"And my passion for music came back, thanks to you. You're my muse."

I wasn't expecting that, but it's the ultimate compliment when someone calls you their muse. Clara Wieck was Schumann's muse. The universal language of music was their personal language of love. He turns up the stereo volume and bobs his head to a series of drum kicks.

"That's my jam." He gets up. "Let's go for a swim." He opens the door, walks outside, and jumps into the pool. I stand in the doorway watching him swim to the surface before he goes underneath again. I take off my cover-up and step in. The water reaches up to my neck. I see him swim toward me just beneath the surface. He pops up and follows my lead, letting the water reach his neck.

"Where's your man?" he asks.

I remember Gregory and the promise I made to him before he left.

It's been a couple of weeks, and I still haven't heard from him. Maybe he's forgotten about me.

"He's around," I hear myself say.

"Really? He's around here?"

"No," I respond and leave it at that.

The music takes his focus off me for a second. "Damn. I want a LinnDrum like that. You hear those drum kicks? That's sexier than a mofo." He bobs to the rhythm then submerges himself underneath. I see bubbles rising to the surface. I swim toward him, and underneath the surface, I see him dancing. I swim to him, and he reaches out to me. We play this game of cat and mouse before I swim back to the surface. He pops up. I notice his eyes traveling the course of my bikini. In that moment, he grabs me, and we kiss, wild and passionately. I feel his lips kissing my neck and my chest with fierce urgency. I close my eyes. My legs turn to jelly. I'm weak from the sensation of his touch and held captive in a spell. I wrap my legs around him and cling to him as we ascend the steps of the pool, still kissing each other. He opens the door to the pool house where the music is still playing. Still kissing me, he closes and locks the door.

Sixteen

The phone rings, startling us both. JB gets up and quickly answers. I'm checking out the shape of his butt and the tone and definition of his body. With the phone still in hand, he turns, and we make eye contact.

"I haven't made a decision," he says in an official tone. "Sports World gets the exclusive if I decide to go pro." He turns and while still holding the phone, he walks into the main room of the pool house. I feel a throbbing sensation between my thighs. When I look at myself and wipe, I notice blood on the towel. I stand, but the soreness makes it difficult for me to walk. When I get to the bathroom, I close the door, turn on the shower, and allow the hot water to cleanse me. Out of nowhere, emotions overtake me, and I start crying. Sliding down the wall, I hold myself. I look up and see JB's silhouette behind the shower door glass. He opens it and sees me sobbing on the floor. He steps in, closing the door behind him. He reaches down to give me a hand. He adjusts the water flowing from the showerhead.

"Talk to me," he says.

"This feels so weird."

"I've been fighting the urge until I just couldn't anymore."

"I've got to go. If we get found out, it won't be good."

He sighs. "You're not leaving me," he says. "Call and tell them you're spending the night with a friend."

And so it begins. I tell Cassandra I'm hanging out with Ursula, and she feels slighted because she wasn't invited. I'm thinking how many more times will I be able to use this lie. When I think Aunt Mary is home, I call and tell her the same thing to which she says, "Be very careful and stay out of trouble."

He cleans up the pool house, gathering up the bath towels, wincing at the sight of blood on them.

"You're still bleeding?"

"No."

I follow him into the main house as he carries the towels into the laundry room.

"Where are your parents?" I ask.

I'm staring at old pictures. JB must've been five or six, standing with his mother in front of a huge water fountain. It was the early seventies when plaid pants and platform shoes were in fashion.

"My guess is Arizona. They're in an RV driving cross country."

"Cool. How long will that take?" I ask.

"They stretch it over the month," he says.

JB gives me his USC sweatshirt to wear over my laced underwear. I sit at the kitchen bar and watch him mince, measure, and season. He grabs a bottle of beer for himself. I don't drink, so I settle for a glass of cola.

"Cheers to us." We clink glass and bottle. I sip.

On the stereo, soft music plays—dramatic violins, a woman and man duet proclaiming of first love.

"I don't know if you remember, but the first night when you arrived, I didn't want to go home. I slept on Caleb's floor while he stayed awake playing the Legend of Zelda just so I could be near you."

"Really?"

JB puts down his bottle and holds out his hand for me. I take it, and we slow dance to the music. My head is pressed against his body. I hear his heart beating. I close my eyes while my mind replays images of what happened between us hours earlier. He turns me around and wraps me in his arms.

"It's moments like this, you wish the night would never end," he says. I turn, and we spend the moment kissing.

"That night I dreamed about you," he says.

"You did? Was it good?" I ask.

"It was. I think I'll write a song about it. Will you help me?"

The tender way he says it, and the dreamy way he's staring into my eyes, I can't refuse. I know before I said my gift is not free; my time and talent are not free. For JB, I'll make an exception. As much as I inspire him, he inspires me too. When I feel his lips on mine, I hear a section of violins rising like the waves we swam in Malibu. I love his energy. I want to be around it every chance I get.

"I'm hungry. You hungry?" he says.

"Yes. I can't wait to try your food."

For dinner, he cooks pan-seared salmon with Filipino fried rice. As he's cooking, he scoops a spoonful of the Filipino fried rice for me to sample. I blow to cool it before taking a small bite. It's flavorful with a little spice.

"It's good. Your mom said she taught you how to cook."

"She did," he says, eating what's left on the spoon.

"She said she'd give me lessons," I say.

"You can't cook?"

"No."

"How about I give you cooking lessons and you give me music lessons."

"But I want your mother to show me."

"Me showing you will be just like my mother doing it."

I watch him grab two plates along with silverware and dish up each one.

"This looks and smells so good," I say.

"Let's give thanks," he says. I close my eyes and take his hand. I think I'm about to hear a prayer and all I hear is, "Thanks." I open my eyes.

"Is that it?" I ask.

"That's all God wants. He doesn't need a long, drawn-out prayer, which is how my grandma Imogene from Alabama prays."

"What does she say?"

"She thanks God. She thanks the butcher. She thanks the man who drove the food delivery truck. The fishermen—"

"Stop." I'm chewing and laughing at the same time.

"By the time she's finished, we're all done eating."

We laugh, and then there's that awkward moment of silence that really doesn't seem so awkward anymore.

"Is there a song that makes you cry when you hear it?" I ask him.

He chews quietly as he's thinking about it. "No. I mean. When I hear it, I don't cry, I just get a lump in my throat."

"What song is that?"

"Promise you won't tell anyone?"

"Why? Is it cheesy?"

"Kinda, sorta. I mean, you've probably never heard it. I have the record in my room."

"Can I hear it?" I ask.

"Right now?"

"Just whenever."

After dinner, we go to his room. I can tell he tried to tidy it up, but there's still clothing everywhere. I see a lot of shoe boxes with brand-new sneakers still inside. On the wall is a picture of his fraternity's Greek letters and a photograph of him, Caleb, their friend Paul, along with other guys from their fraternity dressed up in tuxedos. There are framed images of him on the cover of various sports magazines. There are basketball trophies and accolades everywhere. He has incense burning to mask the stale odor. I sit on the edge of his bed, and I feel like I'm in a pool.

"Cool. You have a waterbed," I say before lying down and stretching out.

"I see you're liking it," he says with a grin. "It likes you too."

Lying there, I watch as he finds a record to place on the turntable. I hear a soft synthesizer playing a haunting melody and a man's voice singing the first verse. The waterbed makes a swooshing sound when JB lies next to me. He doesn't say a word. Instead, he listens. No bobbing this time.

"What's the name of the song?" I ask.

"'I Want to Know What Love Is,'" he answers. As he's saying the title, I hear the lead singer along with a mass choir. It has a gospel, celestial sound and feel to it.

The volume in the room is at a level where everything is loud and clear. Lying there I think about JB and me and I think about my mother. My emotions run high as I lose myself in the song. There's a moment when the voices overtake the lead singer, and I hear ad-libs declaring, "There's nothing greater than love." I feel those words, and soon tears flood my eyes and roll down my cheeks. JB kisses every one of them. The tears don't stop. Neither do the kisses. There's truth to what Aunt Mary said about liquor stores and legs open after midnight. JB falls asleep inside me.

***

Cassandra enters my bedroom like a lioness waiting for an opportunity to pounce. "Lucy, you got some 'splainin' to do," she jokes using the popular catchphrase from the I Love Lucy show.

"What are you talking about?" I ask.

"You weren't with Ursula last night," she says.

"How do you know?"

"Because I talked to her."

"Why would you do that?"

"Because I wanted to know where you were and who you were with."

"You can't know everything."

She studies me for a moment. "Who is he?" she asks.

"My lips are sealed."

"Is Gregory back from Europe?"

I don't respond.

"Maddie, did you..." She studies my expression. "Omigod, Maddie, you didn't."

My silence is enough for her to read between the lines.

She covers her mouth, "Omigod, Maddie. Why don't you want to tell me? That's special, and I'm your favorite cousin. Tell me who it was, and I promise I won't tell a soul."

"No."

"Was it someone in our crew? Someone like Mona. You know she's into girls, too."

I frown. "Absolutely not. No way."

"I'm going to keep bothering you until you tell me."

I'm not saying a word. I can see her mind racing, then she covers her mouth. "Maddie, did you sleep with Kyle?"

My mouth is open, and words can't get out quick enough. "Are you out of your freaking mind? He's your boyfriend. How dare you ask me that? You know how ridiculous you sound?"

"Okay, okay." She recoils and stares at me like I'm the crazy one.

"If I told you who it was, you wouldn't understand."

"Is it a guy or a girl?"

"Cassandra, you're about to give me a freaking headache. Of course it's a guy,"

"If you won't tell me who it was, please tell me it was good, Maddie."

I close my eyes and think about last night. "I'm not saying a word."

"You don't have to," she says before rising to leave.

I sense she's upset because she's glaring at me as she walks out of my room.

Hours later, after studying my Schumann piece, I walk downstairs to see Aunt Mary and Uncle Frenchy sitting at the bar. She has a glass of wine; he's drinking brandy. I give them both a hug.

"Have you seen Dee lately?" I ask.

"I saw her today. She started her first round of chemo."

I remember my mother's first round of chemo. The ordeal is draining for an adult, so I can only imagine how it will be on Dee.

"How's Rosie? It's been a while since we spoke."

"Rosie's well. She sometimes rides with me to see Dee. By the way, that was thoughtful of you to get Dee a little keyboard player."

"She bang a few notes for you?"

"Of course."

"It's essential to her healing."

"Dee's mother mentioned you showing up with a famous basketball player."

"Who? JB?"

"Oh?"

"JB was kind enough to offer me a ride, that's all."

Aunt Mary sits quiet and sips from a glass of wine. At that moment, my skin feels flushed. It feels like somehow she's putting together pieces of a puzzle in her brain. Or my imagination could be just overanalyzing.

"He's made quite an impression on Dee and her mother," Aunt Mary says.

"From eight to eighty, the ladies love JB," Uncle Frenchy adds.

"I've seen girls scream after him, and I'm thinking, JB? Little ole JB? It's crazy when you think about it," Aunt Mary says.

"He's not even in the pros yet. Imagine the cattle when that happens," Uncle Frenchy says.

"Our son has his fair share of lady fans too," Aunt Mary says. "When he's not crashing here, Caleb also has an apartment near the campus. One day a girl shows up claiming to be his tutor."

"Caleb didn't know the girl. Turns out she was a fan finding a way in," Uncle Frenchy says to me.

"I don't understand it. Nowadays, girls will lie, manipulate, compromise their standards, and for what? Just to say they've been with an athlete." Aunt Mary finishes a glass before pouring herself another.

It kind of felt like she was talking about me.

"According to your parents, you compromised your standards when you married a loud-mouthed pilot." Uncle Frenchy leans over to kiss Aunt Mary on the cheek. "And it was 1965 when that happened."

"Don't make me spit out this wine, Frenchy." Aunt Mary's face is turning red as she glances at Uncle Frenchy and shakes her head.

"I saved you from a life of misery. You were about to marry an ambulance chaser."

They giggle and cuddle, and I'm sure if Cassandra was downstairs seeing this, she would do the fake gag, where she sticks her finger in her mouth and pretends she's about to erupt.

I leave them alone and walk outside to sit with my feet in the pool. So much is going through my mind. I know I made a promise to Gregory, but I haven't heard from him. I'm going to give him a chance to write me a letter, send a postcard, or give me a phone call. If I don't hear from him soon, I will assume he's forgotten or he just doesn't car.

I'm in a hazy mix of emotions, so I busy myself practicing the Schumann piece, and in between that, playing the pieces I composed, particularly the ones I collaborated on with JB. He wrote these words:

I threw away the black book

Don't need it anymore

You made me fall hard

The minute you walked through the door.

I convince myself these lyrics have absolutely nothing to do with me. I can't possibly have that effect on anyone. The other night while listening to music, we wrote songs. He wrote about the dream he had of me. When we finished writing, it must've been around two a.m. He held me in his arms and just started improvising the lyrics. He has a smooth tenor for someone so imposing, and when he sings, he seems vulnerable—open to whatever the universe gives. I play our song while my mind drifts to how the late night ended and early morning began. The energy we have is supreme for a love song. I stop playing and get lost in my thoughts, remembering how our bodies danced underneath the covers. We ascended to heights beyond his bedroom. Hearing him moan and declare, "You're the best I ever had." Feeling our heartbeats in sync. How the room settled slowly into a peaceful lull. These thoughts are causing my thighs to tingle. Vibrations are moving through me. I hold myself and pretend my arms are his.

Hours later, I'm sitting in the den chatting with Aunt Teal when Aunt Mary appears with Rosie. Rosie and I embrace. It seems like ages since we last spoke.

"Did you forget about me?" she asks.

"No. I would never," I say.

"I miss you and Dee being at the youth center," she says.

"To be honest, it's a little difficult for me." I hold my chest, feeling it get heavy.

"We're on our way to see Dee. Come ride with us," Aunt Mary insists.

I grab my things, and we jump into the Chevy Caprice.

On the ride there, she shows her latest sketches. I thumb across a drawing of a young boy, half of his face hidden behind a bandana. I see that same face in a couple of other sketches.

"Who's he?" I ask.

"Dante. I met him at the roller rink."

"Nice."

"Does he roller-skate, or does he just hang out?"

"He's one of the deejays," she answers.

"Wow. That sounds fun."

I didn't want to probe any further. Instead, I look at more of her sketches.

We arrive at the hospital and take the elevator to Dee's floor. The closer we get to her room, we hear her hammering out something on her keyboard. We stand outside the door listening. I try to make out the tune. It sounds like she's trying to play, "Twinkle, Twinkle Little Star." She has the tempo, just needs to find the right keys. The three of us are basking in the doorway, enjoying it. Aunt Mary enters first, followed by me and Rosie. She doesn't stop playing; now that she has an audience, she bangs louder. We applaud when she finishes.

"Am I going home?" she asks Aunt Mary.

"Not today, Dee," Aunt Mary says, arranging Dee's stuffed animals neatly on the bed. "Is this your audience?"

"Yes." Her mood turns gloomy. "But I'm going home, right?"

I can see Aunt Mary doing her best to lighten the mood. "Your audience wants you to stay here until you feel better, okay?"

"Okay."

"Dee, can you play something for me?" I ask.

"What do you want to hear?" she asks.

"Do you know, 'Jesus Loves Me'?"

"Sort of."

I get up and sit on the bed next to her. "My mom used to sing this to me, and it always made me feel better."

I point out the keys for her to press, and I sing along. We do this for a couple of rounds until she plays them without my instruction.

"Wow, Dee. You catch on fast," Aunt Mary says.

"I can play," she says. Her eyes are sparkling. "I want to play it again."

"You need me to point out your notes?"

"No. I got it."

She starts playing. She misses the mark a few times, but it really doesn't matter.

Rosie is so quiet-I almost forgot she was in the room.

"Look, Dee." She shows Dee a sketch of a girl sitting at a piano with musical notes floating from each side.

"That's me?" she asks, pointing.

"Yes. You like it?" Rosie asks.

"Can I have it?"

Rosie places the drawing in her hands. I notice she has a wall full of Rosie's drawings to go along with a banner of everyone's signature from the youth center.

"I like it."

She's doing considerably well despite having had chemotherapy the day before. We continue to entertain her. When dinner arrives, she toys with her green beans. She never touches her carrots, and the chicken is a no-go. What she really wants is the gelatin. Sitting there with her, I think, *why waste time sifting through things you don't want? Toss it all aside and get to the best part, that which is sweet and brings you satisfaction the moment it touches your lips.*

We leave the hospital and find a nice Italian restaurant nearby. Aunt Mary seems preoccupied with her thoughts. She orders a glass of wine and zones out for a second.

"It just occurred to me," she begins. "I spend more time with you girls than I do with my own daughter."

Rosie and I sip cola from our glasses. The reality of her statement sinks in. She seems troubled by it.

Aunt Mary takes a sip. "I never intended for it to get to this point."

"Maybe you guys can talk about it," I suggest.

Aunt Mary clasps her hands, allowing her chin to rest on them. Her eyes flit as she tries to recall. It makes me sad for her and Cassandra.

"She resents the center. It consumes me, I know."

I'm thinking, she's right-but I dare say it aloud.

"I must find a happy medium." Aunt Mary sighs. "I've got to do better."

"What do you have in mind?" I ask.

"A weekend retreat somewhere quiet, somewhere different."

"Sounds wonderful."

She nods. "I need to do this. Just me and her. I'm not worried about Caleb. He's an adult doing his own thing."

Rosie and I nod in compliance. Her spirits seem lifted. We order. The evening turns out pleasant.

***

I look at my aunt, unlike her assistant, Leah, she has no reservations about dropping off Rosie in the rough neighborhood where she lives.

"I'm dropping you off at your front door, and I'm watching you walk inside."

"Mrs. Mary, you don't have to."

"What's your address?"

Rosie rattles it off and sits back shaking her head.

"Yes, I'm aware you do this daily, but we're doing things differently tonight."

We turn into the place called the Jungle, and the hairs on my skin stand immediately. People are loitering, and overhead I see the spotlight of a chopper looming. The energy I feel has me on the edge of my seat. I can't imagine living like this. We pull up to the apartment building.

"I'd like to meet your mother," Mary says to Rosie.

"She's at work," Rosie answers.

"What time does she get off?"

"Eleven."

I glance at my watch. It's 9:25.

"I sit with my neighbor sometimes until she gets off. I'll do that tonight, if it makes you feel better."

I hear a long, drawn-out sigh from Aunt Mary.

"Thanks for everything." Rosie glances at me. "I guess I'll see you around. I notice her expression turns pensive.

"You can always stop by the house to visit," Aunt Mary says to her.

"Sure, I'll do that." She gives me a long, tight hug, almost as if she doesn't want to let go.

"You have a good night, Rosie," I say.

She nods and quietly gets out of the car. Aunt Mary doesn't back away until Rosie is inside.

"God, protect my eaglets." When we come to a stop, I notice Aunt Mary gripping the steering wheel. I reach over the seat to rub her shoulder.

"He hears you," I say.

When we arrive, she finds Cassandra outside sitting by the pool. I can't hear what they're saying, but I watch their exchange. I turn and walk upstairs to my room. The house is dark and quiet. Aunt Teal is probably in her room asleep. Caleb comes and goes, but I would imagine his day involved basketball and interaction with JB.

I open my journal and proceed to write the following:

June 23, 1987 10:30 p.m.

Two days have passed. I can't stop thinking about it. Everything that led to it, and everything that's happened since. That morning he got up and took the dog for a walk. I tried to sleep, but the phones kept ringing. At some point, I started to answer them. One was a sports reporter calling from the East Coast. Another call was from the Philippines. What I gathered, it was a relative who wanted to speak to his mother, Judy. I answer another call, and the voice on the other line replies with, "This isn't Judy. Who is this? My reply, "Who would you like to speak with?" Her reply, "JB." My reply, "He's not here. May I take a message?" Her reply, "Tell him Basha called." I remember hanging up the phone and asking, "Who is Basha?" When he comes back, I don't tell him about the phone calls—don't want him to think I'm meddling in his business.

We kissed and he told me he'd see me later. Now I've convinced myself that
when the time comes be different.

***

It's now Saturday morning. Caleb's dropping off Aunt Mary and
Cassandra at LAX to catch their flight to Acapulco. The phone rings.
I pick up.

"Hello," I answer in a low, soft voice.

"You're even sweet over the phone." It's JB.

He gets right down to business. "Pack a bag. I'm picking you up in
twenty minutes," he says.

He hangs up before I can process and gather my thoughts. We
haven't spoken or seen each other since Tuesday. My intentions are to
call Ursula, go to a spa, and follow up with lunch, but now I'm looking
around the room, thinking, I need to shower. I need to brush my hair.
What am I going to wear?

When I finally see him, all the questions I want to ask are quickly
forced to the back of my mind. He's in Jake's Jeep Wrangler, and Smitty
is in the backseat, tongue dangling, with a smile on his face. JB sits
behind the wheel, his hair curly and wet like he just stepped out of the
shower. His gaze is seductive, naturally. My hair is wet, tousled, and
beachy. I open my pochette to retrieve a pair of sunglasses.

"You look nice," he says.

"Would've been spectacular, if I had more time."

"You can't go wrong if you tried."

"Wanna bet?"

He drives in silence, and I'm shocked. A gorgeous day like this needs
a soundtrack.

"Where's the music?" I ask.

He reaches behind the seat and retrieves an attaché case. He places
it in my lap. "Open it."

I unlock it and see a series of cassettes.

I read some of the titles. I'm not familiar with these artists.

"What do you want to hear?" I ask.

"You see World Class Wreckin' Cru?"

I'm impressed he has everything alphabetized and organized. I scroll until I see the cassette and place it inside the player for him.

The first track plays, and he's bobbing his head with the rhythm. I hear guys screaming and rhyming over drum machines and computerized programming. I've heard of rappers like Run DMC, but that was about the extent of it.

"Me and Caleb wore out this tape our sophomore year." He breaks into the rhyme. The tempo of the song slows, and the woofers in the jeep start vibrating. I must admit, watching him is quite entertaining. Smitty is unfazed, and I get the feeling he's seen it before.

"You and your music," I say.

"Have to admit, you like my eclectic mix, right?"

"Some of it. What I'm hearing now is noise."

"I respectfully disagree. What's noise to you is artistic expression to the next person."

"You call a bunch of guys screaming poetry over syncopated beats artistic expression?"

"Yes." He chuckles.

I try to listen with an open mind.

I cover my ears. He frowns. I eject the tape. He looks at the cassette player and then at me.

"Next," I say.

The traffic is bumper-to-bumper and crawling. Saturday midmorning in L.A., and the sun is a welcoming sight, having burst its way through the dense smog.

I randomly place a tape inside the cassette player. Whatever emanates from the speakers could set the tone or kill the mood. The tune is jazzy with a saxophone intro. I like what I hear, so far. A woman's voice pleads because she wants to know, Is it a crime?

"Good choice," he says to me.

"If I don't like it, I'll eject." I give him the side eye.

"Keep your ears open."

I close my eyes to allow the smoothness of her voice and the winds to calm me. Though, I have so many questions to ask, first and foremost, *where are we going? What's happening between us? Who is Basha?*

We pull into an area where he takes Smitty for a walk. He reaches into his pocket to retrieve his wallet where he pulls out fifty dollars.

"This place has the best burgers and fries. Medium-well, bun toasted, vanilla shake. Order whatever you like." He kisses my lips before walking through a well-worn trail with Smitty leading the way. We are somewhere off PCH in an area with quaint cottages, bright flowers, and topiary. A waitress greets me, and I tell her I want a table for two outside.

JB returns with Smitty shortly after I place our orders. I order just what he wants and the same for myself.

"Are we close?" I ask. "The suspense is killing me."

"We're here," he says.

"Oh," I say. "Not too far off the beaten path without feeling totally isolated." The waitress brings us our drinks.

"Ideal for creative minds like ours."

"How do you know about this town?" I ask.

"It's one of the few places where I can bring Smitty along."

"JB?"

"Yes."

"Why didn't I hear from you this week?"

He takes a moment before answering. "Basketball. It's the wife. It demands most of my time and attention."

"I see."

"I'm sorry if I didn't call." His eyes flit when he's in deep thought. "I don't know if you want me to do that. Suppose Cassandra or Caleb or your aunt Mary answers?"

"That crossed my mind as well."

"You're off-limits to me."

"I've always assumed it was our age difference. You're twenty. I'm seventeen."

"I don't think that's the issue. See—Caleb knows this better than anyone. It's why he's protective of you. I'm the big bad wolf, huffing and puffing. Licking and sticking. I can't help it."

"Wow." My heart drops to Smitty's level. He pulls his chair next to mine.

"I don't want you to think what happened between us meant nothing. It did. In fact, it scared the shit out of me."

I listen as he continues.

"You blew my fucking mind," he says.

"How?"

"The way you make me feel."

"How is it different from other girls?"

"It's real. There's no pretense. The sex is pure. Being your first is a damn privilege."

"But you just said you can't help being a big bad wolf."

"I'm working on it."

The waitress returns with our burgers and fries. The smell of the grilled burgers and the buttery aroma of the brioche buns is a distraction. JB takes a bite. "Ummm," he says. "Tastes almost as good as you."

"Really, JB?" I shake my head before taking a bite. It has a really good flavor. I didn't intend to change the direction of this conversation, but sometimes I express the first random thought that comes to mind. "Did you know Cassandra and Aunt Mary were flying out this weekend?"

JB finishes chewing before he answers. "I did."

"You knew what time Caleb was dropping them off?"

He winks. "I knew I had a narrow window to scoop you up quick, fast, and in a hurry."

Smitty is sitting nearby, his face resting on his front paws, tail wagging, his eyes dancing from JB to me, waiting for us to throw him a fry or something.

"What's the plan?" I ask.

"Let's go with the flow," he says.

After lunch, we drive to the beach and park the jeep on the sand. He retrieves a cooler. It's on wheels, so he rolls it to a spot. I open it to find beer, soda, a bottle of wine, hard-boiled eggs, grapes, trail mix.

I open a blanket to spread over the sand. The breeze off the ocean makes it hard to stabilize, so the cooler holds it in place. He returns to the jeep to grab two surfboards. I take off my cover-up and meet JB's gaze. He drops the surfboards, staring at the fullness of my curves and overflowing cleavage in my bikini.

"Focus," I say, pointing to the incoming waves rolling in our direction.

"You know what you're doing." He puts the surfboards aside and walks back to the jeep with Smitty trailing behind, his tail wagging. He retrieves a Frisbee and throws it out. Smitty runs full speed leaping to catch it before it hits the sand. I watch this exchange for some time while checking out other beachgoers doing their thing. The rush of the waves, the breeze, the seagulls, and their calls stir emotions in me. I put on my sunglasses and watch JB pick up a surfboard, and in his tall, confident-laden gait, meet the waves, and when the big one comes, he rides in on it before falling off. He does it a few more times until he finds that ideal wave. I take off my glasses. I grab a surfboard and join him. Together, we leap over waves, riding on some and crashing off others. Water and its power.

We dry off and take a moment to relax. JB pours pet food in Smitty's dog bowl. He is more than anxious to eat. The evening is slowly approaching, and some of the beachgoers are packing up to leave. JB opens the cooler and grabs a can of beer and trail mix. I reach in and grab a handful of grapes.

"I like the rush when you ride a wave," he says.

"Do you get high?" I ask. Such a random question.

He looks at me with an expression that asks, *Where are you going with this?* "I have," he answers.

"What was your drug of choice?"

"Pot, 'shrooms, acid. Stuff I did in high school. Why?"

"I never understood how or why people chase a high."

"God gave us natural highs, like when you get in a good workout at the gym and you can't wait to get back the next day, or when I'm on the court and I make a fade-away jumper with two seconds left in the game and the crowd goes wild, or the high you get when you've just made love to a virgin."

I stare at the sun's reflection over the waves. "It doesn't matter if a high is natural or not. At some point, you have to come down and deal with reality."

"What are you dealing with?" he asks.

"I can't put it into words."

"Does it have anything to do with us?"

"Some of it."

"You want to talk about it?"

I nod. "How would you define us?" I ask.

He takes a moment. "Girl and boy. Family friends. Bond over their love for music. Develop feelings for each other they never knew they had."

We sit and allow those words to register. The breeze sweeps strands of hair across my face. He stands and extends his hand to me. I take it and allow him to whisk me off my feet. He's such a showoff, using my body like a barbell, lifting and lowering me, flexing every muscle in his arms. When he's done lifting, I sit on his back, legs crossed, posing like a beach-babe while he's underneath doing push-ups. I count seventy-five. He's making my five-foot-three-inch, 155 pounds feel light and sexy. Minutes later, we are holding hands and spinning around until we are dizzy and exhausted.

Sunset finds us wrapped in a blanket. I'm safe and secure in his arms. We don't need music right now, not when the waves roll like an orchestra of timpani and crash like cymbals.

"Finish telling me about all the things you're dealing with," he says.

"I don't want to dampen this mood," I say.

"Okay. Just know I'm all ears."

"I really miss my mother."

"I'm sorry."

"She enjoyed sunsets as much as I do."

"Do you ever feel her spirit sometimes?" he asks.

"No."

"Not once? Did you feel like she was watching over you?"

"I honestly don't remember."

"Have you ever felt the Holy Spirit?"

"Can't say I have."

"You talk to God?"

"It's been a while."

"My grandmother Imogene used to sing 'Jesus is on the Mainline' in church.

I rest my head against his chest.

"When I was a kid, I really believed I could pick up the phone and dial Jesus."

We both chuckle at the notion.

"My daddy says, 'God hears your prayers, talk to Him. He's always there,'" I say.

"You sound doubtful."

"More like disillusioned."

"God meets you where you are. Everything is according to your faith."

"I feel like every day is a battle—angel on one shoulder; devil on the other."

"I feel you on that." He chuckles. "I've got a devil on my shoulder right now whispering in my ear."

I turn to face him. "What is it telling you?"

"The ocean isn't the only thing that's going to be wet around here," he says with a mischievous grin.

I pull up the blanket so we aren't exposed. Luckily, the crowd from earlier has thinned out. Only people left are lovers taking an evening stroll.

"Are you sure you want to do this here?" he asks.

"There's hardly anyone around."

"If we get busted, what are you going to say? The devil made you-do it?"

We laugh and kiss before I hold him close and take the ride.

Seventeen

The cottage has a Southern charm to it with its trellis of bougainvillea and red door. Inside, the decor is antique, and sitting in the middle of the bathroom is a stand-alone tub. JB is impressing me without even trying. He fills the tub with lavender bath soap and instructs me to relax while he takes Smitty for a walk.

He comes back minutes later with a cassette player in hand. He plugs it up, presses play, and the sounds of the soothing female voice from earlier fills the room. He takes off his shirt like a striptease, rolling his pelvis in a seductive circular motion. He turns his back and grinds, hugging himself as if his arms belong to a beautiful stranger I can't see.

Still in the vein of a striptease, he slides off his shorts and underwear, exposing his bare, taut butt. The warm water seems to be heating up, and steam quickly covers the mirrors, then he turns around, giving me a full-frontal view.

"Room for one more?" he asks.

"I'll make room."

He steps in and sits on the opposite end.

"This place is a hidden gem. How did you find it?" I ask.

He clears his throat. "I plead the fifth."

"I see."

I can tell he's reading my expression. I'm not upset, though in the back of my mind, I want to feel this place was sought out especially for me. Now all I can think is what other girl sat in this same spot and watched the same striptease.

184 - T. WENDY WILLIAMS

"Penny for your thoughts?" he asks.

"There's someone I've known for a while. Just two weeks ago, he and I became closer. He left on a boating expedition for Europe, but before he left, he asked me if I would be his girl. I said yes."

"Is he coming back?" JB asks.

"I don't know."

"What are you going to do?" he asks.

"I don't know."

Now he's quiet and staring at the treble clef pendant resting at the apex of my breasts.

"Penny for your thoughts." This time I ask.

"I'm leaving Tuesday for a couple of weeks. I can't really go into details because it's basketball related. I want you to know that road trips can get very crazy for me."

"Crazy? How?" I have an idea, but I want to hear what he says.

"The girls. The clubs. The parties."

"I heard about it. I know about Basha too."

The look in his eyes is curiously intent.

"Are you seeing her?"

"Not at the moment."

"What does that mean?"

"I'm doing me. She's doing her."

"I still don't understand."

"I care about her. We're cool. We're just taking a break."

"What happens next?"

"We break for good, or we get back together."

"You would get back with her if the opportunity presented itself?"

"Let's say this: It's the right thing but not really something I'm pushing for."

"What would make you return?"

"Not saying it's happened, but if she got pregnant, I wouldn't leave her."

The lump in my throat eases its way to my stomach. I have a sick feeling.

"I tell myself, 'Maddie, you should've never let him kiss you at the pool that day. You should've stopped him, grabbed your things, and went home.'"

"You have regrets?" he asks.

I didn't really know how to answer him.

"I don't regret a thing," he begins.

"What happens between us?" I ask.

"We write about it." He laughs. "Add a melody."

I'm not laughing. I don't find it funny. He notices the serious look in my eyes.

"I'm afraid of what happens between me and your family if they find out about us. They know my reputation. You're sweet, little innocent Maddie. You're supposed to be that way until marriage. You don't get involved with a guy like me."

"But I like being with you."

"I like being with you too," he says.

"The song about us. You have a title for it?" I ask.

He nods and brings me in close for a kiss. "Maddie, my love."

It's like watching magic happen and hearing the voice of God when the portals of creativity are open. With my eyes closed, I listen while he sings:

I don't give a damn about the other girls
All I really need is you.
Your body is the spark that ignites my world
You make all my dreams come true.

An orgasmic sensation flows through me. It feels the same as it did the very first time it happened between JB and me.

"Open your eyes," I hear him say.

When I do, I see his brown eyes connect with mine. I look at his lips, the way his mouth moves, his teeth, the wickedness of his tongue.

Can you trust me?
Do you want to be with me?
I swear I'll be good to you
All I really need is you

He stops singing and studies my expression. He does that a lot. My guess is it's all inspiration for the next song. The water is getting cold, and our bodies are turning into prunes. After drying off and quickly slipping into our pajamas, we sit in the center of the bed. He has his composition notebook, and I have my folder with my compositions and sheet music. Once the tape player stops, the room is silent, but our thoughts are in sync.

I write down melodies as he sings. Often, he stops to look at the sheet.

"You've got to teach me how to read music."

"Once you learn, I'll become useless. Then you won't need me anymore."

He looks up from his notebook. "You're my muse. I'll always need you."

He grabs our notebooks and sheet music and places them on the nightstand beside the bed. He then gets up and turns off the light. It's completely dark, and the next thing I feel is his lips kissing me ever so gently.

***

Cassandra and Aunt Mary arrive home with bags of souvenirs. Caleb is behind carrying their suitcases in each hand. Cassandra's giving me the evil eye, upset I still won't tell her who I was with. I greet Aunt Mary with a warm hug, and she gives me a bag with souvenirs.

"Thank you," I say while looking inside to see everything wrapped neatly.

"We needed that." Aunt Mary looks at Cassandra.

Cassandra gathers her suitcase and bags and walks upstairs. I'm right behind her.

"I'm happy for you and Aunt Mary," I say, following her into her room.

"It was nice. Food was great. I snuck in a couple of tequila shots."

"How did you do that?"

"I went to the bar when Mom wasn't looking, gave the bartender a ten-dollar bill and had him fill my glass with the clear stuff."

"But couldn't she smell it on you?" I ask.

"If she did, she never mentioned it."

She pauses and looks me over from head to toe. "You look cute. You have a date?"

"No."

"Still won't say who he is?"

I don't respond.

"I know for sure it's not Gregory."

"And how do you know that?"

"I hear he and Ruger are now in Nice."

"Where did you hear that?"

"First, tell me who the guy is."

I sit on the edge of her bed. Silent.

"Has Gregory written to you?"

"No."

She sighs and sits next to me. We are both quiet, staring ahead. There are questions running through our minds. I know her mind is burning with one question.

"Who is he, Maddie?" she asks in an almost pleading fashion.

My silence is deafening.

The following morning, I look up and see Cassandra dressed and joining me and Aunt Mary and Aunt Teal for breakfast. She notices me staring at her rather strangely.

"Are you, okay?" she asks.

"I don't believe this. Are you going to the youth center with us?"

Cassandra frowns. "Calm down," she says, pretending to be annoyed by my excitement.

"Cassandra's helping out with the younger group. I'll need you to take the older ones," Aunt Mary says to me.

"This is going to be so much fun now." I'm cheering and clapping.

We get to the youth center, and once everyone arrives, I observe Cassandra with the younger group. I feel a lump in my throat when I think of Dee. I turn my attention to my group. I'm not much older than them. Their assignment is to write one page on a subject that interests them.

"I want to write about a famous black painter, but I don't know any," Rosie says.

"I think I can help you," I begin, remembering my grandmother Magdalene's friend, the painter, Beauford Delaney.

"My grandmother was a writer in New York with a Black newspaper during the 1920s. Are you familiar with the Harlem Renaissance?"

"No," she answers.

"A lot of Black artists and writers came out of that period." I notice the others stop to listen as I explain to Rosie. "You guys heard of Langston Hughes?" I ask.

They look at me with blank stares.

"What about Zora Neale Hurston?"

Again, blank stares.

"You guys like poetry?" I ask.

"I do," Rosie says.

I turn to Rosie. "When you get the chance, look up Beauford Delaney. He's a famous Black painter. I also want you to find a poem by Langston Hughes."

"Where will I find that?" she asks.

"Mrs. Mary has a library here." I point to a shelf of encyclopedias.

"Maddie, your shoes are cute. Where did you find them?" one of the girls asks. The other five girls and the two guys at the table crane their necks to get a peek at my shoes.

"I don't remember," I reply, looking at my pair of white Keds.

"You do. You just don't want to tell us," another girl says.

"Honestly, I don't remember."

"You're kinda fly," one of the boys says. He's slouched in his chair.

"What are you writing about?" I ask him.

He sits up and covers his paper. "Nothing."

One of the girls looks over his shoulder. "That's a love note," she says.

They laugh and tease him. She reaches in to try to take it; he holds up his arm as a shield.

"Anyone want to share what they've written so far?" I ask.

"We want to know about you," says the girl who had asked about my shoes earlier.

"Me?"

"Yes. You come here looking fly and cute. Your hair is always pretty. You play the piano very well. What set you claim?"

"What?" I'm confused.

"She wants to know what neighborhood you live in," Rosie leans close to tell me.

Before I can answer, a different girl answers.

"I bet you stay in the Hills. No, you look like you're from Ladera Heights or View Park."

"How did you determine that?" I ask.

"Some people you can tell they're not from around the way," she says.

"I live nearby," I answer.

"And that's all they need to know," Rosie says to me.

"Rosie, I heard your mother put you out and you're living with Dante now," says the same girl who inquired about my shoes.

The rest of the girls and guys sitting at the table respond with collective, "Oohhs."

Rosie sits straight up in her chair. I notice her light-brown complexion turning red. "That's a lie, Tatiana."

"Dante friends with my homeboy, and he told me y'all been kicking it." Tatiana keeps talking.

I notice Rosie's fists ball up, and I feel the tension in the room.

"Tatiana, be quiet," a girl sitting next to her advises.

Miss Vanessa, the volunteer teacher, arrives before things can escalate. "Thank you, Maddie, for filling in for me," she says.

Everyone sits up straight in their chairs and continues quietly with their writings as if they've been doing this all along. I glance at Rosie, and she's seething—her eyes are still on Tatiana. She looks as if she wants to lunge across the table at her. Tatiana said a mouthful. Now, I have questions, and I hope Rosie is willing to give me answers.

Eighteen

"Please don't tell Mrs. Mary," Rosie says to me when we're alone.

It's after closing at the center, and Aunt Mary, Cassandra, and Leah, Aunt Mary's assistant, are down the hall in Aunt Mary's office. Rosie sits at one of the tables and listens while I practice my Schumann piece.

"What Tatiana said, was it true?" I ask.

"Yes."

"Mrs. Mary can help you," I say.

"The state'll put me in foster care. They did it before."

"You live with your boyfriend and his family? His mother's okay with that?"

"Yes."

"The night when you asked if you could spend the night with Leah, were you living at home?"

"No. My momma had just put me out that morning."

"Why?"

"Some days she's nice, and some days she's really violent."

"Is she on drugs?"

"No, but she smokes bud sometimes."

"What is that?" I ask.

"It's like weed."

She stands and places her pencil and sketchbook inside her backpack. "I'll see you tomorrow, and please remember what I said."

I sigh. "Okay."

"I like living with my boyfriend, and I don't want to leave."

I watch her walk out, closing the door behind her.

When I arrive home, there's a huge floral arrangement waiting for me in the foyer with a note attached.

"Those are beautiful," Aunt Mary says.

Cassandra picks up the note. I gently take it out of her hands. I open, and it reads: I can't go another day without you. See you soon. GW III.

"The sender has great taste. This arrangement is exquisite." Aunt Mary studies the exotic-looking flowers and the designs etched in the crystal vase.

"It's from Gregory," I say.

Cassandra smiles. "See. He didn't forget about you. He cares."

"Gregory. Remind me. Who is he again?" Aunt Mary asks.

"Mom, Gregory Washington," Cassandra says.

"Washington, yes. Now, I remember. Greg and Celeste's son. Where is he?"

"He's in Nice, in the South of France," I answer.

"What's he doing so far away from home?"

"His family has a home there."

"I see." She takes one more look at the arrangement. "The Washingtons are a good family."

Aunt Mary leaves us in the foyer. I give Cassandra the note. After reading it, she glances at me. "You don't look too excited."

"I don't know, Cassandra." I touch and smell the roses. "'See you soon.' What does that mean?"

"Maybe he's coming here, or maybe he'll send you a ticket to France."

I want to see Gregory. I miss him. I want to relax with him on his boat or wherever and see how far things really go with us. I want to see JB too. I miss him too. I want to go back to that little cottage across from the beach and sit in the middle of the bed in our pajamas and write songs and listen to him sing. I like how they both kiss me and hold me and look at me. I like how they smell. My thoughts are filled with episodes where I'm lying underneath JB. It's nightfall, and the stars twinkle with whole notes, half notes, and quarter notes. My thoughts drift to Gregory and his smile. He doesn't smile often, but when he does, he has the whitest teeth, and his lips are full, and his kisses are sensuous and intense.

The following day, Cassandra and I ride with Aunt Mary to UCLA to see Dee. She's had her second round of chemotherapy, and she looks tired. I sit on the side of her and hold her hand. I feel her give me a little squeeze. Aunt Mary sits on the opposite side of the bed.

"I want to play something, but I don't know how she'll react," I say.

"Just play soft," Aunt Mary suggests.

And that is what I do, playing Mozart's, "Piano Sonata No. 11 A major K 331." Aunt Mary is quiet. Her eyes are closed as she sways slightly from side to side. Cassandra is asleep, sitting in a chair across the room. Dee's eyelids are heavy as she fights to stay awake but eventually falls asleep—that is until I stopped playing.

"Why did you stop?" she asks in her sweet little singsong voice.

"I thought you were asleep," I say, squeezing and rubbing her hand.

"I like the song," she says. "Can you play it again?"

I glance at Aunt Mary, who winks. Then I proceed to play. Dee sits up and studies my hands, watching them glide over the Casio keyboard.

"Can you teach me how to play that?"

"Of course." I take her fingers. They are cold to the touch. I warm them with my hands before we proceed to touch the keys. I see her eyes light up, and we do this for twenty minutes until she's drowsy again, and this time she falls asleep.

***

The following day, I'm sitting at the piano practicing my piece when I hear the doorbell. When I'm practicing, and I have the piece memorized, I play with my eyes closed. This is how I focus on the melody, the phrasing, and the tempo. My eyes are still closed, and I smell the freshest of scents, light and airy, like I imagined how it smells in paradise, then I feel soft lips kissing the back of my neck. It startles me, and my heart races. I open my eyes, turn and see Gregory standing with more roses and a gift in his hand. We hug, kiss, and cling to each other. We're squeezing and holding our bodies so close, I fill his heart pounding against mine. We find a spot in the far corner of the room to sit. He sets the flowers and gift aside so we can continue kissing. We stop often to take a breather and just stare into each other's eyes.

"Hey, you," he says finally.

"I thought you had forgotten me."

"Can I explain?"

I nod and listen.

"I'm in the middle of the English Channel on a Maxi yacht with twenty other guys including Ruger. When I finally think I have some down time to write or send you a ticket, I'm swept into another race."

"I get it. You didn't have the time."

"Hope you like the flowers I sent you. They look nice in the foyer," he says.

"I do, and they smell good too."

He's holding a gift in a red box with gold trim. "My apologies," he says, giving it to me. "Open it."

"You didn't have to," I say.

"I know," he replies with a deadpan expression that can be curt, or depending upon the situation, endearing and funny.

I open it to find a diamond-studded eighteen-karat gold bracelet with a small golden screwdriver.

"It's gorgeous," I say. "A simple 'I'm sorry' is okay."

"I don't do anything simple."

"I should know this," I answer.

Gregory takes the screwdriver to unscrew the bracelet. When it opens, he places it around my wrist and secures it in place with the screwdriver. I hold it up to admire it. A sparkle from a diamond catches my eye.

"I love it."

"I knew you would."

"What are you going to do with the screwdriver?" I ask.

"Keep it."

"You better not have an Inspector Gadget—type spy camera inserted in one of these diamonds."

He smiles and shakes his head. "Now that's funny."

"I was practicing my piece. I have a concert next month."

"Wow. This time, can I get an invite?"

"We'll see."

I'm checking Gregory's look. He's stylish and dapper, even in relaxed settings. Nothing's out of place; it's almost too perfect.

"Can we go to your boat with no-name?" I ask.

"Now?"

"Yes. Now."

I notice a smile emerging. "If we go out, it'll be a while before we return."

"As long as you have me back before 11:30 tonight," I answer.

He chuckles. "I remember now. Your aunt's curfew."

I pack a bathing suit and a change of clothing along with my composition notebook and staff sheets. Aunt Mary and Cassandra are at the youth center, Uncle Frenchy is on a trip and Caleb's out of town-so I inform Aunt Teal that I'm hanging out with Gregory, Ursula, and Mona. She's sipping on a glass of wine, watching one of her soap operas.

"Have fun, be careful. It was nice meeting you." She says to Gregory.

Outside, parked in the driveway is a white exotic-looking sports car.

"Nice. What kind is it?"

"Ferrari Testarossa."

He opens the door, and I sit inside. The bucket seat with its soft leather enfolds and holds me like a long-lost friend.

"You love the finer things in life."

"How you know me." He winks.

We leave the neighborhood, and as we ride, I notice there's no music playing.

"You have tapes we can listen to?" I ask.

"No."

"Why not?"

He looks at me and shrugs then presses a button. "Radio is all I got."

Static comes over the speakers, and he presses buttons, changing from station to station until we hear a broadcast of a random song played loud and clear.

"Have you eaten a Fatburger?" I ask.

He adamantly shakes his head. "No. Have you?"

"Yes. I had one with chili, cheese, and an egg."

"That sounds gross."

"That was my initial reaction, but it's actually good."

"No, thank you." He shifts gears, keeping his eyes on the road.

I'm riding, but my thoughts are running wild. I'm thinking just how different he is from JB when it comes to music. Seems Gregory couldn't care less. The radio just plays a random song, and it's just background noise. There's no dancing, no head bobbing; right now, I'm kind of missing that. We get to his boat, and he closes the door and locks it. Soon, everything comes off, and we don't leave the boat for a very long time.

Nineteen

I arrive home close to my 11:30 curfew, and Cassandra is still awake in her room. She hears me enter, and soon she appears and finds a spot on the edge of my bed. She's looking at me. I can tell curiosity is getting the best of her.

"I'll tell you everything once I'm finished with my shower," I say to her.

Her eyes widened. "Okay. While you're in the shower, I'm going to load some popcorn kernels in the air popper. I don't want to miss this." She runs out of the room.

I close the door to the bathroom and undress, looking at the reflection of my naked body in the mirror. There are dark red marks covering the side of my neck. Gregory's sucking grew intense. I take a washcloth, soaking it in cold water, and apply it to the spot on my neck. I can hear the conversation when Cassandra sees it—or worst, Aunt Mary. I turn on the shower and step inside, feeling the hot water massage me. I lather my body with soap, washing my breasts and between my legs. The soap stings a little, and I tilt the showerhead so the pressure flows right to the soapy areas. My mind drifts to those moments when I'm with Gregory or JB, and those feelings of euphoria take over. I'm rising and falling at the same time. I'm throwing pillows; I'm ripping sheets from the fitted pockets. I'm moaning and crying, going out of my mind. *What have I gotten myself into? I can't continue this*

I dry off and put on my robe. I grab my hairbrush and when I open

196

the door, Cassandra is sitting on my bed with her bowl of popcorn, waiting.

"So?" she begins, munching.

"Gregory's back in town." I say.

Her eyes widened as she rises to her knees to move so I can sit at the edge of the bed. I give her the brush and close my eyes.

"When did he fly in?" she asks.

"This morning."

"Did you see him?"

"Yes."

"Tell me everything." She grabs strands of my hair to brush.

"I can't tell everything."

"Then give me the highlights."

"We spent the day on the boat," I say.

"Did you go fishing? Swimming?"

I smile, feeling the hairs on my arms stand, just thinking about what happened with Gregory and me.

She leans over to check out my reaction. "You're smiling, so I'll assume you and Gregory did the deed."

"The deed? Is that what you're calling it?" I ask.

"You already know. But what's freaking me out about you, you still won't tell me who the other guy is. You have had sex with two guys in two weeks. Maddie, I'm shocked."

"Me too," I say when the reality of her statement hits home.

"What's gotten into you? Let me rephrase that: *Who's gotten into you* besides Gregory?"

"I'm still not saying."

"You've been turned out," Cassandra says, gathering my hair and brushing my edges.

"If that means I like it, then so be it. I think about it all the time now. It's scary."

"Wow, Maddie."

"I know I've got to stay focused on my music."

"You don't want to be like our friends Ursula and Mona. Ursula's seeing Harry and a guy who used to be our camp counselor, and Mona is seeing Ruger plus she's messing around with her esthetician."

"That's wild," I respond.

"They may be our friends, but they can't keep their legs closed."

She stops brushing my hair. I turn around to face her and grab a couple of popped kernels. She notices the marks on my neck.

"Omigod," she says. "He's a freaking mosquito. It takes a while for those marks to disappear."

"I'll just say I'm allergic to something."

"People know passion marks when they see them." She laughs. "What were you thinking?"

"I wasn't," I admit. A sparkle from my bracelet reflecting off the light catches her eye. "Wow. Pretty." She takes my hand and examines it up close. "He gave you this too?"

"Yes. It's his way of apologizing for not communicating with me while he was away."

"I noticed fresh roses downstairs," she says.

"Another apology gift," I answer.

"Wow." She pops a kernel in her mouth. "Who do you like better?" she asks.

"I like them both."

"If you had to choose one."

"I don't want to think about that, Cassandra."

"You've got to choose one."

"I guess I choose Gregory."

"Why?"

I didn't want to say a lot about JB without giving away clues. Cassandra is smart. She's like a detective.

"Gregory's better for me." Even as I say it, I am not truly convinced—yet.

"Omigod, Maddie, please tell me I'm wrong." She taps my hand, startling me a bit.

"What?"

"Is Jake the other guy?"

"Good night, Cassandra." I push her away.

"That means no, right?" She's backing away from me.

"Yes."

"Yes, as in the answer to my question, or yes, you are seeing him?" She stands in the doorway awaiting an answer.

"What do you think?"

"I've run out of clues. Guess I'll never know." She turns and walks to her room. I close the door and grab my journal.

July 3, 1987. 12:52 a.m.

All I wanted was rest. Now I'm restless. Finding myself in a situation I never imagined. I was too young to talk about it when Mother died, and Daddy never mentioned it. He just assumed that I'd be so consumed with music that sex would never cross my mind—at least not until I was twenty-one, maybe. Truth be told, it never crossed my mind either, then JB kissed me and carried me inside his pool house. The way he handled my body, and the way my body responded, I can only describe it as something so extraordinarily beautiful— like a feeling I only experience when I'm on stage. I want that feeling over and over. Now that JB isn't around, I'm getting that feeling from Gregory. I'm craving it. Almost like an addiction. I've got to get control over it before it gets control over me.

I can't manage to get out of bed with these marks covering me. Facing Aunt Mary, the eaglets, and the rest of the staff at school is something I'm not willing to do. Aunt Mary enters my room, and I pull up the covers.

"Good morning." She sits on the edge of my bed.

"Good morning."

"Did you get fresh roses too?" she asks.

"Yes."

"Your friend, he's quite generous, isn't he?"

"He is."

I'm nervous, and I pray Aunt Mary doesn't feel me shaking underneath the covers. I have them pulled all the way to my neck.

"You and your friend have plans for the Fourth?"

"I haven't given it much thought."

"Frenchy's flying in today, and we have plans to celebrate in Palm Springs. It's usually a family thing, but Caleb and Cassandra feel they've outgrown it. I'm extending an invitation to you, but I sense if they aren't going, you won't want to either."

"Thank you, but I'll stay here."

"I kind of figured that," she says. She studies me for a second, and I get the sense she feels something is going on with me.

"You and I don't get to chat that often," she says. "I'm still amazed at how you managed to graduate so early. You're top of the class. You have a full class load and a busy concert schedule."

"I guess I was driven" is my answer.

"Keep that drive, Maddie," she says to me. "Don't let anything or anyone take you off course." She kisses my forehead before leaving the room. Meanwhile, I'm still buried up to my neck with covers wondering if I'm strong and willing enough to keep that drive.

Hours later, Gregory calls.

"Thanks to you, I can't go anywhere," I answer.

"Why?"

"You left marks on my neck."

"Wow. I couldn't help it. You reminded me of a sweet and juicy summer peach."

"I'm staying in until they disappear."

"No. You're going to the closet, you're picking out something nice, and we're going out."

"Where, Gregory?"

"Wherever you want."

"But I don't want to go."

"Staying home's not an option," he says, "This weather's too perfect."

"I've got to practice my piece."

"Bring it with you."

"You won't take no for an answer."

"Do I ever? I'll be over in an hour," he says before hanging up.

I'm lying there listening to the dial tone with the receiver in hand. I glance at the clock. It reads 10:47, Aunt Mary and Cassandra are already at the center now. I put the phone on the cradle and open the door to the closet to search for the perfect outfit—one that will allow me to accent it with a scarf. I see a white short-sleeve linen shirtdress. I open the dresser where I keep the scarves, and among the pashmina and silks, I notice my mother's Hermes scarf. I'm going to need more material—the square isn't going to work for me—so the pashmina it is.

A little over an hour later, I'm downstairs looking in the mirror. My hair is curly and hanging past my shoulders. My lips are shiny with pink gloss. Aunt Teal passes through the room and notices me.

"Looks like you've just stepped out of the pages of a fashion magazine," she says with admiring eyes.

The scarf accents my outfit and conceals what I want concealed. I glance at Aunt Teal. It seems she never leaves the house. All she does daily is watch television and do house chores.

"You think my dress is too short?" I ask.

"That's the style these days." She finds a seat on the sofa.

"I'll take that as a yes," I answer before studying myself from all angles in the mirror.

"You've got a date?"

"I do. His name's Gregory."

"I met him the other day. He's the one who sent you all those nice roses and flowers?"

"That's him."

"He seems like a nice fellow. He dresses well. Smells good too."

I hear the doorbell. "That's probably him."

"I'll get that." Aunt Teal walks through the foyer and opens the front door.

I hear her and Gregory chat with small talk when he enters. He's dressed in a T-shirt with pastel linen pants, wearing slip-on loafers with no socks.

"I wish I had a camera so I could snap a picture of you two. You complement each other so well." Aunt Teal's eyes sparkle.

"Thank you," Gregory says. "Are you listening, Maddie? We

complement each other. Like peanut butter and jelly. Like the sun and moon. Like Kermit and Miss Piggy."

"Okay, okay, okay," I say, stopping him before he goes further.

"Aunt Teal, a pleasure, as always. I promise to have her home before she turns into a pumpkin." Gregory takes my hand, and we walk to the front door.

"Be careful and enjoy," Aunt Teal says.

Once inside the car, Gregory eyes my ensemble. "Wow. Beautiful as always."

I remove my scarf and show him the marks he left on each side of my neck. His eyes widen.

"Thank you, Gregory Washington III." I tie the scarf.

"I'll admit it, I got a little carried away."

"A little?"

"I'm sorry. Look, some theatrical makeup will do the trick."

"Hopefully I can find a match for my skin tone."

We glance at each other. He's checking out my skin tone. I'm looking at him, admiring the pastel colors against his roasted chestnut brown skin. He starts up the engine and we drive through the neighborhood and out onto the busy boulevard.

"You look nice," I say, breaking the seconds of silence.

"You find me irresistible?" he asks.

"Of course I do."

We come to a stop at a traffic light. He puts the car in neutral and leans over to give me one of those passionate kisses. It lasts until I hear horns blaring from the cars behind us.

Minutes later, Gregory valets the Ferrari, and we're in and out of shops on Rodeo Drive. We walk into a fashion showroom, and the saleslady knows him by name, greeting him with a warm smile. I notice a beautiful black dress on display.

"You like it?" Gregory asks.

"I love it," I say, admiring the design, but that's all I can do. I can't wear it. It's too small.

In the showroom is a display of high-end European fashions. On the walls are mounted black-and-white photos. Captured in the photos is a guy, very eccentric in appearance, surrounded with angular, swan-like models.

"That's Max V," Gregory says, pointing to the gentleman in the photo. "My mother won't attend an event unless she's wearing a Max V ensemble."

The saleslady smiles. "Max owes a lot of his success to your mother. The year she was nominated for a Tony, she wore a dress of his. Keep in mind, this was the early seventies, during a time when designers weren't dressing Black celebrities. Your mother stepped on the red carpet wearing his designer gown. It became one of his signatures the following spring, and thanks to her, Max became a household name."

"Wow. I never knew that," Gregory says.

Looking at the clothing I think, Max V's designs are for petite body frames like Gregory's mother. I'll have to starve myself if I want to fit into any ensemble of his.

"I understand it's your mother's birthday today," she says to Gregory before walking behind a display counter. She retrieves a black rectangular box decorated with a red bow on top. There is a card attached. She hands it to Gregory.

"Compliments of Max V himself who sends greetings all the way from Nice."

"Thank you," Gregory says.

"You didn't tell me it's your mother's birthday," I say to him.

He shrugs it off. "Ooops." Is his response.

We leave the showroom, and our next stop is a Japanese restaurant for sushi.

"What's the nicest thing you've ever done for your mom on her birthday?" I ask once we are seated.

"One year we flew to Seville. Mom loves flamenco, so we threw her the biggest birthday celebration with flamenco performers and food and sangria for days. She still talks about it."

"Is she home?" I ask.

"I don't know."

"You don't know anything, do you?"

Gregory smiles."I know your weak spot."

"Shut up." I give him a shove.

"I know you like Tiffany Blue."

"You remember?"

"Yes. I know you like sunsets. I know your birthday is Valentine's Day."

I smile. I remember telling him this a while ago.

"I know a lot more than you think," he says.

"What am I thinking now?" I ask.

"Duh. You're always thinking about me."

"Wrong. I want to get your mother a gift for her birthday."

"You really don't have to do that. She has everything—diamonds, clothing, yachts, cars, me."

"And now you're home, so she probably has a headache."

"That wasn't very nice." He pretends his feelings are hurt.

Our order is taken, and moments later, hot tea arrives. I take a sip, cooling it, careful not to swallow while it's still piping hot.

"So, what are you going to do when I leave for New York City in the fall?" I ask.

"I'm going back to Europe, and this time for good," he answers.

"Why?"

"In Europe, I don't worry about LAPD pulling me over to check my ID. Second, the women in Europe don't grab their purses and cross the street when they see me coming. Third, I don't get mistaken for the cleaning crew when I'm checking out my boat. The only issue I'll have is finding a good barber."

"I guess that'll be the end for us," I say.

He shrugs. "That's a strong possibility."

"You wouldn't fight for us?"

"I'll miss you," he says. "I'll miss you a lot."

"No college?" I ask.

"I'm not wasting my time, especially when there's a position waiting for me with my dad's company."

"I see."

"You don't really need school either."

"Stop."

"With your repertoire and talent, why be a student when you can be on the payroll teaching—I'm talking about a handsome salary with benefits?"

"It looks and sounds good when you hear 'Juilliard-trained concert pianist.'"

"Suit yourself."

I sip my tea quietly until a colorful platter of sushi is placed in front of us. An overwhelming feeling consumes me. The multiple colors in the platter can't distract from it.

Twenty

Hours later, we are inside Gregory's family's house. I hear laughter and voices, and I follow Gregory into the entertainment area where his mother, Celeste Nobelle, and several other women are gathered, sipping champagne.

"Getting started without me?" Gregory jokes as we enter, and he presents his mother with the gift from Max V. She's smiles, and I see where Gregory gets his nice white teeth from. She notices me and reaches out to give me a hug.

"Happy birthday," I say to her.

"Thank you." She has a warm and firm hug.

Gregory then greets each one of the women with a hug, calling them all Aunty. They weren't biological aunts, only friends of his mother's from the entertainment industry. I only recognize Aunty Carolyn. Gregory introduces me to the rest.

"She is phenomenal on the piano," his mother says to the other ladies.

"I recall," says one of the aunts.

I feel bare, not having a gift to give his mother, but then I have an idea.

"May I play something for your birthday?"

"Oh absolutely," she says. With a champagne flute in hand, she leads me to the piano.

I sit and open the cover and begin to play the birthday song for her. Soon, all the aunties begin to sing along, holding their champagne flutes, cheering and showering her with love.

"Thank you. Merci beaucoup," she says to everyone.

Gregory is holding a champagne flute about to bring it to his lips when one of the Aunties gently takes it away from him. "I was just smelling it," he says to her.

Soon, his mom and all the aunties talk of their experiences on Broadway and in Hollywood. She asks me if I know a certain song. Some songs I know, some I don't. The songs I know, I accompany her as she sings in dramatic fashion. I think the champagne is taking its effect on her. I begin to play Schumann's "Toccata in C major, Op.7" piece, forgetting how much digital work went into it, and when I finish, my hands and arms are sore. I spin around to hear applause.

"I love your interpretation," I hear.

"You have a flawless octave technique."

"We want more," they say.

I dig into my repertoire and Debussy's "Arabesque No. 1" comes to mind. I close my eyes, and my fingers take on a life of their own. With every sway and every note, I'm swept into the world Debussy wanted so much for me to interpret. I finish to another round of applause. I stand and bow.

"We love you." Celeste Nobelle blow kisses my way. One of the aunties, tall in stature, approaches me. She tells me her name is Colette and she's a writer for a leading magazine, and she would like to ask me questions. I never imagined my day would include a birthday celebration, and not just any celebration. Celeste Nobelle is a legend of the stage from Broadway to London to Paris, and she is so sweet and nice.

"You play beautifully, Maddie," Colette says. "May I ask you questions about your playing style?"

"Sure," I answer. I love to talk if it deals with classical music.

"Would you play other music?" she asks.

"No." I'm emphatic about that.

She asks if I recorded music. I tell her there are two live recordings where I performed piano concerti. The first was recorded when I was fourteen; the second around my sixteenth birthday.

"How old are you?" she asks.

"Seventeen," I tell her.

"You're special. I want to schedule an interview with you—soon."

"I love interviews."

She nods and joins the rest of the women. I look around searching for Gregory.

"May I use your restroom?" I ask Celeste Nobelle.

"Yes. It's down the hall on the left," she says.

I step out into the corridor, and I notice Gregory sitting at the foot of the stairs. He beckons me with a head tilt to follow him upstairs.

"How big is this house?"

"I don't know, fourteen thousand, maybe fifteen thousand square feet."

"If I'm not back, won't they start looking for me?" I ask.

"Please. In five minutes, they'll be wasted. They'll forget you were even here."

"Your aunty Colette wants to schedule an interview with me."

"Cool."

He opens a door. Upon entering, I notice a spacious living area to the right. Across the hallway to the left looks like a library. I see a giant Haitian flag encased in a frame mounted on the wall. We walk farther down the hall, and there's a game room with billiard tables, arcade consoles, and a fully stocked bar.

"Your parents okay with this?" I say, pointing to a display of various wines and spirits.

"I can't recall the last time my parents were up here. If it were a problem they would have mentioned it." he answers. He walks across the hall and opens the door to a bedroom. "For the dudes who get wasted." I imagine when he and the yacht crew are together, the ruckus they cause. I follow him down the hall to another room.

"Finally, where the magic happens," he says when we enter his bedroom. It's open and massive, and it's neat and clean. On the walls are framed movie posters like Purple Rain, Karate Kid, Back to the Future, and Beverly Hills Cop.

"Your room is nice," I say.

He stands there. "I wish you didn't have to go home."

I glance at my watch. It's 8:26 in the evening.

"Want to watch a movie?" he asks.

"Sure."

He has a library of VHS tapes.

"Have you seen The Karate Kid Part II?"

"No. I haven't seen the first one."

"What?" He looks shocked. "We've gotta watch it—now."

He searches until he finds the movie. He then puts the tape inside the VCR. We don't make it past the opening credits. Often, we stop and watch for a brief minute. The main actor is cute, and I want to follow the storyline, but Gregory and I are preoccupied. With each other.

Hours later Gregory and I walk downstairs and I hear Celeste Nobelle and all the aunties, laughing loud and singing out of tune. I don't want to leave. The baby grand in the entertainment room is calling my name, but I know if I start playing, I will lose track of time, and right now I have an hour left before I turn into a pumpkin.

***

Aunt Mary, Uncle Frenchy, and Aunt Teal left for Palm Springs about ten o'clock this morning. Thirty-minutes after that, Cassandra's boyfriend, Kyle arrives. I haven't seen him since he stopped volunteering at the youth center.

"Hi, stranger," I say, following him to Cassandra's room. She has outfits lying across the bed, trying to decide which one to wear.

"What are we doing today?" she asks.

"Gregory says we can hang out with him on the yacht," I say.

"You think he minds if I call Mona and Ursula and see if they want to hang out too," Cassandra says.

"I don't think he'll have a problem with it." I say.

"I'm bringing the booze," Kyle says.

"Where will you get that?" Cassandra asks.

"Outside in the trunk. I've got two twelve packs of Budweiser and a couple of bottles of vodka I stole from my parents' liquor stash."

"Oh, hell yeah." Cassandra's eyes are sparkling.

"And you can't have a celebration without red solo cups. I grabbed a pack of those too." Kyle does a little happy dance.

"What time does the party start?" Cassandra asks me.

"I'll give Gregory a call," I say.

They nod, and I get the feeling they want me to leave so they can be alone.

Afternoon comes, and I ride with Kyle and Cassandra to Marina del Rey. Parking at the marina is difficult, so we circle a couple of times before finding a spot to park. Fourth of July colors of red, white, and blue are visible everywhere—on banners, balloons, clothing. Docked boats are filled with revelers, celebrating, waving American flags.

We see Gregory descending the ladder from the upper deck when we arrive.

"I just got fuel, and it's enough to take us to Catalina and back," he says before giving me a kiss.

"Before we leave, what do you have to eat?" Cassandra asks.

"There you go. Is that all you think about?" Gregory asks.

"We're not starving out in the middle of the ocean."

"Relax. I've got it," Gregory says.

"What do you have?"

"Check in the galley."

"I bet you don't have barbecue," she says before going inside.

Kyle turns to Gregory. "I've got my boom box, drinks, and bags of ice inside a cooler in the trunk of the car."

"Do you need a hand?" Gregory asks.

"Yeah, man."

Gregory leans in to give me a kiss. "Can you hold it down until I get back?"

"I'll try."

I watch him and Kyle walk away until I can no longer see them. People passing smile and wish me a Happy Fourth. My mind wanders a lot. At that moment, I think of Dee, Rosie, and JB. A feeling of guilt comes over me. In the case of Dee, I feel guilty for not spending enough time with her like I promised myself I would. With Rosie, I sense she's giving me signals and instead of me helping her, I'm ignoring her. With JB, I feel like I'm not fighting enough to give the relationship a chance. Our situation is not ideal; he admits he has a problem controlling his urges, not to mention his situation with Basha, but now I'm with Gregory, and although it looks as if I've moved on, I still think about JB.

I think about him a lot.

Cassandra walks outside. "Okay, I'm shocked he really has good food. It's not barbecue, but it will work."

Ruger and Mona arrive, along with Ursula and a guy I recognize as the camp counselor. They all are tall and attractive. Heads turn with curiosity. Mona and Ursula both give me a hug.

"I've missed you. Why haven't you called?" Mona asks.

"And we're supposed to have lunch," Ursula adds.

"Lunch? Not without me." Mona frowns.

"Of course it wouldn't be without you," Ursula says.

"And not without me," Cassandra says, squeezing between us.

"Gregory's baaaack," Mona says.

"That's why we haven't heard from her," Ursula says to Mona.

Mona says with a smile, "You finally got your cherry popped."

I roll my eyes, embarrassed she's saying this in front of everyone.

"You're blushing. How cute." She's giggling.

"Have you been drinking?" Cassandra asks her.

"I had a little something on the way over." She blows into her hand and smells it.

Ruger scoffs and climbs the ladder to the upper deck.

"Where's Gregory?" Mona asks me.

"He and Kyle went to get something."

"Maddie, you and Cassandra remember Oliver? He used to be our camp counselor." Ursula takes his hand. Oliver extends his hand to us. I remember Oliver. All the girls were crushing on him. He's wearing a muscle shirt and beach shorts. He has smooth light-brown skin and wears his wavy hair cut low.

"Oliver, admit it, when we were in camp, weren't you checking us out too?" Mona asks.

Oliver stares at her for a minute. "Hell no." He frowns.

"When did you and Ursula hook up?" Cassandra asks.

He and Ursula glance at each other. "We were both extras on a set," he says. "I knew I recognized her, but I couldn't remember where."

"So, you asked her out?" Cassandra asks.

He smiles. "Something like that." He and Ursula exchange more glances. I sense a strong attraction between them. Mona reaches inside a leather knapsack and pulls out a small bottle of vodka and a bottle of Perrier.

"I'm ready to get this party started," she says.

"Can we at least wait for Kyle and Gregory?" Cassandra asks.

Ursula grabs Oliver's hand. "We have to use the restroom," she says, opening the cabin door. Oliver's smile is big when they enter.

"He's still hot," Cassandra says, fanning herself.

Mona and I agree. I wonder what happened with her and Harry the comedian. He was cute and fine too.

"I'm going inside to change," Mona says, "and I might sneak a peek at Oliver."

"Omigod, Mona. You're a mess," Cassandra says.

I find a seat. The winds bring a cool breeze, and I'm glad I have on my coverup. One, to keep me warm and two, so everyone won't notice the marks that are slowly fading. Last night when I was entertaining the aunties, I was praying my scarf wouldn't fall. How embarrassing it would have been if they saw the marks.

Cassandra and I find a spot on the lower deck to relax. We remove our coverups, put on sunscreen, and lie down and close our eyes. I think I drift off for a moment when I am awakened by laughter and talking coming from inside the cabin. I look, and Cassandra is now lying on her stomach. The sun gives her a rich honey tone. I get up and climb to the second deck where Gregory and Ruger are. Gregory looks up. I notice his eyes travel the length of my bikini.

"Oh my," he says, staring at my cleavage. He grabs the crotch of his swim trunks. "You've gotta go. You're making it hard to concentrate."

"What are you doing?" I ask.

"Our safety prechecks," Ruger answers.

"Go, Maddie. Please," Gregory says, sounding flustered.

"May I sit behind you and watch? Promise I'll be quiet."

I listen to him and Ruger chat. "Can you check the water levels in the bilge pump?" Gregory says to him.

"Sure. We checked the anchor. Checked gas bottle fittings and piping. Gas alarm works. Radio works. Checked the seacocks," Ruger rattles off.

Gregory is writing in a book. "Fuel is good. Winds'll be out of the northwest at thirty miles per hour," he says. Now he's pressing buttons.

"You're using autopilot?" Ruger asks.

"Yes. Unless you want to take the helm," Gregory says.

"Fuck, dude. Give it a go. I'm checking the bilge." Ruger glances at me, "I almost forgot you were there." He descends the stairs.

Gregory sits next to me and continues to write.

"What are you writing?" I ask.

"My logbook. Every destination I've traveled, every mile covered, the winds, engine checks, fuel, oil, observations, the crew." He hands it over for me to see. I flip through random pages and see entries from three years ago. I read the words, Amalfi Coast, Croatia, Cyprus.

"The last time we were here, I wanted you to take me sailing, but you had other things on your mind," I say to him.

He nods with a smoldering-eye gaze and a wink. Ruger returns.

"Bilge is clean and dry," he says.

Cassandra ascends the ladder. "There you are," she says to me.

"Cassandra, please do a huge favor for me," Gregory says to her. "Tell everyone to grab a drink and meet here."

"Do I have to?" She sits next to me.

"I said, please," he answers with that deadpan expression of his.

Cassandra scoffs. "You should've hired a crew," she says before descending the ladder.

Minutes later, everyone's gathered around holding red cups. Mona pops open a magnum of champagne and fills everyone's cup, even mine.

"Cups up," Gregory tells us. "Cheers to a good time. I don't have a name for the boat, but knowing some of you, I might come away with one before the day is over."

"Freak-Nasty," Kyle yells.

"Speaking of freaky, if you find yourself occupying one of my berths, all I ask is that you use a condom. I've got you covered. Regular Trojans for people like Kyle."

Everyone laughs.

Kyle sneers. "Why are you clowning me? You must wear them, too, if you have them."

"No. I sport the Magnum." Gregory adds, "XL."

"XL. Whatever," Cassandra says.

Everyone else talks and laughs among themselves.

"Happy Fourth of July, America. You kicked ass and took names and did a lot of foul shit, but you gave us a day to come together and get fucked up. Drink up," he says. I watch everyone turn up their cups and drink. Mona finishes her cup, then drinks what's left in the Magnum. After the last drop, she licks the top of the bottle.

Gregory puts down his cup, and he and Ruger prepare to detach the boat from the dock. I pour all my champagne into his cup before joining the rest on the lower deck. Cassandra and Kyle are cuddled together, Ursula and Oliver are in another corner cuddled together. I'm sitting on the opposite side when Mona sits next to me. She's holding her cup.

"Why aren't you drinking?"

"I don't drink."

She notices the marks on my neck. "Wow, Maddie."

"He was very happy to see me."

"Do tell," she says with a wicked smile.

"Mum's the word," I answer.

She sits quiet for a second and sips.

"Are you going to Sardinia with Gregory?"

"No," I answer. "Are you going with Ruger?"

"Yes. You should come too."

"I can't go. I've gotta stay and focus on my concert with L.A. Phil. I have rehearsals starting this month."

"Sounds exciting," she replies. The bikini she's wearing is high cut with a triangle bottom. "When I return from Sardinia, I'm flying to New York. I've signed on with a modeling and talent agency, and I've already got bookings plus an audition for a tv show."

"That's cool, Mona." I nod.

I feel the boat moving, and soon, we are sailing down a crowded waterway along with other ships, kayakers, and people on personal watercrafts.

"I'm going to the upper deck to join Gregory," I announce. "There's not much happening down here."

"I'm following you," Mona says. We leave Cassandra, Kyle, Ursula, and Oliver. On the upper deck, Gregory is at the helm. Ruger sits next to him, observing the scenery.

"It's crazy out here," Gregory says, paying close attention to the other boats.

We cruise past a large yacht packed with revelers. They wave and cheer. I imagine boats numbering in the hundreds. Some zoom past us as Gregory's yacht picks up speed. We sail over vast, rippling currents. The winds are blowing our hair. I'm getting a little chill. Gregory notices me shivering and motions for me to join him, and it becomes just what I pictured. Me standing at the helm and him close behind, guiding me while trying to keep me warm.

"I see you're handling this like a pro."

"Where are we going?"

"Wherever you want to go."

"Surprise me."

We sail along, and it smells of fish and sea salt. I look out and see dolphins move forward gracefully in and out of the water. I feel Gregory's lips brush against my ear.

"Whisper something sweet," I say to him.

"Ma chère Maddie, je ne veux jamais que tu partes."

I'm like hot candle wax in the palm of his hand. He continues, "Je veux nager nu avec toi."

"What did you say?"

"I said, I never want you to leave. Then I said, 'I want to swim naked with you.'"

I turn to look at him. "Not in this water. It's too cold."

He laughs and rubs my arms. "Think you can handle this while I go and grab a jacket?"

"You'll let me steer it?"

"It's on autopilot, so technically, it's navigating itself. Just make sure you don't crash into another boat."

"I can do this."

I glance at Mona and Ruger, and they're making out like they're the only people around. I turn my attention to steering and admiring the ocean view. I look out, and I think I see a whale's fluke descend into the blue. Minutes later, Gregory returns with a jacket and drapes it over my shoulders.

"Really? Right here?" he says to Mona and Ruger. I notice her top is off, and she's sitting on Ruger's lap.

"Okay. We're leaving," Mona says, not bothering to cover herself.

Ruger turns to Gregory. "It's gonna be a long evening."

"If I need you, I'll know where to find you," Gregory replies.

We are now alone, and he motions for me to sit on his lap. "You sure? I'm not too heavy?" I sit on his lap, wrapping my arms around him.

"Please. I can single-handedly bench press your weight."

"Now I know you're joking."

We hit patches of rough seas. Gregory holds me tight. He has one arm wrapped around me. With the free hand, he's pushing buttons, and the boat gradually decreases its speed, and soon, the yacht comes to a complete stop. Behind us, the mountains look like a hazy silhouette in the far distance. He presses another button.

"Time to anchor my baby."

"How deep is it?"

"According to the depth finder, about forty-feet."

I hear laughter and talking coming from the lower deck.

"You know how long I've been wanting to be with you?" he asks.

"How long?"

"From the moment I first saw you."

"And when was that?"

"Like five years ago."

"Five years. Wow."

"Yeah. You were always elusive—that rare pretty diamond sitting in a showcase with armed guards standing by to protect it. A guy wonders, How do I get a diamond like that? But you wouldn't give me the time of day, except one time. It was the last day at camp. You wore a yellow dress. We kissed—or was it more like a peck on the lips. Remember?"

"It was a good riddance peck," I say, laughing at the memory.

"I didn't want to wash my face for a long time after that."

I caress the outline of his face; he closes his eyes. I sense my fingertips are relaxing. I feel his one hand rest around my waist. His other hand starts on a journey, traveling peaks, valleys, and the tunnel. The minute I release and scream, a flock of sea birds scramble. Their wings flap as they fly in many directions. He holds me close until I finally come to my senses. I open my eyes, and he's smiling.

"Are you finished?" he asks, mimicking my expression.

"I am. You're so silly."

We join the rest of the crew on the lower deck. Oliver and Kyle are swimming in the ocean. A stereo boombox blasts a song. A woman sings of being a nasty girl. Ursula and Cassandra are dancing and singing with red cups in hand. Gregory jumps in the middle of them and starts shaking his behind and waving his hands. Cassandra pushes him away. The momentum from her push brings him to the edge of the boat.

He leans over and yells to Kyle and Oliver, "Look out for those sharks."

He dances his way to me, urging me to dance. Because he insists, I move my hips and my shoulders and soon my feet. Cassandra joins me. We dance until the song fades. Gregory climbs the ladder to the upper deck. Ursula, Cassandra, and I clap and bow as if we put on a performance.

"Have you swum the ocean?" Ursula asks me.

"No."

"Come on. You've got to."

"It's too cold."

"Come on, Cassandra. Let's do it."

"I need a shot of something that'll warm me up so I won't feel the initial shock."

"All I have is vodka," Ursula says.

"Give it to me straight up." Cassandra holds out her cup for Ursula to fill it.

Cassandra tosses it back and makes a face as it goes down. She and Ursula walk to the bow of the boat, and together they plunge into the ocean with a big splash. Once Cassandra comes up for air, I hear her scream before she swims out to Kyle and Oliver who are floating on their backs. Ursula is a few strokes behind her.

I go inside the cabin, and just as I'm about to walk into the galley, Mona is walking out. We collide.

"Omigod, Maddie, you startled me," she says, and she's totally nude.

"Why don't you put on a robe?" I say.

"I don't have one."

"Get a blanket or something."

"Alright. Alright. Alright. You sound like someone's mother." She closes the door. Meanwhile, I'm in the galley, and I see beef shish kebabs, fruit, pasta, chips, and more champagne. I try the kebabs, and the beef is mouthwatering. Gregory joins me, and we feed each other kebabs and fruit. He squeezes the juice from a strawberry onto my lips then licks it.

Late evening, we watch the sun set from the top deck. It's beautiful how it vanishes behind the horizon and all the colors—purples, blues and oranges—emerge and give the sky an ethereal glow.

We gather and couple-up on the lower deck. We talk about our days in camp and some of the people who attended and the counselors who worked with us. As we get closer to the marina, in the distance, fire-works as far as I can see light up the night sky, and for thirty minutes we watch in awe like children. When it's all done, the skies and air are filled with smoke. Gregory and Ruger guide the yacht to the dock and soon afterward, everyone leaves. Gregory and I are now alone, and since there's no one home to make sure I'm there for curfew, I spend the night.

Twenty-One

That Sunday, I get Cassandra to drive me to UCLA Medical Center to see Dee. In the gift-shop, I find a beautiful brown crochet doll with curly crochet locks. When I walk into her room, I stand frozen. The doll falls from my hands to the hospital floor. Cassandra bends to pick it up. I feared this day, seeing Dee without hair and life draining slowly from her face. She's now breathing with the help of oxygen. I sit next to her, taking her hand. She is awake but heavily medicated.

"Hello, Dee."

Cassandra finds a seat. I notice the keyboard lying underneath a row of stuffed animals. I get it, plug it in, and play Brahms' "Lullaby." As I play, I look into her eyes, and she's staring at the movement of my fingers on the keyboard. I play it soft so that it's soothing to her ears. Moments later, she's asleep, and all that's heard is the constant beep of the monitors, and in the distance, someone paging a nurse over the intercom. I put the keyboard aside to hold her hand. It's cold but not freezing. I rub her head gently, like I used to rub my mother's. I hum, "Jesus Loves Me."

Felicia, Dee's mother, enters. We embrace.

"How is she?"

"It's spread to her lungs."

I hold Felicia's hand. Felicia seems numb and tired.

"She will get through this," I say.

"Pray for her."

"I will. I played a little for her before she drifted off to sleep."

"Thank you for doing that. She was playing until a couple of days ago. This last round did a number on her."

I sit next to Dee's bed, and I rub her head and hold her hand.

Cassandra stands to join us, introducing herself to Felicia, and somewhere in their conversation, she tells her she's Mary Honoré's daughter.

"Your mother is heaven sent," Felicia tells her.

"I know," Cassandra responds.

I embrace Felicia. "Call Aunt Mary's number if you need me, and if I'm not there, I'll get the message."

Felicia appreciates our presence and embraces us again. She doesn't want to let me go.

"I don't want her to suffer like this," she cries. "I feel so helpless."

I rub her back, listening to her cries. Cassandra rubs her back. She's blinking back tears. At that moment, Aunt Mary arrives, a little tanned with her hair pulled into a bun. She embraces us. Her being in the room just makes it seem like everything will be better. She sits on the edge of the bed next to Dee.

"Dee, you're an eagle. You can rise above anything, baby-girl," Aunt Mary announces in a calm, soothing voice. She beckons for Felicia who walks over and takes her hand. "Don't give up on your child. She still has the will in her to beat this. You've got to believe it too." Felicia nods and wipes away her tears. Cassandra and I stay a little longer until Aunt Mary decides to leave.

Once inside the elevator, she studies us for a minute. "I see you two have had some fun in the sun," she says, referring to our tans.

Cassandra is red, I'm a shade darker than my usual tone.

"You, too, Mom. You, Frenchy, and Aunt Teal lay out by the pool?"

"We played golf," she answers. "What did you two do?"

Cassandra and I glance at each other, seeing who will be the first to answer. "We spent the day hanging out with our friends on Gregory Washington's boat," Cassandra answers.

"Maddie, is that your friend who brings you flowers?" Aunt Mary asks. The diamond from my bracelet catches her eye. She takes my hand to examine it.

"Another gift from Gregory Washington? He sure is generous. What have you been giving him in return?"

The elevator door opens, and people are there waiting for us to exit so they can enter. The brief interruption gives me a chance to gather my thoughts. I really don't want to talk about it, though I kind of get the feeling she already knows. We're walking, and I hear her say, "I'm waiting."

"Nothing. I gave him nothing," I answer.

"Ummm-hmmm," she responds, giving me a sideways glance.

Once outside, she turns to us. "I will see you ladies at home." She walks in the direction of her car.

"I guess we'll be going home," Cassandra says to me.

We're zipping through traffic, which is still a lot for a Sunday. We're driving down Crenshaw Boulevard on our way home when I see someone familiar.

"That looks like Rosie," I say to Cassandra.

"How do you know?"

"I recognize her bright red sketchbook."

Cassandra pulls the car over, and I roll down my window. "Rosie."

She looks over her shoulder. There's a scowl on her face that quickly vanishes once she recognizes me and Cassandra's car.

"Maddie," she yells and runs to the car and reaches inside to give me a hug.

"Where are you going?" I ask.

"Can I ride with you?" is her answer.

"Sure. Get in," Cassandra says.

I get out and adjust the seat for her to climb in. Once inside, she gives Cassandra a hug.

"Where are you going?" This time Cassandra asks.

"On my way to catch the bus to the skating rink."

"Which one?" Cassandra asks.

"Skateland."

"Where are your skates?" I ask.

"They have skates."

"I usually go to Hollywood to skate." Cassandra says.

"Can you take me to Skateland?"

"We're supposed to be going home," Cassandra says.

"Oh," Rosie says, sitting back in her seat. I think of her living situation, how she's staying with her boyfriend and his family.

"I'll ask my mom if we can go," Cassandra says.

When we get home and ask Aunt Mary, she looks at us and adamantly shakes her head.

"No way. That's in Compton."

"Mrs. Mary, it's really safe. They have security, and they have metal detectors so you can't get in if you're strapped. Nobody's thinking about gangbanging. Everybody skating and having fun." Rosie says.

"I take it you're a regular customer," Aunt Mary says.

"Yes. They know me," Rosie answers.

"Where's Caleb and JB? Maybe they can take us," Cassandra says.

At the mention of JB's name, my heart pounds.

"Even if they were here, I wouldn't want them in Compton." She takes a moment to study our reactions. We're all quiet. Rosie's staring at the floor, twisting her lips from side to side.

"Now I'd prefer the safer rink in Hollywood," she says. "You have my permission to go there. What are my rules again?"

"Be home before 11:30," Cassandra and I answer.

"I trust you to do the right thing," she says.

Later when Cassandra drives out of the neighborhood, she glances at Rosie.

"Tell me how to get to Skateland."

Rosie's face lights up. "For real? We're going?"

"I asked you how to get there, didn't I?"

"Okay. You don't have to say it like that." Rosie sucks her teeth. "It's at 135th and Central."

The area looks just as scary as the area around the youth center. My palms are sweating, and I'm feeling a little nauseous. My nerves are jittery. Cassandra parks the car, and I see a crowded parking lot with people and cars and guys dressed in red with red bandanas.

"My boyfriend deejays here," Rosie says.

We get to the entrance, and a sign reads, NO CAPS—NO COLORS. We pass through a metal detector just as Rosie mentioned earlier. Once inside, the music is loud, and on the floor people are rolling on their skates. I look to my left, and I notice a group of guys standing along the wall staring at me.

"Dayum you're fine," someone says.

I follow Cassandra and Rosie to a counter to retrieve skates. Rosie and I both wear a size seven. Cassandra wears a size nine. We put on our skates, and I admit it's been a long time since I've put on a pair of roller skates, but once I get the rhythm, I'm rolling along with the rest of the crowd. Rosie takes off ahead of me, skating backward, bending her knees, crossing over, and weaving around people. She looks like she's gliding. As Cassandra and I skate along, I'm watching people whiz past us. I smell cologne, perfume, and hair product. Guys wear Jheri curls, gold chains, and Laker jackets. The girls are wearing two-tone acid wash jeans, Laker jackets, gold triangle-shaped earrings dangle from their ears. I stop to watch a group of people dancing.

"What's the name of that dance?" I ask Cassandra.

"I think it's called the wop." She does the dance.

I just stand, observing. Sometimes I wish I knew all the popular songs and the dances that go with them. I always feel like I'm out of place. I notice Rosie talking to a guy standing behind the deejay booth.

A cute guy wearing a black-and-white Adidas tracksuit approaches me. "You want to dance?" he asks.

I don't want to be rude and say no. "Maybe after this song," I tell him.

He nods and walks away. I move to another location before the song ends. I have no intentions on dancing with anyone.

At the end of the night, I spot Rosie still talking to the guy behind the deejay booth.

Cassandra and I approach her.

"Dante, these are my friends, Maddie and Cassandra."

He nods. "What's-up?"

"Hi." Cassandra speaks. I just wave.

"Rosie, we have to go," Cassandra says to her.

"I'm going to leave with them. I may or may not be home," Rosie says to him.

"Cool," he answers.

Rosie follows us to the car and gets inside. The parking lot is jam-packed with people. It's like a party outside. Rosie leans over the seat.

"You guys think Mrs. Mary will be okay with me spending the night?" she asks.

"She shouldn't have a problem," Cassandra answers.

"Okay. You liked Skateland?"

"Yes," Cassandra answers.

"What about you, Maddie?"

"I liked it. Would I go back? Probably not," I answer.

"Come on, Maddie. You know you were looking at the guys with the finger waves," Cassandra says to me.

"No way." I laugh.

"Compton guys are soulful," Rosie says.

"I notice a lot of people wearing red," I say.

"That's because this is Blood territory," Rosie answers.

We finally make it out of the parking lot and onto the main street.

"Is that a gang?" I ask.

"Yes," Cassandra and Rosie both answer.

A car zooms past us followed by a trail of police cars, with lights flashing and sirens blaring. The speed from the cars causes debris to fly. Something cracks Cassandra's windshield, startling us.

"Omigod," Cassandra cries, driving slower.

"Are you okay?" I ask.

"Yes, but my freaking windshield."

I notice a crack.

"Hurry and get us home, please." I feel my heart racing.

It's 11:18 when we enter, and thank goodness the house is dark and everyone has gone to bed. Rosie follows us upstairs to our rooms.

"What are you going to say to Aunt Mary when you see her tomorrow?" I ask when she walks into my room and sits on the edge of the bed.

"I'll tell her it was late, and Cassandra didn't want to drop me off."

I see her reach inside her backpack and pull out a toothbrush and a change of clothing.

"May I use your toothpaste?" she asks.

"Sure," I say.

She walks to the bathroom suite where Cassandra stands at the mirror rubbing her face with facial cream.

"Where are you sleeping?" Cassandra asks.

"In Maddie's room at the foot of the bed," she declares.

"I hope you don't snore," I joke.

"I hope you don't kick me," she says. "I'll kick back."

"Don't worry. I'll sleep in one spot all night."

After we say goodnight, turn off the lights, and get comfortable under the sheets, Rosie says, "Maddie, I found a Langston Hughes poem."

"Good," I respond before yawning.

"I like the poem, 'Mother to Son.'"

"That's a really good one."

"One day, if I have a son, I'll say that to him."

I yawn again. "Good."

"Good-night," she says finally.

"Good-night, Rosie."

***

Aunt Mary left first. Cassandra, Rosie, and I leave shortly afterward in the car with the cracked windshield. When we arrive at the center, Aunt Mary is all smiles as she gathers the older group of children in a corner to talk to them about what to expect in the summer leadership camp. A donor is sponsoring all of them. Right now, she's still missing permission slips.

"Please, I'll need your parents' signatures. I wouldn't want you to miss out on this opportunity," she says.

She has me and Cassandra explain to them what to expect from the experience. I glance at Rosie. Earlier, she admitted to me she forged her mother's signature on the permission slip.

During a break, she and I sit at a table and snack on sliced apples while we talk.

"I never want to go back home," she says to me.

"You don't have another relative you can stay with?"

"They're just as crazy."

"How long do you think you can keep staying with your boyfriend and his family?" I ask.

"Until he makes enough money from deejaying and moves us out of the J's." I listen while she continues. "I know someone who can get me a job at Mickey D's too."

"A job? But you're not old enough."

"It doesn't matter. I have my ways of doing things."

"What does that mean?"

"I know people who can help me."

"I don't want you to get in trouble."

"I won't," she says.

She sketches a picture of herself sitting in a tree in the middle of the forest. I sit and watch her sketch from start to finish.

"What's the name of your drawing?" I ask.

"I don't know. Here." She gives it to me.

"It's beautiful," I say, taking it and studying the details.

"If I get a job, I won't be coming here anymore," she says.

"What about camp?"

"I'm still going, but after that, I'll probably be working."

"Rosie, you have to tell Mrs. Mary so she can help you."

"I don't want her to know. Please don't tell her. Please," she whispers.

I worry about her the rest of the afternoon.

Twenty-Two

Colette, the writer with the magazine, and I are sitting at the piano in the entertainment room of Gregory's family's home. She has a notepad and pen with notes jotted down. I've done interviews in the past, so I've got a feel for how these things go.

"I remember talking to Nina Simone, and she said, 'All I ever wanted to be was a concert pianist,'" Colette begins.

"Imagine if she had gotten that opportunity. If race and sex discrimination hadn't played a part," I answer.

"Had she performed just classical; she wouldn't be who she is."

"I respectfully disagree. She would've been the best to ever interpret a Bach piece."

"In America, few people of color perform classical music. Why do you think that is?"

"Culturally speaking, Black people are drawn more to music that's reflective of their experience. There are exceptions."

"What attracted you to classical music?"

"My mother. She was a classically trained pianist, and she saw something in me when she took me to see the great Martha Austin. I was on the edge of my seat the entire time. There was magic in her fingers, and I said, 'Mother, I want magic in my fingers just like her.'"

"I felt the same when I saw you play. I was told Schumann's toccatas were the hardest to master, but seeing you play made it look effortless, like there was magic in your fingers."

She had no clue how sore my hands and arms were.

"When was your first concert?"

"I was twelve. It was a piano solo with the Houston Symphony."

"Do you remember the piece?"

"I think it was a Mozart Sonata. I remember it had three movements, and everyone was blown away because I was young, and the piece was fifteen minutes long."

"Impressive. Do you remember how you prepared?"

"At the time, my mother was dying of cancer, so I practiced every day, sometimes three to four hours, as a form of therapy."

"The music was therapy for your mother?"

"I think so."

"Did she see your performances?"

"Yes," I answer, recalling the last performance before her death.

"Do you remember what you played?"

"Again, it was probably Mozart." I was ready to move on to something else. I think she could sense that as well.

"Please, play something," she says.

I wish I had a dollar each time someone told me that. I play Schumann, the piece that blew her away the other night.

When I finish, she stands and applauds. "The magic is in your fingertips," she says before sitting down. As we talk, I continue to play other pieces softly like background music.

"I know you won't agree with me, but I can see you playing other art forms."

I think of JB at that moment.

"Like Nina Simone and others with classical backgrounds, you can incorporate the influence and blend it with jazz."

I sigh, and I recall we talked about this once before.

"I play classical as an homage to my mother. She had dreams of performing in concert halls, and as much as she wanted to show her talent and gifts, the world was not ready."

I continue playing as Colette allows my statement to sink in.

"The world missed out," I say, "and she had all the credentials."

"She lives through you."

"I am her wildest dreams." I smile.

Colette's photographer snaps a candid shot of me sitting at the piano. He snaps another shot of me playing, zooming in on my hands moving along the keys. Then he wants me to pose with the piano in the background. He snaps one shot of me smiling directly into the camera. He just happens to capture a shot of me glancing at Gregory appearing in the doorway.

"How do you find time for romance when you're constantly performing?" Colette asks.

I shrug. "I take the summer off. I don't know."

"You give her flowers, you take her out on the boat, you watch the sun set," Gregory answers.

Colette smiles. "Thank you, Gregory, but I specifically asked Madeline."

"She would tell you the same," he says.

Colette turns to me. "Our magazine is national with just over a million subscribers. Our aim is sharing hidden gems to a broad audience of music and culture lovers."

"What do you think they'll say about the pretty Black girl who performs classical music?"

"When I'm finished, they'll love you, and they'll want more," Colette declares with a nod.

"Sounds like music to my ears," I reply.

"When will the magazine be on the newsstands?" Gregory asks.

"In four to six months, usually." Colette responds.

After they pack their cameras and leave, Gregory and I are alone.

"I was on the phone with my dad, and he wants me to fly to San Jose."

"Why?"

"I told him I wasn't going to Stanford in the fall, and when my regatta in Sardinia is over, I'm moving to France for good."

"What did he say?"

"He gave me an ultimatum: If I don't go to Stanford, I can forget about the regatta and any other regattas for that matter, so I told him, just let me skip college altogether and work for him. My father doesn't have a degree, yet he's a multi-millionaire. Now, I've agreed to go to a week of training in San Jose."

"What kind of training?"

"Like an apprenticeship with the company."

"What will you do?"

"It's too technical to describe."

"Okay."

"I want you with me." He takes my hand.

I sigh. Not again. "Spend a week with you in San Jose?"

"Maybe a couple of days."

"What do I tell my aunt?" I ask.

"You'll think of something," he responds.

"When are you leaving?" I ask.

"Tomorrow," he says.

"When are you coming back to L.A.?"

"Next month."

"Will you attend my performance?"

"I wouldn't miss it."

I sit at the piano; my mind has a million thoughts running through it. I realize I haven't practiced my Schumann piece in nearly a week. I want to go with Gregory, but I wish I didn't have to lie to Aunt Mary about it.

* * *

When I see Aunt Mary, I tell her about Mona's family's Malibu beach house. I go on and on about how beautiful and peaceful and how much being on the beach really helps with my creativity.

"Will Mona be there?" she asks.

"Yes. She and Ursula will be there."

"How long do you plan to stay?"

"Two days, three days-tops."

She studies me for a beat. "Where's Mr. Gregory Washington?"

"He's out of town, working for his dad."

"I see," she answers, still studying me.

I stand for what seems like eternity waiting on an answer from her.

"When was the last time you talked to your father?" she asks.

"It's been a while," I admit.

"Why?"

"Daddy's busy."

"He's never too busy for you."

"I'll call him."

"When?"

"Soon," I answer.

"Yes. You can go to Malibu."

Finally. I nod and smile. "Thank you."

Once inside my room, I pack a suitcase, and then I realize I need to tell Cassandra my plans.

"Hey, I'll need you to drop me off at Gregory's in the morning."

"Why?"

"He's going to San Jose for a week to train with his dad's company, and he's invited me to come along."

"Did you ask Mom?"

"Yes, but I told her I was hanging out with Mona and Ursula at Mona's family's beach house in Malibu."

"Okay."

"So if Aunt Mary asks you why aren't you hanging with us, just tell her you didn't want to."

"How long will you be gone?"

"A couple of days."

"That'll be fun," she says.

"I've got to finish packing," I say before returning to my room.

I didn't know exactly what was in store, so I packed a couple of durable evening dresses in case we go out. I sit on the floor for a moment and think, I never imagined a summer like this. It's like I'm watching myself outside my body, and I have no control over what happens. I could have told Gregory no like I did when he asked me to go to Europe. I didn't tell him no this time because I want to be close to him. I like the way he smells and how he feels. Crazy is a word I could use to describe my summer up to this point. Risky comes in a close second.

The following day, I'm sitting on a small airplane with Gregory and one of his dad's associates who looks at me rather strangely.

"Talk to my dad if you have a problem," Gregory says to him.

The associate doesn't say a word. During the flight, he sits at a table near the front of the plane reading. Meanwhile, Gregory and I are in the rear. As soon as the plane takes off and makes a sharp turn, I feel it dip. I unbuckle myself, get out of my seat, and sit on Gregory's lap, and it's where I remain.

"I feel your heart racing," he says.

"I've never flown in a small plane before."

"Are you scared?"

"A little."

I feel another dip, where my heart feels like it's coming out of my mouth, and I squeeze Gregory for dear life.

"I don't like small planes. I don't like small planes." I close my eyes and pray. Gregory finds it amusing, and I'm nearly in tears. When we land in San Jose and the door opens, I want to kiss the ground.

"I'm driving back," I tell Gregory. He can't stop laughing. He's in tears.

I follow him and the associate to a waiting cab. An airport concierge follows close behind with our luggage. We get inside, and the associate gives a manila folder to Gregory.

"The address is inside," he says. "Call if you have questions."

Gregory opens the folder and reads it. The driver stares at him from the rearview mirror. Gregory rattles off an address, and we drive off. Gregory continues to read over his packet of information while I sit staring out the window. On the radio, a song called "Tender Love" plays. I remember hearing it once while making out with JB. Looking at Gregory, I realize music doesn't move him—to him, it's just background noise.

I'm glad to see a piano in the house where the company has him staying.

234 ~ T. WENDY WILLIAMS

"Did you know this place had a piano?"

"No."

I sit and play my Schumann piece just to hear how it sounds on this piano.

"Hey, let's go check out the company car," Gregory says.

"Company car?" I'm still playing and listening for twang and flaws, but the sound is rich and clear.

I stop and follow Gregory downstairs to the garage area. A sports car just like the one JB drives is parked inside.

"Just a Porsche." Gregory looks disappointed.

"It's nice. I like it. Let's go for a ride," I say.

We change clothes and go zipping down winding two lane highways. I see cypress trees and giant California redwood trees. I smell eucalyptus, and I am in awe looking at nature's beauty. The drive takes us to jaw-dropping views of the coast. The Porsche navigates narrow, winding roads, and I can't imagine how roads are paved on the side of mountains in the first place. There are sections that have no guard rails, and the only thing preventing us from careening off the edge is Gregory's steady hand on the wheel. He finds a spot designated for sightseeing, and it's where we park and watch the sun reflect off the waves and huge ships sail in the distance.

"Can you tell me a little more about the training?"

"It involves shadowing the top VC's at my dad's firm."

"What's a VC?"

"A venture capitalist—someone who provides money to companies in exchange for a stake in that company."

"I see. Is this what you really want to do?" I ask.

"No, but I can't be a bum who sails all the freaking time—living off my parents' money."

My thoughts drift to Aunt Mary's youth center. "You think your dad's company can make a charitable donation to my aunt's youth center?"

"Yeah. They always do," he answers.

"I see you running your dad's company one day."

He nods, and I can tell he's imagining it too.

"Guess what?" he asks.

"What?" I answer.

"I've got a surprise for you."

"Can you give me a hint?" I ask.

"I know you'll like it."

"You know for sure?"

"Like they say in the 'hood, fa sho."

"What do you know about the 'hood, Mr. Beverly Hills?"

"My dad's from Oakland. Does that count?" he asks.

"No." I think about the roller rink. "I went to the 'hood the other night."

"What?" He looks concerned.

"I went to a roller rink with Cassandra and this girl from Aunt Mary's youth center."

"Why?"

"It was a new experience. I wouldn't go back, though."

"If you see me in the 'hood, I'm just passing through on my way to pick you up or drop you off."

"You can't drop a teeny, tiny hint about the surprise?" I ask.

"No." He drives and glances at me and winks.

And he was right. I totally liked my surprise. On a marquee I see, An Evening with Concert Pianist Martha Austin, San Francisco Symphony and Chopin.

My face is aching from grinning so wide. We have lower-level box seats, and the minute the curtain is up, I'm drawn into the magic of Martha Austin the way I was when I was a little girl and my mother took me to see her for the first time. I'm so into her that I forget about Gregory sitting there. The sound of the orchestra behind her performance swells and ebbs like waves on a beach. I close my eyes and picture myself playing "Waltz in D-flat major, Op. 64" along with her. I look and see Gregory's trying his best to stay awake, and before Martha Austin strikes the last note, Gregory is asleep. The cheers and applause from the audience wakes him.

"Wow. Some performance," he says clapping.

236 - T. WENDY WILLIAMS

"It was, if only you were awake to see it."

He's slightly embarrassed. "How about we go and meet her and tell her how great she was?"

"I don't want to. I don't want to know what she's like off stage."

"Why? You think she's mean?" he asks.

"Just want to admire her from afar."

"You think she knows about you?"

"I'm sure she's heard of me, though, in her mind, I'm probably not on her level."

"You won't know unless you talk to her."

"Another time. Maybe when she's at one of my concerts." I wink.

Afterward, we eat dinner, and during the ride back from San Francisco, Martha Austin's performance gives me inspiration, and a melody pops in my head. When we finally arrive at the house, I grab my composition notebook and get a sheet of staff paper and sit before the piano. I hear the notes, and I'm jotting them down, looking up often to see if what I'm hearing is right.

I play and write and erase and ponder and write some more and play. It's now one a.m. I must get this song out of my heart and into my head. I like it in C major, pure and innocent and naive.

"Hey, you." Gregory's standing in the doorway. "You want to make music, or you want to make love?"

"Give me a minute."

"Your minute's up by the time I'm in the room."

"I need one last measure in place."

I play until I get the sound I'm satisfied with. The lyrics I formulated keep getting jumbled with Gregory's words, *you want to make music, or you want to make love?* Up until three weeks ago, I was satisfied with just the music. Music was the blueprint of my soul, the blood flowing through my veins. I bled Chopin's etudes, ate Mozart's sonatas for lunch. Then something happened: rhythms flowing from a different beat blend with my crisp, sharp tones, and the music changed. Music needs daily passion, the kind that holds you with a grip so firm it's suffocating. You start with every intention of making love, but the music stokes you and licks you like the sweet juices of a black cherry and leaves you desiring more.

I rise from the piano with my piece in hand and place it in a binder along with my other compositions. I see this in two movements, and I call it, "Lost in the Music."

***

Gregory is up and out of the door by eight o'clock. I spend the morning practicing and writing new music before I walk outside on the balcony for fresh air. The house is nestled high in the hills, and below us are other homes that look like white palaces sitting in an emerald paradise. I grab my sheet music and begin to create, drawing inspiration from my summer experience. I go from being a virgin to having been with two guys in a span of two weeks. I sit, and I compare them. One is tan, tall, rough, rugged. He sweats, he sings, he loves music. The other is dark-brown, average height, refined, clean-cut, and wealthy. I shouldn't be falling for anyone right now. I imagine once I get to Juilliard and see a guy I like, I'll eventually fall for him, too. As much as I convince myself to not get too much involved, there's a part of me that's saying, *It's too late, Maddie.* I've allowed JB to kiss me in areas I promised to hold sacred until my wedding night. That day on the yacht with Gregory, I became a summer peach in the palm of his hands. I promise, I am not a slut. I'm just behaving like one right now.

Gregory arrives late that evening, and we go out to dinner.

"How did it go?" I ask.

"I watched two VCs, and their day involved a lot of talking over the phone."

"Think you'd like that?"

"No, but again, I'm no bum. I've got to know the ropes."

"Did you see your dad?"

"Briefly, then he was off to another meeting with a start-up company."

"Your father lives in San Jose during the week, and he flies home to L.A. on the weekends?"

"Yep," Gregory answers.

"How does your mother feel about that?"

"She's busy too. She's back and forth from L.A. to New York to Paris."

"I don't know if I could stand the distance."

"It's worked for them all these years."

"You know that'll be us in the fall. Me, living in New York City, and you're God knows where."

"We'll be like my parents. We'll make it work," he says.

"What if it doesn't? What if I meet someone new? What if you meet someone?"

He stares at me for a minute, pondering my questions before slicing a piece off his bone-in rib-eye and eating it. Chewing in silence. My guess there's a million-and-one thoughts running through his mind.

"I don't want to imagine what it's like without you," he says.

I notice during the drive, he holds my hand, squeezing it tight. Later that night, he doesn't want to let go. He's intense—from his kisses to his touch. It feels as if we're in a marathon going from the bedroom to the bathroom and from the bathroom to the balcony and from the balcony to the stairs. This is the first time I've seen and felt him sweat, whatever pent-up frustration he has he lets it out, and when I come to my senses, I look around, adjusting my eyes to the darkness and realize we're in the room with the piano.

"Maddie."

"Yes."

"Promise you'll always be my girl."

Next, I hear him snoring, and all I think about is getting on the next flight back to L.A.

Twenty-Three

For nearly four hours, I meet with the conductor and other members of the orchestra. This is the ice breaker where I get a feel for them and vice versa. We are a month out. Only two rehearsals and a possible third on the morning of the performance.

"Fresh face and phenomenal. I look forward to this," the conductor says to me once our meeting adjourns. Walking the hall on the way outside, I think, *you've done quite well for yourself, Maddie.*

A cab sits idle across the street. Times like these, I wish I had a vehicle. "Can you take me to Crenshaw?" I ask once I approach. He glares at me like I speak a foreign language. I don't see another cab in sight, so desperate, I reach inside my pochette and pull out a twenty-dollar bill. With that, he unlocks the door.

Once we take off, he asks, "What's a pretty girl like you doing in those parts?"

"Those parts?" I repeat.

I know what he's getting at. I just want to hear what he has to say.

"Have you been watching the news? There's a lot of bad elements over there."

"I don't watch television, and furthermore, I teach piano to the best and brightest in those parts."

"Be careful is all I'm saying."

"Thanks for the tip." I say with an eye roll.

***

He drops me off at the youth center, and I receive a big welcome from the staff.

"Wow" is all I can say. The children who recognize me rush up to give me love, knocking me over. I'm lying on the floor covered with children. Their laughter and their scents fill me up. Cassandra pulls them off one by one and gives me a hand.

"You're interrupting my class," she says.

"I can help you, if you'd like," I say to her.

The older group is away at camp, so I'm free to help.

"Who wants to go outside?" Cassandra asks.

Everyone raises their hand. It's good to see Blaze and Damon and the others I recognize. My heart sinks when I think of Dee. Outside, they roam, just as helicopter choppers circle overhead. Cassandra and I sit on a couple of benches.

"I still can't believe you're here volunteering," I say to Cassandra.

"I'd much rather be around the younger group."

"Fun, aren't they?"

"Bad as hell, especially those two." She points to Damon and Blaze.

"I hope the older kids like camp and get as much from it as we did."

"How did your meeting go?" Cassandra asks.

"It went well."

I hear the squeal of brakes followed by rounds of gunshots.

"Get down," Cassandra shouts.

We both fall to the pavement. I hear the children crying and screaming, and I'm praying none of them are hit. The only thing separating and surrounding the children's play area from the busy thoroughfare is a fifteen-foot chain-link fence. In the distance, I hear a car speeding off and exhaust flaring in its wake.

I lie there. My heart's pouring out of my ears. I look up and notice Damon ten feet from me covered in blood and crying out in agonizing pain. Some of the children are crawling on their hands and knees to me and Cassandra to shield them. I see blood trickling down little Jessica's arm. The door opens, and Aunt Mary runs out followed by Leah, Vanessa, and the rest of the staff. She grabs Cassandra and me.

We both reach out to hug her. She's examining us, her eyes dancing and searching us for wounds.

"Damon needs you," I scream.

She rushes to his side. A puddle of blood forms around him. Blaze is nearby screaming. One of the staffers puts her arms around him to console him.

"He's gonna die," he yells.

She takes him inside. Cassandra and I gather some of the children and bring them inside.

They are crying; we all are crying.

Cassandra yells, "It's my fault. I shouldn't have taken them outside." The center, once a place of refuge, is now filled with anguish and sorrow. Minutes later, the paramedics arrive, and I've seen this before, where Aunt Mary is once again rushing an eaglet to the hospital, only this time, there's blood everywhere.

***

Uncle Frenchy bursts through the doors of the waiting area with Caleb and JB. He sees Aunt Mary and grabs her, hugging her. He's broad, six-five, and imposing. She looks so tiny and fragile engulfed in his arms. I hear sobs escaping her.

"I'm here," he says, holding and kissing her. Cassandra and Caleb join them, holding and consoling their mother.

I'm crying, and a number of things are the cause; seeing JB stirs a whole other set of emotions. He's staring at me with dreamy, expressive eyes. I try not to stare back. Uncle Frenchy reaches out to embrace me. Caleb does the same. I'm trying so hard not to look at JB, but he can't resist grabbing my hand and hugging me too.

"You okay?" he whispers.

I don't want the hug to linger, so I pull away. I wipe away tears.

"I'm okay," I lie. I'm not.

I had hoped I could get away with not seeing him—his touch, his scent, his energy. I watch JB embrace Aunt Mary. I can't be alone with him. Not even for a minute. *I'm Gregory's girl.*

"How is the boy?" Uncle Frenchy asks.

"The bullet shattered his tibia, and the doctors are working to re-construct it," Aunt Mary answers.

"You think they'll be able to save that leg?" Uncle Frenchy asks.

Aunt Mary sighs. "I want to be optimistic, Frenchy."

"What did the police tell you?"

"They found two dead on the sidewalk adjacent to the playground. Suspected gang members."

Uncle Frenchy rubs the fine hair on his head. "Damn, Mary. You can't go back."

"But Frenchy—"

He stops her mid-sentence. "Find another way to reach these children."

Aunt Mary still has Damon's blood on her clothing. Her eyes are weary and tired. I see her nodding and agreeing with him.

"When I end my trips, the last thing I need is to get a phone call like this. I'm grateful to God you all—" He gets choked up.

I swear it's the first time I've seen him this way. I get emotional all over again. While hugging Uncle Frenchy, I steal a glance at JB. His face is flushed, and he stands with hands buried in his pockets. He's fighting back tears.

"I should've stayed inside," Cassandra says again.

"Don't do this to yourself." Aunt Mary wraps her arms around Cassandra.

She and Caleb and Uncle Frenchy surround Cassandra, embracing and soothing her. Aunt Mary takes her face in her hands.

"Baby, you did nothing wrong," she says. I see Cassandra's shoulders relax when Mary takes her in her arms and rubs her hair. They find a seat as Aunt Mary continues to console her.

Damon's mother arrives. Aunt Mary stops consoling Cassandra so she can console her. Uncle Frenchy isn't leaving her. Cassandra and I still have traces of blood on our clothes. Leah, Aunt Mary's assistant, gives us a ride home. Caleb and JB branch off into another direction. I am somewhat relieved until we arrive home and I see JB's car parked at the edge of the curb. That's when my palms sweat and the hairs on my arm stand erect.

I walk down the hall to Caleb's room. His door is opened slightly. I hear him talking. I tap it gently.

"Hold on," he says, and seconds later, he appears. I notice the telephone receiver in his hand. "Everything okay?"

"Yes. I was just checking." I'm looking over his shoulder. "I saw JB's car."

"I thought he left," Caleb says.

"He's not in there with you?"

"No."

"Where is he?"

"Wherever he is, he knows how to let himself out. Are you good?" he asks.

I get the sense that I'm interrupting something.

"Yes."

He nods before closing the door.

I hear water pouring from the shower head in the bathroom suite Cassandra and I share. I walk to the window to glance out, and I see JB below lounging by the pool. It's almost like he knows I'm watching and he's waiting on me. I'm hesitant about joining him. I imagine how Caleb would react if he sees us or Cassandra—once she gets out of the shower. Before I realize it, I walk outside to the pool. JB's gaze follows me from the time I step out until I sit on the spot next to him.

"I missed you," he says.

"How was your basketball trip?"

"Long. I'm glad to be back."

I was glad to see him, too, but I didn't want my feelings to show.

"What did you do while I was away?" he asks.

"Remember when you asked if I had a boyfriend?"

"Vaguely" is his response.

"Well, I told you I did, and your response was, 'Is he around?'"

He sits quietly as I explain.

"I was with my boyfriend this entire time."

"Where is he now?"

"Sardinia," I say. My bracelet catches his eye.

"How long?" JB asks.

"I don't know. Two. Three weeks."

We both sit quietly, searching for words.

"How are you and Basha?" I ask.

"She's still doing her, and I'm still doing me."

"What does that mean?"

"We talk, we hang out, we go through the motions."

"I see."

"You thought I was blowing smoke when I said you blew my mind."

"Those are just words."

"Not to me."

"You'll say anything."

"I'm tired of talking. When I came off the road, I hung out with Benny, and he let me use some studio time. I played a little something on the piano and recorded it."

"That's nice. My boyfriend isn't really into music. It kind of makes me sad," I confess.

He sits quietly, taking in what I just said.

"I want you to listen to this song." He stands and extends his hand to me. I am reluctant. "I promise I won't bite." He says.

I take his hand and let him lead me outside to his car. He opens the door for me to get in. I watch him stroll around the front to the driver's side. He opens it and sits inside. He turns the ignition and puts a tape inside the player. The tape hisses, and then I hear melodies, a string of notes blended together. The key is C minor. I listen quietly, paying close attention to his styling and the way he structures his music, then I hear him singing next to me:

Your eyes are all I see

Yearning with passion as you look at me

I hold and squeeze your body tight

And love you throughout the night.

Your kisses melt me like ice

I'm a big, bad wolf
But you've made me think twice
All night with you
All day too
There's nothing else I'd rather do
Than spend my time being with you

The entire time he's singing and the music is playing, he's looking at me, and I'm trying not to look back. Instead, I look at the bracelet sitting pretty on my wrist. I'm fingering the diamonds and telling myself, *When the song ends, get out of the car.* There is an interlude where he displays piano prowess. I love it. I really do.

"Did you just think of those lyrics?" I ask.

He responds with:

All night with you
All day too
There's nothing else I'd rather do
Than spend my time being with you

On the player, he's dazzling the piano keys. Sitting next to me, he's miming the piano parts. His fingers are traveling up my arm. This sensation is overwhelming.

"All I need," he says. "Your love is all I need. Your kisses. Your mind. Your body."

"You have Basha," I tell him.

"But I want you," he says. "Today just put all that in perspective. Life is short; tomorrow isn't promised."

"Bye," I say, opening the door.

He grabs my hand with a firm grip, pulling me back.

"How much do you want to be with this guy?" he asks.

"I don't want to talk about it."

"Just tell me, and I'll leave you alone."

"I don't know. I mean—He's nice. He really likes me."

JB releases his grip. "Does he kiss you all over the way I do?"

"I have to go." As I get out, he grabs my hand again and pulls me back inside. "JB, please don't do this."

"What am I doing?"

"You know what you're doing."

"Tell me, huh? Does he sing sweet melodies to you?"

"Yes. Yes." I'm getting angry for entertaining him this length of time.

"Liar," he says.

"He kisses me. He takes me sailing on his yacht. He remembers my birthday. He knows my favorite color."

"A yacht, wow." He sits back. "You sure it's his? People in L.A. be frontin'."

"Oh, it's definitely his," I respond.

"You say he doesn't listen to music, and it makes you sad."

He reaches in the backseat and retrieves that worn-out composition notebook with the fold across the cover. "Every word in this book is about you. From the way you walk, talk. The way your eyes sparkle when you hear a song you like. How you look at me when I'm kissing you. I'm lost in your world, and I can't seem to find my way out. I'll say this: I don't want to find my way out."

I listen while he continues.

"Right now, I just want to kiss you. All over. Promise I won't miss a spot."

He takes my hand and presses it against his lips, kissing it. "You want it too." He says.

I'm nervous, hoping no one sees us. It's crazy what's happening to me right now. He does tricks with his tongue, never taking his eyes off me. I get flashbacks, and I remember how I responded and how much I enjoyed it.

Get out of the car, Maddie.

"I can't be with you. Bye, JB." I open his car door, and this time he doesn't reach for me. Walking to the front door, I hear his engine start, and he drives off just as I enter the house.

I finally take my shower. Sitting on the edge of the tub, I let the hot water massage me. I watch the white lather from my soap turn pink from the traces of dried blood still left on me from the shooting. I let it roll down my body and down the drain. I take mental note this is how I feel: emotionally drained.

Twenty-Four

The shooting is on the news. When they show footage, yellow crime scene tape is tied to the fence and blood is on the sidewalk. I turn off the television, and it hits me all again. The image I see when I close my eyes is Damon screaming, lying in a pool of blood and the blood trickling down Jessica's arm, and I hear screaming and crying, and I see the children crawling on their hands and knees like little soldiers in battle. I hear that cabby's words ringing in my ears, '*There's a lot of bad elements in those parts,*' and I wish for a moment he was wrong. These are not all bad parts. It's just now and then, you get a cluster of bad people. Cassandra walks in and sits on the bed next to me.

"I looked for you earlier. What happened?"

"I went out for a walk to clear my head."

"You went alone?"

"No. JB was nice enough to walk with me."

"Kyle's on his way over."

"How is he?"

"He's freaking out."

I take her hands.

"I've never prayed so hard for anyone in my life, Maddie. I hope they're able to save Damon's leg."

"Just keep praying."

"I feel really bad for Mom. I don't know how she'll recover from this."

"Aunt Mary's strong. It's going to be tough, but she'll be okay."

"Heard from Gregory?" she asks.

"No."

"Are you able to call him?"

"Not if he's somewhere on a boat."

"He didn't leave you a number?"

"He knows this number if he wants to talk."

"I'm going downstairs. Kyle should be here any minute."

I'm left in the room, and it's where I remain the rest of the day. A dreadful feeling creeps in, and when that happens, I don't want to move. I don't want to eat. I barely want to get out of bed to use the restroom. I just want to lay there, and if I sleep through the night, I'm good.

**

I awake to Aunt Mary's voice. Its raspy nasal distinction is soothing and calm. She rubs my hair.

"How is Damon?" I ask.

"They tried all they could to reconstruct his tibia. They may amputate it."

Now I feel guilty. Maybe if I had used that time to teach the children new piano techniques, they would have been inside, safe.

"The police report described a turf war between rival gangs."

"What are you going to do?"

An exasperated chuckle escapes her. "Part of me wants to continue. The other part is saying, 'Mary, you've done enough.'"

"You'll find a way. You always do."

"I don't want to hear, 'I told you so.' A lot of people in my circle doubted I'd last this long."

"Just focus on all the good you've done, Aunty. The good outweighs everything."

I notice her eyes blurring with tears. "Thank you. I needed to hear that." She gives me a warm, tight hug.

Aunt Mary called my father, and one of his parishioners, who happens to be a pilot, flew him private overnight with our assistant, Gilda, and a couple of staffers from the church. When I see him and we embrace, I turn into a twelve-year-old girl. I'm clinging to him, sobbing. His embrace is strong and warm. Everyone gives us a moment; I hear a few sniffles. He looks at me. I see his eyes brimming with happy tears, then he brings me back in for another hug before he gathers everyone into the living room, and with joined hands, he leads us in a prayer. He prays for restoration of our minds, our bodies, and our spirits.

"Heal this land, Father. You alone can do it," he says.

When he's done praying, there's a collective sigh of relief in the room—like out of all the prayers, God really heard this one. Daddy and I find our own private space to sit and talk.

"I'll stay as long as you need me to," he says.

"I'm happy you're here. I miss talking to you," I say.

"We can talk now. I'm all yours," he says.

At that moment, I want to pour out my heart and tell him every-thing—I mean everything. Instead, we talk about music.

Later, he and the staff meet up with Aunt Mary at the hospital, and we visit Damon. I feel better when I see he's in good spirits. Daddy prays for him and spends time speaking words of encouragement. Watching Daddy minister, I'm reminded just how handsome and soft spoken he is in these settings. We leave there and travel across town to UCLA to see Dee. Felicia is present when we arrive. When she's introduced to Daddy, she's trying to hold it together. Gilda sits and chats with her as Daddy goes over to pray for Dee. She's wearing a beautiful red bandana, but she's heavily medicated. Once Daddy finishes his prayer, I sit and hold her hand. While everyone else is talking and chatting with Daddy in the waiting area, I get alone time with Dee. I play something I wrote, and I see her blinking, and for a second, her eyes open, like they're trying to adjust to the lights, and for a split second, she looks at me before her eyes move downward to the keyboard.

"Would you like me to stop?"

Her eyes close, and my guess is yes. I stop and unplug the keyboard, putting it back in its place. I study her wall of get well wishes. JB left an autographed picture of himself in uniform, and it reads: *To Dee: My number one fan.* For reasons beyond my control, I get misty-eyed.

Daddy, Gilda, and the staff are staying at a hotel near the Beverly

Center. That night, the six of us dine in the hotel's restaurant. It isn't too crowded.

"Mary, Mary, Mary," Daddy says. "Your sister told me crazy stories, and I didn't believe her."

"She had one extraordinary imagination," Aunt Mary replies.

"Tall tales she doth tell." Daddy chuckles as he reflects.

"I see a lot of Evelyn in Maddie. They both possess that colorful creative right brain," Aunt Mary says.

"Her brain never had an off switch," Daddy says.

"No, it didn't," Gilda adds.

"She talked me off the ledge and told me, 'Mary, the Mays are about mission. Spreading education, culture, and wisdom to the forgotten ones. And who does society forget? Poor Black children.'"

Daddy nods and listens.

"You had no idea how taxing it became sitting in that office listening to rich kids with everything complaining about nothing. So what? Daddy took away the keys to the Porsche. You should thank him; the roads are a lot safer." Aunt Mary vents.

I take two more bites of salad before pushing away the plate.

"So Evelyn did some research on nonprofits with services that cater to those in at-risk communities. Together, we drew up a proposal for the center and came up with a mission statement: *To boldly go where eagles soar.* We used an eagle—the symbolic nature of it—to inspire and influence, and when it spread its wings how majestic and free and beautiful it is."

The room is quiet as she goes on to explain. "So Evelyn says, 'Mary, you've got to serve the people. I'll help you anyway I can,' and together we found a place, and we got donations and pledges and support, and the eagles started coming. One of my first eaglets is now pre-med at 'SC. He said I inspired him to go to medical school. Here is a kid from the roughest part of town, well on his way to greatness because of the center and all the wonderful programs and services we provided for those babies."

Gilda nods before taking a sip of her drink.

"Frenchy says I need to find another way to reach the children. He says I can't go back." Aunt Mary puts down her fork and rests her chin against her hands. I see her mind working.

"Mary, it's not what you want to hear, but he's right," Daddy says.

Aunt Mary shakes her head. "I can't let the streets win, Eugene."

"Choose your battles wisely—something Evelyn always had to re-mind me." Daddy says.

Aunt Mary sighs.

"To everything there is a season, Mary," Daddy begins. "There's a verse that says there's a time to get and a time to lose; a time to keep and a time to cast away."

"I'll need a prayer before the night ends." Aunt Mary forks her dish.

"We can pray now," Daddy says. "I feel this tugging at you, and the Bible says where there's two or three gathered in my name, I will be there in the midst of them. Only God can give you the answers you seek. You've got to trust Him. You must find a quiet place so you can hear Him. When He speaks, you'll know His words, and they'll be plain as the day."

I feel that, and I am moved to tears. Gilda puts her arms around me and brings me in close. Her scent is familiar, identical to my mother's. While Daddy's praying and everyone's head is bowed, I sense something happening behind the scenes between him and Gilda. They seem closer now than ever since Mother's passing. After dinner, it's just Daddy and me. In his hotel room, we find two comfortable plush chairs with ottomans. Daddy is drowsy. His body clock is two hours ahead, but he will stay up all night if it has anything to do with me.

"May I ask you a very personal question?" I begin.

He's rubbing his eyes. "Oh, dear."

"Are you and Gilda together?"

He's nodding off with his hand resting on his cheek. "I want to talk to you about that. Gilda and I have always maintained a professional relationship. However, out of respect for you and your mother, any other relationship we're aiming to forge, we wouldn't proceed without your blessing."

I'm listening, and I think about it. "Does she make you happy?"

"Maddie, there are no words." His eyes are closed, and his hand is still resting on his cheek. "And I know from the outside, it doesn't look appealing. Gilda and your mother were college roommates, sorority sisters. She was the maid-of-honor at our wedding. When your mother was alive, I always looked at Gilda as a true friend, a gem, someone who enjoyed taking care of business and made life easy for me and Evelyn."

"And when Mother died?"

"I still looked at her in that way. I loved her professionalism and decorum. She and Evelyn were cut from the same cloth. I saw how she took care of you and handled your business. I observe how you are with her; you seem okay with her."

"I love her, Daddy, and yes, you have my blessing."

He clasped his hands together in a prayer pose. "I've prayed for this day," he says. I give him a great big hug and a kiss on the forehead.

"Be happy. You deserve it," I say.

The next morning when I see Gilda, we sit and talk.

"You make us both happy," I say to her, and tears are flowing.

I see Daddy, and he reaches out and embraces us both. We are all wiping away tears. I know Mom is somewhere smiling. She approves. I feel this in my heart.

***

Dad and Gilda leave, and the following day is the first practice with the orchestra. I'm learning all the cues from the conductor. Hearing that massive sound in the rehearsal hall with the orchestra, I feel the adrenaline I get from an actual performance. I play my solo, remembering every note, granting its proper phrasing. Closing my eyes, I imagine Schumann playing this for his wife, Clara—her listening to it for the first time and him wanting it to sound perfect to her ears. Afterward, I sit and chat with some of the musicians. We've spent years honing our craft, attending the best conservatories. We go to sleep and wake up with our instruments. We eat and breathe music. I lose track of time. It was close to nine P.M., and this time, I called Aunt Mary to pick me up.

It's strange yet comforting to have Aunt Mary around the house now. Between breaks of practicing, I'm listening to her phone conversations, and I'm hearing that May fervor, always wanting to save the world. Neighbors I haven't met this entire time are now stopping by. Aunt Teal brings out the silver tray tea service for those like Mona's mother and Ursula's mother and a couple of city officials and a congresswoman who represents the district.

I'm not in the room but sitting at the bar.

"I need a new location, preferably one not in a danger zone but close enough for children from those areas to attend," I hear Aunt Mary saying.

"Good luck with that" is Mona's mother's response.

"Mary, just set up practice in Beverly Hills like you did before." That sounds like Ursula's mother.

"There's a new generation who could use your counseling."

"This eighties generation is a different animal," Aunt Mary replies.

"Mary, I love your optimism and your determination, but in reality, the area is dangerous, and we can't take any more chances."

"I'm not going back to Beverly Hills," Aunt Mary says, sounding exasperated.

"Try Burbank or West Hollywood for Christ's sake—anywhere but the Crenshaw district."

"Hey, you're being harsh on my district." That sounds like the congresswoman.

"Soror, what is your district doing about the gangs and the crack cocaine? Seems it's gotten worse under your watch."

"I'm doing my part. The challenge lies in getting the community to do theirs."

"Upping police presence won't help. Studies show they make matters worse," Aunt Mary states.

Cassandra joins me at the bar. "Eavesdropping, I see."

"Just listening."

"I talked to Mrs. Palermo," Cassandra begins. "Mona's in Sardinia."

"She mentioned she was going when we were on Gregory's yacht," I respond.

"Did you get a look at Mrs. Palermo and Mrs. Woods?"

"Not a good one."

"Too much plastic surgery. Mrs. Palermo is losing her nose. It's starting to look like a face with holes."

"Awful," I say. I'm so tempted to walk into the room just to see for myself.

Upon Aunt Mary's recommendation, Cassandra and I go for a walk. The doctor in her says walking is good for your heart and mind, and it also helps get some Vitamin D from the sun. I need the exercise. I still haven't found a dress for my performance. I really liked the dress I saw in Max V's showroom in Beverly Hills. I'd have to starve myself to wear it. Our walk takes us to a park with never-ending steps. I walk them but get winded after a short time.

"Neither of us is in shape," Cassandra barks.

We keep walking, and I notice a couple with a dog like Smitty descending. The sun is behind them, so it's difficult to make out until we're close up. It's JB wearing no shirt, glistening with sweat, and behind him a girl—tall, slender, brown complected with attractive features.

"JB. Basha." Cassandra rattles off her name with familiarity.

So that's Basha.

"Hi," she responds.

She's movie-star gorgeous. I notice her sweating and glistening too. Her breasts are prominent for such a small frame. Her shorts are so short. I don't want to look, but I imagine you can see her butt cheeks.

JB doesn't make eye contact with me. Instead, he busies himself with Smitty who can't resist my familiar scent. He happily wags his tail. I bend to pet him, and he licks my face.

"He really likes you," Basha says.

"Enough, boy," JB says. Kneeling, he steals a quick glance.

"Well, wish us luck," Cassandra says.

"You haven't broken a sweat. You're still good," JB says. He nods goodbye and continues downstairs, conversing with Basha.

"I guess they're back on again," Cassandra says once they're far off.

"She's his girlfriend?" I ask. I already know the answer.

"She's the visible one. He's just stringing her along, and she's foolish because JB does whatever with whomever he pleases."

"What?" Instantly my heart feels weighty.

"JB, Caleb, their friend Hollywood with the video camera, Jake—all are just nasty."

"Define nasty." This I want to hear.

"They have girls everywhere. I hear them joke about girls waiting in the hotel lobby after the game and sneaking upstairs to their rooms. JB's hitting her from the back, and Caleb's hitting the same girl from the front."

"Hitting?" I get a visual.

My stomach churns, and I take the stairs slower than I did initially. I had an idea this was what JB meant when he told me he was a *big, bad wolf*, but to hear it from Cassandra just makes it all seem worse. I hate myself for getting caught up in his looks and his charm and how we both love the piano.

"It doesn't help that they're in a fraternity. They call JB Wolf. Caleb's name is Floyd, and Paul, they call him Hollywood. If you watched Revenge of the Nerds, you'd get an idea of what I'm talking about."

I feel a lump in my throat, remembering JB saying how much I inspire him to write music. His tablet is full of lyrics he says are all about me. I can't help feeling it's all just words used to flatter me to get what he wants. I see how quickly he can move on and not so much as speak to me. Right now, I'm hurt. I know I told him I was moving on, but I sometimes say things I really don't mean.

***

It's late Wednesday night, two weeks to the day since I spoke to Gregory. When I answer the phone, I hear:

"Bonjour, mon amour. Tu me manques."

"How are you? And what did you just say to me?"

"I said hello, sweetheart. I miss you," he answers.

"I miss you too. When are you coming back to L.A.?"

"I'll be there in time for your performance, I promise I won't miss it."

"I had the first practice. My solo tore the roof off the place. When I finished, they gave me a standing ovation."

"I swear I hear you playing that in my sleep."

"No way."

"It's stuck in my brain."

"Tell me about Sardinia. How did it go?"

"We came in second."

"I wish I could've been there. Next summer you and I are sailing together. Are you with me?" I ask.

"I'm way ahead of you," he says.

"I wish I could kiss you."

"In two weeks, you can kiss me how you want for as long as you want."

I go to sleep smiling.

***

Aunt Mary, Cassandra, and I walk into Damon's hospital-room. The doctors aren't able to save his leg-so they amputate it. We find him sitting up in bed.

"How's my warrior?" Aunt Mary says. "Talk to me. What are you thinking?"

He thinks about it. "When I get my leg, I'm going to learn how to run faster."

"Hey, that's great. You'll do it. You know why?" Aunt Mary asks

"Why?"

"Because you believe you can," she answers.

"I'm an eagle," he declares with a smile.

"You are, and what do eagles do?" Aunt Mary asks.

"They soar."

"That's right," Aunt Mary says.

Cassandra and I observe their interaction. When we leave, I notice her holding on to her mother and Aunt Mary putting her arm around her.

"Talk to me," she says.

"I'm not okay," Cassandra says. "All I hear are gunshots, and all I see is blood."

Aunt Mary holds her, and they embrace. Cassandra melts like a small child in her mother's arms.

I'm standing watching them thinking, *I've got to stay strong. I can get lost in my music, and I'll be alright.*

"Why is he doing better than me, and he's the one who got shot?" she asks her mother. Then she answers her own question. "I'll tell you why: You were so busy teaching other children how to soar, you never taught me."

Aunt Mary walks her until they find a women's restroom where the three of us go inside. Aunt Mary locks the door. Her arms are open like, *Now let it all out.*

"I wish you spent as much time with me as you did with them." Cassandra cries.

"I regret every second I spent away from you. I thought if I gave you the luxuries of life, that was enough. Now I know it's never enough. When we went to Acapulco, I promised you I would be more present and whatever you needed—whether it be a listening ear or a trip around the moon, anything to make you whole and feel loved—I'm willing."

"I just need it all to go away." She grabs her head.

Aunt Mary and I embrace and hold her. I feel her tears rolling down my arms, and I hurt for Cassandra.

"Just make it go away," she repeats.

Aunt Mary schedules appointments for me and Cassandra to meet with psychiatrists. I tell myself I don't need it. I can find a way to be stronger. Music is that way. I have two hundred compositions. I express myself through music. I go and waste an hour on the couch. Cassandra wants the pain to go away. They prescribe medicine, and all she does is sleep. I practice all day, and when I stop to check on her, she's asleep. The next day, I'm practicing, and when I stop to take a break, she's asleep. She's breathing, but she's asleep.

Uncle Frenchy, loud and boisterous as he can be at times, checks in on her.

"Chère!" He's pinching her ear and pulling her toes, but she doesn't flinch. "Cassandra!" He shakes her.

"Whuuut, Frenchy?" The grogginess from the medication has her sounding like a zombie.

"Mary!" When he yells, his voice carries so the entire house hears it.

Aunt Mary appears moments later. "Frenchy, let her rest."

"What is she taking?" he asks.

"Sertraline. It's used to treat post-traumatic stress disorder."

"Don't give her anymore." He removes a strand of hair from Cassandra's face. She looks like a baby doll with her rosy cheeks, freckles, and lush lashes.

A long, tired, exasperated sigh escapes Aunt Mary. Before I fall asleep, I say a prayer for her. God, please give her strength and guidance. I say a prayer for Cassandra, that she finds peace and a way to cope without medication. I say a prayer of healing for Dee, and a prayer for Damon. It's been awhile, but I have no doubt God hears me.

I go and see Dee. She's lost weight, and her eyes are sunken. I never imagined her cancer getting this aggressive. I'm not giving up hope. I hold her hand and listen to the machines. I plug in the keyboard and play a song for her, one of my songs. When I'm finished, I hold her hand and pray to God to take away the suffering.

Twenty-Five

I check on Cassandra. She's sitting in bed with a dazed expression. It pains me to see her this way.

"Hey," I say, taking her hand and holding it. "How are you?"

She manages to smile. "Much better. I haven't slept like this in ages. Where have you been?"

"I went to see Dee."

"How is she?"

"She's lost weight."

Cassandra is quiet. I bury my face in my hands. "I have to stay hopeful," I say.

"That's all you can do," Cassandra answers.

I think about my performance coming up in two weeks, and I still haven't found a dress.

"Once you're better, you think you can help me find a dress for my performance?" I ask.

"Sure," she answers.

"Let's go outside and sit by the pool." I insist.

"Yeah. Why not?" She replies before slowly moving out of the bed.

Outside, Caleb is swimming, moving above and below the surface with ease like a pro. It must be four o'clock in the afternoon. The summer sun is beaming on us. Thank goodness there's a breeze. Cassandra and I sit. She looks at me.

"You seem well. What's your secret?"

I take some time to gather my thoughts. I don't want to sound preachy, and I don't want to sound condescending. Classical music is my therapy. It works for me. It may not be that simple for her.

"I don't know" is the best I can do.

"I really wish there was such a thing as a magic wand," she says. "If I had one, I'd make all bad things disappear—crack, AIDS, gangs, guns."

Caleb gets out and dries himself with a towel.

"Are you good, cuzzo?" he asks.

I think about it before I answer. "Yes" is my reply, knowing inside, I'm about to die.

After Caleb finishes drying himself, he grabs Cassandra. He has her in a headlock, taking his knuckles and playfully kneading her forehead aggravating her, obviously.

"Stop," she yells, sounding like she did when they were much younger.

"I love you," he says. "You have to say it back."

"No," she says, trying her best to maneuver out of his grasp.

"I'm not letting you go until you say it."

"Alright," she yells.

"Alright what?" he teases.

"I love you," she says through clenched teeth.

"I can't hear you. What?" He leans over with her head still locked in the crook of his arm.

"I said I love you. Let me go. For real, I'm about to vomit," she screams.

He releases her, ruffling her hair. She swings at him. He ducks out of her reach. They play fight, pretending to box.

"Too slow," he teases.

She tries to jab. He catches it.

"Come on, lightning."

"Don't you have practice?" she asks, trying to sneak in a lick.

"I want to hang with you and cuzzo?"

Cassandra pretends to vomit.

"How often do we hang out, we three?" he asks.

"It's been a while," I recall, thinking back to last month in Malibu.

"We're so busy, we forget about each other."

"I actually like it when you're busy—at least you're not bothering me." Cassandra playfully rolls her eyes.

Caleb, with his quick athletic reflexes, grabs her and puts her in another headlock. "You don't mean it," he teases.

"I promise I'm coming out swinging," she says with her head trapped in the crook of his arm.

"In your dreams," he says, chuckling.

"Maddie, help." She feigns exasperation.

"I'm loving the brother-sister bond," I admit.

"Take him to New York with you, please."

He releases her and shakes his head, chuckling at his little sister's antics before entering the house.

"I need to find a dress for my concert, and the one I want is a size five."

"I'll call Ursula, and we can browse a few boutiques."

"Can you call her now?"

"Sure. Why not?"

A short time later, Cassandra and I meet Ursula, and we drive to five boutiques looking for a dress until I finally find one, and it fits snugly on me. I stand looking at my reflection in a three-way mirror. Cassandra and Ursula are on each side of me. Cassandra gives a thumbs up. Ursula not so much. She rubs the front of my dress near the stomach area.

"What?" I ask.

"I'm only saying this because you're my friend, but you could lose a few pounds," she says.

I turn to the side and notice a stomach pooch in the front and my big, rounded butt in the back. I sigh.

"Mona and I diet. You only drink water and you only eat salad, and you stop eating after six P.M."

"You think it will help me?" I ask.

"Yes. It helps. If I know I have an audition, I'll do it, and I lose the weight just like that." She snaps.

"Think I should get it or wait?"

"Get the dress. It'll motivate you to lose weight."

I turn around to see how it fits from behind. I see a roll of back fat—not much but enough to where it's noticeable.

"What do you think, Cassandra?" I ask.

"I like it. I like the illusion top with the dramatic back and how it flares at the knees,"

I turn to look at it again. I'm going to buy it, and after I do, I'm going on a strict diet.

***

That night, Uncle Frenchy treats us all to dinner at a Japanese restaurant. I've never laughed so much at airline stories, and he has plenty to entertain us with.

"Frenchy, you should write a book," Cassandra suggests.

"What would I title it?"

"The World of Flying, According to Frenchy," Cassandra says.

"Too lame," Caleb responds.

"How about Frenchy's Passport Adventures?" Caleb gives me the thumbs down. "You have something better?" I ask.

"I do, as a matter of fact," he begins. "Captain Frenchy. Let that alone be the title."

All he gets is blank stares from us.

"I thought you had something profound," Cassandra answers.

"Keep the title simple yet catchy," Caleb explains.

Aunt Mary sits quietly, sipping sake. There's a calm resolve about her. She looks so refreshed and revived wearing makeup, and her hair is down and straightened. There are moments when I see her beaming at us, and my guess is she's grateful.

"I've got one, Frenchy: Stranger than Fiction." Cassandra goes on. "What do you think?"

"You're onto something." He winks. "Mary, you'll help me write it?"

"I've got my own book to write." she answers.

"Excuse me?"Uncle Frenchy says.

"I've got free time now to reflect. Who knows, maybe I'll dust off my passport and start traveling with you."

"You don't know how long I've been waiting to hear you say that," he says.

Cassandra rolls her eyes.

Uncle Frenchy, sandwiched between the two, reaches around and puts his arms around them both. He kisses Cassandra's forehead, aggravating her in the same manner Caleb did earlier.

"We should find time and make it a point to do this once a month," Aunt Mary suggests.

"Give me a date in advance, and I'll fly from New York," I say.

"Wow" is Caleb's response. "I'm down the street, and I don't know if I can."

"Yes, you will," Aunt Mary says. Her affirmative tone has him convinced he needs to be present.

Uncle Frenchy holds everyone's attention, so they hardly notice that I'm not eating. I sip genmaicha, a green tea, and eat miso soup.

"Caleb, have you made your decision about whether you want to go pro?" Uncle Frenchy asks.

"I have, and I've decided I'm staying in school."

"Wonderful," Aunt Mary replies.

"Okay. Okay." Uncle Frenchy nods. "Is that official?"

Caleb nods.

"Are you happy with your decision?" Aunt Mary asks.

"I want to see how the year plays out with the team and work on getting that NCAA championship title," he answers.

In an instant, I think of JB and whether he'll stay in college or decide to go pro. I think of JB the rest of the night. It's strange and unexplainable that I just have to write music about it and I don't fall asleep until early the very next day.

August 12, 1987, 10:12 a.m.

The weeks seem to fly, but I keep busy practicing the piece. Other times, I'm exercising and walking with Cassandra and Aunt Mary. We went to Runyon Canyon and hiked only halfway, stopping to sit at a bench in an area Aunt Mary calls Inspirational Point. How apropos because while sitting there next to her and Cassandra, a melody flows through my mind. It has all the

characteristics of a symphony. I see it written in four parts. The first move-
ment in a sonata, the second movement slow, the third movement in "simple
triple" meter, and the fourth returning to a sonata. I'll name this symphony,
"Cassandra's Heart." I opened my backpack, pulled out my sheets and my
pencil and wrote down my notes. Marking and erasing, listening for what I
think is it and jotting it down.

Dee is still fighting. Will she win? A battle like this is tough, even for the
strongest. I give her a kiss on the forehead, and I hold her hands close to my
heart, and I kiss them. While waiting for the down elevator, another elevator
opens, and JB emerges alone, holding a bouquet of balloons. We speak, then I
step on the elevator, press the key for the lobby, and watch it close. In my heart,
I feel this is the last glimpse of him before I leave in two weeks. Who knows?

* * *

I'm playing my piece when the door opens, and Aunt Mary appears smiling. "My apologies for interrupting, but there's someone here I think you'd like to see."

Upon hearing that, my heart rate soars, and I feel the hairs on my arms stand. I open the door, and not far from me is Gregory dressed in a cool white polo top with khaki cargo shorts and leather boat shoes. I notice he has a fresh haircut and gone are the whiskers and the glasses. He and I are both trying to remain calm in front of company.

"I'm leaving." she says with a wink. "Good seeing you, Gregory."

"Likewise," he says, watching her walk out of the room.

We're alone now, and we embrace, and I inhale his scent. I want so badly to take him to my room.

"I'm upset with you," he says.

"About?"

"Why didn't you mention the shooting?"

His question blindsides me. *Bad news does travel fast.*

"I don't know. I mean, you were five thousand miles away—on a boat."

"Doesn't matter. I have to be here to protect you."

"I'm fine now."

He looks at me like, Really?

"Stop," I say, looking away.

"I don't know what I'd do if anything happened to you."

"That sounds like a song. I need to write it down." I run to the piano where I keep my notes. "Say it again. What you just said to me. You remember?"

Gregory finds a seat and relaxes with his legs crossed. "If I lost you, life would have no meaning...I don't remember."

"Never mind." I walk over and sit on his lap.

"Now I remember. I don't know what I'd do if anything happened to you."

"What happened to the glasses?"

"I'm trying a new look. I'm wearing contacts. Do you like them?"

I nod and spend the next minutes cuddling, and kissing. I've convinced myself that he's the one I want around. I must get over that he's not into music and he tolerates it because of me. In two weeks, I'll be in New York City, and he'll be somewhere between San Jose and Nice. We'll write each other letters; he may surprise me one weekend and fly to New York. Depending on where he is, I may spend the holiday break with him. Who knows?

I need to send a list with the names of ten guests to the people at L.A. Phil for comp tickets. Let's see, number one on the list: Gregory. My dad, Gilda, Aunt Mary, Uncle Frenchy, Cassandra, Caleb, Aunt Teal, Rosie, and the tenth spot is up for grabs. Maybe I'll leave it empty.

Gilda, me and Daddy's assistant, calls and tells me Juilliard wants me to call and confirm my attendance for a weeklong orientation. It's a reminder my summer break is slowly ending, but not without a grand finale.

Twenty-Six

My alarm sounds off around 7:15. I snooze it twice before I get up to wash my face and brush my teeth. I look at my reflection in the mirror and smile at the wave of confidence enfolding me. I grab my robe and head downstairs to join the family for breakfast. I'm usually the last one out of bed. I say greetings to everyone and take a seat next to Caleb. Aunt Teal is scrambling eggs.

"Scrambled soft, please and thank you," I tell her.

Aunt Mary sips from her flute of sparkling orange juice. "I was watching a commercial for Time magazine, and there's a song playing. It's called, "Turn! Turn! Turn!" by the Byrds...I'm sitting and watching the beautiful images, and I think, Where did I hear those words? Eugene, your daddy," she says to me. "I heard those words from him."

"What about the song makes you think of Eugene?" Uncle Frenchy asks.

"When he was here, we talked about the center, and he agreed with you that my season is up, and it's time for me to leave, whether I want to or not."

"Mom, maybe you can do something in conjunction with the university," Caleb says.

"Caleb, I love the way you think, baby."

"You'll have loads of free time to write a proposal," he says.

I notice her eyes sparkling. Caleb sets her creative wheels into motion.

"I can help too," Cassandra adds. I get her needing to feel a sense of purpose.

"Yes. We're a team, honey. I'll bounce ideas, and I need your honest opinion."

"I'll give you nothing but honesty, Mom." Cassandra says.

Aunt Teal places a plate of hot scrambled eggs in front of me. The smell, along with my nerves, makes me nauseous. I take one bite out of a slice of toast, and I'm done.

"Someone has a big night tonight," Uncle Frenchy says.

"How are you feeling?" Aunt Mary asks.

"I'm so nervous I can't eat."

"Come on. You've done this before," Uncle Frenchy says.

"It's the feeling that everything's come down to this moment."

"I can't wait," Cassandra says. "I'm excited for you, cousin."

"Aunt Teal, I'm sorry. My nerves," I say, giving her my plate of barely eaten eggs and toast to take away.

My final practice with the orchestra is at 10 a.m., and Gregory is coming by to pick me up for that. I go upstairs and turn on the shower, feeling my stomach twist into a knot. I know the piece, so why can't I control this feeling? It's agonizing. When I step in the shower, the heat nearly takes my breath away, and I can't hold it any longer. I step out of the shower, fall to my knees and bless the toilet, and when I'm done, I lay my head on the seat, and that's where I spend the next twenty minutes until I will myself into the shower.

***

I gather myself together when Gregory arrives in the Corniche convertible. He takes my dress, which I have inside a garment bag and places it in the trunk of his car. He opens the door for me, and I sit inside. I'm so over this day. I want it to be done so my nerves can return to normal. Once he's inside, he gives me a gift.

"You shouldn't have," I say.

"I know," he says, starting the engine. "Open it."

I hold it next to my ear and shake it before I open it and find inside a magazine with a male model gracing the cover. I see where he's already added a bookmark to the page featuring my article. "Wow," is all I can say.

"I managed to get a proof from Aunty Colette. The issue won't hit the newsstands until November." Gregory says.

"Classical American Beauty" the headline reads.

"Teen sensation is the next big thing in the world of classical music." I read aloud. The prominent photo for the article features the candid shot of me sitting at the piano the moment Gregory catches my eye when he stood in the doorway. My eyes are radiant in the black-and-white photo. I'm glad they chose that particular photo for the lead. It captures an honest emotion.

"She talks about your mother's influence on you. I didn't know your mom was your teacher."

Flipping through the pages, there's another photo of me sitting before the piano. I think it was taken when I played the Schumann piece. You can see my intense expression. I flip to another page to see Gregory and me, and the caption underneath reads: A summer break makes time for romance with boyfriend Gregory Washington III. In the photo, we are sitting on the staircase at his parents' home, and my head is resting on his shoulder. I'm looking into the camera, and he's looking at me. The black-and-white photos summon a romantic mood.

"Yes. She opened my eyes to the world I know and love."

Colette goes on to write about my playing style, describing it as magical in the vein of concert pianist Martha Austin and spellbinding like legendary concert pianist Andre Watts.

As I'm reading I hear, "You've got to be kidding me. You've got to be fucking kidding me."

I look up. "What?" I look around, and in the side mirror, I see flashing lights from a police car, and Gregory slows down and pulls over.

"Maddie, could you open the glove compartment and get my registration, please?"

For a moment, the article made me forget about the nausea, but searching for his registration and seeing the cop car triggers it again. Gregory turns on the hazards, and when the cop approaches the car,

Gregory presses the down button of the power window. He looks straight ahead; the expression in his eyes is cold.

"Sir, I'm going to need you to step out of the car," the officer says, his hand resting on the gun in his holster.

"First, would you like to know who I am and who the car is registered to?" Gregory asks.

"Are you trying to do my job, sir?"

"Just do what he says, Gregory," I say as I look at the clock and see I have thirty minutes until the start of the rehearsal.

When Gregory gets out, the cop has him put his hands on the hood and pats him down.

"Can you tell me what this is about?" Gregory asks.

"You fit the description of a suspect—black male driving a stolen Corniche convertible."

"I've got one word for you, officer: registration. We could have avoided all this."

Gregory opens the door and sits inside. I hand over the registration for him to give to the officer.

"Don't need it. You best be on your way."

Then he proceeds to shoo off the car with a dismissive wave.

"Gregory's so angry his nostrils are flaring.

"Let's go," I say, taking his hand.

We pull off, and for the entire drive, he is seething, cursing at other drivers, honking at pedestrians to hurry and cross. I'm so relieved when we arrive at the rehearsal hall.

"What's the game plan?" he asks.

"Rehearsal ends at two. I'm staying at the Ritz downtown. The room's registered under my full name. The show starts at 7:30."

He nods as I rattle off my list.

"I'll see you later, and no peeking at the dress."

"Why would I do that?" he says with a wink. "I know what's underneath."

"See. That's all you think about." We kiss, and I make a dash inside.

For the next four hours, I play my part, the orchestra plays its part, and we both take our cues from the conductor. Playing allows me to forget about my nausea, but during one of the breaks, I run to a restroom far from everyone and lock the door and pray to the porcelain god. I pray to the real God too: Just let me make it through the performance. God, I worked all summer to get to this point.

***

I meet up with Daddy and Gilda for afternoon tea. I still have three hours until my performance. Gilda presents me with a box. Its design looks familiar, and when I open it, I recognize the diamond earrings inside. They were my mother's.

"I love you," I say before embracing her.

"Oh, I love you too. I packed them because I knew you'd want a piece of Evelyn on stage with you."

"I do," I say, admiring their sparkle and brilliance. "Thank you, Gilda. You are a godsend. I sense Mother knew she didn't have to worry. As long as I had you and Daddy, I'd be left in good hands."

"You hold me in such high regard," she says.

"Wedding plans soon?" I ask.

Glancing at each other, they smile.

"What?" My eyes dart back and forth, gauging them closely.

"We're old school. Let's enjoy our courtship. It's a remarkable thing," Daddy says.

"If you decide to marry, would you like a big or small wedding?"

"I want a small wedding," Gilda answers. She looks at Daddy. "What about you?"

"Small, intimate. No more than ten people on the gazebo in the backyard at sunset," he answers.

"I'll be the one playing 'Ave Maria' in the corner," I say.

Gilda's fanning back tears. "You have hair and makeup coming in thirty minutes. You'd better go."

We hold each other for a long embrace. She smells so much like Mother, it's weird. I don't want to let her go.

"See you later, Daddy." We hug and kiss.

***

Around 6:30, Gregory arrives with the dress. He's dapper in an Italian-style suit, wearing leather designer loafers with no socks. He comes bearing more gifts.

"I'm your world-class errand boy, but only for today. My services expire at midnight."

"Thank you."

The hairstylist puts the finishing touches on my hair. My makeup is done natural—not too heavy on the eyeshadow but lush and thick on the lashes. When she's finished, I retrieve the dress.

"I can help if you want me to," he says.

"Just be dazzled when I walk out, okay?"

I emerge ten minutes later, all pulled together. Gregory's mouth drops along with the hairstylist's and makeup person's. I walk the room modeling, showing them all angles of the dress.

"Damn. Why didn't I think of hiring a photographer?" he says.

I find a mirror and turn to get a side profile. I'm wearing a girdle, and it's tight, but I'm not going to focus on that or the fact that I haven't had an appetite. I'm not going to let nausea get the best of me, not on my special night.

When the hairstylist and makeup artist leave and it's just me alone with Gregory, we take a moment to hold each other in silence. It's moments like this when no words are necessary. I'm in the moment, and Gregory feels so good.

"You ready?" he asks.

"Always," I answer.

I grab his hand, and we meet up with Daddy and Gilda. I introduce Gregory to them as my boyfriend.

Daddy's eyebrows raise, "Really? Boyfriend?" he asks Gregory.

It's difficult to tell if he's serious or just taunting Gregory.

"Maddie, you haven't told them about me?" Gregory asks me.

"Of course, I have." I answer

"Actually, you haven't." Daddy says to me. He glances at Gilda, "Did she tell you?"

"I don't recall." Is Gilda's answer.

"Daddy. Gilda?" I say.

"We're just giving you a hard time." Daddy says to me.

He and Gregory shake hands. "Nice to meet you, sir." Gregory says.

I notice Daddy and Gregory are the same height, about five-foot-ten.

"I believe you're the first boyfriend I've ever met." Daddy says. He turns to me, "I'm sure you've had other boyfriends but I've never met them."

"Because I never had a boyfriend." I use air quotes when I say boyfriend. "I was always too busy practicing the piano and performing."

"I notice the air quotes." Daddy says to me.

"Me too." Gregory announces.

"It simply means, there were boys who liked me, and we happened to be friends. That's all." I say.

"Okay," is Daddy's response. He looks at Gregory. "What's special about you?"

Gregory smiles showing his beautiful white teeth. He appears to be blushing. "There's nothing special about me. Maddie is the special one."

"She is, indeed." Daddy says.

"I tell her she's rare, like a diamond." Gregory says.

"You're sharp." Daddy taps him on the shoulder.

"Thank you." Gregory answers.

"Daddy, let's go." I grab his hand.

Gregory gives us a lift for the short distance to the performance hall. Inside, the place is busy with people milling around socializing, waiting for the performance to start. Daddy, Gilda, and Gregory follow me to a green room area where I greet more people affiliated with L.A. Phil and some concertgoers who are usually patrons of the arts. It doesn't matter how many times I do these events, my nerves just won't give me a break. I'm poised, but underneath I'm a mess, and it doesn't stop until I walk onstage.

***

When I hear my name and the name of the toccata announced, I emerge from stage right, and I hear applause—the sound of thousands. I look and see a sea of faces from the orchestra level up to the highest balcony and those sitting in the box seats. The piano is black, and the lid is open. I sit before it and place my hands in position. I close my eyes, and I begin. I feel Schumann's presence, and I embody every note, every phrase, every octave as he would. I think of my mother and imagine myself as her if she had been given this moment.

I've always wanted magic hands, and now my hands are just that, weaving magic into the ears of thousands. When I'm finished, I sit and soak in the moment, my heart beating in tandem with the thunderous applause. I try to stand, but I feel weak, so when I finally do stand in front of the piano, I use it to hold me steady. I receive applause, and someone gifts me with a large bouquet of red roses. I take them, and the smell triggers my nausea. Suddenly, my vision is blurred. I feel light-headed, and all I need is a glass of water. When I take one step to exit the stage, my legs betray me, and I see the room go from right side up to sideways as my body hits the stage. I look up and see the stage lights blink on and off, and that's the last thing I remember.

***

Daddy and Aunt Mary are in the emergency room with me. I'm hooked to an IV, and the doctor says dehydration. I can see that leading up to the concert I didn't eat or drink much. I wanted a perfect-fitting dress to match my perfect-playing skills. I needed to lose my stomach. I thought if I drank too much water, I'd be saddled with water weight. If I ate too much, my stomach would get bigger. Then he ran another test. After he's finished, the doctor looks at me then at the nurse in the room. She looks at my chart, and I notice her eyes dance across the page.

"Miss Richardson, you are eight weeks pregnant," I hear.

The doctor and nurse observe my expression—or lack of it. I see shock on Daddy and Aunt Mary's faces. Right now, I want to scream, but what good will that do? I do the math, and eight weeks ago was a day in June. It happened with JB. I am numb. Daddy and Aunt Mary are looking at me for answers. The rest are gathered in a waiting area down the hall, anticipating news of my diagnosis. Gregory is there, and it hits me. I'm flushed, my ears are ringing, and the tears start flowing.

I want them to stop, but they continue their course. The nurse and doctor excuse themselves, leaving us alone.

Aunt Mary takes my hand and squeezes it. I see her fighting back tears. She's searching for words, probably wondering, *how could this happen on my watch?*

Daddy stands next to her, traces of gray in his goatee, and thanks to me, it will be snow white before it's all over with. We should be talking about my performance, but here we are, trying to find words. Figuring out the next move.

"Eugene." Aunt Mary says to Daddy, "believe me, I laid down the rules. I trusted Maddie enough to respect them. She gave me no reason to suspect she was doing anything else." I see a tear roll down her cheek. "I'm sorry I've let you down. You have every right to be upset with me."

"Jesus Christ." He looks upward, taking a deep breath. "Getting upset won't change anything. What happens from this moment forward is my only concern?"

They both look at me, and I feel as if I am in a soap opera that Aunt Teal watches where there's cheesy dramatic music, only I'm the star. *What happens now?*

Aunt Mary moves aside, and Daddy takes my hand, I reach for him and bury my face in his chest, and I hear myself sobbing. *How could I be so careless? I'm so scared. I'm so sorry.* I've let him down, and to me that is the worst feeling in the world.

"Mary, can you tell the boyfriend, Gregory, to come here, please?" Daddy says to her.

"No," I scream.

They stare at me, visibly shaken at my sudden outburst. I feel like I'm about to hyperventilate.

"I don't understand," Aunt Mary says. She glances at Daddy for his reaction.

"Maddie, why are you saying no?" Daddy asks.

"Because Gregory's not the father." It hurts me to my core to say that.

I see their reaction: the pain, disappointment, and frustration. At this very moment, I want to crawl into a hole and stay there. Forever.

Daddy just stands there for a moment. Visibly hurt. He takes me and rocks me. Listening to me sob.

"God said before you were formed in your mother's womb, I knew you. I know the number of hairs on your head. God's Word says, Madeline May Richardson, I know the plans I have for you. Plans to prosper you and not harm you, plans to give you hope and a future. Life's not over. There are more mistakes to come and lessons learned from them. You need to make this right by all parties. First, let the father know. The responsibility shouldn't rest entirely on your shoulders. Second, as hard as it is, you're going to have to tell your boyfriend. The worst thing you can do is involve him in this situation and not be upfront with him."

"But I don't want to hurt him," I cry.

"Maybe you should've thought of that before." Daddy's tone has an edge to it.

"I don't want to lose him." I look at Aunt Mary, hoping she'll say something, anything.

"Maddie, who's the father?" she asks.

"JB," I whisper.

"Who?" Both Daddy and Aunt Mary ask.

Aunt Mary stands frozen in shock. Daddy is looking at her reaction and back at me.

"JB? Who is that?" Daddy asks.

"Caleb's best friend since middle-school," Aunt Mary answers. She's shaking her head in disbelief.

"I'm sorry" is all I can say.

"You know him, Mary?" Daddy asks.

"I do. He's like a second son."

"Was it consensual?" Daddy asks me.

"Yes," I answer.

"How old is he? Is he in school?" Daddy asks.

"He's twenty. Same age as Caleb. He attends USC. He and Caleb are on the basketball team," Aunt Mary answers.

"Twenty? He's a little older, and I'll assume much too experienced," Daddy says.

"He was someone who I thought I could trust around the girls. He's like family," Aunt Mary explains.

"Is he close to graduating? What does he plan to do?" Daddy asks me. Silence.

"How well do you know him, Maddie?" Daddy asks.

Again, silence.

"My God." Daddy sighs. "Mary, think you can set up a meeting tomorrow? I'd like to meet this young man and his parents."

"Sure. I'll get on it right away," Aunt Mary says before leaving me and Daddy alone.

"Maddie, did it ever occur to you that while you were being careless, something like this could happen?"

Again, silence. I can't stop the tears from flowing.

"Tonight, I sat in that audience like any proud father, amazed at the talent you possess in those fingers. I would have never imagined the evening turning into this."

"Gilda's going to be hurt when she finds out," I say.

"Yes, she will."

"Daddy, I don't want it."

"That's not your choice to make."

"But it's my body."

"You are a minor. I still make the decisions."

"You all seem to forget I'm about to be on my own, living like an adult."

"I'm not so sure about that now, Maddie. If you're careless under your aunt's supervision, just imagine what happens when you get to New York."

"It won't be like that."

"Like what?"

"I won't be careless anymore. I want this over and done with, so I can go on with my life."

"That's my and your mother's legacy growing inside you. You terminate the pregnancy, you terminate our legacy, and for the life of me, I can't sign off on that."

"What good is a legacy if I don't want it?" I feel light-headed.

"Imagine if your mother felt that way about you," he says.

Sometimes I wish she had flushed me out into the unknown, to a place where I wouldn't feel so much pain.

"I can't do this." I shake my head.

"Yes, you can."

"No."

"You can and you will." The authoritative tone in his voice has me convinced I can.

Aunt Mary returns with Gilda who rushes to my side.

"Don't ever scare me like that again." She holds me. She looks ravishing in her navy-blue dress, accented with a pair of eye-catching diamond earrings. "You're supposed to take better care of yourself. You know that."

"I know. I know. I'm sorry."

"I come with love and concern, that's all."

"What did you think?" I ask.

"You made that toccata look like a walk in the park, and we both know it's not."

"I wish I could do it all over again. That wasn't the finish I had in mind."

"Listen, you've learned your lesson. Next time, do better."

"Next time? You have more concerts scheduled?"

"I've gotten quite a few phone calls over the summer. There are possible concerts scheduled in December, during the winter break in DC and Philly."

Listening to Gilda who's always scheduled and booked my events talk about the possibility of other concerts, I feel tears falling.

"You want to talk about it?" she asks.

"I'm pregnant," I say to her.

She pauses and just stares at me. She glances at Daddy for confirmation. He nods and lowers his head.

"Oh, Maddie." Her pitiful tone is unbearable. She continues to hold me. "Eugene, what are we going to do?"

"I know what we're not doing," he answers.

This feels surreal, and I tell myself, *you can wake up any moment now. See, it was just a dream, a bad dream.*

Aunt Mary stands with her arms folded and shaking her head. "I let you down, Gilda. God, I let my sister down."

"Aunt Mary, it's not your fault," I say to her, "You trusted me, and I lied. I lied to you so many times about where I was and who I was with."

She closes her eyes as the tears roll down her cheeks. Gilda reaches over and brings her in for a hug.

"You have an idea if they'll release her tonight?" Daddy asks Aunt Mary.

"They will," Aunt Mary answers. "Granted they'll monitor her a few more minutes before she's released."

"We will not talk about this to anyone outside this room. We will tell all our family, friends, and colleagues from L.A. Phil, who are sitting in the waiting area, it was dehydration, and it was." Daddy says to Gilda and Aunt Mary.

Daddy takes my hand. "You are having this child. You and I will talk to the father and his family."

"Just got off the phone with the mother. She, her husband, and JB will meet in my home at one o'clock tomorrow afternoon."

"Very well." Daddy turns to Gilda. "Pregnancy aside, Maddie has gotten herself in a predicament of sorts. You see that nice gentleman we met earlier, the one who she introduced to us as her boyfriend?"

"Yes," Gilda responds.

"He's not the father."

Gilda's mouth drops. At that moment, I wanted to bury myself.

"We'll meet the father tomorrow. In the meantime, Gilda, we're walking to the waiting area to tell everyone goodnight."

"What about Gregory?" I ask, feeling my heart get weighty.

"He'll need to go as well." Daddy's tone is authoritative and definite as he and Gilda walk out of the room. I'm alone with Aunt Mary.

"I have to know: Were you having unprotected sex with Gregory too?" she asks.

"No."

She sighs.

"I'm scared. I don't want to face Gregory. I don't want to face JB. I don't want this baby, Aunt Mary. I didn't plan for this."

"Let me share something with you: I married Frenchy when I was twenty. I was pregnant with Caleb at twenty-two. I was a senior in college with plans to attend medical school that fall."

"What did you do?"

"When Caleb was born, I took a year off. That first year of motherhood was rough, and many times, I wanted to give up on my dreams. I kept pushing, I got back on course. I eventually went to medical school."

I am so overwhelmed, I break down. Aunt Mary, who's wearing a beautiful off-the-shoulder dress, literally gives me her bare shoulder to cry on. I hold on to her. I'm exhausted. I want to go home with her and go upstairs to my room, get in bed, and stay there for as long as I can.

Twenty-Seven

I'm awakened when Cassandra jumps in bed and gives me a tight squeeze.

"Maddie, your fall made the eleven o'clock news?" Cassandra says. She looks at me. "Omigod, your eyes are red and puffy."

"I'm sorry. All my guests dressed up just to spend the evening in the hospital."

"I'm glad you're okay. That fall looked painful," Cassandra says.

"I honestly don't remember it."

"What happened?"

"Dehydration," I answer, and then it hits me, then tears blur my eyes.

"Gregory dropped me and Caleb off and stayed up to wait for you. He left shortly before you arrived," Cassandra says. "He says he's coming by today to see you."

My body pulsates when I hear that. I have a flushed feeling. I can hear my heart beating, and it feels like it's pouring out of my ears. It's all in my fingertips. The nausea makes a return, and I rush the toilet. I'm hurling and crying.

"Maddie." Cassandra kneels so that she's next to me.

"I've really messed up this time," I cry.

"You fell, so what? Accidents happen," Cassandra says.

I sigh and flush the toilet. Cassandra grabs a cool hand towel to wipe my forehead.

"Maddie, I couldn't believe it. Reporters were downstairs in the hospital lobby trying to find out information about you."

"Really?" I respond.

"People from the symphony dropped in too," Cassandra says.

I nod as I feel the constant flow of tears. "I'm pregnant," I say to Cassandra.

"What?" Cassandra's aqua-colored eyes appear to pop out of her face. Her mouth is open, like one big-O.

"You've got to be kidding," Cassandra says.

I use the hand towel to wipe my face.

"Omigod, Maddie." Cassandra covers her mouth. Her skin is flushed, and a tear rolls down her cheek. "What are you going to do?"

"I don't know," I whisper.

"Will you tell Gregory?"

The thought makes me wish I had found out about the pregnancy in a different, more secretive way. I could have gotten rid of it without anyone knowing. What's crazy is that I didn't notice I stopped having a period. I didn't keep track of it. Before JB, I was a virgin. I recall the only time JB and I didn't use a condom was the day in the pool house. Everything happened in a whirlwind. I was ecstatic—out of my mind—and I had no sense of control.

"I have no choice," I say, regarding whether I should tell Gregory.

"I never imagined this happening to you," Cassandra says, wiping away her tears.

"I'm sorry I let you down," I cry.

Cassandra comforts me with a hug. It takes my mind off what I'll be facing later today, if only temporarily.

"Will you and Gregory get married?" she asks.

"No," I answer.

"Why not?" Cassandra asks.

I turn to Cassandra. "Remember when you kept asking who the other guy was?" I take a deep breath and exhale. "It's JB."

"What are you talking about?" She asks.

"JB's the father." I answer.

Cassandra gasps and covers her mouth with both hands. She shakes her head. "No, Maddie," she cries. "No. No. No." She rises to her feet.

I just sit as the tears flow and listen as she goes on.

"I can't believe this, after I told you about him."

"Please. You're making this worse."

"Gregory's coming over. What are you going to tell him?" she asks.

"The truth," I answer.

Cassandra wipes her tears. "I feel really bad for you, Maddie."

I'm imagining my life in two versions. In the first version, I'm at Juilliard, carefree with no responsibilities, coming and going as I please. The second version is me with a baby, living God knows where, but I'm sad and angry, and more than likely, alone—a victim of so many choices gone wrong. God, I don't want that.

"I need some time alone," I tell her.

"I cannot believe this, Maddie. JB? Does mom know?"

"Yes."

"Do Frenchy and Caleb know?"

"I don't know."

"I'm leaving. I'm hanging out with Kyle. I don't want to be anywhere around when you give Gregory this news."

She leaves me in the bathroom. I lock both doors and stare at my reflection. How will I do this? I can't perform while pregnant. I can't go to school pregnant. I can't have a baby. I feel more tears. Then I hear, *Shhhh. Stop. You will have this baby. You will eventually go to Juilliard. Where is it written that you can't do both? Do you know who you are? I didn't raise you the first twelve years of your life for you to crumble at the first sign of a challenge.*

I look around the bathroom. Yes, I'm the only person inside, but I hear a voice. It's loud and clear, and it sounds just like my mother's. Her cadence and tone. *Life is precious, and when I had it, I fought every fiber of my being to keep it. It had a purpose. It brought joy. It taught lessons. It created laughter. It even held a grown man together many nights when his world was falling apart. Your little friend, she's across town right now fighting for it. Her life brings happiness, joy, and meaning to everyone around her. Your other little friend almost had his life taken away, but he fought because his life has a purpose, and his testimony will inspire another life. We are all here for a purpose. We all matter, big or small. I want you to enjoy the life growing inside you. It will fulfill you in ways you can't imagine. You will look into your child's face and shudder at the notion of wanting to kill it. I'm not ready for my grandbaby. I want you to be ready, and when the time comes, you will.*

I stand, listening and waiting for more. I want to hear more. Whatever happens from this point, I'm ready to face it.

Later that day, Daddy and Gilda arrive first. Daddy is dressed in a leisure jacket with linen trousers and soft leather loafers. Gilda complements him with a women's leisure jacket with shoulder pads and linen trousers with flat slippers. She has roller set curls that bounce when she walks. I can tell by the red in their eyes and the puffiness around them, they didn't get a good night's sleep either. When Aunt Mary asks Daddy how he's doing, he replies, "I'm holding it together."

About twenty minutes later, the doorbell rings and in walks JB's parents. His mother is carrying a rectangular container with something that smells of fresh coconut.

"Where's JB?" Aunt Mary asks.

"He's coming," His father, James replies.

Seconds later, the door opens, and JB appears. My heart does somersaults, and when we make eye contact, all the hairs on my skin stand at attention. Aunt Mary introduces Daddy and Gilda to JB's parents. When Daddy's introduced to JB and they shake hands. Daddy replies, "Nice, firm handshake."

"My pops says a handshake can tell you everything you need to know about a person," JB replies.

"Indeed it does," Daddy replies. We follow Aunt Mary to the dining room where Aunt Teal has the table set. My heart races. It's the fear of the unknown. When we sit, there are seven of us, and I'm wondering if Aunt Mary's informed Uncle Frenchy. I wonder if Caleb knows. I'm sitting across from JB, and while Daddy's engaged in formalities with JB's parents, JB and I are back to the awkward stage.

They heard about my performance last night. JB's mother, Judy mentions even seeing it on the news. Then Daddy says a prayer, and while everyone's heads are bowed and eyes are closed, JB and I are staring at each other. He's pensive, and when Daddy nears the end of his prayer, JB closes his eyes and opens them as if he had them closed for prayer all along. When the food arrives, we eat in silence briefly until Daddy begins.

"JB, tell me about yourself."

JB quickly glances at me before answering. "What would you like to know?"

"Enlighten me," Daddy says.

"When I'm not playing basketball, I write and make music. I'd like to eventually write and produce songs for different musical artists."

"I see."

"Love for music is something Maddie and I have in common," he says.

"Interesting. Mary tells me you attend USC. Are you a music major?"

"No. Business major."

Daddy looks at me. "Maddie, did you know that?"

I shake my head and slice my brisket.

"Will your business degree intersect with your musical aspirations?" Daddy asks.

JB nods and chews silently.

"In basketball; what position do you play?" Daddy asks.

"Power forward," he answers.

Aunt Mary, Gilda, and JB's parents stop talking and listen to Daddy and JB's conversation.

"See yourself turning pro?"

"Eventually," JB answers.

"See yourself becoming a father?" Daddy asks.

A frown appears on JB and Judy's faces.

JB glances at me like *why is your father asking me this?*

"I don't understand," JB answers.

"The other night when Maddie was rushed to the hospital, we found out something that blew us all away."

I notice JB's eyes lingering on Daddy's every word.

"First, we find out she's dehydrated. Second, we find out she's eight weeks pregnant."

"Pregnant?" JB stares at me.

"What?" JB's parents answer together.

"Maddie is pregnant," Daddy says. "She says you are the father."

JB pushes away from the table and holds his head in his large hands, his tan complexion turning red.

"JB, please tell me this man is lying," JB's father, James says.

JB lifts his head and glances at his father. "He's not."

There is a collective sigh of disappointment from his parents.

"Honey, no." His mother moans.

"I want you all here because I don't believe in abortion and adoption is not an option. This matter shouldn't be swept under the rug," Daddy begins. "James, Judy, like you, I'm shocked, and I'm disappointed. However, right now, they don't need us to exacerbate. They need us to help them figure this out."

JB's head is still between his hands, and I don't know if he's angry or crying. His mother gets up from the table and comes to his side.

"Honey," I hear her whisper. His head is still between his hands, and I notice him rocking quickly back and forth. My guess, a combination of nerves and shock.

Tears blur my eyes. JB finally lifts his head. "Maddie, we need to talk, just you and me," he says.

I look at Daddy, who's next to me and Aunt Mary who's sitting to the right at the head of the table.

"Talk," Daddy says, patting my hand and pulling out my chair for me to stand.

"Excuse me," JB says. His mother stands to the side, giving him space to move.

Together, JB and I walk out of the dining room and down the hallway. Just when we're about to open the patio door and walk outside to the pool area, Caleb enters with Gregory behind him.

"Hi, Maddie. Gregory's here to see you," Caleb says.

Gregory's eyes light up when he sees me, and naturally, he walks up and gives me a hug and looks into my eyes.

"I'm glad you're okay," he says before kissing my lips.

I'm trying to seem normal to him but given what's happened in the last twenty-four hours, seeming normal is exhausting.

Gregory notices JB and nods. "What's up? I'm Gregory." Gregory extends his hand.

"JB."

They shake hands, and right now, I feel faint.

"Bruh, when did you get here?" Caleb asks JB.

"About thirty minutes ago," JB answers, and he's looking at me, anticipating my next move.

"Please, just give me a second," I say to JB before taking Gregory's hand and walking him toward the foyer.

"What's happening, Maddie?" Gregory's expression turns serious.

"This isn't going to be easy for me. I never meant for any of this to happen. I know I made you a promise I'd wait for you, but I didn't, and while you were away, I was with JB. First time with him, I wasn't careful, and—"

"Wow, Maddie." He walks to the door, shaking his head, blowing air out of his mouth.

"I'm so sorry." I feel dizzy and faint. All my worst fears are happening at once.

"You weren't careful. What? You're pregnant?" he asks.

I nod, feeling tears roll down my cheeks. He paces the foyer with hands clasped behind his head.

"You're pregnant?" he asks again.

"I am."

He takes a minute for it all to absorb.

"Are you keeping it?"

Again, I nod.

"Where does that leave us?" he asks.

"We can't be together anymore," I reply. A sob escapes me.

"It's like that?" he asks, his eyes brimming with tears.

"I'm so sorry."

"I never imagined you'd do this, Maddie."

"I never meant to hurt you, Gregory. I never meant for any of this to happen. When you were away and I didn't hear from you, I thought you forgot about me."

"What? Maddie, I was in the middle of the ocean. There wasn't a day that passed that I didn't think about you." I notice his voice growing louder.

"Let's go outside," I suggest.

"No. I want to have a word with JB."

"Gregory, please." I hold him back. My hands are pressed against him. I can feel the firmness of his pecs flexing underneath his linen shirt. "Please don't."

"Why can't I talk to him?"

"I don't want you to."

"Just let me have one word. Okay, two words."

"Gregory, please leave."

"Really? Leave?"

I open the door, and we step outside. "I don't know what else to do, Gregory."

"Is this really how it's going down?"

I nod.

"I need to talk to JB." He pushes past me. I grab him. "Please don't make this harder. Just leave, Gregory. Please."

"You are breaking my heart for real this time," he says.

"I'm so sorry." I cry.

"I can't believe you did this to me, Maddie."

I look at the bracelet on my wrist and finger the diamonds. "Do you have the key?" I ask.

He scoffs, "I thought I did."

"Can you find it?"

"Guess I'll be forever searching, Maddie," he says before walking to his car. He stops and turns around. Walking toward me, he grabs and pulls me in close for a long, lingering, intense kiss. His fresh scent, his soft lips, the peppermint taste of his kisses, I'll miss. Though, deep down, I have this feeling I haven't seen the last of him.

***

JB's outside sitting on a lounge chair by the pool. I join him.

"You know while you were with him, in the back of my mind, I'm thinking, is this really my baby?"

"How dare you."

"Weren't you with him too?"

"We were careful. He made sure of it."

"Damn, Maddie."

"I've got orientation next week at Juilliard."

"What are you going to do?"

"I'm going. Aunt Mary recommends I sit out a year, but I don't want to. Gilda has performances lined up. I want to keep going. I don't want to stop."

"You're living in New York; I'm living in L.A. How will this work?"

"I don't know."

He sighs. "I gotta do what I gotta do."

"Are you still with Basha?" I ask.

"Not anymore. We're done."

"Really?"

"Really," he answers.

"JB, I'm scared."

"Remember the day at the diner when I told you I had you."

"Yes."

"I meant it."

He places a hand over my stomach. "I have both of you now."

The patio door opens, and out walks Caleb. He looks suspicious.

"What's up?" he asks JB.

"Sit. We have something to tell you." JB points to the empty lounge chair next to ours

"I don't want to." Caleb walks up and at this point, JB stands. Now he and Caleb are nose to nose.

"Bruh, have a seat," JB insists.

Caleb looks at me. "Maddie, what is this about?"

"Please let JB explain," I say, wringing my hands.

He notices and frowns. "You okay?"

"Caleb, listen, I really care about your cousin and I want to be with her." He takes a deep breath. "She's pregnant."

Caleb turns red, and he shoves JB. "What? You've lost your freaking mind."

I stand and sandwich myself between them. "Caleb, stop." I hold his hands.

"Why, man?" Caleb asks. He looks hurt too. "All the girls in L.A., you screw my cousin?"

"Maddie's different from them." JB's skin is red again, and his chest is heaving.

"You don't deserve her." Caleb says. I'm still sandwiched between them.

"I'll be good to her. I'll take care of her. I promise."

"How?" Caleb's question pierces my ears.

"I told Maddie don't worry, I've got her."

Caleb scoffs, "I'll believe it when I see it." He shakes his head and walks back inside.

"Now what?" I ask.

"We go back and strategize," JB says.

When we meet with our parents, I sit, not believing this is happening but coming to accept that this will be the way it is. Aunt Mary wants me to stay in L.A. just until the baby is a year old. I don't want to. I'm ready to go to New York.

"Who'll take you to your weekly check-ups in New York?" Aunt Mary asks.

"I'll go by myself," I answer.

"Once you have the baby, then what?" Daddy asks.

"I'll figure something out."

"Now is the time to plan," Daddy says.

"I'll take care of the baby," JB's mother says. She turns to me and takes my hand. "You go off and do your music. JB, you call up that sports agent and tell him you're going pro."

His father looks at his mother and shakes his head, "You haven't discussed this with me."

"Get on board with it, James. We have a grandchild coming," she says.

JB sighs. "The plan was to stay at USC, get my degree, then go pro."

"The plans changed. Now plan on changing diapers and warming bottles," His father says to him.

Then Daddy says, "Call me old-fashioned and not up to date with the eighties way of thinking, but I'm not a fan of children born outside of marriage."

"Wow Mr. Richardson," JB begins, "no disrespect, but I'm already overwhelmed with the pregnancy. Now we're talking about marriage?"

"Time's ticking. You've got seven months until the baby arrives," Daddy adds.

"I understand," JB says. He turns to me. "I just need to process all of this."

My head is spinning too as I imagine life seven months from now. Not only will I have a baby, but the possibility of a husband, and this is really blowing my mind.

Daddy says, "Maddie, if you want to continue performing, the optics are better if you're pregnant and married. Think about it."

"You're holding a 12 gauge up to my son's temple." JB's father says. "Now, I understand you're a minister and you have your beliefs, but these kids aren't ready."

JB is silent, and I can see he's lost in his thoughts.

Daddy folds his arms and glances at JB's mother, "You know that's a really kind gesture of you offering to take on Maddie and JB's responsibility, but they've made their bed, no pun intended."

"Fair enough." I hear his mother say.

"I'll call the sports agency and tell them I've made a decision," JB says. "I'm declaring myself eligible for the '88 draft."

"I'm going to New York as planned," I say.

Daddy shakes his head, "Maddie, No. Juilliard is on hold for at least another year."

"But Daddy—"

"No, listen. L.A. is where your emotional support is. The father of your child is here. I can't in good conscience send you off to New York, miles away from home, pregnant and alone." Daddy says.

I break down, it's not what I want to hear. Especially when I've worked so hard to get to this point.

Daddy holds me and I cling to him. A list of *what ifs* race through my mind. *What if I hadn't kissed JB that day. What if I had taken a moment to ask JB to wear a condom. What if I had waited for Gregory like I promised him I would.* I never meant to hurt him, I never meant for any of this to happen. I hear Daddy whispering a prayer: "Father God. He who knows and sees all—Your word says be not dismayed, for I am God, I will strengthen you, I will help you, I will uphold you with my righteous hand."

While still holding on to Daddy. Another hand grabs mine and gently squeezes it, I look over Daddy's shoulder and see it belongs to JB. Now we embrace. I feel the energy from him, now flowing through me. We never imagined this moment: surrounded by our parents, planning a future—way off the mark—far different from what each of us had in mind. I release from his embrace and glance at Aunt Mary and Gilda; I see the hurt on their faces. I look at JB's parents-put in a situation, they had no idea they'd be in.

"I agree with your Daddy and Aunt Mary." I hear JB say, "It's best you stay. I'll need you to stay."

"What do we do now?" I ask him.

JB sighs-it's a long exasperating sigh.

Daddy chimes in, "I get it. A lot is coming at you two at once—JB, you know about teamwork and what it takes to win. You apply that same concept to you and Maddie's situation. She's your teammate, now."

JB nods.

"I'll need to talk with JB and Maddie, alone." Aunt Mary says, "Can you all give us a minute or two?" she tells everyone else. It appears they've finished eating and they leave us alone. Aunt Mary sits at the head of the table, JB and I sit next to each other to her left. JB and I hold hands.

"I did not see this coming." Aunt Mary says, "JB I've always held you in high regard, like my own son—I looked to you more as a brother, a protector to Maddie and Cassandra."

JB lowers his head.

"Why did you put yourself in this position?" she asks him, "can you articulate that to me?"

JB answers, "I stopped looking at Maddie like a girl and started looking at her like a woman."

"JB. She's a seventeen-year-old girl." Aunt Mary's words are definite. "And because of what you two did, she's forced to become a woman."

She stares at us, giving JB and myself a minute for her statement to register.

"Babies, are what you two are. You don't understand the magnitude or responsibility of parenthood. I was twenty-two when I had Caleb, hell I didn't understand it."

The weight and reality of her words bring tears to my eyes.

"I'm trying to respect your father and not exacerbate but I'm going to break it down from the perspective of a psychiatrist who specializes in the behavior and minds of children—you will be overwhelmed, you will want freedom to do as you please, you're young, that's what young people do; all of that stops, the second this child is born."

JB and I sit quietly.

"There are driving manuals and in basketball you have a playbook; parenthood is a different ball game and my advice going forward is that you get mentally prepared for it."

"You're scaring me," JB says to Aunt Mary.

"Don't get scared, just get prepared."

I feel JB's hand squeezing mine tightly.

"Now your Daddy wants you married." Aunt Mary says to me, "you've got no business marrying any more than you need to be having a child."

"Can you talk to him? Convince him that we don't have to do this. We can go somewhere and get this over with and no one outside our circle will ever know."

"You want an abortion?" JB asks me.

"Yes." I answer, "If we did that, you can finish school, then go pro the way you planned, and I can go to Juilliard the way I planned. We won't have to get married. We can be normal."

JB stops me mid-sentence, "Are we a team?" he asks.

"Yes." I answer.

"We're teammates, we're in this to win, right?"

"Yes."

"I'm not losing. I'm not losing you or this baby, Maddie."

"You sure that's what you want?" Aunt Mary asks JB.

"Yes," he answers.

I turn to JB, "Really?" I ask, "are you feeling pressured or obligated?"

"Be honest." I hear Aunt Mary say to JB.

"I-want-you, Maddie." he says looking directly into my eyes.

For a split second, I forget Aunt Mary is present. JB's words resonate with me.

"You accept the responsibility of being a father on your terms?" Aunt Mary asks.

"I'm all in." JB says.

"What about you, Maddie?" Aunt Mary asks.

I nod. A tear rolls down my cheek.

"Why are you crying?" Aunt Mary asks me.

"Because I'm scared." I answer.

"Why are you scared?"

"I won't be a good mother. I won't be a good teammate."

"How do you know this?" Aunt Mary asks.

I shrug because I don't know what to expect.

"I suggest you do some research on parenting." Aunt Mary says to me, "Because both of you are about to get a real-life experience in child rearing."

JB and I sit quietly, allowing her words to resonate. Aunt Mary calmly stands and walks toward the door's opening and turns to us. "Now that I don't have the youth center to go to, I'll be available to talk. Often." she says before leaving me and JB alone.

He glances at me and reaches out to wipe away a tear from my cheek. I take his long, slender hand and kiss it.

"We can do this," he says.

"Yes, we can." I say aloud, though inside I'm feeling different, like I'm about to be in over my head.

"I really want you." he says, his voice is low and soft.

"I know." I whisper.

We enjoy this quiet time, alone in the dining room. I wish it would last, but it won't. Soon we'll resume our conversation with our parents and deal with reality. We have roughly seven months to try and figure this out.

T. Wendy Williams is a native of Huntsville, Texas and a 1996 graduate of Sam Houston State University. Lost in the Music is Williams' third novel. She is also author of Mile High Confessions and Happily Never After, both novels were featured in Essence magazine and the New York Review of Books. Williams is proud wife to husband; Joseph, and loving mother to their children; Layla, Miles, and Lance. Currently, Williams resides in Suburban Houston where she is writing her fourth novel.

Connect with T. Wendy online:

Instagram @twendywilliams

Twitter @twendytheauthor

Facebook @twendywilliams

Website: www.twendytheauthor.com

Acknowledgments

Thank you God, the Creator. Thank you to my husband; Joseph, for your wise input and listening ear. Thank you to my children; Layla, Miles, and Lance for being loving and patient. Thank you to my mother; Bobbie, for your many words of encouragement. Thank you to my mother-in-law; Willie Mae, for keeping my house in order while I wrote. Thank you to my sister; Tawanna, for your valuable input and honesty. Thank you to my brother-in-law; Richard, for helping me with the "techy" side of things. Thank you to my editor; Chandra Sparks Splond, I'm so glad I chose you to help with this project. Thank you; Brittnee Bennett, Gary Prevost, Cynthia Sledge, and Gaven Lucas for being available to answer my questions and providing me with research information. Last but not least, thank you to my readers for your patience and support. I promise I won't take this long to write the next book.